NATURE'S LEGACY

APPRENTICE SCOUT BOOK 2

ALI INGS

ALI INGS

CONTENTS

CHAPTER I

The dirt was warm and damp, clinging to her palms as she laid her hands on either side of the sapling. Aili opened herself to the energy of nature. Redirecting a touch of energy, she flowed it up into the sapling, all the way to the leaves.

"Feel that?" Andvari knelt beside her, the knees of his trousers growing damp.

Aili nodded. "A fungus? It feels like a fungus."

"That's right. I figured you'd identify it that easily. Now, what would you do about it?"

Releasing the energy, Aili sat back on her heels. "I didn't sense any Darkness. It's just a regular fungus. Hang on." She closed her eyes and opened herself to the forest. Stretching her awareness across the magic in the forest, Aili examined the trees and soil. "It's everywhere. Thin, though. Where'd it come from?"

Andvari smiled. "Let's find out, shall we? What do we know so far?"

Aili rubbed her chin as she stared at the little sapling. "Well, it's affecting the leaves and parts above the soil. The soil has a healthy growth of good fungus, though it's not as thick as I'd expect."

"So, the fungus is probably airborne, right? It might be harming the beneficial fungus in the soil, which could explain why that's not as strong. What would you do about it?" Andvari stood and brushed the dirt from his hands.

She focused on the dirt on his knees. A touch of energy and the soil particles fell back to the ground. "We should follow the air and see where it's coming from. This time of year, it comes from the west. Might it be from a farm?" Aili turned west and peered through the trees. "If so, they need our help before planting season. If it's from a seed or leaf a bird dropped, it could be from anywhere."

He folded his arms across his chest and smiled. "That's a good thought, but it's the wrong time of year. It would also take longer to spread from a single small source like that. With how well we watch the forests, and how fast this was caught, the odds are it's natural from cultivated land. We can treat it without magic, since we caught it early."

Aili looked up at him. "You're happy right now."

"It feels good to get back to basics." Andvari grinned and turned his face into the dappled sunlight from above. "I spent most of my early Scout days doing this. We wandered the forests and watched the balance of life. I loved the challenge of identifying plant or animal diseases. That and preventing animals from spreading where they don't belong."

She leaned back on her hands, bracing against her straight arms. "Plant diseases I get, but why wouldn't animals belong somewhere?"

"Remember those tiny fur-footed mice down south? They're the primary food source to a thriving weasel population. Imagine they got loose in the rainforest. There, they'd mainly be predated by hawks and eagles. Those birds also eat plenty of other things. With how fast the mice reproduce, and how few predators they'd face compared to down south, soon there'd be thousands of mice, or more. They'd strip plants of leaves and seeds before the plants could grow strong and reproduce. They could even destroy other species that way."

"I could happily do this for the rest of my life." Aili stretched out on her back and stared up at the sky. The thick leaves protected her from the strongest sun, leaving her in the comfortable shade. "If I ever get this whole Darkness situation taken care of, that it."

"We will. It's our duty. Now, time to go make a remedy for this." He stretched his hand down to her.

Taking his hand, she bounced to her feet. "Really?" She dashed over to her pony, grazing the long grass under a nearby tree. "We're going to make it ourselves? You don't just have a massive vat of this stuff sitting around?"

Andvari walked over and stroked his horse's shoulder. "Of course we do, but where's the fun in that? Back to basics, remember?"

She vaulted onto Leya's back. Andvari swung up into Charger's saddle, a tall horse to match his own height. He picked up the reins. Guiding the bigger horse back towards the camp, he led Aili and Leya through the trees.

"Did Ilia ever teach you potions for plants and gardens? Maybe one to deal with fungal infections?" He glanced down at her as she rode up beside him.

Aili grinned. "One of the first potions she let me make by myself, in fact. These are harder to mess up, she said." She let her thoughts wander through memories of Ilia's workshop, and all the hours she spent there as a child. The sounds and smells filled her mind — flowers drying as they hung from the ceiling and potions bubbling in cauldrons.

Pulling herself back to the present, Aili let her gaze wander over the rolling hills and meadows. They emerged from the forest and entered the grassy fields around the camp. The wildflowers weren't blooming yet; it was too early for that, but the grasses were already growing long.

Leaving the horses at the stable for Jordi to look after, they headed across the camp to the healing centre. The potions lab shared the building and had its own entrance.

Aili darted up the wooden steps. She stopped at the top, turning to look around at the camp.

The main hall towered over the camp, except for the enormous warehouse beside it. Both had multiple stories. The stables were hidden behind the hall. Bunkhouses for most Scouts and support staff ran around the edge of camp, with workshops mixed in. A group of Scouts trained in the grassy area in front of the hall, where Drill took place.

Once Andvari caught up, she headed inside. Waving to the herbalists, Aili wandered to her favourite brewing station. This corner had windows looking out in both directions. She could watch the meadows beyond camp from here.

Andvari took a large cauldron from the space below the workstation. "Do you need a recipe, or do you have it memorised, too?"

Aili turned from the window and leaned against the counter. "I'd prefer a recipe, but I can make one if I need to." She turned to the shelf over the counter and ran her finger along the book spines. Finding the recipe book she wanted; she pulled it down. Flipping through the pages, she stopped. "How about this one?"

He leaned over and had a look. "That's a good choice. Gather the ingredients. I'll get this boiling."

The massive cupboard had everything she needed. Aili collected bottles and tucked them into a wicker basket. Taking them to her workstation, she weighed and portioned out the ingredients, setting them in little glass dishes. Aili arranged them in the order she'd add them.

"There. Now we just go down the line, adding them when it's time." Aili put the bottles back in the basket.

"A trick Ilia taught you?" He wiggled his fingers. The fire in the firebox grew more intense.

"Yeah. When I was really little, she'd prepare them for me. I still got to add them myself, though. Over time I got to help prepare more by myself. Mostly I had to grow big enough to use the scales." Aili grinned. The memory was fuzzy, maybe not even real, but it was vivid all the same. She was tiny, scooting across a table, knocking bottles everywhere.

"We have our rolling boil. Ready?" Andvari tilted his head towards the cauldron.

"You're making me do all the work?" Aili poked him lightly in the side, her finger hitting hard muscle. "Wait, that's probably a good idea. You did turn someone blue, after all."

He stared at her, eyebrow raised, his mouth open.

Aili grinned. "It's fine. I got this." She picked up the first dish and tipped the contents into the bubbling water. "Stir."

Andvari picked up the stirring rod. "One minor mistake, turn a Scout blue, and nobody ever lets you live it down." He shook his head as he mixed the ingredients in.

She dumped the next pair of ingredients in. "Hey, it makes you more human. You're so good at your job, it's nice to know you fumble and mess up like the rest of us." She dodged his elbow, laughing as she grabbed the next dish. "So, how do we distribute this? The fungus is in more than one spot."

"We have our ways." He chuckled.

***

"Are you serious?" Aili pressed the trigger and laughed. A blast of potion sprayed across the ground, flowing from the end of the nozzle. "This is awesome." She paced in a lazy circle, spraying a fine mist of remedy over the undergrowth.

Andvari smiled and shook his head. "Hang on. Let's get everyone and everything organized. Aili, take the end. Everyone, line up." He called the last instruction loudly enough for the group to hear.

The Scouts formed a line, their sprayer packs on their backs. Each held an applicator wand. Aili moved to the end of the line.

"You all know the routine, but we're going over it for our newest helpers. Walk as a group, staying in line. You're all responsible for your own strip of land. Take a moment and find your reach." Andvari stood before the group, watching and waiting.

The line spread out as the Scouts waved their wands slowly from side to side.

"Here, hold your wand towards me as if you were spraying, like this." The young Scout Apprentice beside Aili showed her.

"Okay." Aili copied her motions. She stepped away until their spray would just barely overlap.

Andvari walked over and stood on her other side. "I'll stay here, and Kyson has the other end. Call a halt if anyone sees anything unusual, or you have a problem with your sprayer. Ready?" He waited a moment, but the group was silent. "Go."

Following the group, Aili activated her wand. She swung it back and forth as she advanced with the others, leaving a light coating of potion on everything she passed. Someone picked up a tune, humming softly. Soon the group was singing an old song to the tune. Aili smiled and sang along. Ilia used to sing this while working in her workshop.

They stopped a few times and returned to the wagon. A Scout there refilled their packs or handed out snacks. The canteens were labelled with each Scout's name, and full of their favourite drink. Aili's had apple juice and refilled itself like the others. She stuffed a few extra snack bars in her pockets on the breaks, too.

***

Water dripped from her as she stepped out of the tub. A touch of magic and Aili was dry, the water returning to the tub. The aroma of herbs clung to her, a result of the bath salts that would prevent her from getting sore. Aili tidied up after herself and pulled clean clothing on.

"I thought we could eat here this evening." Andvari nodded towards the desk. A tray held two plates full of food. "It's been a while since we walked all day like that." He settled into his desk chair.

Aili picked up the second plate and settled on the large trunk near him. How many early meals had she eaten here, perched on the trunk at the end of his bed? "I'm surprised there's not another way, like mounting sprayers on air boxes or wagons."

Andvari laughed. "There is, if we're treating crops or fields. The trees prevent getting an even coat on the ground, so in the forest, we walk."

"Is this what being a regular Scout is like? Way too much walking with a pack on my back?" Aili scooped up some lentils and veggies.

"Sometimes the pack is a shoulder bag instead." Andvari grinned. "It's not all tracking wayward mages and fighting Darkness. Not for most Scouts. It's tending forests and finding lost hikers. Oh, don't forget all the surveys, either."

Aili dug into her supper. After all the walking, she needed it. Her experiences as a student weren't normal; she knew that already. Most Scouts had never hunted the Darkness and ended up in combat like she had, not even some senior Scouts. What would her life be like if she were a normal student? Would she be in the city somewhere, attending classes at a school with other young mages?

"You're deep in thought." He picked up his teacup. Waving a finger, he directed a cool breeze around the teacup, cooling it.

Aili swallowed the last of her meal. "I was just thinking about everything we've done. What's it like being a normal student? What did I miss, and where would I be?"

He took a sip and set his cup down. "It's interesting to think about. There's no way to really know. I can tell you what being a normal student is like, though. At least, normal for a student with a Scout teacher. Also, how people usually join us."

Aili leaned back on her hands, still perched on the trunk. "Please. How did you end up here?"

He told her about his village and how the Scouts often stopped by or passed through. "I loved tending the animals, but as a shepherd I mostly dealt with just the sheep. As a Scout, I get to work with so many animals. Anyway, one day a pack of wolves passed through. They saw the sheep and attacked. I got a barrier up around my flock and sent a call for help. A pair of Scouts were nearby, and they chased the wolves off."

"You put a barrier around an entire flock of sheep while young?" Aili smiled and shook her head.

He laughed. "Yeah, they weren't sure to believe it at first, either. My flock was a good size, too. I always kept them safe. Well, they told someone in their camp. The very next day a Scout came and offered me a position. They said anyone with barriers like that needed a mentor to help make the most of their skills. I couldn't argue with that, so I joined the Scouts."

Aili got up and set her plate on the tray. "Do you ever miss it? The sheep and fields and all?"

He smiled and leaned back in his chair. "Sometimes. I love what I do now, though. I don't regret coming for a moment.

She sat on his bed by the window, letting the breeze flow over her. He told her about his early Scout days. She got to hear about life as an Apprentice Scout and how he met Kyson. She listened raptly to the tales of her mentors being young and carefree.

CHAPTER 2

The water rippled as she tapped the surface, dipping her fingers in. Lifting her fingers, she watched the cold water drop back into the pool. With a thought, every drop fell from her skin, leaving her clean and dry. She rolled and sat, pulling her cloak tightly around herself.

Andvari sat under a tree, leaning against the trunk. He was the smart one, sitting out of the spray as he watched the water tumble down the rocks forming the falls. He's been awfully quiet so far. Her brow furrowed as she looked him over.

Andvari smiled and shook his head. "I'm fine. I was just thinking."

Aili wandered over from the edge of the pool, smiling as she settled in the sunbeam's warmth. "What about?"

"About your training, mostly. The crystals. Also, the growing taint. Ultimately, every forest in the country is my responsibility. Mine and the Commander's. Until recently

12

it was easier. There was no taint and Darkness to deal with. Now, I hope I'm up to the task." He stared at the water where it rushed into the pool.

Aili leaned against his side. "I know the feeling. What happens if I fail?"

Andvari met her gaze. "Then you try again. We keep trying until we succeed. That's all we can do."

"What if I die?" she whispered.

He wrapped an arm around her, hugging her to his side. "If so, you die knowing you did everything you could. You would have tried your best."

"What if you or someone else dies because I wasn't good enough?" She rested her head on his shoulder as she blinked back tears.

"Aili, sometimes people die. Sometimes it doesn't matter how hard we try. That's just life. Magic gives us an advantage, but it's not a guarantee everything will work out in our favour."

She lifted her head from his shoulder. Hoofbeats? Stretching her senses out, Aili smiled. Kyson was coming on horseback, bringing someone she didn't know well. Who? They were vaguely familiar.

"Frida."

Aili glanced up at him. "Is that today? We haven't dealt with the Darkness since her last visit." She straightened up and smoothed her hair with her hands.

He shook his head. "She wants to meet with me. Her checking on you gives us a good excuse nobody will question."

Trickster came into the light, carrying Kyson into the clearing around the pond. A small Scout horse carried Frida behind him. They dismounted beside Charger and Leya, where some choice grass kept the horses busy. Kyson swiftly untacked the horses and let them graze.

Frida walked over. She slid the pack off her shoulder and sat in the grass facing Andvari. Staring at the backpack, she was silent for a long moment.

"Is everything alright?" Andvari reached over and took her hand.

Frida blinked up at Andvari. Her gaze looked unfocused, like she was staring through him. Aili reached for her shoulder. Frida shook her head and focused. She met his gaze.

"I'm okay. I think so, anyway. We've been digging into the situation and trying to learn more. There are a few colleagues I can trust." Her hand shook as she opened the backpack. "We did a full inventory of the secure room. Another artifact is missing."

Pulling a book from her pack, Frida opened it to a marked page. She handed him the book and pointed.

Andvari scanned the list. "Another pin? Rei is studying the one we brought back. Are they related? They look so alike."

Kyson settled on the grass with them.

"The design is the same. They were probably made by the same person or people. It was so long ago, before magic changed, so who can say?" Frida pulled another book out and opened it.

Aili gasped. The glossy pages showed the water pin she recovered. A few paragraphs gave some details about the artifact. "The Great Tides?"

Frida nodded. "There were four pins made, one for each element. This book is private information, available only to high level public defenders and researchers. Whoever took the pin knew what they were getting. They probably had access to this information." She turned the page.

This page showed an almost identical pin. Instead of the deep blue crystals, this one had the light blue crystals of Air Magic. Aili leaned closer. "The Grand Circulation. Wait, that's that air current thing that affects the weather, right?"

Kyson dropped his face into his hand. Shaking his head, he looked up at Aili. "I sometimes wonder how much you listen when I try to teach you something."

She stuck her tongue out at him. "I listen. I just don't always remember boring details like names in my brain. The air current flows around the planet and carries the wind, moving warm ocean air over the land. It affects the climate. I was listening."

"Someone took that from the vaults?" Kyson leaned closer to see the page.

"Not just that one, but this one, too." Frida tapped the facing page.

"The Solid Foundation," Aili read. Little emeralds covered the pin. She leaned against Kyson to read the first paragraph. "Wait, someone could raise mountains with that?"

"Maybe once. No mage alive has that kind of power." Andvari stared at her for a moment. "Well, only one I know of, and I hope she knows better than to try."

Aili raised her hands and shook her head. "I would love to see the pin, but you can't raise a mountain without affecting the land across the continent. I remember those lectures vividly." She stared off at the waterfall as her thoughts raced. "Why would someone want them? Who's trying to control nature?"

Kyson rested a hand on her knee. "You can feel artifacts, especially the old and powerful ones. Do you feel anything at all from them?"

She shook her head. "Not a thing. I had to be in the north before I felt the one across the water, though. If that distance is the same for all of them, I'd need to go west before I felt these two, if that's where they are. That's assuming they're still in Athia."

Andvari rubbed his chin. "We could have Dinna fly you around. You could cover the entire country in a day."

Aili stared at him. Her jaw dropped.

"She's ready to see the crystal storage. That's out west," Frida suggested.

"True." Andvari got his thoughtful look, the one where his mouth twisted slightly in one corner. "That should put you close enough to feel them, if they're out west."

"Why these, though?" Aili gestured at the pictures. "I mean, I guess the air pin would let you control the weather, but that can't end well. Why the earth pin?"

Andvari shrugged and shook his head.

"I'm more interested in who had access to the vault and how they got these out. The security is tight. You'd need to know what you were looking for and where it was. You'd need to get in and out with the appropriate paperwork and permissions. Who's the traitor on the inside?" Frida closed the book and tucked it back in the pack.

Andvari handed her the other book, which she also put away.

"Rei got in. I'll ask if he remembers how." Andvari folded his arms over his chest. "It might give us some insight, as he has similar permissions, being one of our elite and researchers."

Frida's hand shook as she fastened the buckle on her bag. "I don't want to believe someone I work with is capable of this, but what else could it be?"

"Someone from the Council?" Kyson suggested. "They also can get permission to go in the vaults, in some cases, anyway."

"Either way, we'll figure this out. You have our support. You also mentioned having people you trust?" Andvari nodded to Frida.

Frida smiled. "Three I trust completely."

"I have many Scouts who can help, all across the country. We can even involve the younger Scouts, without letting them know every detail. They'll help keep watch."

Kyson sighed. "What about investigating the Council? Is it likely someone from the CDF is involved without a Council member backing them up?"

Andvari shook his head. "Possible, but not necessary."

"I feel like such a traitor, investigating my own people." Frida rubbed her temples.

"I know the feeling." Andvari rested a hand on her shoulder.

"It wouldn't be the scary man who chased me across Athia, would it?" Aili fidgeted, gripping the emerging grass between her fingers.

"Scary man?" Andvari raised his eyebrow. "Which scary man?"

"He was there when you were taken. Sharp eyes, like an eagle, and his nose has that angle compared to ours." Aili drew the shape over her nose with her finger.

Frida laughed. "Commander Grinnon is the most highly respected public defender in the city. He's responsible for the elite forces and is my boss. He's the CDF equivalent to Andvari. I did a mind scan with his permission, and he held nothing back. He's on our side."

"But he was so persistent," Aili whispered. She stared off at the waterfall. She'd never forget the way he chased her, not if she lived as long as Ilia.

"They call him the Hound, because he follows his targets to the edge of the world if needed. He would never have hurt you. He wanted you to come home safe, too." Frida took her hand and squeezed it. "He told me after we brought you back how he admired your ingenuity and dedication to your mentors."

"He's not mad at me?" Aili curled up and wrapped her arm around her legs. "He always looked so angry."

Andvari nudged her. "You used to think that about Kyson, too. Now look at you two. You tease each other like family. You've risked yourself to save him, and how many times has he saved you?"

Aili sat quietly for a long moment, her mind whirling. "Alright, if you say so, I accept he's on our side. He's still intimidating."

Kyson snorted. "You used to think I was intimidating."

She rolled her eyes. "That was before I knew you. Now I know you're just a big softy who acts tough."

"They always like this?" Frida smiled. She glanced between Aili and Kyson.

Andvari shrugged and nodded. "Pretty much, now. Brings life to the missions and makes running for our lives more fun."

"I'll send copies of information on all four pins to you directly when I get back. I shudder to think someone might ever locate the Eternal Flame pin, but we definitely need to get the other two back. I've got special information here for you, too. Keep it secure. It's personal information on everyone who can access the rooms without needing paperwork done first. It might help narrow our search."

Frida took a large and thick envelope from her bag. She passed it to Andvari.

He took the packet and tucked it into his mailbag. "What support do you want from us?"

"I'll keep digging into our people with my group. If you can learn what you can about the artifacts, maybe even trace them, that would help. I don't know how you found the water pin, but nobody else I know could have done that."

Andvari smiled at Aili. "We'll see what we can do. Aili, what do you need for that?"

"Can I see where they were stored? I might learn something that can help me." Aili held his gaze, willing him to say yes.

Frida laughed. "That's a good puppy dog face. I can get you special permission to enter escorted. Andvari and Kyson can already petition to access the vaults, but you'll need temporary permissions."

"That'll help." Aili nodded. "I hope."

"I'll go get that arranged." Frida stood and slung her bag over her shoulders. "Thanks for the help. I can't imagine trying to do all this with only the four of us, even as high ranked as we are."

Andvari stood and clasped her hand. "We all want Athia safe and prosperous. We're happy to help."

"I'll escort you back." Kyson got up and walked over to the horses.

Aili stared at the water where it flowed into the pool below, causing a mist that spread over the pond to the edge of the bank. Tracking two artifacts? That shouldn't be a problem, but should she have felt them already? How close would she need to be? Can the others really not sense them at all, not even with a spell? What if she couldn't find them?

He settled on the grass beside her. Draping an arm around her shoulders, he pulled her lightly to his side. "You'll be fine. We're here to help."

Aili rested her head against his shoulder. "I wonder if mother knows anything?"

"Do you want to ask her?"

She nodded, her head moving against his shirt. "She said I could contact her by finding certain trees spread across the forests, as well as seeing her directly. I found one near here. What do we do first, though? Go see the vault, find mother, or visit the crystal storage place?"

"What do you think?"

Aili sighed. "I think my life was easier before my magic was active."

Andvari chuckled. They sat quietly as they watched Kyson finish tacking up the horses. The big man steadied the smaller horse as Frida swung herself up into the saddle. It wasn't graceful, but Aili reminded herself they barely ever rode horses. Kyson mounted Trickster. They rode off through the trees, disappearing from sight.

"Why now? Why has everything been good for a few hundred years, and now it's starting again?" She closed her eyes. The mist didn't reach this far, but the air was still moist and thick.

"I don't know. We are here to help, though. It's what we do. We're Scouts." His arm tightened around her briefly before relaxing again.

Aili grinned and opened her eyes, looking over at him. "We are, aren't we?"

"We should also go back." He gathered the last of his papers and stuffed them into the mailbag.

"Just a few more minutes? It's easier to think out here than in camp."

He chuckled. "Sure. A few more minutes. Then we go back."

CHAPTER 3

A ili looked up from her book. Andvari strode into the room, right to his desk overflowing with papers. He had more paper in his hands.

"Frida works fast. She's already got us clearance to go see the vaults." He filed the papers in a slot, and they disappeared, heading who knows where?

"So soon?" She set her bookmark and sat up on his bed, the warmth of the sun through the window on her back.

"Kyson and I already have clearance. She just needed to get you set up. Let's go tack up the horses. If we leave now, we can get back today before dark." He grabbed his light cloak from the hook by the door.

Aili tossed her book aside. She dashed to the door, stuffing her feet into her boots and grabbing her cloak. Jogging behind him, she pulled her cloak on as they headed to the stable.

Kyson looked up from beside Trickster. "Beautiful day for a ride." He snugged the glossy black horse's girth before patting him on the shoulder.

Andvari went into Charger's stall. Jordi was already there, tacking up the massive horse.

Jordi tightened Charger's girth. "I put some day provisions in your saddlebags, along with emergency rations and supplies."

"Thanks. We plan on being back today, but who knows what we'll find?" Andvari slipped Charger's bridle on.

Aili grabbed Leya's saddle and entered the pony's stall. "You're all beautiful and brushed," she cooed to the pony. "Thanks, Jordi."

"I had help." Jordi grinned and nodded towards the tack room.

A slender girl brought Leya's bridle from the tack room. "You're leaving again? Can we go for a ride soon?" She tucked her long blond hair behind her ear.

Aili embraced Silla, hugging her around her thin shoulders. "Absolutely. I don't know when yet, but I'll make time if I have to." She took the offered bridle. "Thanks. How's Meeka doing?"

Silla grinned. "She's great. Jordi is letting me try mounted games with her now."

Aili eased the bridle over Leya's head. "Those are so much fun. I look forward to it."

Kyson led Trickster from his stall. Andvari and Charger followed. Aili took Leya's reins and left her stall.

"Have a safe trip." Silla waved.

Aili swung up into her saddle and waved back.

"Ride on." Andvari guided Charger down the road, heading for the city beyond the fields and meadows.

***

Andvari slowed Charger. He nodded to the guards at the city gates. "You've been quiet the entire ride. Are you alright?"

Aili nodded. She focused on the road ahead, packed with people and horseless wagons. "I'm fine. There's just a lot to think about."

"I'll say. Your thoughts are a jumbled mess." Kyson eased behind her as a wagon loaded with crates rumbled past.

Aili looked over her shoulder, narrowing her eyes at him.

Kyson shrugged. "Can't help it. Mind mage. Your thoughts are so crowded they're spilling into the link."

"When you're ready to talk, we're here." Andvari smiled down at her as he eased the big horse through the crowd.

People stepped aside for the horses. Andvari turned off down a quieter street, away from the wagons and bustle of the main roads. They passed the market down an alley, weaving through the back streets of the busy capital.

Aili smiled and perked up as they turned into one particular alley. Leaving the last of the crowds behind, they rode to the far end. Double doors opened, and a couple of people in Scout uniforms stepped out to greet them.

"Darik!" Aili leapt from Leya and ran for him, wrapping her arms tightly around his waist.

"Aili," he gasped, hugging her back. "Can't—breathe."

She loosened her grip but didn't let go. "Sorry. How've you been? What're you doing here? They're not working you too hard, are they?"

He laughed as he rubbed her back. "I'm fine. I'm doing what I was meant to do. The cheeky little lady looks good." Darik caught Leya's reins as the pony wandered over and butted his pocket with her nose.

"She's doing great. Glad to go for a ride. You're looking after her while we're here?"

"Of course. She can use the fourth stall on the left. The other two can use the fifth and sixth stalls." He nodded to Andvari. "Recruit."

Andvari grinned and bowed his head for a moment, though he didn't salute. "Good to see you looking well. Once we get the horses settled, we'll be off. I don't know how long we'll be."

Darik nodded. "Understood."

Aili led the pony into the stable and to the assigned stall. The hay feeder was full, and the bucket was clean and filled with fresh water. She untacked the pony. Leya shook as Aili took her saddle off, letting a cloud of loose pony hair fill the air near her.

"Darned shedding season," Aili muttered.

With a thought, she called the breeze from the open door. The pony hair collected in her little air funnel and travelled to the muck bucket across the aisle. With a last glance at the hay and water, both full, she stepped from the stall. Setting her tack on the rack outside the stall, she took a deep breath.

"Ready?" Andvari held her gaze.

Aili shifted from foot to foot. "I guess?" How will she feel going back into that building? She wasn't sneaking in this time; she was using the main door like a normal mage.

Kyson chuckled. "It'll be fine. Nobody is chasing you this time."

Andvari draped his arm around her shoulders and steered her to the door. "We're with you. Just stay close and tell me if you need anything. You're here on official business."

She nodded. "Okay. Let's get this over with."

They left the Scout headquarters. City noise hit her as she stepped into the alley. He led her through the alleys. They crossed a few streets, weaving among the crowds until they got into the next alley. She grew up in this, but didn't miss it at all. She moved closer to him as they joined the last street heading to CDF Headquarters.

Stopping at the bottom of the steps, she looked up at the open double doors. The brass handles shone in the sunlight. The wide stone steps looked inviting enough, if she hadn't known what was inside.

"You okay?" Andvari stopped beside her.

"This feels so weird." Aili met his gaze.

"Coming back here?" Kyson nudged her shoulder lightly. "Or not running from the law?" He grinned at her.

Aili elbowed him in the ribs. "I've been in most public buildings often. Not this one. The first time I was here, well—"

"You broke in, found us in a restricted area, and ran." Andvari laughed. "This time you're an invited guest. The sooner we go in, the sooner we can leave."

She marched up the stairs. "Fine. Let's do this."

Andvari and Kyson caught up with her as she passed through the door. She slowed as she stepped inside. It didn't feel like the same place, though it looked the same. Lanterns of mage-light glowed, casting a soft light around. It reflected off the white stone floors. Stained-wood chairs and desks made the place seem less cavernous, more welcoming.

She touched the leaves of a potted plant. "These weren't here before."

"Those were added a week ago." A young woman smiled at Aili from behind a tall desk. "Scout party?"

Andvari smiled. He stepped over to the desk. "Here's our clearance." He set the papers on the desk.

The plant pulsed with energy. It was happy. The mage-light lamp over it had extra wavelengths, mimicking the sun. Someone recently watered it.

"Aili, ready?" Kyson had his arms folded over his chest, leaning against the pillar near her.

Andvari watched her as she turned towards him. Another man stood beside him. Her breath caught in her lungs. Those dark eyes that could stare a hole through a mountain watched her.

'Best behaviour, both of you.' Andvari glowed in the link. 'We represent the Scouts when we're out in public.'

'So, no making faces,' Kyson teased, growing warm in the link. 'Aili, you're fine. He's not going to throw you in the cells.'

She forced her feet to carry her to Andvari's side. Each step was harder than the last.

Andvari wrapped his arm around her shoulders, pulling her close. "You remember Commander Grinnon?"

Aili looked up into those piercing eyes. The last time she saw him, he was scowling at her. Jeril protected her and kept her safe. Andvari was here, though. He would give his life for her, so she was safe, right?

"It's nice to meet you properly." Commander Grinnon bowed his head to her. He wasn't scowling. His expression was so neutral, she couldn't read it. What was he thinking?

"And you," she stammered.

"Frida has kept me fully informed. If you'll come this way?" He turned and walked across the entrance hall, towards the back stairs and lifting platforms.

Andvari kept her moving. Kyson stayed behind her. Her stomach flopped. Maybe this would be a waste of time, and she should just go?

'You're fine.' Soothing flowed into her through the link from Andvari.

'You weren't there.' She blinked back tears as she let them see her memory. Back in the tower with Jeril, Herta, and Rei, Aili fought the mages. She vividly remembered his anger when Jeril stood up for her. That scowl was seared into her memory forever.

They passed into a back hallway, turning down another hall. Aili recalled the map she had memorized so many months ago. She hesitated as the tugging feeling pulled on her. That hallway? She barely resisted the pull back then.

'What's up?' Kyson brushed warmth against her in the link. 'Your thoughts are a total mess and it feels like static.'

Aili opened the link and let them feel what she felt. 'This hall isn't on the map available in city records.'

"It's been a while since the Scouts and Civic Defence Forces have worked together." Commander Grinnon stopped at the end of the hall.

"Before both our time, for cooperation like this," Andvari agreed.

"It is reassuring to know that cooperation is still possible." The commander looked down the hall. He rubbed his chin.

Aili peered down the hall past him. It seemed to go on forever, with no doors or turns. That wasn't possible, was it? The far end seemed fuzzy, like it was out of focus. She closed her eyes and reached out with her awareness.

"A glamour?" Aili opened her eyes.

Commander Grinnon raised an eyebrow and looked at Andvari.

Andvari smiled and shrugged. "Her magic is different. Always has been. That's why she's here."

The commander glanced at her band, visible above her shirt collar. She gripped her cloak. Don't fidget, she reminded herself. He's only looking at the odd colours. Everyone does. Nobody else has a gold core, not even Ilia.

"Yes, there is a glamour, but most mages can't detect it. They either see it, if they don't have clearance, or they don't sense it at all. Your clearance should prevent it from affecting you." He stared at her.

"What do you see, Aili?" Andvari nodded down the hall.

"It looks like it goes on forever, but the end is fuzzy. It pulls at me. Part of me wants to follow it, but only part." Aili rubbed her temples.

"That's part of the protective magic. If someone without clearance walks down the hall, they keep going to a room that will hold them until we arrive." Grinnon frowned at the hall. "It shouldn't affect you here, though."

He led them a few steps down the hall. The surrounding magic changed, the glamour still there in the background, but new magics shimmered on the walls and floor. She recognized the privacy spells and silencing spells.

"We can speak completely freely in here." Grinnon glanced at Aili. "This is the highest security area in the entire city. The vaults are down this hall. We hold artifacts few people know exist, and we'd like to keep it that way."

Andvari lifted his chin slightly. "She has full clearance as a Scout. Aili understands secrecy and discretion."

'What, I do?' At least in the link, her communication was private.

Andvari smiled at her. 'Yes, you do. Our commander adjusted your clearance before our mission down south.'

'Does this mean I get access into the restricted sections of the records?' She stood taller, straightening up.

Grinnon nodded. "Alright. This is the vault the pins were taken from." He turned a corner and gestured at a door. "What do you need to do?"

Aili pulled herself free of her thoughts. "What?" she stammered.

Kyson hid his grin with his hand. 'Focus. You were going to look around? Feel for magic?' He nudged her in the link.

"Right, I just need quiet. If you two want to help, you might make more sense of what I feel than I might." Aili held her hands out.

Andvari took her hand. "You lead."

Kyson took her other hand.

"Can I get closer?" Aili tried to keep her voice from shaking.

"You can go wherever you need, as long as I'm with you," Grinnon agreed. He held her gaze, but his expression was softer finally.

He really doesn't look so scary now.

'He's not.' Kyson chuckled in the link.

'Stop listening to my private thoughts.'

'Don't think so loud.'

'Focus, both of you.' Andvari floated between them in the link. 'When you're ready, Aili.'

She walked towards the door, taking slow steps. Keeping her eyes open, she opened her senses as well. The magic symbols from her senses shimmered against what she saw with her eyes, covering every surface.

'I know these spells. They were set ages ago and are still strong. Nobody has altered them.' Kyson directed her attention to some of the symbols.

'Great. What about those?' Aili directed her attention to the floor, where many coloured traces of footprints glowed. "How many people can access this, if it's so secure?"

Grinnon followed, matching her pace. "A couple dozen can come and go freely, but their passing is detected by magic when they enter the hall. Records exist for that. A few dozen can get special permission, like you were given, and their passing is also noted."

"Where is the magic sensors for that? I haven't felt them yet." Aili reached back down the hall.

"They are at the entrance, where we first came in."

"Am I missing them?" Aili searched at the end of the hall.

Andvari tugged at her senses. She relaxed, letting him focus her attention instead.

"Only because they're not there." Andvari pointed to where they should be. "There are faint traces of it, but barely detectable."

"What?" Grinnon spun and marched back down the hall. "Can you prove it?"

CHAPTER 4

"Aili, will you let him look?" Andvari squeezed her hand lightly.

"I can link him in like a normal Master Mage working," Kyson offered. "I'll let him see what he needs."

'You'll protect me?' She pressed her lips together and tightened her grip on their hands.

'Absolutely. He won't feel a thing from you. I'll let him see what I see from you, and only what he needs.' Kyson squeezed her hand back.

"Okay."

Kyson held his hand up. Commander Grinnon turned his back. Kyson's skin seemed lighter against the black CDF robes. Aili turned her focus back to the magic, letting Andvari direct her senses again.

"This is remarkable. You see this all the time?" Grinnon's voice was quiet and soft, almost breathless.

"Mostly if I focus or look," Aili admitted. "I can sort of turn it off and on now, and not get so overwhelmed."

"Look here." Andvari pointed out the traces of magic, where a spell once had been.

"There should be a border all the way around. You're right. It's not there. Are you sure she would sense it?"

"Positive. She can even feel types of magic we can't." Andvari squeezed her fingers lightly again.

She took a few slow breaths and waited, keeping the link open. They examined the entire entryway for every spell.

"What was it supposed to look like?"

'Like this.' Andvari drew the pattern in her mind, laying it in place over what she saw. 'It would detect everyone entering or leaving. See how it works?'

She looked a little closer, trying not to pull her attention from where Kyson was helping Grinnon. 'Oh. Yeah, I see. How powerful would the spell have been? It looks like it might even detect those with invisibility potions and spells.' Wait, would it have detected her had she come this way that day, so many months ago?

'It might have. You're lucky.' Kyson chuckled.

"Might have what?"

Andvari sighed, so softly Aili wasn't sure anyone else noticed. "Apologies. We can communicate through the link to an extent. Aili was asking about the spell and how it worked."

Commander Grinnon backed out of the spell. He looked at Aili like a hawk assessing something small and furry. She suppressed a shiver as she wrapped her arms around herself.

'Drama much?' Kyson warmed the link. 'You've impressed him. Nothing more. He's not going to eat you.'

Aili took a step back, bumping into Andvari. He steadied her with his hands on her shoulders.

Grinnon shook his head. "We should examine the vault. I want to know what else changed, if possible. Can you detect all magic down the hall and in the vault?"

She nodded. "I might not know what I'm looking at, though."

Taking her hand, Andvari guided her toward the vault. "I'll help. I know more about the spells and will likely notice if something is unusual."

Opening her senses, she started scanning as they walked. The magic was fairly continuous, the spells reaching the entire length of the hall.

"Are there supposed to be any spells spaced down here?" She looked closer at a section of the wall.

"No. There should be more spells at the door to each vault, and inside the vaults. Cleaning spells will be everywhere, so cleaners don't need to come in here. Most of the security is at the start of the hall and at each vault." Grinnon kept pace with Kyson, following behind them.

Aili stopped at the end and turned left. "They were in that one?" She pointed to the second door down.

"Yes. Was that a guess, or do you feel something?" Grinnon crossed his arms over his chest.

"I feel something." Aili shared the sensations with Andvari in the link.

'I'm not sure what that is,' Andvari admitted. 'It's too faded. Can you look closer?'

Aili sat on the floor. Closing her eyes, she searched for the trace. 'Footsteps.' She focused on the pattern, looking for the track. Aili opened her eyes. 'It's power like mine, kind of, but tainted by Darkness. What's the opposite of a Nature Mage? Is there such a thing?'

"Follow it." Andvari helped her up.

"Follow what?" Grinnon stepped closer.

Aili waved her hand and focused. The footsteps appeared on the floor like faded shadows on the white stone tile. "That's as good as I can do. It's a strain to do that much."

"Come on." Kyson took her other hand. He walked with her, watching as the footsteps appeared a foot or so ahead of them.

The footsteps faded completely once she was a foot or so past them. Aili gripped his hand tighter as they passed the first vault, practically glowing in her senses with all the magic inside. The footsteps kept going, not stopping until the next door.

"They go in, but don't come out? How did they get back out?" Aili frowned down at the footsteps at her feet.

Grinnon kneeled beside her. Holding his hand over a footprint, he cast a few spells. Shaking his head, he stood again. "I can't detect those at all. How are you doing it?"

Aili looked to Andvari. 'Help?'

"Confidential?" Andvari moved closer to Grinnon.

Grinnon nodded.

"She's a full Nature Mage, the first one in maybe four hundred years. Her ability to use magic is nothing like ours. She is tied to the planet and can tap directly into the energy that flows through it. What she's detecting is a power like hers but tainted with Darkness." He rested a hand on her shoulder.

Grinnon was silent as he rubbed his cheek. His gaze flicked to the door of the vault. "That explains why it was so difficult to track you. Does that mean you can track whoever this is?"

Aili shrugged. "I can tell where they've been. My ability to sense their magic depends on what they were doing."

"Can you tell how they got in?" Grinnon gestured at the door.

"Can I touch it?" She stared up at the door, her nose wrinkled. It had so much magic in it, it might take a month to untangle the spells.

Grinnon nodded. "Your clearance and the paperwork should have disabled the trap spells for you."

She stepped forward and placed her hands on the door, diving her senses right into the magic. The door was thick and solid metal. The walls were thick stone with metal bars pressed inside by Earth Mages. Magic shimmered everywhere, spells for protection and security.

"Were there more detection spells here?" Aili pulled her hands from the door.

"Yes. Are they also gone?"

Aili touched the door again. "Yes, but something else feels off—"

Keeping her fingertips against the wall, Aili kept going down the hall past the door. A few feet down the hall, she found the footprints again. Had they jumped or been thrown back somehow? The footsteps stopped at the wall, pointing right at the stone.

"Here. They went through here." Aili tapped the wall.

"The wall?" Grinnon narrowed his eyes at the spot. "How did they get through the magic?"

"Like the Grandmaster?" Andvari stepped closer and cast a few spells at the wall. "We couldn't detect her transportation spells, but we could detect her. Only you could feel her move."

"What's that?" Grinnon raised his eyebrow.

Kyson paced slowly behind the group. "We were on a mission almost a year ago. We ended up at some ruins protected by magic only Aili could sense. Or so we thought. Some artifacts also revealed the magic. The former Grandmaster of the University found an artifact of ancient days and made her way inside. We witnessed her teleporting through magically protected stone walls."

"Nobody informed us?" Grinnon frowned.

"It was in my full report. I don't know what the Scout Commander chose to pass on." Andvari touched the wall beside her hand. "Can you tell how they went through? Was it teleportation, or did they use something else?"

She closed her eyes and searched for that familiar feeling. Was that it? Aili looked closer, closing in on the essence. A pattern slowly revealed itself to her, an intricate web of magic on the wall, with the twist Darkness left in living things running through it.

'I don't know what this is.'

Kyson moved right behind her and rested his hand on her back. He entered the link fully. "It's a variation on the magic used to send food between kitchens and dining rooms. This one has a few modifications, though."

"What? What does it do?" Grinnon stepped right beside them, facing the wall.

"I can copy it out, if you get me some parchment and a quill. Aili, can you focus that long?"

She nodded. "I'll need a big meal after this. This stuff takes more focus to detect."

"I'll arrange it. I'll be right back." Grinnon strode off, turning the corner and disappearing down the hall.

"You can relax. Save your energy." Andvari rubbed her back.

"Who can use this kind of power, though?" She went and sat against the far wall, staring at the spot. "Is there someone like me out there? Like me, but using Darkness? How? Where did they come from?" She rested her chin on her hand.

Andvari sat beside her and let her lean against his side. "I don't know."

"That was a spell, though." Kyson tapped his chin as he thought. "That wasn't how you do magic. That was definitely a spell, but with taint. Whoever it was, I bet they started as a regular mage."

Aili sighed and rested her head on Andvari's shoulder. Was that better or worse? Someone like her. How rare was that? Not even every century. That's how rare. If it were a regular mage who was tainted and changed, was anyone in danger of becoming something else? How might it change her friends? She shivered.

"We can't see the tainted magic. You can, probably because of your tie to nature. I wonder if they can detect you?" Andvari hugged her to his side.

She closed her eyes and sighed. More unknowns. Perfect.

Footsteps approached. She looked up as Commander Grinnon came around the corner. Aili sniffed the air. The aroma from the bag in his hands made her stomach growl. He also had a roll of parchment tucked under his arm. Handing the parchment and a quill to Kyson, he passed the bag to Andvari.

Andvari opened the bag. "Take a moment and eat. The spell will wait for you."

The pastry inside still steamed lightly. Aili accepted the food and tore into the snack. The cheese and herbs mingled on her tongue. She smiled as she wolfed it down, ignoring the heat. He gave her the second one. With the edge of her hunger gone, she savoured this one as Kyson unrolled the parchment on the floor.

"Do you want me as an intermediary, so you can focus on drawing?" Andvari set the bag aside.

Kyson nodded. "If she focuses on the pattern, you can share what she sees. I'll get it down. Just channel it for me, so I can use both hands and move a bit if I need."

With the pastries gone, Aili moved back to the wall. She licked her lips as she pressed her hands lightly against the wall. Andvari knelt beside her. His hand was warm and solid against her back. When she glanced over, he had his other hand on Kyson's back as well. The big man knelt before the parchment, leaning down with quill in hand.

Pulling the pattern up, Aili focused on locating the magic. Quill scratched on paper as he sketched the design. She looked closer where he directed her attention, showing the smaller and increasingly complex lines of the spell. How did the mage hold a pattern so intricate in their mind to cast it?

"Done." Kyson straightened up and stretched his arms high over his head.

Aili slumped against Andvari. He pulled the bag close and handed her the last pastry. She demolished it in seconds.

"Do you have experts who can assess this?" Andvari pointed at the parchment.

Grinnon nodded. "My top security spell team will have it done within hours. Whatever changes they made to this spell, my people will detect and decode them."

"What happens if you cast that and imbue it with your Light, like they used Darkness?" Kyson nudged her gently.

"If I try it, I want more of those pastries. They're amazing." Aili straightened up and focused on the wall.

The corners of Grinnon's mouth turned up. "Try it, and we can go to the Elite CDF dining hall. You can have as many pastries as you like, and anything else there you want."

"Deal." Aili stood, facing the wall. Closing her eyes, she reached for the magic. Tracing her pattern over theirs, Aili released her magic. Her inner light shone through the pattern, filling it with power.

The wall melted away, revealing shelves within the vault. Two spaces were empty, where boxes once sat. Feeling for the shelves, Aili sensed residual magic from the artifacts.

"What the—" Grinnon reached towards the wall.

Stopping before he touched it, the commander picked up the quill. He stuck it in the gap, passing it almost into the vault. Aili grabbed his arm and pulled as the wall reappeared. The quill clattered to the floor at their feet.

"Interesting. It created a gap just long enough to grab the items. How would they know exactly where they were, though?" Andvari touched the solid wall, his fingertips pressed to the stone. "They must have had access at some point, or know someone who does."

"They may not have known." Grinnon headed for the vault door. "There are more illusions inside. It won't change for whatever reason the person is there for, but all other artifacts will look like they're in different places each time. We always record why we're in there, and the last full inventory was last spring. The magic works on everyone." He tapped his chin as he looked at her. "Or does it?"

Aili tugged Andvari's sleeve. "Can we get more food?"

"In just a moment," he assured her. "Can you test this before we go?"

Aili nodded. "Food right after."

"Agreed." Andvari steered her over to the door.

Commander Grinnon opened the vault. The door swung in. Aili stepped through the doorway. She grabbed a shelf and Kyson's sleeve as she swayed. The room shifted and turned in front of her. Her magical senses saw a solid and steady room, but her eyes saw the room literally spinning in front of her. Aili closed her eyes, leaning against Kyson as he wrapped his arms around her.

"What's wrong?" Andvari's fingers rested on her forehead. His soothing magic flowed into her, easing the urge to be sick.

Steadied by her friends, Aili reached out with her senses. There were so many powerful artifacts, she couldn't tell where one ended and another began. A few glowed stronger, but mostly it was a blur of blinding magic. The power pressed in on her from all sides.

"Out," she pleaded, reaching for the door with her hand.

CHAPTER 5

Kyson supported her as she stumbled from the room. "You're out. What happened?"

She opened her eyes. Aili took a few slow breaths before straightening up. "I might know why they went through the wall. If they're even a bit like me, they couldn't have gone in there. I'm not sure how they would have experienced that room, but it was too much. Maybe ask Rei what someone tainted feels around them?"

Andvari cradled her cheek in his hand. He peered into her eyes. "Are you alright?"

She nodded. "Food."

"Come. The Elite dining hall is on the upper floor." Grinnon picked up the empty bag and the parchment.

They followed him down the hall, Andvari's arm around her. She leaned on him. Each step got steadier as she left the hall behind. Soon she was walking beside him without help.

"I'll be fine." She poked his side. "You can stop giving me that look."

Andvari raised his eyebrow.

"I felt better once I left the halls."

The corners of his lips turned up.

"Okay, the dizziness just passed moments ago. Once I've eaten, I'll be good as new. Perfectly normal."

"Normal. Right." Kyson chuckled.

"Normal for me, mister."

Her steps slowed. She knew where they were going. Aili stared at the lift platforms. No. Not these. How many flights of stairs? Maybe she'd be fine until they got back to the Scout headquarters. Lots of stairs there.

"You'll be fine. Ignore the sensation of the space below you. Focus on those delightful pastries above you." Andvari guided her onto the platform, his arm firmly around her.

She gripped his shirt. Focusing inside herself, Aili touched her inner lights. Going deep enough, she could somewhat diminish her outer awareness.

"Is she okay?"

"Yeah." Andvari rubbed her back. "She's just very aware of the open space below the platforms. It's not a pleasant feeling."

Their voices sounded distant, like she was hearing them underwater.

"Last time she was here, she escaped down the stairs." Kyson laughed.

Aili peeked up at Grinnon from around Andvari's side.

He had an unreadable expression again. That horrible assessing expression. "You were here. That breeze. You, right?"

She nodded and stared at her boots. "Yeah." Shuffling her feet, she tucked farther behind Andvari. "Sorry?"

He shook his head slowly. "Would you be willing to write out how you did it? It might help us track this other individual. Andvari can make sure I get your report."

Aili nodded. "I won't get in more trouble?"

Andvari smiled. "Consider it a way to make amends. You can include how you snuck into the other buildings, too, as a bonus."

"Other buildings?" Grinnon raised his eyebrow.

The lift stopped. Aili dashed off the platform. The men followed her.

"This way." Grinnon headed towards a hall.

Aili glanced around. It was a lot like the floor she stopped on, but not quite identical. The offices should be over there. The other floor had an open meeting area right near the lift, but this one didn't. She could smell the dining room already, though.

They followed a hall around a corner. Aili found herself in a room with immense windows overlooking the city. Tables full of food lined one wall, full of platters loaded with a bit of everything. There were pastries and snacks, as well as full meals, and even a soup pot. Stuffed bread pockets filled a tray beside the soup pot. One table was entirely teapots and cups.

"Have whatever you like, as much as you like." Grinnon gestured at the table.

Aili darted over to the table and grabbed a tray. She piled a bit of everything on it, including three more pastries. Taking a cup, she selected a sweet tea from all the enticing choices.

Instead of long tables and benches, there were thickly padded chairs around round tables. At one end, there were some armchairs by a fireplace with a fire crystal inside. Those chairs had little end tables. Two of the chairs were occupied, one by the towering man called Theron. The woman she didn't know. Aili went to the nearest table and sat.

"I'll get my people on this right away." Grinnon tapped the parchment. He turned to the people in the chairs. "We learned some interesting things down there."

Aili turned her attention to her food. The sandwiches had shredded veggies in a thick sauce. She licked the sauce from her fingers. The slight tang made her smile. Dill? Her tea gave off heat. Aili set a breeze around it. Even with her magic, it would need time. Aili picked up a pastry.

"How do we form a defence against someone who can bypass every security spell we have?" Theron shook his head.

"Aili's going to help with that." Grinnon turned to look at her.

She froze, her pastry halfway to her mouth, and stared wide-eyed at the Master Mages all staring back at her. Andvari grinned.

"Vinnia, how do you feel about forests?" Grinnon addressed the woman.

"I don't have any advanced bushcraft, but I enjoy nature, Sir."

"You will be my representative. Go with them when they leave. Work with them. These three can know anything you will pass on to me, or anything else they need to follow this criminal. Hold nothing back. We'll be in touch daily, so we can keep everyone up to date on what we're learning."

She straightened in her chair and bowed her head. "Yes, Sir."

Andvari smiled. "Can you ride a horse?"

"A—a horse?" she stammered.

"That's fine. We have horses for brand new riders. You'll be fine." Kyson walked over to the drink table and poured himself some tea.

"What will I need?" Vinnia tapped her fingers on the arm of her chair in a random pattern.

Andvari rested a hand on her shoulder as he knelt beside her. "Bring what you like to be comfortable in camp. We're pretty informal. We'll provide you with clothing of an appropriate colour for when we leave camp. You'll stand out in a forest, otherwise."

Aili snorted. "That's for sure. Even without my senses, I noticed every last one of you."

Andvari glanced at the ceiling and shook his head.

Kyson smirked. "Do you even know why they wear the colours they do?"

Aili took another bite of pastry as she went silent. She chewed and swallowed her mouthful. "Okay, we wear green because we blend in. We don't want to be seen. They wear colours that stand out, so they must want to be seen."

Grinnon almost smiled, the corners of his eyes crinkling slightly. "Yes, we do. Sometimes, when things are stressful, we can calm them just by showing up and being calm ourselves. People see our black robes, with or without the colourful trim, and they know we'll help and keep order. They calm just with us there, and it makes our jobs easier."

Aili took another bite while considering this. "While we're in towns, it's like that. If someone needs help, they see us and smile. They run to us."

Andvari grinned and stood. "Exactly. We're recognizable in towns because we no longer blend in. Same thing for them. They want to be seen."

Vinnia stood. "I'll get my things. Where should I meet you?"

"Do you know where the Scout Headquarters are? A few blocks down?"

Aili smiled at the way Vinnia had to look up to him. Most field Scouts were tall. At least the men were. Mind you, so were the CDF mages, too. Theron could easily look Andvari in the eye if they were both standing.

Vinnia nodded. "Sure do."

"We'll be there once Aili's done eating the CDF food supply for the week." Andvari grinned at her. 'It's fine. Take your time. I know how hard you worked.'

'Not listening.' Aili focused on her food, though she couldn't hide her smile as she shoved more sandwich in her mouth.

"I'll be right back. Help yourselves to anything." Grinnon gestured at the food table before turning and leaving, the parchment in his hands.

Andvari walked over and poured a tea. Kyson took his tea and sat with Theron. Vinnia left quietly. Once Andvari filled his teacup, he joined them. Aili ignored them, her attention still on the delicious food in front of her. The CDF ate as well as the Scouts, but their cooks used different spices.

Grinnon was back in minutes, just as Aili finished her plate. She drained her teacup.

Andvari stood. "Looks like Aili is ready. Thank you for the opportunity to come and see the magic, and for ensuring she had food after." He touched palms with Grinnon in a gesture Aili hadn't seen before.

Grinnon bowed his head. "Thank you for sharing what you've learned. Vinnia is fully trustworthy. She will stay in contact with me and can pass information securely."

"Great. We'll keep you fully updated. Aili?" Andvari nod-ded to the door.

Aili stood with her tray in her hands. "Ready."

She took her tray to the last table and set all her dishes in the containers. They did this part pretty much the same, so she figured it out easily. Kyson brought the teacups over, setting them with hers. She walked with him to the door, ducking to the side to avoid a couple of CDF mages coming in. They glanced at her as they passed. She scooted out behind Kyson, moving around him.

Kyson chuckled and shook his head. 'They aren't going to do anything to you, you know. They don't walk around and randomly torture people for fun.'

She marched down the hall after Andvari, heading right for the elevators. 'Maybe not, but I'd like to go home now.'

"As soon as Vinnia joins us, we'll ride back." Andvari rest-ed a hand on her shoulder, squeezing lightly. "You really should get more used to the other branches of law enforce-ment. Sometimes we do need to share information or work together to solve a situation."

"Other branches? There's more?" Her thoughts flowed back to Dinlark, and sneaking into and out of the city there. The guards there wore different uniforms. "Of course. Each major settlement has their own, don't they?" Aili stepped onto the platform. Her stomach lurched. She grabbed Andvari's sleeve.

He set his hand on her back and eased her nausea with a simple spell. "Most mid-sized settlements, too. Often, they'll be branches from the nearest major group. The capital is unique in not having any branches. The Scouts look after the farmland and area around the capital. That's why we have a building here."

She leapt off the lift and onto the solid floor. Taking a moment to root herself and touch the stone, Aili took a deep breath. "How often do you interact with them?"

Andvari stepped calmly from the lift. "Me personally? Hardly ever. I have someone on my staff who handles all joint cases. They make sure whatever Scouts are in the appropriate area know what they need." He led her through the entry hall.

She dashed beside him, her short legs unable to keep up at his pace. Speeding up at the open doors, she ran down the steps and stopped in the sun. Aili turned and waited for them to catch up.

"Eager to get back?" He smiled as they headed for the alley.

Aili walked calmly with him at a pace she could easily walk all day. She shrugged. "Sometimes it's nice to be home."

They made their way through the alleys and back streets, taking the quietest path.

Vinnia waited just outside the stable door, a small bag over her shoulder. She smiled as they approached. "I thought I'd wait for you here. The breeze is pleasant."

"That's fine." Andvari smiled back at her. "I sent word ahead, so the horses should be ready for us." He opened the wide doors and walked in.

The horses were tied in the aisle, all tacked up and ready. Each had a hay net keeping them busy. A small horse Aili didn't know waited at the far end beside Leya. Leya whickered at her. Aili darted over and rubbed her shoulder as Andvari guided Vinnia past the other horses.

Darik came from the tack room and walked over to the unfamiliar horse. He patted her dark rump. "This little girl is a sweetheart. She knows her job and will keep you safe."

Vinnia reached up and touched the little horse on the neck. Her hand almost shook. Her fingers sank into the soft winter hair. "Hi."

"If you have any questions or feel uncertain, ask any of them." Darik nodded at her and the others. "Especially Aili. She knows horses and can help." Darik winked at Aili.

Aili grinned and waved. "Happy to help." She walked around Leya to the little mare and rubbed her forehead. "How are you today?"

She sank her powers into the horse and touched the mare's heart. Images of the countryside flashed through her mind.

'Yes, we're leaving the city.'

Happiness and warmth flowed into her.

"You really are a Scout horse." Aili smiled at Andvari, knowing he felt the exchange through the link. "When she finally comes back, consider letting her spend some time in a camp for a while."

Darik laughed. "She told you, huh?"

"Uh huh." Aili patted her shoulder. She turned back to Leya and rubbed her forehead.

"Can you talk to them?" Vinnia stroked the horse's shoulder and neck.

Aili glanced up from checking Leya's girth. When she glanced at Andvari, he nodded. "Yes. It's not talking with words like we do, but I can communicate with them."

"I've heard so many stories of what you can do. Each is wilder than the last."

Darik smoothed a leather strap. "There you go. She's all ready for you." He tucked the spare leather into a keeper. "Once you're mounted, I'll adjust your stirrups for you."

"Aili, take Leya out and mount up. Darik will get Vinnia settled and ready, and you can help her when we get going." Andvari untied Charger and led the big horse out behind Kyson and Trickster.

Taking Leya's reins, Aili brought her out into the sunshine. She leapt up into the saddle without using the stirrup. Leya snorted, staring longingly at her hay net.

"You can have more later. It won't kill you to go without eating for a little while." Aili stroked her neck.

Leya snorted.

Vinnia laughed. "It's like she's talking back to you."

Aili shrugged and grinned. "She is."

Darik brought the little mare over beside Aili. He set the reins over the horse's head. She stood still as he showed Vinnia how to mount, swinging effortlessly into the saddle.

"Just like that. Don't worry if it feels awkward. That's normal until you get used to it." Darik held her bridle. "Whenever you're ready."

CHAPTER 6

Vinnia stepped up beside the little mare. She set her foot in the stirrup. With a little effort and a tight jaw, she swung up into the saddle. Fit and athletic, Vinnia made it look easier than many beginners. She lowered herself into the saddle and let out a breath.

Aili held her hands up a little. "Hold the reins like this. She'll stay beside us, so you can relax while you learn."

Andvari mounted Charger, making it look effortless. "We'll teach you as we go. By the time you get back, you'll be riding confidently." He glanced at Kyson, mounted and ready to go. "I'll lead. Aili, stay beside her. Kyson will ride rear."

Aili touched the little mare with her abilities. 'Stay with me,' she whispered through her magic. She turned Leya to follow Charger. The mare turned with her.

"The more you relax, the easier the ride will be," Aili advised. "All you have to do is let your hips follow her motion. Keep her between you and the ground." She smiled at Vinnia. A smile could go a long way with a new rider.

"That's it, huh?" Vinnia smiled back, though it almost looked like a grimace. Her fingers clenched around the reins.

"Yeah. Breathe. It helps. Slow and deep, like meditation. Wiggle the fingers a bit and relax. She knows what to do."

Vinnia took a breath and let it out. "Okay, this isn't so bad. She really is following you."

"She will. All the way to camp if you need. She's a good girl." Aili reached over and patted her shoulder in front of the saddle.

Andvari led the group down the alley. Staying on quieter streets as long as possible, they finally joined the crowd on the main road. Aili kept the little mare close to her. The crowd gave them room, respecting the uniforms and recognizing them as law enforcement.

"The city looks different from the back of a horse." Vinnia glanced down each side street they passed. Her black robes with colourful trim stood out among the crowd.

"I don't think I've ever seen anyone from the CDF ride before." Aili searched her memory but was drawing a blank.

Vinnia shook her head. "It's not a skill we train. We don't use horses in the city. We have wagons and even flying transports for anything we need." She sighed in contentment as they left the city gates behind, riding out between fields and crops already, a faint smile on her face.

Andvari dropped back beside Vinnia as the road widened. Aili slowed Leya and joined Kyson. He took the time to show Vinnia some compass spells, as well as spells to locate water. Aili watched what she could. Kyson showed her the patterns through the link. The trip seemed so much shorter heading home.

"Before we go out into the bush, we'll get you out on some basic exercises. I want to make sure you can find any Scout or camp and can survive for a day or two if the worst should happen." Andvari perked up as he pointed ahead. "You'll see our camp in just a few moments up there."

They crested the rise. Aili's smile mirrored theirs. Home. What would Vinnia think of it? The city was significantly larger and made of stone. The camp was made entirely of living wood. It sprawled, covering a hillside, with plenty of space between buildings. The sun reached almost everywhere in camp, except behind a few of the tallest buildings.

"It's so quiet." Vinnia almost whispered.

They passed through the dome protecting the camp. The magic was a warm tingle to Aili, strong, but welcoming. The others didn't even feel it.

"This is the second largest Scout camp. We have a fraction of the capital's population, and plenty of space to spread." Andvari gestured at the hill hiding half the camp from the road. "The pastures and many gardens are back there, behind the camp. The stables as well. We'll show you around."

The horses carried them along the road, through the camp. Scouts practiced combat and arrest skills in the main square outside the command building. Support staff weaved and carved and made things in the grassy space around their workshops, enjoying the warm sun. Students gathered together in another open space, learning new spells from a Scout and Border Guard.

"There's less rushing here." Vinnia turned in the saddle, taking it all in. "A slower pace of life."

Kyson nodded. "We do trade with businesses, but mostly we're self-sufficient. Our support staff can make nearly everything we need. We only have to send away for specialty items."

"Like the communication mirrors?" Aili looked up at him.

"Yes. The small ones we carry are made here or up north. The large ones, like the one in your room, those are made in the big cities."

"Those are herb gardens?" Vinnia pointed to the tended beds of flowers and other plants beside the herbalism workshops. "Medicinal or culinary?"

"Both," Andvari confirmed, as they rode past. "Our herbalists tend them with help when needed. Much of our food is grown on farms nearby and by independent farmers in the area. We help them with their crops and livestock. They give us a portion of their harvest." He pointed to the long warehouses. "Two of those are just food storage."

They rounded the command building and rode back to the stables. Leya whickered at Meeka, who grazed in a paddock nearby. Meeka lifted her head and called back.

"I'll put you out once you're brushed," Aili promised, patting her withers.

"Kyson, would you get Vinnia settled while we take care of the horses? Any of the guest quarters are fine." Andvari halted Charger in front of the stable doors.

"Sure." Kyson stopped Trickster beside the little mare. "You dismount like this." He talked her through dismounting, showing each step. Landing lightly, he patted Trickster's shiny black hair.

Aili dismounted and held the little mare's reins. "I'll look after her for you."

Vinnia smiled as she slid from the saddle. "Thanks." Her feet hit the ground, and she winced as she straightened up. "I appreciate it." Vinnia untied her bag from behind the saddle.

Jordi came out and took Trickster's reins. "Welcome back. I got the big lad."

"Thanks." Kyson waved as he led Vinnia to the nearby command building.

They took the horses inside and tied them in the aisle. Working together, they had the horses untacked and groomed swiftly. Aili led the smaller two out, following the bigger horses and men to the paddocks.

"There." Aili slid Leya's halter off. "Told you I'd be quick."

"I'll check how they're doing. Why don't you start that report for Commander Grinnon?" Andvari closed the gate behind her. "Don't leave anything out. They are our allies, after all."

Aili hung the halters on the hooks. "I guess."

Andvari chuckled. "Bring the paper and write out here if you like. Where you write it doesn't matter."

She dashed towards the door. "Great."

"Once you're done, you have the rest of the day off," he called after her.

Aili pumped her fist in the air. Finally, some serious time to read. She wanted to try a new potion in the herbalists' workshop, too. It's been a few days since she walked in the woods. Some time with her sword would let her work on form four. How was she to choose?

***

In the end, she read for a while before trying the potion. Leya deserved a break after taking her to the city. This morning, he still had meetings, so she went for a ride in the forest after breakfast.

She stroked Leya's neck as they wandered through the trees. Where was she even going? Aili closed her eyes and felt the breeze brush over her skin, still cool this early. Her hips swayed with each step the pony took. Aili pulled her cloak tighter around herself.

Opening herself, Aili stretched her awareness over the nearby forest. The grass pressed up through the soil, some already emerging from winter slumber. Tiny animals darted around, collecting the food they stored away over the winter.

What would spring feel like up north, across the sea? That land was almost all brick and stone. How dead must it feel? She wouldn't be upset if she never left Athia again. That place was so cold and lifeless.

Something pulled at her, tugging at her heart. Aili opened her eyes and peered through the trees. Leya perked up and whickered.

"What is it, girl? Do you feel it, too?" Aili closed her eyes again and sought the sensations. "Let's go find it."

With a light press of her leg, Aili turned Leya towards the warmth. It wasn't so much a pull as an awareness of home, like how it feels when you've been away, and someone has a mug of tea ready for you. Aili braced on Leya's withers as she leaned forward.

Could that be it? Aili rubbed her cheek. That tree felt different somehow, like it wasn't just waking for spring. Aili leapt from Leya's back and ran to it, touching a nearby branch. Did something make it wake early?

Images flashed through her mind. She saw a tree with rich, warm brown bark. It sat in a clearing, surrounded by the tallest trees she'd ever seen. A woman sat under the tree, sheltered by the branches. She looked right at Aili and smiled.

'Mother?'

'Yes, child. I'm here. You found one of my sentinels.' The woman opened her arms to Aili.

Energy pulsed into her through her hands and feet. The breeze blew around her with more warmth than she expected. 'How many trees like this exist?'

The breeze circled her like a hug. 'One in every forest away from my heart. More in the larger forests. You found the closest to you and your camp. Touch a sentinel's trunk and it will be like you stand before me.'

"Why didn't I notice this tree before? I've been through here many times.' Aili ran her fingers through the long needles, her other hand still touching the bark.

'I woke the tree so I could speak to you. I need your help, if you are willing.' The image in her mind stepped forward and hugged her. The breeze caressed her skin.

'How can I help?'

Her mother smiled. 'You are growing stronger and more confident each time I see you. I think you're ready.'

'For what?' Aili reached through the branches and touched the trunk.

Her mother took her hands, or so it felt. 'To cleanse the Darkness. All my children have this gift, you included. Ilia is capable, but her focus is on another task. I ask this of you. There is a collection of crystals. Your mentor knows about it. With their help, it is time to cleanse them. The Darkness is building, and you must stop it before it awakens fully.'

She rested her head on her mother's shoulder. 'I'll do what I can. There's something else going on as well. Something they're trying to deal with.'

'The artifacts. I know. I can feel them.' She brushed a lock of hair back from Aili's face, her fingers warm on the girl's skin. 'It's all connected. Cleanse the Darkness, and the rest will follow.'

The image faded, leaving Aili with her cheek pressed against the tree trunk. Her arms threaded between the branches, hugging the tree. She pulled back carefully, untangling herself from the thick branches. A trace of warmth lingered on her cheek.

Cleanse the Darkness. Everything else will fall into place if she does? If they were more worried about the missing artifacts, would they stop to let her cleanse the crystals? Andvari had the power to make many things happen. She needed to speak to him first.

Aili leapt onto Leya and turned the pony back for camp. Once back, she left Leya in the larger paddock with Charger and Trickster. Aili headed for the command hall. He'd probably be there, either in his room or in a meeting somewhere.

Andvari came down the stairs as she headed for their room. "There you are. Come. We have a meeting."

"Wait, we?" Aili turned around and walked with him back towards the meeting rooms.

"Yes, since you're here, I want you to come to this one. It affects you and your abilities, so it's only right you're there." He looked through the papers he carried.

She glanced in the usual meeting rooms as they passed, heading for the far end of the hall. Andvari turned into the meeting room usually reserved for officers and the most senior staff. She hesitated before following him inside.

Padded chairs waited in a loose semicircle around a wooden table, all facing the massive wall screen and mirror. Smaller than the briefing room, only the most senior staff used it. She'd been in here maybe twice ever, unlike the normal meeting rooms.

"Take any seat you like." Andvari waved vaguely at the chairs as he set the papers on the table.

"Can I talk to you quickly while we wait?" She fingered the hem of her shirt, her gaze at her feet.

"Of course. What's on your mind?" He turned and faced her, his full attention on her.

"I spoke to my mother." She met his gaze. "She wants me to do something."

Aili explained how she had found the sentinel tree and talked to her mother. He listened to everything she had to say before responding.

"She didn't give me any more details than that. She might not know. It wouldn't be like her to hold something important back."

Andvari tapped his chin. "I see. She think's they're related somehow? Thanks for telling me. Grab a drink and we'll see how the meeting goes. We might have more to talk about after."

Kyson wandered in. He grabbed a tea from the snack table and took a chair near the end. Setting his tea down, he closed his eyes. Aili poured herself some apple tea. She wandered over to join him.

Andvari selected a darker tea. He set it beside Aili and sat. "We're just waiting for a few more people."

Aili brushed her fingers over the soft fabric covering the chair. The table was smooth and highly polished. The wood grain stood out with whatever stain they used, a complex contrast of dark and light.

An older Scout escorted Vinnia in. The head of the Border Guards followed them. What was his name again? She knew him by sight as they ate meals at the same table. She rarely talked to him, not like Andvari did. They all took something to drink and settled around the table as well.

CHAPTER 7

"Now that everyone is here, we'll begin. We have a few pressing problems right now, one of which affects everyone." Andvari gestured at the wall.

An image of the pins appeared on the wall where a map of Athia had been moments ago. He nodded to Vinnia.

Vinnia stood and approached the wall. She stared at the images for a long moment in silence before turning back to the table. "These were stolen from our vaults. It would take either an immensely powerful mage, one with magical augmentation, or someone with access. We need to get these back and find out who took them."

"We know Aili can sense their power from a distance, as she sensed the water pin from across the channel. Given what we know about her range, and everywhere we've travelled in the last year, it's safe to say the pins are not in the eastern half of Athia." Andvari gestured at the wall, and the map appeared with red marks all over it.

Aili stared up at the map. Had she really seen so much in just a year? Not even a year, but close? Probably half the map was shaded red. Of course, he allowed for her range in detecting the magic, so it looked bigger than it was.

"How long have the pins been missing?" The border guard crossed his arms over his chest. Broso. That was his name. What was his family name again?

Vinnia shook her head. "A full inventory is only done annually. They were all marked as being there last spring."

"What if they were taken recently?" Kyson frowned at the map. "It's possible they could be somewhere, moved there after we passed by. She wouldn't feel them then."

"I considered that," Andvari admitted. "Given that the water pin was causing problems just being where it was, the others might do something similar. The Scouts would have noticed if it were in the north. Too many experts are stationed up there. I think it's most likely here in the southwest somewhere."

"Near the crystal storage?" The last Scout shook his head. "That could be it. The magic around the storage might overwhelm the magic in the pins or affect our ability to notice something different."

"Nothing crossed the land borders. We'd know. You're sure they weren't taken somewhere by ship?" Broso picked up his mug and took a sip.

Andvari shook his head. "While we can't be completely sure, there's a reason to believe the pins are still here in Athia. She would have noticed another pin while we were getting the first one. No ships have gone anywhere else. A few research ships have left, but none made landfall anywhere. We started checking all the ships as they left the moment we returned with the water pin."

Maybe I should start making a travel journal, she thought to herself. All those places I've been, and it's only my first year.

"It's not just hunting the pins, though. We need to know who took them." Vinnia paced in front of the map. "We need to stop them from taking anything else."

"What do you think we should do?" Andvari turned to Aili.

"Me?"

He chuckled. "You're the one who can feel the artifacts. You're also the one who can cleanse crystals."

"Um—yeah. I guess." She opened her mouth and closed it when no sound came out. Shaking her head, she shrugged. "If the artifacts are probably in the southwest, and the crystal storage is also in the southwest, that might be a good place to start. We should go. I might feel something as we get close."

Andvari smiled. "I'll make the arrangements. We'll stay in the camp at the crystal storage, using it as our base. Aili is right. Just by being there, we may learn more, or she could feel something that helps. We'll leave at first light. That gives us the rest of the afternoon and evening to pack and get ready. We'll also take Vinnia into the forest and practice a few spells before we go. Aili, you can help with that."

She nodded. While she didn't use spells like they did, there were other ways to help. If he was teaching a tracking spell, she could lay a track with ease.

"I want to know immediately if your people find any trace of artifacts anywhere." Andvari nodded to Broso.

"Will do." Broso nodded back at him.

"I'll inform the camp and ensure they have plenty of supplies." The other Scout pulled out a small notebook. "How many are going?"

"Four. The three of us and Vinnia."

Aili searched through her memories. Who was this Scout? He was senior in rank, or he wouldn't be here. Andvari talked to him all the time, but she never had to go to those meetings.

The Scout nodded. "It'll be done."

"I'll get gear for Vinnia packed and ready," Kyson offered. "That'll give you more time with her out in the forest."

"Thanks. Aili, grab a snack if you need. We're heading out once you're ready and will meet you at the stables." Andvari stood.

Everyone took this as their cue to leave. Aili got to her feet. Wait, he's the camp commander. All camps had one. While Andvari ran the Scouts, he ran this camp specifically. She met the camp commander at a smaller camp to the west once. Before that, she didn't even know it was a thing.

Grabbing a couple of snack bars on her way past the table, she followed the others from the room.

***

Andvari stopped just inside the treeline. "Have you spent much time in a forest before?"

Aili slid from Leya's back. She removed the rope bridle and tucked it in her backpack.

Vinnia eased from the small mare and smiled when her feet touched the ground. "We'd go into the forest on my days off and just walk around."

Aili glanced at Andvari. He had already shown her a few spells on the ride to the camp. Perhaps he wanted her to practice them?

"Her specialties will be combat and control magic," Andvari explained to Aili. "We'll make sure she's comfortable with a few Scout spells. She'll need something to track in a forest with, and a way to always find the camps. Where she'll really shine is when we find whoever we're tracking."

"Okay." Aili nodded.

"First, you need to always find a camp, no matter where you are. We'll practice the spell as much as you need. This one will work using your senses. If you feel warmth or heat, that's a Scout. Cool or cold is a camp. Work it like this." Andvari cast the spell slowly, chanting out loud for her.

Vinnia cast the spell. "Interesting." She turned to face the camp. "It feels unusually cold, but isn't making me cold. Does it get more intense the closer I am?"

Andvari grinned. "It sure does. I imagine with us standing so close, you probably feel like you're standing next to a fire."

Vinnia nodded. She took a few steps away and faced them. "Yes, over here it's still hot, but not nearly so intense. I can't tell the difference between you, though."

"No, you won't be able to. At least most people can't. Only a few with healing skills can, and only sometimes. However, if you're in the bush and need help, any Scout can assist you. It won't matter who you go to. Even a new apprentice can help, and they can get backup swiftly for you."

Aili sensed the spell as Vinnia dissolved it.

Vinnia cast the spell again and let it drop. "Thank you. I'll remember this one."

"Show me your compass spell again?" Andvari requested.

"I prefer this one." Vinnia held her hand out flat in front of her. She took a thin wooden stick from her pocket and set it on her palm. With a whispered incantation, the stick rose slightly off her hand, spinning for a moment. Soon, the white pointed end aimed right at the camp.

"Excellent. We've used that spell with twigs or leaves as well, so if you lose the stick you're not lost. Now we make sure you can track someone in the forest. Have you ever adapted a city spell?"

Vinnia shook her head. "I've never needed to. Any fugitives I've chased, I've caught within sight of the city. Farmer's fields aren't that hard to track in."

"I'll show you a basic forest tracking spell. This one works as long as you have a reference point for someone, some place you know they've been. While I intend you to always be partnered with a Scout, if something happens and you get separated, we want you prepared." Andvari nodded to Aili. "She'll set a track."

Vinnia watched closely as Andvari cast a spell. "We have a similar one. I see where it's different, though."

"This one will work anywhere, even where magic is stronger, or where wolves roam. It doesn't have to filter out other tracks, since it's set on a single track, so the range should be about twice as far as usual." He turned to Aili again. "A simple wide loop. Don't bother hiding the track. Just jog and be back in a couple minutes."

Aili took off through the trees at an easy jog. Her muscles warmed as she went. Aili smiled. Moving felt so good. She missed training in tracking. They didn't do so much now that she was so good, and they had other things to focus on.

Watching him cast spells when teaching others always taught her so much, too. While she didn't cast spells like they did, simply reordering the magic around her instead of casting from her own energy, she could use their patterns to focus her intentions. Sure, she could just wish something to happen, and it would, but magic was easier to control when it was ordered. The more she focused, the more she could do.

Heading in a slow and wide circle, Aili kept them in her senses as she jogged. Vinnia cast the spell, and they set off, following her track. By the time she made it back, they were already catching up.

New magic flared; a spell cast with incredibly familiar magic. They changed direction, heading right towards her. That spell was focused on her or anyone else in the area, letting them find her directly. The downside of that spell was that you couldn't tell people apart with it. There were ways around that, too. Another spell would locate all Scouts. Cast that first, and the caster could rule out a lot of life signs in a forest.

They weaved through the trees as they approached, Vinnia leading. "Okay, I can work with those." She smiled.

Andvari chuckled. "As we go, we'll teach you more. That'll get you started if anything happens on our first mission, though. I'd hate to have to explain to your boss if something went wrong because we didn't prepare you."

Vinnia saluted, her hand and arm crossed over her chest and on her opposite shoulder. "That was great. Thanks. Any more and I might not remember right now."

"Let's go back. We all need a good meal, and we want to be rested for tomorrow. We leave at first light." Andvari led them back towards the horses.

***

"Oh, we get to fly?" Vinnia rushed over to the air box and circled it, her fingers touching the glossy wood.

"That's right." Dinna patted the sloping front. "First class comfort in this one."

Aili sighed. She was leaving poor Leya behind again. Mind you, she didn't want Leya around the Darkness and crystals, so maybe flying was her best choice?

Andvari wrapped his arm around her shoulders and steered her closer. "Come on. The sooner we get in, the sooner we're there."

She dropped her bag in the back, behind the seats. This transport was larger than any other she'd been in. The seats were padded and thick. They even reclined. If she was lucky, she could sleep the whole way. The whole way where, though? They were going west. That's all she knew. This camp was hidden somehow.

Andvari tucked his bag in the back beside hers. Kyson strapped the bags all in place. Of course, an Air Mage would smile, she thought to herself. He'll be in his element up here. Literally. Aili shook her head as Kyson moved farther up the air box, to where Vinnia stood beside it. He held his hand out to her.

"Thanks. Just climb over?" Vinnia leaned against the side. She bounced over, Kyson helping support her.

How could anyone be so excited to fly? Then again, Vinnia was scared of horses, the same way Aili felt about flying. Maybe she wanted to fly like how Aili always wanted to ride?

Andvari finished adjusting the cargo straps. "There. That'll hold no matter what."

Aili let out a deep breath, calming her body and mind. She leapt the side and walked up the centre aisle between the seats. She stared at the seats, her brow furrowed.

"You sit in them. That's how seats work." Kyson nudged her side lightly. His powerful hands moved to her shoulders. Turning her, he pressed down.

Aili landed on the soft cushion. She gripped the armrests. Was it really just because of how tied to the soil she was, like Andvari suggested? Being high up, she felt ungrounded.

Andvari sat across the aisle from her, Vinnia in front of him. He reached across the aisle and rested a hand on hers. "It's fine. Not everyone takes to flying, just like some people never get comfortable riding. Slow and deep breathing. It's a splendid chance to meditate, if nothing else."

Meditate. Right. Darik taught her one for moments just like this. It calms wild emotions. She crossed her legs on the wide seat and leaned back, resting her hands in her lap. Taking slow breaths, she counted to herself as the box rose into the air.

CHAPTER 8

S omething jostled her. Aili blinked and looked up. Andvari nodded ahead, past Dinna. She sat up and peered around Dinna. Aili blinked again. It's been ages since she fell asleep meditating. Her focus was better than that. At least it means she calmed herself well. Too well.

The forest stretched out in front of them, covering most of the west. From Dinlark towards the north to Mithlan on the southern coast, trees filled much of the space. A few wide swaths of fields and meadows broke the solid mass of forest. The land gently rolled, except to the south, where mountains rose higher than they flew. Wait, was that a valley ahead?

Aili opened her senses fully and felt for the land below her. They weren't close enough yet, but the valley almost shimmered in her senses.

"Enchantments?"

Andvari nodded. "Many. This is the most protected place in all of Athia. It's more secure than the Council building or any vaults in the cities. We'll pass through many layers of magic here."

As they flew closer, she picked out the first layer of magic. A vast dome covered something, like the domes over most camps, but stronger. Beneath the magic, she sensed people and wooden buildings. The camp? Another dome was beyond the first, larger and stronger.

Dinna aimed the transport at the closer dome, gliding down to just above the trees. Aili gripped the armrests as they skimmed down into the treetops. Her skin tingled as they passed through the dome and into camp.

She shook her head. They emerged from the trees and into the clearing. From the outside, the dome made it look like the forest was undisturbed, like there was no clearing. The camp was smaller, with only a few scattered buildings, and quiet. Dinna brought the transport down in front of what should be the main hall.

"We'll settle in before we do anything else." Andvari leapt over the side, landing with a spring in his step. "This camp is a little different from the others, so take some time and get used to it."

Aili scrambled over the side and pressed her palms to the soil. She closed her eyes and soaked in the energy from the precious ground.

A smaller hand rubbed her back. "I won't take it personally." Dinna winked at her. "You did better than last time."

Kyson snorted. "She slept through the last flight, too."

"Yes, but last time you tossed her into the transport. This time she got in on her own." Dinna helped her up.

Aili brushed the dirt from her palms. Her cheeks burned.

Dinna hugged her. "It's fine. Don't let him make you feel bad about not taking to the sky. Have you tried any flight magic?"

Aili shook her head. "Levitation is bad enough. Why would I want to fly deliberately?"

Dinna grinned. "It's the first thing I'd do if I could."

"You're the weirdest Earth Mage I ever met." Aili narrowed her eyes at the woman.

"Look closer." Dinna tapped her neckband.

Aili leaned closer and examined the little crystals set in four clusters. They were emerald like any other Earth Mage, but each had a tiny blue core. Aili blinked and rubbed her eyes. She'd never seen that before. Sure, Ilia had three emerald crystals and a light blue one, but each was a solid colour. Maybe neckbands were more diverse than she thought.

"That was amazing." Vinnia took her bag from Kyson. "Thank you."

"You're welcome." Kyson slung his own bag over his shoulder.

Andvari handed Aili her bag and set his own over his shoulder. He led the group up the steps and into the main hall. It was similar enough to the others as far as she could tell, though only two levels high, and smaller. The dining hall was through the archway to her right as she came in. Upstairs would be personal quarters, as they always were.

"The guest accommodations are where most of the front meeting rooms would be," Andvari explained. He nodded past the stairs. "Also, game rooms and lounges, and a few work rooms."

Aili followed him past the stairs, Kyson and Vinnia behind her. She glanced into a room and saw sofas and tables with chairs. A man sat at a table, weaving a basket from grasses. He smiled and nodded to her as she passed.

"These guest rooms are designed for a Scout partnership. We'll be splitting up." Andvari turned down a side hall. "Aili, you'll share with me. Kyson will stay with Vinnia. He can assist with anything she needs. When we're on missions, you'll be Kyson's partner, though. I'll partner with Vinnia in the rare event we need to split."

"Okay." Aili shrugged.

"When working with other branches of law enforcement, the most senior or skilled mages will partner with them. It helps cover any differences in job-based skills," Kyson explained. "He's technically more senior than I am, since he doesn't mind paperwork."

Andvari opened a door. "You two will stay here. We're right next door."

Kyson led Vinnia inside. Aili followed Andvari to the next door. She grasped the cool metal doorknob and turned it, opening the door. The room was smaller, with enough room for both beds and a desk, but still comfortable. Trunks sat at the end of each bed as usual, ready for their belongings. They still had a private washroom as well.

"It's weird not being on a cot in the corner." Aili walked slowly towards the window.

Andvari chuckled. "Which one would you like?"

"This one. It's closer to the window." Aili dropped her bag onto her trunk.

"You're a full Scout now, even as an apprentice. You can choose to stay with us or have your own room when we travel. Well, actually, you'd stay with one of us and the other would get their own room. We're more senior, so it's a perk." Andvari opened the window between the beds and looked out.

"Wait, what? So, all this time I've been sharing your room, I've been intruding on your space?" Aili slumped onto her bed.

Andvari knelt and took her hands. "I don't see it that way. When you were a new student, you needed to be close. If anything happened with your magic, I needed to be close to help. You're like family and I like having you around. I don't mind, and I never did."

She stared at him. What was she to say to that?

"One day you might even have a student of your own. You'll need to share your space. You'll know what I mean, when that day comes. At first, you'll be figuring things out, but once they've been around a while, it's like they've always been in your life. You'll notice when they're not around."

"Me? A mentor?" Her brain froze. She'd never be able to help a spellcaster. Unless she had a half-sister to teach, being a mentor wasn't likely.

He got that thoughtful look, the one where he stared off at nothing for a moment. "Okay, probably not, but you never know. You might be asked to watch a more advanced student for another mentor." He leaned closer. "That's when they can be a bit annoying."

Aili laughed. She covered her mouth with her hand, hiding her grin.

"Technically, any time a mentor teaches a lesson, they have temporary guardianship over those students until the lesson is over. I can see having you teach new Scouts tracking and other skills, so it's not that unreasonable, is it?" He stood and went to his trunk, opening it.

"I guess not. Okay, hang on here. I just realized something." Aili sat straighter, pinning him with her gaze. "I'm a full mage, and no longer your student. Not like I was, though you are still my mentor. When normal mages become apprentices, they get assigned an experienced partner. They also get a roommate. I haven't."

He stopped and stared at her, his open bag in his hand.

"What?" Aili raised an eyebrow. "What's that look for?" Opening the link, Aili reached for him, but his warmth was distant. "What aren't you telling me?"

He dropped his bag in his trunk and sat on the bed across from her. "When apprentices are assigned partners, that partner is their mentor. You're in a unique position because of your magic. I'll stay your mentor until you're a Master Mage. I already understand you and your magic. I already have a partner, so nothing changes for us. We work as a team instead of a pair. It's been done before, it's just not common."

"Oh." It made sense, but she just got the feeling it wasn't everything. What wasn't he telling her?

His warmth filled the link, no longer distant. Andvari reached over and took her hand, squeezing gently. "You're different because of your abilities and being a Nature Mage. Kyson's not just my partner, either. Despite appearances and his disdain for paperwork, he does help me run the Scouts."

'I heard that.' Kyson shimmered in the link.

Aili pressed her fingers to her mouth, over her smile.

'Well, I'm not wrong. It's a good thing I have others around who are actually good at paperwork to help with that part.'

'I simply prefer to use my talents in other areas and ways that benefit the Scouts.'

Andvari laughed. 'Whatever you say, partner.' He stood again. "I'll be right back. Dinna hasn't left yet, and I want to talk to her for a moment."

Aili stood and stretched. Picking up her bag, she opened her own trunk. Stuffing her belongings inside, she tucked the bag in the corner. Unpacked and unsure, she closed the lid and sat. Taking a moment, Aili looked at the pictures on the walls. Each camp and room had unique pictures, but they were always scenes of nature and the forests.

One painting caught her eye. She got up and walked over. Aili knew that camp. Whoever painted it had been there. Her home. The eastern camp stretched across the painted hillside, as seen from another hill she stood on herself just days ago. Did a Scout paint these?

Tearing herself away from the painting, Aili headed for the door. He went outside, probably. She wandered back towards the main door, taking her time and memorizing where her room was. This part was a little different, with side halls in places other camps didn't have. Brushing her fingers over the warm living wood, Aili found her way to the main door.

Andvari was just coming back in, followed by Kyson. "Did you want to eat first, or clean up?" He nodded toward the archway into the dining room.

Her stomach rumbled. Aili looked down at her belly. "I guess I'll be eating first."

Kyson half-snorted as he suppressed a laugh. "Be right there. I'll check on Vinnia." He squeezed past Aili in the hall.

She stepped back, giving him more space to go by. Her stomach growled again.

"Let's go eat before people think the dragons are coming back with that noise." Andvari headed for the dining hall.

Aili followed him through the archway. She sensed the silencing spells that kept the noise inside as she passed through, but didn't hear the usual buzz of voices once inside. Walking down the short hall, she turned into the dining with him. Stopping short, she looked around.

The room was half the size she expected, even for how small the camp was. It was a fraction of the size of her home camp's dining hall. A few tables were surrounded by chairs instead of benches, enough for a couple dozen people. Wide windows made the room look larger than it was. A small group of people sat at one end of a table, talking and eating.

Andvari stopped at the food table. Grabbing a plate, he added some scoops from the platters and bowls. "Coming?"

Aili shook her thoughts free and followed. "Yeah. Sorry." She scurried over to his side, ignoring the people watching her now.

The usual wide selection of dishes awaited her, but the bowls and platters were so much smaller. She couldn't resist the basket of fresh buns. Taking a couple, a couple more appeared in the basket to replace them. Last, she took a bowl of veggie stew, still steaming and ready to go. Aili picked up her tray.

Vinnia followed Kyson through the entrance and joined her at the food table. "Look at all the choices. You eat better than we do."

Andvari smiled. "We get the freshest produce from all the farmers we help. Being able to work with naturally preserved foods and fresh foods, well, that's a big draw for a culinary mage. Help yourself. There's always plenty."

Aili added a cup of tea to her tray. It smelled like normal apple tea, but with something added to it. What, though? Once it cooled, she'd taste it and find out.

Andvari led her group over to the table with Scouts already sitting there. At larger camps, he'd take her to a separate table, where senior officers sat. Here, it looked like everyone ate together.

"Hey, boss. How've you been?" An older woman gestured at the chairs. "Pull up a seat. We were just debating the merits of different types of barriers. I know these youngsters would benefit from an expert's advice."

He set his tray down beside the woman and pulled the chair out. "Sure. What's the consensus so far?" Andvari settled in the chair.

Aili sat beside Andvari. Kyson and Vinnia joined them on the other side of the table, beside a younger man. She tore open her roll and looked at the small group. The older woman and an older man sat with three younger Scouts. Her breath caught as she saw the youngest woman at the far end of the table. She was almost Aili's age with light brown eyes and a quick smile. She nodded to Aili. Aili returned the smile and nodded back. Someone so young out here, of all places? She was an apprentice, not a student. The young woman had the same shoulder patches Aili had on her own clothing.

'Don't ogle,' Kyson teased in the link.

'What? No, I'm just—' Aili stared at him across the table. Her cheeks heated.

'Just what?' Kyson raised an eyebrow.

CHAPTER 9

'I didn't expect to see anyone even close to my age here.' Aili stuffed a massive piece of bun into her mouth. The hot butter burned the roof of her mouth.

Andvari rested a hand on her knee. Soothing magic flowed, easing the sting of the burn. 'Steady, now.'

"—so, we're debating which is better. Do we use a general shield against any attack or are we better off matching the shield to the element." The older man raised his teacup towards Andvari. "Let the highest skilled shield expert give his opinion."

"Sure." Andvari took a sip of tea. "It depends on skill. Any shield is better than no shield. If in doubt, throw up our general-purpose shield. Now, if you have a chance to see what kind of mage you're up against, if you can see the crystals in their neckband, that does give you an advantage."

"What about against someone like her?" The young man nodded at Aili's neckband. "I've never seen those colours in a neckband before."

She glanced up at Andvari. Having missed most of the conversation, the urge to put up a bubble and sneak out overwhelmed her.

Andvari chuckled. "Aili is one of a kind, magically speaking. Fortunately for you all, she's on your side, or you would have reason to worry. She does have an attack that can go through our standard shields, but she won't use it against you."

The older man turned his gaze on her. Aili stared down at her bowl of stew.

Andvari rested a hand on her shoulder. "She's helping us develop new shield spells for everyone. Since she became my student, we've learned so much more about magic. In training, master mages have been able to defend against her, so once we perfect those spells, we'll share them with you all."

"New magic?" The young woman perked up and smiled. "You're her." She stared at Aili.

'Her?' Aili glanced at Andvari. 'Her who?'

"Yes, Aili is the Nature Mage." Kyson laughed. "She's here to cleanse the crystals. While she's doing that with Andvari, Vinnia and I will be working on new spells to protect against the Darkness. You all can help with that."

'Everyone is staring.' Aili picked up her spoon. Her hand shook.

"Who wants a few special training sessions while Kyson and I are here?" Andvari raised an eyebrow and smiled.

'Thanks.' Aili sent gratitude and warmth down the link to him.

His warmth flooded back to her. 'Any time. You'll get used to it, though. You can't hide it anymore. Not with your crystals changing like that.'

Aili ran her fingers over her neckband. Slender strands of braided metal held clusters of four crystals together, spaced around her neck. Instead of glowing solid with one of the four elemental colours, hers also had gold cores. Aili had never seen gold in a neckband crystal before.

'Eat. I thought you were hungry? Unless the burns in your mouth took away your appetite?' Kyson nudged her foot with his under the table.

"Any magic in particular you'd like to practice?" Andvari asked the group. He had their full attention now.

"I'd like some time with Kyson." The older woman picked up her teacup and took a small sip. At a glance, Aili noticed the light blue crystals in her neckband. The metal was platinum. She was a Master Mage. "I'm working on advanced levitation."

"We'll make time," Kyson assured her.

"I'd like to practice my arrest and control skills," the young man requested. "I don't get much chance to work with people I don't know well, so I'd like the challenge."

"Me, too," the slightly older young woman added.

Andvari smiled. "How would you also like a chance to see the CDF techniques?" He tilted his head towards Vinnia.

"I'd be delighted to help. It's what we train the most." Vinnia raised her teacup to the young Scouts.

He turned his gaze to the young woman. "What about you?"

She squirmed for a moment, glancing down, before meeting his gaze again. "I'd like some practice with tracking."

'Now's your chance. Dazzle her.'

Aili glared at Kyson. She pressed her fingers to her burning cheeks. 'She probably already thinks I'm an awkward fool.'

"I love a good tracking lesson, and I know Aili does, too. We'll set aside time for that as well," Andvari promised. "Once we've eaten, we're going into the dome, though. We'll be here at least a week, I expect. I'll do up a schedule for everyone."

'Eat,' Kyson urged through the link. 'If you end up doing any cleansing or magic, you'll want the energy.'

Aili focused on her plate, and the food still sitting on it. Cleansing Darkness took a lot of energy, possibly more than anything else she could do with magic. If anything went wrong when they were in that dome, she had to be ready to protect them.

"You can stay while we go into the dome," Andvari told Vinnia. "Feel free to explore and get used to the place. Any Scout can help if you're trying to find something or need something. As long as you're here working with us, you're considered one of us."

Vinnia nodded. "I appreciate that."

***

The magic sparkled and shone in her senses — an enormous dome that covered the entire valley. The magic was so thick it was hard to see inside. She held her hand just inches from the dome. "I've never seen anything quite this powerful," she whispered.

Andvari handed some papers to the Scout at the gate, a narrow opening into the dome where the magic felt different. "Everything is in order. Let us know when you are ready."

"Yes, Sir." The woman took the papers and stepped into a tiny building beside the dome. It was barely big enough for a table and chairs.

"Mages have been adding protections here for a few hundred years. They waited for the next Nature Mage to arrive and cleanse it all." Kyson rested a hand on her shoulder.

Aili pressed her lips together as she stared at the dome. "I've never read anything about this. How do you know?"

Andvari stepped closer to her, his presence in the link growing stronger. He was examining the barrier through her awareness, so she let him in fully. "I'm not sure anyone outside the most senior Scouts knows. We were the group Ethala Minis started, after all. We supported her work and watched the planet with her, carrying on when she left."

Aili crossed her arms over her chest and stared up at him. "So, who else knows I'm some kind of 'Chosen One'?"

Andvari shrugged. "Only the most senior Scouts. The Commander, Kyson and I, Darik, and a handful of others. Uh, the camp commanders anywhere you've been. Gavi and the most senior healers. Don't forget Hana and Kaj, those we worked with down south—"

"So, basically everyone I've met so far?" Aili raised her eyebrow.

Andvari and Kyson shared a look.

"Yeah, that's probably about right," Kyson agreed. "I mean, not absolutely everyone, but nearly everyone you've met or worked with has been higher ranking."

"Jordi," Andvari added, counting off on his fingers. "Oh, and Frida and a select group of the CDF. Ilia. Your father now, too." He raised another finger for each person listed.

"On the bright side, the average mage on the street has no idea." Kyson patted her shoulder. "Even most Scouts think you're just some kind of prodigy, and don't really know what's up with you."

Aili rolled her eyes. "That makes it so much better. At least Dinna doesn't know, or everyone on the planet would."

Andvari chuckled. "You'd be surprised. She can keep secrets when needed, or she wouldn't be trusted to fly between camps like she does. She carries confidential messages all the time. She's also the gossip pipeline for any information that isn't secure, though."

The woman emerged from the small building. "Everything is ready. You may step through." She touched the gate.

The gate swung open away from them. The energy field around it shifted. Instead of a solid barrier, it was now more like a curtain, just big enough for them to walk through.

"I can't loan you the medallion for this. You're going to have to tough it out." Andvari gestured at the opening. "We're right with you. Keep walking, and you can do this." He offered her his hand.

"I can do this." Aili slid her smaller hand into his. "It's not like the border. This magic doesn't hurt. It's just a bit overwhelming with how powerful it is."

"Let's go." He walked forward with her, heading right for the opening.

She walked with him. Her second step carried her into the energy field. Her nerves tingled, though not with any discomfort. Aili took a slow breath and rolled her shoulders as she walked. Her hair fought her braids, like lightning was about to strike. Wait, she couldn't feel where her body ended, and the energy began. How thick was the barrier?

Warmth rushed through her. 'Walk, child.'

Aili blinked. All she saw was white. 'Mother?'

Feeling rushed through her as she stumbled from the barrier. The energy hummed behind her.

Kyson slung an arm around her as she slumped, holding her up. He walked her a few more steps into the dome. "Are you alright?"

She took a breath and straightened up, her hand still tightly gripping Andvari's. "I think so. I've never felt that before."

"That energy matched yours. Not perfectly, but enough I felt it rush into and through you. I felt it in the link, but it was so strong, I couldn't get to you." Andvari pulled his canteen out, uncapped it, and handed it to her.

Tipping the canteen back, she swallowed the sweet, herb-filled water. He steadied it for her as her hand shook.

"Thanks. How did you know I'd need it?"

Andvari smiled. "Ilia suggested you might."

"That's the strongest one. The others should be easier." Kyson rubbed her back.

"Others?" Aili looked down the path. She gasped. "Oh."

Aili no longer saw a reflection of the forest on the barrier. Instead of thick and healthy trees, the land here was almost barren. The forest was sparse, and there were no animals here. Plants were smaller than they should have been. Even the trees didn't stretch so tall.

"What happened?" Her hand trembled. She let Andvari take the canteen as the contents sloshed. "The trees—"

"The Darkness affects it. We're not completely sure why, as we can't feel it like you can. What we know is nothing grows well inside the outermost dome. None grow at all inside the innermost dome." Andvari tucked his canteen away. "The watch camp isn't far."

He took her hand. They walked to the next energy field. She took a deep breath and stepped into it beside him. The energy moved into and through her, but not as strongly. She still felt her body, knew she was walking, and could sense Andvari distantly in the link. They stepped through and into the dome.

Aili looked back over her shoulder. "That wasn't so bad. Why so many barriers?" She reached for the dome with her senses.

They waited as she touched the dome.

"Magic lesson time." Andvari waved at the dome. "Can you tell what this one is set to do? Why did they put it up?"

She closed her eyes and looked for any pattern in the magic. While the base was pure nature magic, there were plenty of spells added over and woven into it. "It's less wild than the first one. Those are spells for protection. It's like the magic in the cloths when we wrap crystals or contaminated things."

"That's right. Older and stronger, but the same spells. What about the first dome? Can you tell me anything about it?" Andvari turned and looked back at the largest dome.

Aili shook her head. "It wasn't spells. That one is pure wild magic, like I get from nature. It has mother's power all through it as well, and someone else's? Ethala?"

Kyson nodded. "So, the stories go. There's mention of it in private histories. Did she mention it in her journal?"

Aili's eyes widened. "That's this place?"

"Yes. When you're ready, we have to walk down to that camp there." Andvari pointed at a small building in a small stand of trees. "We don't use magic in here, so no wagons. The first barrier keeps all animals outside the dome. It only allows Scouts deemed worthy or safe in here."

Aili walked with him towards the building. "Who decides who's worthy?"

"Nature magic and your mother, as far as we can tell." Kyson fell into step beside her.

"What? Really?"

"Well, the barrier, but we all know who put it there, right?" Kyson smiled at her.

"Has anyone ever been turned away? How many people have been inside here?" She stared at the next dome, down past the camp. Camp? It was a single building, and not a big one either.

"A few. Nearly everyone who has gone through the proper channels has been allowed in, but every now and then someone can't get past the gate." Andvari draped an arm around her shoulders.

She quickened her pace. "How long has this been here?"

"Ethala set it up not long before she disappears from history. So, maybe 400 years, more or less."

Aili looked up at Andvari. "Disappears from history? That doesn't sound good."

Kyson shrugged. "Nobody really knows what happened to her. We presume she died, but there's no grave. Nobody wrote about it or seems to know."

Andvari walked up the few steps and opened the door. Aili followed him inside. Two Scouts played a board game at a table in the first room. An archway led into something like a cloakroom. Another door led somewhere else, probably the larger back area of the building.

"Hey, Boss. Have a good trip?" An older man stood and stretched. He wore normal Scout clothing. His dark hair was peppered with grey and neatly trimmed.

CHAPTER 10

"A beautiful day for a flight." Andvari smiled, stepping over to clasp hands with the man. "How is everything here."

"The usual." The man shrugged. He turned to Aili. "The Nature Mage?"

"Hi?" Aili met his gaze.

Kyson grinned. "Aili, meet Mowen. He runs the camp here."

"It is a pleasure to finally meet you. What can we do for you?" Mowen bowed his head to her.

Aili glanced over at Andvari. 'What?'

"She'd like a tour first. Aili just learned about the camp and is still forming her plan." Andvari smiled. 'It'll be fine. We're here to help.'

'What do you mean help?'

"Of course. Would you like a tea first, or would you like to see the holdings?" He gestured at a small dining table, where a teapot steamed on a hotplate.

'What do you mean help?' Aili pressed through the link. She stood as tall as she could, doing her best not to fidget. "I'd like to see the holdings, I guess?"

'Confidence, Aili. They'll respond best to a confident leader.' Kyson nudged her in the link.

'Leader? Hold on here. What aren't you telling me?'

"This way." Mowen headed for the cloakroom. "We'll get dressed before we go in."

He opened a wardrobe and selected an over-robe. The soft cream cloth glowed to her senses, full of magic. She took the offered robe and pulled it on over her clothing. The robe flowed with each movement, almost weightless despite how thick the fabric was.

Andvari tied a scarf over her head, covering her forehead and hair. He tucked her braids in as he wrapped it down around her neck. Kyson dressed the same way, wrapping his own scarf in place. Mowen handed Andvari clothing before taking some for himself. They also put gloves on, but Andvari shook his head when Mowen offered gloves to her.

"Now we're ready, we can go." Mowen led them out a side door.

Kyson followed Mowen.

Aili hesitated. She glanced back at Andvari before trailing after Kyson. 'Leader? You better explain, mister.'

Andvari lightly tapped her back, pushing her to catch up. 'You're a Nature Mage. You'll never be a normal Scout. What's the mission and purpose of every Scout?'

'To protect the forest and those who live there.' She hustled until she was a couple of steps behind Kyson.

'And?'

And? Was there an and? Aili sifted through her memories, but nothing came to mind. She remembered the oath, clear as day, but it didn't help either.

Kyson filled the link with warm amusement. 'Didn't you read the handbook I know he eventually got for you?'

'Of course I read it.' Aili glanced at the few trees and plants as they walked the packed dirt trail. The only difference between the trail and the dirt beside it was the many footprints.

'What about the section on Scout history, and how they were founded?' Andvari prompted.

Ethala Minis, her half-sister, started the Scouts. They helped her look after nature and guard the wild places.

'Yes, she actually led the Scouts. She was in charge. It wasn't an honorary position.' Kyson glanced back over his shoulder at her.

'Wait, you don't mean—'

Andvari touched her through the link with an energy hug. 'We do. As you're growing into your powers fully, you'll have us all to support and help like they helped her back then. The older Scouts especially will look to you as leader.'

'WHAT?' Aili tripped.

Andvari steadied her with a hand on her elbow, keeping her from hitting the ground. "Take a moment and breathe. You're fine."

She clung to his shirt as she drew in a breath. Her, lead the Scouts? She didn't know how. Why her?

Andvari cradled her cheek in his hand and held her gaze. 'Unless you choose another, I'll still be there, doing my job as always. I take care of it just fine, right?' His soothing magic flowed into her, steadying her.

'Yeah.'

'I'll keep doing it until you replace me, or I retire. I can run the Scouts for you and make sure people are where they need to be, just like I already do. When it comes to facing the Darkness, they'll look to you for guidance. Even I can't dissolve the Dark like you do. I only know how you do it because of the link. You'll lead, with my help. You're not alone.'

"Are you alright?" Mowen stepped beside her. He watched Aili, his face lined, and his brow furrowed.

"She's fine. Being an unusually strong Earth Mage, Aili doesn't fly well." Andvari relaxed his grip as she straightened up and let go of his sleeve.

"I'm fine. I just needed a moment. That's the last dome?" She turned to the magic barrier before them, only a few dozen paces away.

"If you're sure. Yes, you'll see it once we're through." Mowen turned and walked to the barrier.

'Wait. Ilia is also a Nature Mage. Why isn't she in charge?' Aili walked over and touched the dome. The surface rippled like water under her fingertips.

'Technically she is, until you are ready. She accepted care of the Scouts after Ethala disappeared. She chose me to do the daily running and the Commander for political liaison.'

Aili met Andvari's gaze. 'She chose you?'

Andvari smiled. "If you're ready, we just walk through." 'Walk tall, like you know what you're doing. We're right behind you.'

She straightened up and nodded. Mowen led the way through the barrier. Aili winced as her spine popped. Taking a deep breath, she stepped through the barrier. Her nerves tingled again, but she was through in a couple of steps.

This place was a desert, with a sandy, dry soil and no plants at all. Crystals waited in piles, sorted by size. Every one of them had a purple tint, some so deep they were nearly black. Some piles of smaller crystals near her were short, but some near the far end were towering mountains of taint.

One pile caught her attention immediately, pulling her to the far end of the dome. A stack of crystals as thick as her arm and easily as long glowed almost black. She touched her inner lights, flooding herself with protection as she knelt beside the pile.

"Protect yourself well from those," Andvari advised.

Aili nodded. She stretched her hand out and pointed. Light flooded the crystal, flowing from her hand. The Darkness stared back at her, not shifting at all. Aili called her light back, wrapping it around herself.

'How am I supposed to cleanse those?' She stood, crossing her arms over her chest. She glared at the crystals. "Where did those even come from? I didn't know they made crystals that big."

"Those came from the university in Dinlark." Mowen stayed behind her but came closer.

"What were they doing? Seriously, how did they get these?" She frowned down at the thick crystals.

"They were experimenting with growing crystals large enough to power shields around cities, very much like the one around this camp. Something went wrong. They couldn't draw energy from the crystals."

Aili rubbed her cheeks. "Okay, but how did they get so much Darkness inside? Surely, they weren't experimenting with Darkness?"

Closing her eyes, she opened herself to the energy around her. Keeping her Light shield up, Aili felt for the energy. It was flowing. The Darkness was being pulled from the smaller crystals into the larger ones.

"Oh, that's not good. There's an energy flow in here."

Andvari joined her in the link, his presence bright. 'I see it. It's so slow, I see how easy it would be to miss. Over time, especially many years, a lot of energy can move this way.'

'It explains how the crystals at this end are darker and more tainted.' Kyson flowed into the link.

Aili opened her eyes and looked around again. "I can't do anything about this today. We should go back. You three aren't protected like I am, and this place is powerful. I need a plan."

Andvari nodded and gestured at the exit. Aili walked beside him through the piles of crystals, back to the edge of the dome. Glancing up, she blinked. Were those shadows moving around over them? Barely there, misshapen forms of what could once have been mages faded when she focused on them. She shivered. She'd seen a shadow before.

"Are you okay?" Andvari laid his hand on her shoulder.

She nodded. It might just be her imagination running wild. This place was creepy, and it made her nerves burn in a weird way. The purple glow reflecting from the crystals didn't help, either. Even the dome had a purple tint in here, probably from the crystals, as the magic in the dome was untainted.

Marching through the dome, she held her head high. The air out here still tasted stale, but it was less thick and stuffy than in the innermost dome. Closing her eyes, she sent her awareness down into the soil.

The taint was below her, though not as strong as in the crystals. It stopped at the lower section of the dome. It wasn't so much a dome as a sphere. The soil below was healthy and untainted, beyond the protective magic.

"I need to go for a walk or something. Out there in the healthy forests." Aili stared up at the next dome, and out into the forests beyond. "I need to touch nature and feel."

"We can do that." Andvari walked her back to the building.

Once inside, Aili happily shed her protective clothing.

Mowen handed small vials around. "Here. Everyone drinks one when they come out of there."

She uncapped the vial. Sniffing the opening, Aili recognized some ingredients right away. Others she just couldn't identify. "Ilia brews these?"

"Some of them," Mowen agreed. "She works with a potion master in the Scouts based in Dinlark. They supply the rest." He opened the cupboard and showed her the collection of bottles inside. "Between them, we have all manner of protective potions. If someone is exposed directly to Darkness or there's an accident, we can start treatment immediately."

Aili darted closer and examined the labels. Most had a warning not to assess the potions with magic. Her fingers twitched. She didn't dare assess them with her abilities, either, just in case. They'd never tested whether that also affects sensitive potions, and she wasn't about to ruin a whole cupboard full of them just because she was curious.

"Uh, potion master?" Her brain caught up with the rest of the conversation. She turned to Andvari.

"We have a couple in the larger centres. You met a few up north. The one in Dinlark is closest to here." Andvari shrugged. "We can go see them soon. It's not far by flight. Ilia supplies the east directly. Now, do you still want to go walk the forest and think?"

"Yeah." She turned from the cupboard, glancing back at the assortment of potions.

"All the way out of all the domes?"

Aili nodded. "Ideally. I need to stretch my senses out."

Andvari turned to Kyson. "If you want to go back to camp, we'll join you when we're done."

"I'll come. It's a beautiful day for a walk." Kyson grinned and stretched as he stepped back into the sunshine.

The slope rose gently as they headed up the hill. Aili let her thoughts turn in, going over everything she recently learned. She was going to lead the Scouts? Not fully, not like she feared, but she was supposed to guide them? In some ways, that made her legs shake more than having to cleanse the crystals.

"If you want to talk out loud and sort your thoughts out, we're here to help." Andvari stayed at her pace as they approached the final dome. "I was going to start talking about all this anyway, but gradually. It's a lot, isn't it?"

She nodded. Her thoughts stilled as she stared at the barrier ahead. Once they crossed this, they'd be back in untouched forest. Her hands tightened into fists. It almost overwhelmed her the first time. They weren't passing at the gate. Did they just walk through or something?

"Yes, just keep walking."

Aili glanced at Kyson

He shrugged. "Your expression changed when you looked at the barrier. I hardly need your thoughts leaking into the link to tell me what you were thinking. Mind Mage, remember? We learn to read people without magic as well."

Aili smiled and shook her head. Standing tall, she took a slow breath. At least this time she knew what to expect.

Andvari took her hand and kept walking. Aili let him lead her through, her focus on walking at a steady pace. Her vision went white, and her body numb. No, one foot and then the other. A few more steps and she felt his hand on hers again. More steps and she was through.

The forest welcomed her with a light breeze and cheerful birdsong. The sun warmed her cheeks, stronger outside the domes. Sending her energy down, Aili spread it through the soil. She walked from the barrier, touching everything she could.

Slumping down onto the grass, she rolled onto her back. Aili stared up at the sky through the branches above her, the sun landing on her in little dappled patches. She opened herself fully, soaking in the energy of the soil and plants, and even brushing over some birds and mice.

"Are you sure you're alright?" Andvari sat in the grass beside her. "You've never been around that much Darkness before."

CHAPTER 11

A ili met his gaze, noting the way his forehead wrinkled slightly. "I'm fine. You're right. I've never seen that much Darkness all in one place. I learned something in there, though."

"What?" Kyson lowered himself gracefully to the grass on her other side, folding his long legs as he crossed them.

"You know I'm blessed with the power of Light, or however that works, right? It was a gift from Mother, and it protects me from the Darkness." Aili stared up at the tiny patches of blue above her.

"Right?" Andvari leaned back against his hands.

"But it's not many Lights, no matter what it looks like. It's one light that shows up in many places. It's a single thing, like sunlight. Even though the sunlight comes through those branches in many places, it's still the same light."

Andvari nodded slowly. "And the Darkness?"

"It's the same." Aili sat up. "It flows and moves and shifts, but it's still just one thing in many places, not many little things."

Kyson rubbed his chin. "How does that help us? Does it make the Darkness easier to deal with, or harder?"

She sprang to her feet. "I don't know. I need to walk more."

They caught up within a few steps. Aili marched away from the dome, deeper into the forest.

"Even as strong as it was, the Darkness still moved away. It stayed at the edge of my Light." She wiggled her fingers, tapping them to her thumb. "It's like how a shadow can't survive in the light. Even a tiny candle or ball of mage-light can banish a shadow."

"Darkness is harder to cleanse than that," Kyson pointed out. He stayed at her side, matching her pace.

"Yes, for regular mages. You have a sliver of Light inside you, a tie to the land and its energy through your magic. You're not like a candle, though. Not like the protective clothing or my inner Light." Aili worried her bottom lip between her teeth for a moment. "For me, cleansing the Darkness isn't necessarily easy, but it is simple."

"Scouts cleanse with that potion, as long as they weren't Dark-touched directly. Has Ilia ever shown you that potion before?" Andvari stepped wide around a tree, moving closer again once they passed.

Aili shook her head. "She never even talked about the Light and Darkness when I was small. I wonder why. Can I see the recipe at some point?"

"Sure. I might have to send for a copy, though. I don't think it's in any potion book in the general records."

"If I'm going to cleanse that mess, I need a way to keep the Darkness from just sneaking into another crystal or something. I'm not powerful enough to cleanse it all at once. I need to trap it a bit at a time so I can banish it properly." Aili stopped and rested both palms on a tree.

"What keeps it from coming back?" Kyson picked up a leaf and turned it over in his hands. "If you move a candle, the shadows can shift and change, even grow. How do you keep the Darkness from doing the same?"

She shook her head. "It's like I dissolve it with Light, more than banish it. It can do the same thing to a weaker Light, though. That's how people become tainted. Normal mages aren't strong enough to deal with all but the weakest Darkness on their own. They need potions and protective clothing." Aili pushed away from the tree and headed back to camp.

"We know your abilities are different. That's what lets you deal with the Darkness. Do we know why or how, though?" Andvari tapped his chin. "I can ask Gavi if he's felt anything different about you. He's healed you deeply before."

"Well, my Light comes directly from Mother and ties me to her. Your Light is more like something you're given, but that direct tie is gone. I wonder if I could make a charm or something to store a bit more connected Light for you?"

Andvari grinned. "Should we maybe ask the only person alive who still knows how to make charms?"

"I think that's an excellent Idea." Aili quickened her pace. The camp was in sight.

They passed through the smaller protective dome around camp. She'd never made a charm before, but she didn't find her power until after she left the city. Was this something she could even do? Could she protect her friends?

Looking up, she headed straight for the steps. There was something comforting about the camps being laid out so close. This one didn't quite feel like home, but it wasn't so different, either. Only the northern camp was different, simply because of how big it was. It held both a massive healing centre and a research department unlike anything anywhere else. Why didn't he make that his main camp? Why go east?

"I like the quiet and sometimes need to go into the city." Andvari shrugged and opened the door.

She raised an eyebrow as she walked past him. Did she need to adjust the link if her thoughts were sliding through so easily? Aili made her way to her bedroom and settled at the end of her bed.

"Did Ethala ever write about the camps? Anything about how they're set up, or why, or anything like that?"

Andvari nodded. "Even this place has a small archive. You can now access all Scout records and read anything inside them. I think I know what book you want. I'll go get it."

He left quietly. Aili lay back, stretching out on the bed. She was going to be in charge. When she first became a student, he made it sound like she had so many choices in her life. She could have almost any career she wanted.

'Girl, just say it.' Kyson prodded her in the link with his energy. 'Your thoughts might be quiet, but your emotions are screaming.'

'If you have a question, just ask. I won't be upset or offended,' Andvari assured her.

'When did my future go from nearly endless possibilities to running the Scouts?'

'The day you took the oath and joined us officially.' Kyson warmed in the link, almost a laugh but not quite.

'You can still change your mind and do something else,' Andvari assured her. 'It probably seems like a lot right now, maybe too much. That's why we were hoping to ease into it. Your apprenticeship won't be learning Scout skills. Darik already taught you those. It'll be learning how to lead and deciding how you want to run things. It'll be learning how to work with me, or whoever you choose to run the daily affairs of the Scouts.'

Oh. Aili rubbed her cheeks. That really didn't sound too bad.

'You don't have to make any decisions now,' Andvari reminded. 'Most apprenticeships are around five years long. There's no set timeline, though. You have all the time you need. You're not alone, remember. I have an entire staff spread across the country helping me, and you have me.'

'Your small mirror can contact Ilia, even from here. If you want to use the larger one, I'll help you,' Kyson offered. 'He'll need time to find the book in the archive. The smaller archives aren't always as orderly as the massive ones.'

'Good idea. I'll meet you both in our room when she's done.' Andvari pulled from the link, now just a background presence like always.

She stepped into the hall, closing the door behind her.

Kyson came out of his room. "It's still back here." He led her deeper into the building, towards where the communication centre usually is, but through halls the other camps didn't have.

An older woman looked up as they entered the room. She had light blue crystals in her band, typical of communication specialists. "I'll be with you in a moment."

Her attention turned back to the parchment on the table before her.

The room was much as she expected, just smaller. It had one of the big mirrors on the far wall. Spread around the room, she noticed the crystal ball, a bowl of water with a perfectly calm surface, the table with the parchment, and something she hadn't seen before.

Aili turned and examined the wall nearby. A wooden grid had labelled slots with letters in them. Some had names of people in the camp here, a few with letters still in them. Other larger slots had camp names over them. Those slots were empty. One large slot had Andvari's name on it.

"We send letters to someone by putting the letter in the slot for the camp they're based in," Kyson explained. "If I wanted to send you a letter, I'd address the envelope with your name and place it in the eastern camp slot."

"Would it be waiting for when I get back?" She touched the wood, sensing the magic in it. It had spells she didn't even know existed.

Kyson smiled. "No, it would be redirected here, because that's where you are. All that paperwork we do before we travel is at least partly so the spells can find us, no matter what. It's also linked to our mirrors." He touched his chest, where his small communication mirror hung under his shirt.

"He has his own slot." She touched the letters spelling Andvari's name.

"His goes straight to the mailbag when we travel."

"That's wild. What about when I write my father? He's not at a camp."

Kyson pointed to a massive slot below the rest, so big she didn't realize it was part of the system. "In here. It goes to a central post depot in the capital. They redirect it from there, out to all the cities, towns, and regions. It's some of the most complex magic in the country. The University think they have that title, but they're wrong. This is far grander than anything they have."

"The post office hires the most talented mages in every generation." The woman set a stack of parchment on another desk. "Keeping that magic in shape is a full-time occupation. Now, how can I help you?"

"I'd like to contact Ilia in the capital." Is that how she was supposed to ask? She so seldom used the communication rooms, she wasn't sure.

The woman smiled and walked over to the mirror. "Sure thing. She's on speed connect. I'll be just a moment." She touched the mirror frame, and a menu appeared on the glass. A few touches later, and the mirror went cloudy.

Images formed on the glass as the cloudiness cleared. Ilia stood in her workshop. Herbs hung to dry, as always.

Even just seeing it, she knew the smells surrounding the old woman. A self-stirring cauldron worked in the corner, blending a bubbling mixture.

"Aili, dear. Are you alright?" She stared at Aili with those light grey eyes and the assessing gaze of a healer.

"I'm fine," Aili assured her. "I just went into the dome and now I have questions."

Ilia nodded. She pulled a stool over and sat in front of the mirror, where she was still in easy view. "What's on your mind?"

"Charms. How are they made?" Aili twisted her clasped fingers together in front of her.

"That is a very specialized magic. I can send you a book about it but take care. It's old and can't be replaced if anything happens to it. Thinking of trying a charm or two?" She winked at Aili.

"I want to try. You never taught me as a child, but it takes magic. I didn't know how to use magic back then." She explained what she wanted to do. "Would it be possible?"

"Possible, yes. I'll send you my personal notebook on charms. I'll want it back once you've learned what you can from it, so take good care of it."

"I will." Aili held her clasped hands to her chest. New magic. Just as she was getting truly comfortable with what she could do, now she gets to try new magic.

"If you run into trouble or have questions, call me. I can probably help. I'll send those books right away." Ilia touched the mirror frame, and the surface went cloudy again.

Within moments, the mirror looked like any other, reflecting the room back at her. Aili stared at the space Ilia had been moments ago. Leaving home last year, she wondered if she'd ever see Ilia again. Now, the woman who was most like a mother to her was only a mirror call away any time she wanted.

"We can go get supper now." Kyson nudged her shoulder. "They'll be serving it by the time we get there."

Her heart skipped a beat. Would the young woman be there? Why did she care? Heat flushed through her for a moment. Aili took a deep breath and focused. Ilia was sending books, books so rare nobody else has probably seen them in centuries. Maybe longer.

Her stomach growled.

CHAPTER 12

Her book lay abandoned on the bed. Aili stared out the window. The wood of the frame was smooth under her fingers where she gripped it. Her thoughts wandered, too unfocused to read, too unfocused to even really look out the window into the fading light. She sighed and leaned her head against the cool glass.

The door opened. Andvari's familiar presence filled her senses. Even in total darkness, she'd be able to find him. His footsteps approached. He settled on the bed beside her, facing her. Aili glanced over.

"Sit. We should talk."

She stared blankly for a long moment. Had she done something? Had she forgotten to do something? Was she in trouble for something she didn't even know about?

He smiled and shook his head. "Relax. This is a mentor and student type of conversation about life. We've had plenty of these before, right? This won't be any different."

She sank onto the mattress beside him and leaned against the wooden headboard. "Talk about what?"

"Relationships. Attraction. Consent."

Her cheeks warmed. Did the room get hot suddenly? "Uh—"

He grinned. "Honestly, I'm a bit surprised we haven't needed this talk sooner. Are you alright?"

Aili nodded. Was she, though? She shook her head. "I don't know."

Andvari took her hand. A touch of soothing passed between them, a hint of magic, enough to stop her from burning up. "That's okay, too. Being confused is all part of growing up. Did you want to talk about it?"

She sighed and stared down at her lap. "I don't even know. I can't focus right now. Why? I want to know more about her. I don't even know her. What's wrong with me?"

'It's because you're feeling attraction, Aili. Have you ever been attracted to someone before?'

'Kyson, if you're going to listen in, you may as well join us.' Andvari opened the link fully.

'Hey, I was minding my own business when her emotions burst through the link. Her thoughts are too confused to follow. I'll be right there.'

Aili rubbed her temples, curling up with her feet on the edge of the bed. "It's just so new. It doesn't feel like anything I've experienced before. It's not even like anything I've sensed from you two."

The door opened. Kyson came in. He closed the door and joined them, settling on the end of the bed. "So, Aili's got her first infatuation?"

"My first what?" Aili wrinkled her brow.

Kyson shrugged. "I'd know that feeling anywhere."

"But it's not like when you and Hana spend time together. It's sort of the same, but not." She narrowed her eyes at him.

He rolled his eyes. "Stay out of my emotions. Now, Hana and I have known each other for ages. Longer than you've been alive. We have a strong friendship. You're feeling a mature emotion from me, not one that's brand new. Those are powerful in a different way."

Aili giggled. "Every time you two are together, you get this little warm and happy thing right here." She touched her chest over her heart. "It's like a surge of joy that you can't suppress."

Kyson crossed his arms over his chest. "Yes, much like what I just felt from you. It happens. It's part of being alive. The difference is Hana and I enjoy each other's company and we're friends. I don't have to wonder if she knows I exist or not, or if she likes me back."

Aili opened her mouth. Whatever she was going to say, the words fled her. She closed her mouth again.

"It's confusing, isn't it? The rush of emotions you can't control." Andvari glanced at Kyson before turning fully back to her.

She nodded. "Everything is fine, I'm focused, and it's normal. The next thing I know, my breath just leaves me. I wonder who she is, what she's like, and why she's cute. I think I know partly why. Her energy is different. Not different like mine, but more like yours." Aili pressed her hands to her cheeks. What did she just say? Will he take that wrong?

He smiled and shook his head. "Breathe, Aili. I know what you meant. I can feel it. Your thoughts and emotions are trying to make sense of something that doesn't make sense. It was almost inevitable you'd fall for a Water or Earth Mage. Their magic clearly resonates with yours."

"I don't even know her," Aili wailed, collapsing against him. She buried her face in his shirt.

Kyson eased off the bed. He walked over and knelt in front of her. Resting his hand on her knee, he squeezed gently. "Sometimes it doesn't matter. Sometimes our emotions react without our thoughts. I never told you about my wife, did I?"

She sniffed and straightened up. "No."

"We met at a Scout camp, in a dining hall. We were both still apprentices, both in our last year. I was travelling with my mentor for a special mission, so we were in the east for my first time. There she was, sitting with friends, much like you just experienced."

She pressed her hand to her heart. His pain and joy both flowed through the link, raw and real as the memory flashed through her. She saw his wife as he once saw her. "She was beautiful, too."

Kyson nodded. "Not just physically, but everything about her. Something pulled me closer. I wanted to know her."

Aili touched her lips with her fingers. His memory opened, letting her feel it all. "Did she feel it too? Did she ever say?"

"She did. She shared her memory of that moment with me after we married."

"We're both girls, though. I wasn't expecting that," Aili whispered.

"Young women," Andvari corrected. "You're both adults who can make their own decisions. Which is why we need to talk about consent."

Aili leaned forward, stretching her hand out. She brushed the tear from Kyson's cheek with her thumb. "I already know it's bad to use magic to influence someone." She shivered.

"Yes, it is. Using any form of coercion at all, especially magical coercion, is strictly against the law. It's also morally wrong. There's more to consent than that, though."

"Well, consent is agreeing to something, right? I mean, that is what the word means." Aili straightened up and looked at Andvari.

He chuckled. "Yes. When you're with someone and want to do something together, make sure they clearly say yes. Same thing goes for you. If you don't say yes, they shouldn't push anything on you. You can change your mind, and so can they. Respect that, too."

Kyson stood and stretched. "That goes for any activity. It includes hugs and kisses, holding hands, even spending time together."

"Okay, but we hug lots. Darik always hugged me. How's this different?" She rubbed her chin.

"Intent, mostly, but we also already have a relationship based on care. We're like family. Same with good friends. You hug Jeril and Hana, right?"

"Right, but I can also tell when you all don't want to be approached. It's in your body language."

Andvari smiled. "That's because we all know each other better. How long did it take you to get comfortable with us? We didn't try and hug you right away, did we?"

Aili grinned. "No. You gave me space. I appreciated it a lot."

"You needed it. You were like a scared horse who didn't want strangers close." Andvari grinned back.

"It's pretty simple, Aili. Just ask before touching or hugging, and whoever you're with should do the same. If we're doing training and it's a contact activity, like arrest and control practice, that's different. We know what to expect and what kind of touch is normal. Outside training, ask if you don't know them really well. They should ask you, too." Kyson settled at the end of the bed again.

She nodded. "I can do that. Besides, I don't even know if she likes me that way. Women who like women aren't as common."

Kyson raised an eyebrow. "No, but women who like both men and women are more common than you think. Just get to know her first. You may feel attraction, but that doesn't mean you have to act on it."

Aili stared out the window for a long moment, into the dark forest beyond. "No, I guess not. It's still confusing."

"On the bright side, it's most confusing the first time. After that, it gets easier." Andvari rested his hand on her shoulder.

"You've been through this?" She turned and met Andvari's gaze. In all the time she'd known him, he'd never shown interests in anyone. He didn't even have pictures of anyone from his past.

"I have. It didn't work out. Sometimes it won't. That's okay, too."

"Why not?" Should she have asked that? It was pretty personal, but she didn't sense any pain from him. Not like with Kyson and his family.

Andvari closed his eyes. "I was a Scout. She was meant for city life. She did research in a specialty lab. For us to be together, one of us would have missed on work they love. We'd both rather help our communities. We're still friends to this day." He opened his eyes and met her gaze.

"You've never felt for anyone else?" She tilted her head, focusing on every detail of his expression.

He shrugged. "I need to know someone incredibly well before I develop romantic feelings for them. I also can't have a relationship with someone who works for me. No coercion, remember? They need to feel free to say no at any time without fear of something happening to them. How often do I meet people outside the Scouts?"

"That makes sense. You're not lonely?"

Andvari shook his head. "Are you? No, I'm surrounded by friends and people who care. I care about them in return. Not everyone needs romance to live their lives fully. Now get some rest. Things are going to get busy, starting tomorrow."

Aili smiled as she looked out the window again. Everyone can feel this at some point. It wasn't any less confusing, but talking to them helped her feel better. They could always be friends if Karil wanted that too.

Getting up, Aili retrieved her nightclothes. She sneaked into the bathroom. With a touch on the taps, water flowed into the basin. The soap smelled of flowers and calmness. Her mind wandered as she washed up. All those crystals. She needed a way to cleanse them. The small ones would be easy, but the larger ones? And with so many, how long would it take?

The towel was soft on her skin as she dried herself. Washed and changed, ready for bed, Aili tossed her dirty clothing in a basket and left the bathroom. He was at the desk, reading letters. She slipped into bed and rolled over. The lights dimmed.

"Sleep well."

Aili smiled. "Thanks. You, too."

The quill scratched on the paper, loud in the room's silence. The sound didn't usually bother her. She pulled her leg up and scratched her ankle. Maybe now? Nope, but some meditation breathing might help.

"Can't sleep?"

Aili huffed out a breath. "No."

"What's our motto?"

"Stronger together." She didn't even need to think; the words were burned into her heart.

"That means you don't have to figure out everything by yourself. Need a tea or a sleep spell?"

Aili smiled as she burrowed deeper under her covers. "No, thanks."

Snuggled into her blankets, Aili relaxed into a quiet rest.

***

"Ready, Aili?" Kyson raised his hand.

She backed a couple more steps; the sand giving easily under her feet. They stood in the close-quarters combat practice ring, facing each other. Aili nodded and raised her hand. Vinnia shifted her weight from foot to foot, her fingers curling and uncurling. The woman stood beside Kyson. She had a scanning spell ready.

Aili pointed. A ball of light emerged from her finger, approaching at a quick jogging pace. The light floated towards him at her shoulder height. Kyson chanted softly, his hands moving as he drew a shield. The shield shimmered into life. Aili closed her eyes and opened her senses.

The magic collided. Some of her spell bounced off the shield, scattering harmlessly in the air. Some passed right through the shield. He took a step back as the light burst in front of him.

Aili jogged over. "You managed to block much of it. I could feel what parts worked, though."

'Good catch.' Andvari's presence strengthened in the link. 'I caught it, too. You're right.' He shared it with Kyson as a wavelength chart.

Kyson paced. "Right, I see that. How to adjust it, though?"

"I have an idea," Vinnia offered. She smoothed her hands over her robes. "Most shields are designed to block energy, but she's not sending just that kind of energy at you. Light also moves in waves and it's scattering in the shield. What about adding something like a sun shield?"

Kyson stopped pacing. "It's worth a try." His gaze unfocused as he stared at the sand. "Okay." Kyson looked up at her and nodded.

Aili jogged back to her place a few dozen feet away. She raised her hand. "Ready."

He raised his hand. "Go."

Releasing another ball of light, she sent it at him. Kyson called the shield, taking an extra moment to form it. His magic held in two layers: the shield in front, and a sun shield behind it. Her ball of light hit the shield and partially scattered again. The rest hit the sun shield and stayed stuck against the magic.

She ran over, examining the magic closely with her senses. "You did it."

He frowned at the shield. "I did, but I had to use a Master Mage level spell to do it. We need something friendly to regular mages, and hopefully even our apprentices."

'I have an idea. Try this.' Andvari shared a pattern in the link.

Aili watched the pattern form. It was like a shield he had helped her make once.

"I know a spell that might help," Vinnia offered.

"Cast the spell. Aili will watch, and I'll learn everything I need." Kyson let his shield go, dispersing the magic harmlessly.

Vinnia chanted. Her voice was confident as she drew a circle in the air with her hand. A shield formed in front of her. Aili watched closely, letting Kyson pull her attention where he needed it.

'That's really close to your spell,' she pointed with her attention to where the change was.

'Yes. Hers is adjusted for brightness differently. If I overlay that on Andvari's spell, I bet I can blend them.' Kyson tapped his chin. "Okay, whenever you're ready, Aili."

CHAPTER 13

She darted over to her spot. Taking a deep breath in, she let it out gradually. Aili raised her hand. The light formed on her fingertips. She released it, sending it at him. Kyson cast the shield. The light hit it. Instead of scattering, the shield sucked the light in. It glowed so blinding Aili closed her eyes.

She dashed over, using her magical senses instead of her vision to guide her. Once the blinding light no longer burned through her eyelids, she opened her eyes. Behind the shield, it was shadowy and comfortable, like being under a sunshade. In front, the light glared.

"Well, the shield worked." Kyson touched the edge of the shield with his fingertips. "It seems to have trapped the light like a crystal does."

"It'll trap the Light, yes." Vinnia cast a sensing spell on the shield. "Will it protect against Darkness the same way?

We don't really need to defend ourselves against Aili or the Light."

Aili glanced up at the sun. She paced the back of the shield. "I've been thinking of that. I don't think the Darkness is just corrupted Light. It's like Light, but more damaging. There's a lot of chaotic energy in it. It's scattered, and anything it touches gets scattered, like Rei's brain. I felt it in the inner dome, but didn't know what I was feeling."

"What are you thinking?" Vinnia cast the shield and let it dissipate right away.

Aili sat behind the shield and stared up at it, tucked in the shade it created. "Any spell to block the Light is a start. It needs to be backed up by the ability to redirect or block high-energy attacks. It's like sunlight, I think. It's too powerful without our atmosphere to protect us. I can't be sure, but it feels right." She looked up through the shield at the blue cloudless sky overhead.

"Hmm." Kyson tapped his chin. "Okay, so we need an atmospheric mage."

"Do the Scouts have one?" Vinnia asked.

Kyson grinned. "Sure. Not too far from here. Let me send a request."

'Approval granted. Get whoever you need, and bring them here.'

'Thanks, partner.' Kyson waved his hand, dissolving the shield. The light dispersed as well. "Okay, Aili, you can help me with the paperwork."

"Why me?" She got to her feet and followed him towards the hall.

"Stronger together." Kyson strode back to the hall and up the steps.

"I don't think this counts." She jogged after him.

***

"The best thing I can think of right now is to get some crystals here close to the exit. I can cleanse them, and you can get them out right away. The Darkness shouldn't have time to seep back into them." Aili stared around at the many piles of crystals. So many, how would she manage? Would this take years?

Mowen bowed his head. "We're ready." He stood in full protective clothing, with only his eyes visible.

She spread a cloth on the ground. It was large enough to be a blanket, really. It shimmered with the magic Ilia put there, making the hairs on Aili's arms stand on end. Aili knelt and reached for a handful of small crystals. Holding them before her, she closed her eyes.

Calling her inner Light, she welcomed the glow. The Darkness fled the crystals, heading deeper into the dome. The crystals in her hands were clear and empty. Laying them on a smaller cloth, she bundled them up and handed them to Andvari.

Opening her eyes, she gathered another batch of crystals. This was going to take forever. At least it didn't take any effort. Still, when she cleansed all but the last few, and the dome was still full of Darkness, what then? Was there anything else she could do?

Maybe there was. 'I want to try something.'

'What?' Kyson crouched beside her. 'How can we help?'

'Take my hands.' Aili set the crystals down in front of her on another cloth set by Mowen.

She held her hands out over the crystals, palms away, like she was shoving someone. Kyson knelt opposite her and pressed his palms lightly to hers. She called the Light, sending it between and through both of them.

The light surrounded the crystals, trapping the Darkness inside. It fled, pressing itself into a tiny ball of condensed Darkness between them. She smothered it with the Light. It snuffed out, disappearing completely.

"That worked better." Kyson bundled the crystals in the cloth and handed it off to Mowen.

Aili stood and stretched.

"Do you think that will work with anyone helping you, or only us?" Andvari set a new cloth between them.

"You two for sure. I think it might only be people who I have a strong connection with. If we can cleanse bigger piles, can we still get them out before they're contaminated again?" She wandered to a nearby pile as high as her waist.

"We can bring in more help." Andvari nodded to Mowen, who had handed off the crystals to another Scout already. "With both of us, how big a pile do you think we can cleanse?" He frowned at a pile taller than he was.

"I think this one is a good size to try." Aili pointed at a pile. "We need to be able to stand around it, touching hands."

"Where would you like this?" Kyson pointed at the blanket.

"Beside it? If this works, they can still place the crystals on it and haul it out." Aili pointed at the ground near her feet.

Mowen came back. "Help is coming and they're bringing more blanket-sized cloths."

'I guess it's a good thing I haven't undone the link yet.' Aili braced her hands on her hips and turned. That gigantic mountain of crystals behind her waited.

Andvari chuckled. 'You'll know when it's time. Besides, it has been more useful than not.'

Aili grinned. How many times had the link saved them, letting them communicate when other methods failed? "I guess we wait for help. I don't want empty crystals sitting in here longer than needed."

"They're coming in special wagons." Mowen turned to the dome. "That's them now."

She peered around him. Fuzzy shapes approached, stopping at the building outside the dome.

"How do you think we should do this?" Andvari came closer, standing across the pile Aili waited at.

"Once they're empty, they're safe to touch. If they lay the blankets down beside where we're working, they can pack them up and take them out." She picked up a small crystal, barely bigger than her little finger, and cleansed it in the blink of an eye. "What will you do with them once they're back outside and empty?" Aili handed the crystal to Mowen, who took it out.

"We actually have a storehouse for empty crystals," Andvari explained. "We keep some for Scout use. Many more will be distributed to other groups. Some go to the CDF forces around the country. Others go to the Universities. Anyone can apply for them as well."

The wagons rolled closer again, bringing the people right to the edge of the dome. Four Scouts in full protective gear climbed off and came in. They carried bundles of the protective cloths in their hands.

'Would you like to give instructions?' Andvari offered. 'It'll be good practice.'

She narrowed her eyes at him. 'Fine. As long as you know I lead under protest.'

He laughed. 'Protest away. It gets easier with time.'

"If you lay the cloth down here," Aili pointed beside the pile, "we'll cleanse these. Once we're done, the crystals are safe to touch. Get them on the cloth and take them out. We'll move to a new pile and repeat it."

Two of the Scouts spread the large cloth out. Aili held her hands out. Kyson and Andvari stood across from her, their hands stretched out to hers. She opened the link fully, letting her Light spread among them.

Closing her eyes, she focused on her Light. It was part of her, and she was part of it. The Light pulsed in her, stronger than she'd ever felt it. Closing the Light down and around the crystals, the Darkness faded.

With a pile of clear crystals between them, Aili lowered her hands and stepped back. The Scouts moved in, shifting the crystals onto the cloth. Andvari and Kyson helped, and in moments the cloth was full. She stared at the dirt where the pile once stood. This was really working.

Two Scouts carried the crystals out as the other two placed a fresh blanket where Aili pointed. She walked to the pile and stretched her arms out. Andvari and Kyson joined her, and they cleansed the pile.

"How're you doing?" Andvari stood beside her now, watching as they bundled the cloth and took the crystals.

"I'm good for now. I'll need a snack soon, but this isn't like using magic. This is so much easier. I really just let my inner Light loose and it does the rest. How are you two doing?" She took his hand and touched his energy, a quick and simple healer's check.

Kyson grinned. "I can go all day like this. Your Light energizes me."

Andvari nodded. "We'll have to watch we don't get overcharged or overheated, but we know what to watch for."

"Where next?" A Scout held a cloth up.

Aili led them to the next pile. They set to work cleansing one pile after another. At one point, the wagons left with the crystals, coming back empty a few minutes later. She didn't stop until her stomach growled. All the small crystals were gone, leaving only medium-sized and larger crystals.

"Now is a great time to stop." Andvari stretched and let out a breath. "I need to go ground myself. We can come back after a long rest and a few hot meals."

"Agreed. I'll go discharge myself away from camp." Kyson headed for the barrier.

"Discharge?" Aili jogged over and caught up, walking beside him.

"All Master Mages can store some extra energy safely, as long as we get rid of it within a few hours. How we do that depends on what kind of mage we are. I'll send mine off as tiny bursts of lightning, right into the soil." Kyson let a tiny lightning bolt form on his fingertip.

"I just sit quietly and tap into the deep energy of the planet," Andvari explained, catching up and walking behind them. "How are you doing? I've never seen you use that much Light before."

Aili grinned. "I feel good. A session with my sword ought to do it. I need to stretch and move after all that."

They walked past the two wagons almost full of crystals again, heading for the building.

"What do you do with them from here?" Aili glanced over her shoulder at the wagon.

"I have air transport coming to take them to the storage facility," Andvari explained. "They'll be loaded into crates, enchanted for protection, and held until distributed."

***

Creeping through the bushes, Aili stopped and crouched. Where would a fugitive go if they were running from someone? There. They'd want to stay hidden in the thicker brush, but not so thick they made noise or left sign. She set off, heading for the stream. The sound of running water would cover her movement, too.

She closed her eyes and opened herself to the land around her. Andvari shone like a beacon, strong with her magical link to him. Karil was with him. They'd start catching up if she didn't hustle soon. For a newer Scout Apprentice, Karil was tracking well.

Aili opened her eyes and leapt over the stream. Jogging through the undergrowth, Aili climbed the small rise. Keeping low, she ducked between some boulders and crossed the sidehill. A burst of magic grabbed her attention behind her. Karil knew where she was, roughly, if not with any precision.

Camp was over the next rise. She could make it. Aili scooted between trees and scrambled over rocks. If the forest were thicker and healthier, she'd have more cover. She scowled as she looked around. How was she supposed to cleanse all of this? Darned Darkness.

Dashing around the boulders, Aili stopped. The camp was just a quick run down the path. Something about the dome made her insides squirm, though. What? She closed her eyes and reached for it.

At first glance, everything seemed normal. Or, as normal as she knew. Flowing her awareness over and around the dome, she pressed against it. The dome held firm. Aili shook her head. No, something still seemed off.

'What's up?' Andvari warmed the link.

'I'm not sure. It seems okay, but I don't know. Something just feels off.'

A large hand rested against her back, pulling her partially back into her body. He was behind her already, facing the dome like she was. 'Let me look.'

She took a few slow breaths as she reached for the dome again. Relaxing, Aili followed wherever Andvari focused their attention. He searched for places where the magics crossed, blended, or interacted.

'I see.'

Aili looked closer at where he stopped. The Darkness inside was pressing against the dome, stronger in some places. Those were the spots the magic was concentrating, reacting to the Darkness inside. It flowed up the inside of the dome like vines clinging to a trellis. Tiny cracks were beginning inside, under the pressure.

'Can we fix it?'

He was silent for a long moment, long enough she fidgeted. 'I think we have to. Unless you think you can cleanse everything now, we need to do something about this.'

Now? Even with what she already did, the dome was still two-thirds full. Some piles were so big they'd never cleanse it all at once, or even in a day.

He pulled from the link and rested his hand on her shoulder. "I need to call some people about this. You're not a disappointment just because you can't perform the most powerful magic ever attempted. We need a new plan. Let's go back to camp."

Aili rubbed her eyes. She glanced around.

Karil leaned against a tree, waiting quietly beside them. "Is everything alright?"

Andvari smiled. "You did well. I'll go over everything with you when we get back. How about you and Aili go have a tea and she can give you her thoughts while I deal with something else? I'll join you once I'm done."

Karil smiled at Aili. "I'd like that."

Aili blushed. "Sure. I like tea."

Andvari glowed in the link, his amusement leaking through. "I'll see you two in the dining hall. Let's get back."

They headed down the path in silence. Okay, Aili, focus on how she did. You can do that. Once back in camp, Aili and Karil went to the dining hall as Andvari headed to the communication room.

They stopped at the drink table, and Karil poured a couple of cups of tea. Aili took the offered teacup with a smile and a nod. Strolling to the table right by the window, they sat together. Aili looked out at the forest, the edge of the dome barely visible from this angle.

Karil tapped the table. "I don't know if I love the view or hate it."

Aili turned to her. "Huh?"

"Well, seeing the dome like that, it's a reminder of how we keep people safe, but also that we can't just leave this camp whenever we want. I feel better knowing my being here means people sleep soundly at night, but I miss going shopping with friends, or hanging out and dancing, or even getting an ice cream." Karil stared at the dome.

"Ice cream? Were you up north?" Aili sipped her tea. The hot liquid burned her tongue. Her cup clanked as she set it down. Sending healing into her own mouth, Aili soothed the burn. Smooth, Aili.

Karil grinned. "Yeah. You've been? You know what ice cream is. I did my whole first year there."

Aili nodded. "I love the northern camp. Probably half my friends are there. We were only supposed to be there a week, but things happened, and we had to stay longer. At least I got to train with the best healers in the Scouts."

CHAPTER 14

The barrier crackled. Magic shifted. Aili stared open-mouthed as cracks broke through the dome.

"What's causing that?" Vinnia gripped Aili's shoulder.

Aili shook her head. "It's waking up."

"What do you mean waking up?" Her voice rose, and her fingers gripped Aili tighter.

Wiping tears with her sleeve, Aili turned to Andvari. "I know what they used the earth pin for."

"Mages can't use those pins. We've tried. We feel nothing like what you describe." Andvari wrapped his arm around her and pulled her close. Magic flared at his fingertips as he prepared a barrier.

"Mages can't. The Darkness can." Aili closed her eyes and probed the barrier. "Whoever stole them from the vault, that taint might let them use the pins a little."

The magic held, but the cracks widened. Darkness seeped through, advancing at a snail's pace. The magic is so familiar, but different in small ways. I can feel how they blended the spells in. I can feel her. My half-sister. Ethala.

Darkness struck the barrier near a crack, a tendril of purple energy smashing the dome. Aili threw her hands out, sending Light at the dome. Layering it over the cracks, she pressed her patch into the magic.

"There." Kyson pointed at another spot, where a purple mist began forming at a crack.

The mist formed a tendril. It snaked out and grabbed Edmar, wrapping around his leg. Dragging him towards the barrier, the Darkness writhed. Aili slammed her Light down on the tendril, cutting it off at the dome. She smothered it with her Light, pulling more from the sun.

Andvari charged over and dragged Edmar back. His pant leg smoked. Part of the fabric burned away, revealing charred skin. His eyes glowed purple.

"I can't help him and seal that." Aili poured more power around the dome, sealing every crack she could find.

"Help her. I'll help him." Vinnia knelt beside Edmar.

Andvari set a hand on her back and flared into the link. "We'll create a thin dome over the old one and press them together. Kyson, get everyone we can."

Kyson joined the link, though he seemed distant. Aili couldn't dwell on that. Her focus was on shaping a new barrier. Andvari linked it to the old, weaving the magic together.

Power flowed in through Kyson, though Aili didn't recognize it. More followed, growing in strength every moment. Aili smiled. He was back in camp, acting as a conduit for the mages there. With everyone helping, they stood a chance.

"Go up. I'll seal below the surface." Aili directed her attention to the base and below the soil.

Taking some additional energy from the planet and blending it with the power from Kyson, Aili thickened the Light covering the dome.

'We've got a problem.'

Andvari's hand squeezed her shoulder. 'What kind of problem?'

'It broke through. The Darkness.' Aili directed his attention down.

A thin tendril of Darkness snaked into the soil, reaching down towards the centre of the planet. Branches split off, spreading all around.

He closed the top of the dome and joined her below the soil. 'We'll slow it down. I'll make an emergency call. We'll need help to deal with this. Can we get a barrier around it, even a thin one?'

Aili nodded. Once she finished with the bottom of the dome, she wrapped Light around the tendril. It should run, hide, withdraw somehow, but it didn't. At least the Light kept it from advancing.

She slumped against him. 'That's all I can do.'

He slowed her fall with an arm around her waist, lowering her to the sparse grass. Aili leaned back against his legs. "Are we too late?" She looked over at Edmar.

"He needs treatment now. I can't get rid of taint this bad," Vinnia admitted. Her hand was on his chest, magic flowing, but he was still pale and barely breathing.

Aili crawled over and set a hand on his chest beside hers. Vinnia's magic trapped the Darkness within him but wasn't able to reduce it. Aili closed her eyes and wrapped herself in Light. The Darkness rushed through him, desperate to break free. Why was it different? It was thicker than normal, too.

Andvari knelt beside her. "We're here to help. What can we do?"

She shook her head. "I'll do what I can, but it's not the normal taint we've been dealing with. It's already becoming a part of him. It's like it's invaded his brain and heart."

"Nobody can ask for more than your best." He rubbed her back. "Do what you can."

Closing her eyes, Aili filled herself with Light. Could she even cleanse this? Gathering as much Light as possible, she sent it into his heart. Edmar screamed and thrashed. Aili scrambled back, pulling her Light with her. What just happened?

Vinnia pressed him down, holding him with a spell. Kyson charged through the trees, dropping to his knees to help. Andvari snapped a barrier around Edmar, containing his magic as it flared and burst from him.

"What was that?" Andvari hugged her.

Her body shook. She gripped his sleeve. "I don't know. That should have worked," she whispered.

"We'll get him back to camp. Full containment. He'll need complete decontamination, once we know what we're facing." Andvari stood, helping Aili as she wobbled.

Please, legs, hold me up. Aili leaned against him until she stopped shaking. Why is this Darkness different? Why can it fight back?

"You need rest, too. We'll figure it out." Andvari walked her back to camp.

Kyson levitated Edmar. He and Vinnia escorted the restrained man back to camp, floating him between them. Andvari kept an arm around her, taking smaller steps to match hers. They rushed through the outer dome and back to camp.

Mowen and the other Scouts met them at the edge of camp. They immediately took Edmar through a side door to the secure rooms. Andvari guided Aili along behind them.

"Where are we going?" Aili knew they were heading behind the dining room, near the kitchens, but this camp was different.

"This camp has a special healing centre, because of the risk of Darkness taint. He needs care, and you need some rest and recovery, too." Andvari led her inside.

A woman in the green robes of a Master Healer ushered Edmar into a room. She pointed back at another room. "Take her in there."

Andvari nodded, guiding Aili into the small and bright room.

***

The mug warmed her hands. The hot apple tea warmed her heart. Magic filled the walls, especially to her left. Edmar was on the other side in an isolation room. The sheer power of the magic pulled at her awareness.

Why did her Light cause him such pain, though? How did the Darkness get into his brain and heart so fast? What was directing the tendril in the first place? Whenever she saw something like that, there was always a mage controlling it. Was someone controlling this?

She'd been inside earlier, and the Darkness hadn't been active. Had something changed? The tendril grabbed Edmar. It was connected to the mass of Darkness inside. Did it have something to do with the tendril reaching into the soil? Was someone using the earth pin to affect and control the Darkness inside? Was that even possible?

Aili set her empty mug down. Wrapping the blanket around herself snugly, she stood. How was she going to cleanse him? Slipping out of the room, she glanced both ways. The place was quiet. Nobody was in sight.

Creeping down the hall, she stopped at his door. The doorknob was cold, chilling her fingers to the bone. Cloaking herself in warmth and Light, she turned the doorknob. Aili slipped into the room through the magic barriers.

Edmar lay on the bed, wrapped in blankets that hummed with magic. Only his face was visible. His eyes scrunched closed. His lips pressed together. Even through his eyelids, she saw the purple glow in his eyes. His skin was pale. Too pale.

This could have been her. Her, or Andvari, or Kyson, or anyone. It could be her next time. How was she supposed to stop something that could take over someone like this? She had the best chance of stopping it, might be the only one who could, but what if she failed? This wasn't like a skill test where she could try again with no penalty.

Besides, where should she start? Most Darkness flees her light. This Darkness is so entwined with him, it fought back. If anything, it was like a hissing cat with its back arched. Was it a matter of using more Light? Did she have that much focus?

'Aili?'

She shook her head. She already threw everything she had at it and only caused him pain. What else could she do?

'Aili.'

Would Ilia know something? She's been around practically forever, and cleansed the Darkness before Aili was even born. Maybe one of her sisters faced something like this. Ilia might know how they dealt with it.

"AILI."

'Huh?'

'Come out.' Andvari was close, right outside the door. The link warmed her, and an energy hug flowed around her heart. 'You feel like you need an actual hug, and I can't safely go in there.'

Aili returned to the hallway, passing through the magic as if it wasn't there. He stood waiting. Frowny face. Why did he have to use the frowny face? Aili met his gaze. Andvari stepped close and wrapped his arms around her, hugging her tightly.

She burst into tears. "I don't know how to fix this." Aili wept, her head resting against his chest.

He held her, rubbing her back as she cried.

"Everyone expects me to cleanse this place and get rid of the Darkness. There's so much of it here. I don't know how. I already messed up, and now he's suffering. I can't fix him. I don't know what to do."

"Breathe." He sent warm magic into her. "We'll figure it out."

"What if it's me next time? If the Darkness overwhelms me, who's left to fight it? If it takes me like it took him, uses my powers, what happens to nature and my forests?" Aili sobbed. "I don't know what to do."

"Maybe you don't, but that's okay."

She tilted her head and looked up at him. "How's it okay?"

He wiped her tears with his fingers. "Our motto? It's not all on you. Besides, you have a visitor. Are you ready?"

A visitor? Who would come and see her? Aili nodded. Andvari led her down the hall and through another door.

They left the healing rooms behind, heading for one of the smaller lounges.

"Ilia!" Aili ran across the small room and dropped to her knees in front of the chair. She collapsed across the old woman's lap.

Ilia smiled at her. "I hear you could use some help."

Aili straightened up and wrapped her arms around Ilia. "I don't know how to heal him. I tried the usual way, and it hurt him real bad. His heart almost gave out."

"It's a good thing I'm here, then. How about we go banish some Darkness? Or do you need a tea first?" Ilia brushed some strands of hair back behind Aili's ear.

"I'm ready." Aili stood and stepped back. "When did you get here?"

"Just a cup of tea ago." Ilia nodded at the empty cup on the little table beside her chair. "At least they make it properly here."

Aili pressed a hand to her mouth and muffled the laugh.

Ilia rose to her feet. She adjusted her colourful scarf, tucking some wild grey hair back in place. "Now, where is he?"

"This way." Andvari gestured at the door.

Aili linked arms with Ilia, supporting her as they left the room. "How did you get here?"

"They sent one of those flying contraptions for me. Much more comfortable, though not quite so fast as going by other magical means." Ilia walked with strong and steady steps, not leaning on Aili at all.

"By magic, without an air box?" Aili raised an eyebrow. Wait, she remembered that story. Yikes.

"Be grateful people no longer do that. You might, but it's not worth it if things go wrong. If they don't know you can, you'll never have to try." Ilia smiled at her.

The healer waited outside the rooms for them. She already wore protective clothing.

"Wear this. I made them on the way over. It'll help, though it won't last past this use." Ilia handed Aili a chain with a charm hanging from it. "Mother's power will flow through them. You won't have to draw power to you. It'll come when you call. It'll let us focus on our task." She put another identical charm on.

Aili slipped the chain over her head. It hung over her heart, beside her Scout mirror.

Ilia pointed at Andvari. "Stay out here. The three of us can handle this."

He nodded. His jaw clenched. Crossing his arms over his chest, he leaned against the wall. "Be careful, Aili."

She rested a hand on his arm. "I will. I'll be fine."

"Now, Aili, can you put a layer of Light over us? Is your control for that good enough yet?" Ilia smiled at her and held her hand out.

"Easy." Aili took her hand and created a thin barrier of Light around Ilia. She gave herself a matching barrier.

Ilia nodded to the healer. "It's time."

The healer opened the door. With a wave of her hand, the magical barrier let them through.

Edmar thrashed in the blankets, fighting the magical restraints. His head shook from side to side. The blankets clung to him, the spell keeping them in place.

Ilia walked to the chair beside his bed and sat. She pressed a hand to Edmar's heart. "I see. Yes. I haven't seen a case like this in a very long time. Your sister, Ethala, she was the last to deal with a case this bad."

Aili stepped beside her. "How do we help him?"

"We'll pull the Darkness from him and trap it in a crystal. I hear you've done that before. We'll cleanse the crystal after. First, we have to unweave the Darkness inside him, so it lets go." Ilia set her hand on his forehead.

CHAPTER 15

A ili moved to the other side of the bed and sat on the edge. The healer passed a crystal to her, one big enough to fill her entire hand. It was perfectly clear and empty. Aili set it over Edmar's heart, holding it in place.

"We'll start with his head and chase the Darkness down. We can't leave any behind, though. I will help, but you can lead."

Taking a breath, Aili nodded. She sank into herself and imbued herself with Light. Pulling the Light through herself, she touched his head. Sending the Light down through him, Aili sensed Ilia at work. The old woman took Aili's Light and went through his brain, peeling the Darkness from inside it.

Edmar fought the blankets and restraints, jerking against them. His body twitched; his head rolled back and forth. She pressed down with her Light, advancing on the Darkness in his brain. The tendrils within his brain wriggled down his body, letting go as they fled her Light. His body jerked, pulling against the magical restraints.

"Easy, now," Aili soothed. She went down carefully, feeling his brain as she passed. There were no traces of Darkness left.

His body stilled, though his heart still pounded. The Darkness was being pulled towards the crystal in his chest. What was Ilia doing? It was magic she'd never seen before.

"Focus."

Shaking her thoughts free, Aili pressed on with her Light. Reaching his shoulders, she sent Light down the sides of his arms and back up, chasing some Darkness that fled. She left Light behind everywhere she cleansed, enough to keep the Darkness back.

Easing her Light down his sides, she avoided the middle of his chest for now. Rushing down, Aili filled his legs and pressed up. Darkness gathered near the crystal, writhing and twisting inside him. His limbs were still, flooded with light as they were, but his organs were now intertwined with the Darkness.

Mother, please let this work, she pleaded in her head. Aili sent a burst of Light up from his feet, keeping the Light in his shoulders strong. The Darkness trembled. It fled towards his heart. Ilia grabbed the Darkness with pincers of Light magic and pulled it near the crystal. The crystal sucked the Darkness inside, trapping it.

The crystal glowed so deep purple it was almost black. Aili strengthened her Light around her hand. She lifted the crystal and looked closer. The Darkness swirled inside, bouncing off the smooth sides. For now, the Darkness seemed trapped.

"What now? I need to rest before I can cleanse that." Aili wiped her clammy forehead with her sleeve.

"Rest. I'll have them place this in the dome. You can get to it after a break. This can wait until you're physically and mentally refreshed." Ilia wrapped the crystal in a protective cloth and tucked it into a wooden box. "Go have a rest and a snack."

***

Aili closed the door behind her as she stepped into the sunlight. Ilia was right. A nap and a snack, and she felt refreshed and good to go. Andvari waited for her in the shade nearby, leaning against the building. Her heart thudded against her ribs when she saw who was next to him.

"Today Aili will set a track for us. She won't use any magic to hide her path, but she won't need to. She's one of the sneakiest people I know. We're not tracking her magic. We're going to follow her physical track. I'll show you some spells that will help." Andvari nodded to Aili as he straightened up.

"We're not tracking her magic?" Karil smiled at Aili.

Aili suppressed the urge to wrap her arms around her belly. Her stomach flopped. Why was she nervous?

Andvari shook his head. "No. Poachers and those contaminated by Darkness may choose to avoid casting spells. Any mage tracker, even an absolute beginner, can track a spell. Only the Scouts and the best trackers can follow a physical trail. It takes a lot of practice. Ready?" He raised an eyebrow at Aili.

Vinnia came from the hall, hustling through the door and down the stairs. "Did I miss anything? Sorry I'm late." She dashed over and stopped beside Aili.

"You're coming, too?" Aili smiled at her.

"Are you kidding? I wouldn't miss this. We only track with magic. In a city that's all we have, because of the paved streets. How often will I get this kind of chance?" Vinnia grinned. She tucked her hair back behind her ears.

Aili grinned. "Some day you'll show me city tracking."

"Deal." Vinnia held her hand out, and Aili clasped it. "What did I miss?"

Andvari shook his head. "Nothing. I was just beginning to explain. Aili will lay the track, and we'll follow it without any magic at all."

"Excellent." Vinnia rubbed her hands together.

"Aili, whenever you're ready. Do a wide sweeping path. Stop at a place of your choosing and mill around a bit. Make it long enough and varied for them to see sign in as many places as you can."

Aili turned and jogged into the trees at the edge of camp. 'How easy do you want it?' She reached out through the link.

'Start intermediate. You can get a little harder as you go, but remember, Karil is an early apprentice and Vinnia is a beginner. I can let you know if you need to adjust the difficulty as we go.'

'Got it.'

Focusing on her surroundings, Aili kept her link fully open. She knew exactly where he was at any time with it, much more accurately than just sensing him with her magical awareness. Aili jogged, making no effort to hide her tracks yet.

"Hello, little friends," she whispered as she passed.

Making a wide sweep around camp, Aili headed into what passed for thicker trees here. She stayed just inside the dome around the camp, though.

A bird flew down and perched on her shoulder. Aili stopped, giving her a stable place to rest. Holding her hand up, Aili supported the little bird as it hopped over.

"What's up?"

An image filled her mind when she touched the little bird with her abilities. Her vision was distorted, seeing as a bird would, but she still recognized the landscape as a hillside within this forest. Something was in the forest, and it caused the birds to flee. It was a cave opening in a hillside. The memory made her body shudder. Would she find Darkness inside when she got close?

'How far?' Andvari focused on the image through the link.

The image shifted, growing distant and moving. More of the landscape came into focus. Was she seeing it as a bird would while flying? Soon she saw the camp as well, well enough to judge space and direction.

'Two hills over?' Aili oriented the camp in her mind.

'Looks that way. I'm on my way and I'll bring backup.' Kyson popped into the link.

Aili jumped at his sudden powerful presence, jostling the bird. The little bird puffed up and rustled its feathers. Aili whispered an apology.

'We'll be right there. They're tracking you well, so head that way. Wait for Kyson and the others,' Andvari instructed.

'Okay.' Aili stroked the little feathered back. "We're coming to help. You'll be fine."

The bird chirped and took off, flapping her tiny wings. She headed away from the spot.

Aili turned and jogged to the cave, taking a mostly direct route. She weaved her path a bit to each side as the terrain allowed, keeping the track going. How long would it take Kyson and the others to arrive? Did they have larger transport wagons?

She headed down the hill, looking along the next one. Opening her senses to the hillside, Aili searched for the cave opening. Was that it? Her eyes saw only a shadow. Next to it, in the deepest shadowy part, she sensed the opening.

Jogging over, Aili stopped behind some thicker bushes. Sinking to the grass, Aili leaned back against the rock. Following the tunnel with her senses, Aili closed her eyes. The tunnel was short and led to a single chamber. It was no bigger than a Scout bedroom. Some simple wooden furniture filled the space, along with a trunk. Magic swirled around the trunk. Was that—Darkness?

Kyson approached, a bright beacon in her senses. She pulled herself free and opened her eyes. He approached with Norial, the older woman, and another Scout she met in passing only. Aili stood and nodded as they approached.

"Aili, I know you met Norial. This is Filmat." Kyson nodded to the man.

"Pleased to meet you." Aili nodded to him as she looked at his neckband. A Master Water Mage. "Did you pass Andvari's group?" She turned back to Kyson.

"Even waved on the way by. He'll be here any moment."
Kyson glanced over his shoulder. "As I say."

Andvari walked right over, with the women walking on
either side of him. "What can you tell us about it?"

She explained what she sensed and drew a quick map on
the rock with damp soil from below her. "I didn't feel
any people. There may be more information on that table.
There are papers on it."

"You can tell that?" Filmat shook his head. "Amazing."

Aili smiled and shrugged. "For me, it's normal."

"The Darkness is concerning." Vinnia tapped the map
near the mark where the chest was.

"I can cleanse what little is there before we get close," Aili
assured her. "I can't feel what's inside the trunk, though."

Andvari nodded. "Do it. Don't get tired, or too hungry. I
only have a couple ration bars."

Kyson patted his pockets. "I stocked up."

Aili glared at him.

Kyson smirked. "Hey, I've worked with you long enough
to know. I know what you need and how you burn
through energy."

"How did you find this place?" Karil stared at Aili, a little
wide-eyed.

Aili blushed. "A little bird showed me."

"You can communicate with Animals?" Karil grinned.

Aili nodded.

"Cleanse it. I'll stay with you. Once you're done, we'll all go in and check it out. Karil, stay with Norial. As your mentor, she'll protect you and teach you what to do. I think this is your first investigation?" Andvari held her gaze.

Karil nodded. Aili thought back to her early days with them. Was she that nervous and overwhelmed? Yes, but maybe for different reasons.

"Great. Everyone will look for any information they can. We need to know what they're planning, where they're hiding, anything we can. Be cautious of the trunk, even after it's cleansed." Andvari turned to Aili. "Whenever you're ready."

She took a moment and settled her breathing. Aili walked to the tunnel entrance and stopped, feeling deep inside. She sat in the entrance, her palms pressed to the rock below her.

The Darkness around the trunk swirled and shifted, growing active as she reached for it. Was it aware somehow, or just reacting to her brightness? She gathered her Light and formed a shield, spreading it out. Blanketing the chamber with it, Aili smothered the Darkness. It shivered and quaked as it faded from existence. Was that a scream? Aili shook her head. No, it couldn't be.

"It's safe." Aili stood. "At least, the chamber is. I don't know what's inside the trunk yet."

Andvari stepped right behind her. "I'll take the lead but stay right behind me. Let's go, everyone."

He slipped past her. Aili fell into step behind him, staying close. Keeping her Light up and ready, Aili kept watch, her senses open. Kyson and Vinnia were right behind her, with the others following them. Andvari cast a few spells before checking again with Aili and her abilities.

The end of the tunnel glowed with magic; protective spells left behind by someone unknown. Aili looked closer at the patterns, Andvari and Kyson right with her in the link. Andvari started casting, and a few of the spells faded, the magic dispelled harmlessly. He put a barrier over the others. Calling a ball of mage-light, he sent it into the room.

Two small beds took up one side wall. A table and the trunk were opposite them. The end wall was bare and plain, carved with magic. Andvari headed straight for the trunk as everyone else spread around. Vinnia came with Aili and Andvari. Kyson investigated the table with Filmat while Karil and Norial checked the beds.

Aili kneeled beside Andvari. "I can't see inside. There are spells protecting it."

"I can feel them, even without your help. We need to get this out where we can examine it properly or get everyone else out while we try to open it."

Vinnia cast a sensing spell. "It's shielded well. I can't even decipher much of the magic I know is there."

Closing her eyes, Aili looked again with her senses. Inviting Andvari in, they sorted through the patterns on the trunk. "We shouldn't move this," Aili stated, pointing to a pattern she recognized.

"That's the first layer. Can we look deeper?" Andvari slipped under some spells, exposing more below.

"I found a journal." Norial held up a bound notebook she pulled from under a mattress.

"We got plenty here, too." Kyson gathered some papers as Filmat took a scroll case from the table.

"Bundle it up and get everyone out. Aili, Filmat, and I will open this once it's clear." Andvari glanced over and checked on everyone.

"I can help. We deal with locks a lot," Vinnia offered.

"Can you shield us all?" He rested a hand on Aili's shoulder.

She nodded. "Absolutely."

"Alright. Vinnia will stay as well."

"Everyone else, gather what you found, and we'll go through it outside." Kyson ushered the others out.

Filmat rolled up his sleeves. He stared at the box. Vinnia raised a hand and gathered magic on her fingertips, a spell forming. Andvari stood.

"Shield us. We'll go after the spells one at a time." Andvari raised his hand.

CHAPTER 16

S he shaped her Light, forming an almost solid dome around the trunk. Leaving small spaces for their magic to get through, Aili held it. She could close those in an instant if anything happened. She nodded.

The others chanted, each adding distinct patterns and rhythms as they tackled the spells layered over the trunk. Vinnia's spell worked first, and the first magical protection fell. Andvari took another spell down. Darkness lashed out, shooting up at the dome.

Aili slammed the closest gap closed, blocking its way out. Sending more Light in, she smothered the trunk again. The Darkness winked out at a touch. She waited, but as Filmat took down the last spell, nothing else happened.

"Next Layer." Andvari raised his hand again.

Aili strengthened her shield, adding additional Light to the inner layer. The others began chanting again, each focused on the trunk. Letting their magic through, she remained vigilant, her hands up. While she didn't depend on focusing the way they did, Aili still found it helped her with her magic.

The trunk shook as the second layer of spells fragmented. They didn't stop. Each mage focused on the last layer of protective magic. Filmat was the first to break a spell here. Darkness hissed through, creating a gas that spread inside her protective shield. Aili snuffed it out, slamming the barrier closed while she flooded it with light. Breaking Andvari and Vinnia's spells, she kept the Darkness from flowing out along their magic.

"Got it in time. How are you two?" Aili glanced at them.

Andvari took a deep breath. "That was a bit of a shock, but I'm unharmed. Vinnia?"

Her hand shook, but she nodded. "I'm okay. I haven't had a spell break since I was a student, but we train for that."

"Take a moment and we'll all go after the last spells together." Andvari held Vinnia's elbow, a light support as she also took a deep breath.

"I'm ready." Vinnia straightened up.

Aili opened the barrier, letting their combined spell through. The last seal faded. The trunk waited; all the magical protection gone. Cloaking herself in Light, Aili kneeled in front of the trunk. Andvari stood right behind her, a barrier spell ready.

Unfastening the catch, Aili opened the trunk. It was empty except for a single wooden box. She reached inside and pulled the small box out. It was light, though something rattled, a tiny clinking noise.

With trembling hands, she laid the box on the rocky floor. Flipping the little latch, Aili rested her hands on the lid. The inside was glowing with energy so strong she couldn't feel any details.

'We're here with you. Stay focused. We'll deal with it together.' Andvari crouched beside her, his magic active and ready.

'I know.' She smiled at him before turning back to the box. Whatever was inside, she was ready.

Holding the lid in her fingers, she swung it up on the hinges. Darkness oozed throughout the cushioned interior, a little cloud filling the inside. Aili smothered the cloud with her Light, revealing a tainted crystal.

Andvari took a cloth from his pocket and wrapped it around the crystal. Aili picked up the earth pin from underneath it. The little emeralds glittered in the mage-light. Heat flooded her. Her blood felt hot and thick like magma for a moment, the power of the deep coursing through her veins. With this, she could raise mountains. With this, she could reshape the land at her slightest whim.

'Aili?' Andvari rested a hand on her shoulder, pulling her attention back.

'Huh?' She dropped the pin back in the box. Her body calmed. "What?"

Vinnia picked up the pin, holding it in her palm. Aili fought the urge to reach out and take it. She gripped Andvari's sleeve.

"Are you alright?" He touched her cheek, his magic active and soothing her charged nerves.

She blinked. "Yeah. That was a lot of power."

'We know. We felt it through the link.' Kyson pulsed in the link, pulling the last of the feeling from her. 'Maybe let someone else hold onto that. It doesn't affect any of us like you.'

Aili pressed her palms to the ground and tapped into the energy around her. Her energy stabilized. 'I can imagine now what it was like, back before magic changed. Back when magic and belief were connected, and anything was possible. Having that kind of power, it must have been amazing, and dangerous.'

Andvari sat beside her and draped an arm over her shoulders. "We should put that somewhere safe." He looked up and met Vinnia's gaze. "The Scout vaults?"

Vinnia nodded. "What if it's not just us, though? What if a Scout is involved? I hate to mention it, but it is possible."

Andvari handed her the box. "I know. Even if it is a Scout, they can't get into our vaults in Mithlan. It's locked even tighter than your vaults are, with many more layers of security. So many, only I and those who work there know. I'll alert the Commander so she knows what we've found."

'Is it possible she's involved?' Kyson asked through the link. 'She was alone with the former head of the university, who was a Mind Mage. Could she be affected? She could access the CDF vaults.'

Andvari was silent for a long moment, his presence in the link distant as he thought. 'We could request she undergo a mind scan. I can send Niru. He'll be able to detect any Mind Magic on her, if there is any.'

'And what, you're just going to call her and say hi? By the way, we don't trust you, so if you'd be so kind as to get checked, we'd appreciate it? Isn't she your boss?' Aili shook her head. 'Does it even work that way?'

Kyson laughed, warming the link.

'What?' Aili bristled, ruffling the link.

'Technically she's no longer my boss, though she only had so much say over me anyway,' Andvari explained.

'What? Since when?' Aili took the crystal from him and opened the cloth. It took only a moment to bring her full light onto it and cleanse it. She handed Andvari the clear crystal back.

'Since you became a full mage and learned your place with us.' He took the crystal and held it up to the mage-light.

Vinnia closed the box with the earth pin inside. She cast a spell on the crystal. "It's clean."

'So, who's your boss now?' Aili leaned against his side, her head on his shoulder.

Kyson snorted, clear in the link. 'You are.'

'WHAT?'

'You're the Nature Mage. Ilia has been holding the position for you, but maybe she'd like to rest, right? We're here to support you. All the Scouts are. Now, that means you can form a council of advisors. We approach her and tell her you're ready to start assuming some responsibilities for the Scouts and we're looking at who to include. We'll say you want Niru to check everyone you're considering, given all that you've faced. Kyson and I will also get checked, so nobody feels singled out.'

Aili took the empty crystal and turned it, catching the light and sending beams through the room. 'A council, huh? How many people should I look for? I could use some advice and guidance here.'

Andvari stood and offered her his hand. Aili took it and got to her feet. They all headed down the tunnel.

'That's a good start.' Kyson nudged her in the link. 'That's what we're here for.'

Andvari chuckled. "You'll want someone from each area of the Scouts. A healer, for sure. A field Scout, which could be Kyson if he's your choice. Someone from the cities to act as liaison with the various CDF groups. You could keep the Commander, since she knows her job, or pick someone new. Choose someone from the research and magical theory group. It's up to you but keep it small and diverse. Half a dozen people are reasonable."

Aili stepped into the sun and smiled. The breeze warmed her skin enough to ward off the chill of the cavern. The smile fell from her face. "Wait, I'm your boss?"

He laughed. "Yes. I'm also still your mentor, though, so also no. Nobody anticipated this happening. Are you planning on firing me?" Andvari nudged her lightly with his elbow.

Aili rolled her eyes. "Yeah, because I love paperwork. Especially the kind I don't know how to do. So, how does this all work now? What am I supposed to be doing?"

He led the group back towards camp. Vinnia had the box with the pin under her arm. Kyson walked beside her, both of them behind Aili and Andvari.

"You keep doing what you've been doing. I keep running the Scouts in their daily operations, and we support you. The Commander will do her job until or unless you pick someone new. She is good, so don't make that decision rashly."

Aili nodded. The Commander was there, protecting Andvari and Kyson when they were detained. She checked on them in the middle of the night once, simply because Aili had seen them in a nightmare. She even protected Aili from the University once. Aili hadn't met her often. That might be because she was that good, though.

"I don't know enough to decide that yet, anyway. How do we arrange getting her checked?" Aili looked up at him as they walked.

"You and I will call her together soon. How she reacts might also give us an idea of whether she's loyal or not. We can decide after it's all done."

"Sounds good. Mithlan?"

"The Scout vaults are in Mithlan, in an ancient building protected by magic going back to the golden age." Kyson shrugged. "The highest security vaults, anyway. We have small vaults at each camp for minor valuables."

"So much for some easy tracking training," Aili mumbled.

Andvari shook his head. "Your track was good. They learned as we followed you. We'll try again soon and make it longer."

***

Aili stared out the window into the forest, her food tray on the table in front of her. Was she really even capable of leading the Scouts one day? Before any of that happened, she still needed to deal with the crystals and whatever else was going on around here.

Something yanked her from her thoughts. Magic approached, strong and coming closer. It was familiar, but she couldn't quite place it. Aili set her fork down and stood.

"What's up?" Andvari looked up at her, his teacup halfway to his lips.

Scrunching her nose, Aili closed her eyes. "Magic."

"Let me see?" He set his teacup down and followed her.

Aili headed for the main doors as she opened her senses, seeking the magic still approaching. His presence in the link reassured her. She felt things differently in this camp, with fewer people but stronger protection spells around.

"Oh, that's our help."

Aili held the door for him. "Help?"

Andvari nodded. His footsteps echoed on the wooden steps as he headed down and onto the grass in front of the building. "If we're going to tackle that Darkness, we'll need help. I sent for them. They're here."

Dashing after him, Aili caught up. He stopped near the middle of the grassy field in front of the building, the dome protecting them. She followed his gaze up into the sky, searching for something. Help, he said. Dinna?

An air transport larger than she'd ever seen emerged through the trees, gliding down towards them. It dropped into the dome, descending steeper than she'd ever experienced, heading right at them. Wind whipped at her hair and clothing as it nearly came straight down. Aili ducked behind Andvari for protection, peering around his side.

The air box was huge, easily twice the size of the one that brought her and the others. It touched down lightly in the grass, barely a few feet away. The box was full of people, with every seat occupied. Everyone collected their bags and got out of their seats.

Dinna leapt from the box, landing lightly in the grass. "Thanks, Boss. It's not often I get to fly this baby." She patted the glossy, sloped front.

Andvari smiled at her. "I figured you'd like the opportunity. How was the flight?"

"Smooth. The forests look good until you get close to here. The ring of sickness is widening, though it's slow. The domes still contain most of it, except for one spot. There's a line of sick trees heading southwest." Dinna straightened up and watched everyone disembark from the box.

"I'll have it looked into."

Aili ran over and wrapped her arms around a man who had just exited the box. "Gavi!"

He dropped his bag on the grass and hugged her back, his grip firm and strong. "How are you? How's the training going?"

She let go and stepped back. "I'm doing the readings every day. I'll be a Master Healer in no time." Aili picked up his bag and handed it to him.

He took the bag and slung it over his shoulder. "I don't doubt that for a moment."

"What are you doing here? Don't get me wrong, it's wonderful that you're here, but why?"

CHAPTER 17

G avi laughed and looked over at Andvari. "Seriously?"

Andvari shrugged. "She was busy. I haven't told her yet."

"We're going to help you cleanse the camp." Gavi rested an arm around her shoulders and hugged her to his side.

"That's great. How?" She leaned her head against his side.

"A grand magical working." Hana reached over the side and pulled her bag from the transport. "That's why everyone is here."

Aili looked over the group. She knew most of the Scouts, having worked with many before. What were the CDF people doing here, though? Frida and Theron were talking to Andvari, and two other men she didn't know stood nearby. Everyone who arrived had the platinum band of a Master Mage.

"Hana, it's great to see you. Where's Kaj?" Aili noted again who was here, but also who wasn't. Partners didn't often separate like this, though it wasn't unheard of.

Hana eased her bag strap over her shoulder. Her fiery red hair contrasted with the green bag. "Back at the northern camp. Gavi is more senior, and you only need three mages from each school of magic, so he stayed behind."

Aili looked around at everyone again, paying more attention. Hana and Theron were both Fire Mages, and the other was a Scout from the southern camp she didn't know well. Frida was an Air Mage, but so were Kyson and Norial here.

"Jeril." Aili wrapped her arms around the slender man as he came close.

"Aili." He dropped his bag and hugged her back. "I was hoping you were staying out of trouble, but I guess not, huh?"

"Trouble finds me. It's not my fault." She looked up, way up, at him.

"Did you meet Dax when you were up north?" Jeril nodded to the young man leaning against the transport. "I know you met Edlyn."

The proud warrior woman smiled and nodded to Aili. Dax straightened up beside her and winked at Aili. Aili smiled back and waved.

"I did. Andvari let me go on an underwater survey with them. It was fun, but I almost drowned."

Jeril laughed. "I doubt that, though I don't doubt it felt like it. They never would have let you die." He slung an arm around her as they followed Andvari and the CDF to the main hall.

"Yeah, maybe not, but my lungs didn't know that." Aili elbowed him in the ribs just hard enough to feel him.

Andvari stopped on the steps, Gavi's bag over his shoulder. "Everyone, take a few minutes and get settled. Have some food or drink if you need. We meet at the edge of the outer dome once you're all ready." He turned to Aili. "Make sure you eat well. Take extra bars for after."

Mowen clapped his hands, getting everyone's attention. "If you'll all follow, I'll show you to your rooms. This will be the first time in decades all the rooms will be full."

Aili let everyone else go first and followed them into the hall. She turned off into the dining room, leaving them to sort out who was staying where. Why was the CDF here? There were plenty of Scouts around the country, over three times as many as CDF in the capital city. They must be here for a reason.

Stopping at the snack table, she grabbed a few wrapped meal bars and stuffed them in her pockets. How many would she need? Looking down at herself, all her pants pockets were full. Surely that would be enough? Andvari and Kyson probably had more as well. Grabbing a pastry from the table, she munched on it.

How would they cleanse the dome? It went down into the soil, so she was really cleansing the entire sphere. He must have a plan, or he wouldn't have brought everyone. Aili wandered over and took her teacup. No, not tea. Maybe juice? Grabbing her teacup and tray, Aili set them in bins. She took a glass of juice instead.

After downing the glass, she left it in the bin. She wandered back to the entryway, stopping short at the sight. Aili smiled widely as she held the door open. Kyson escorted Ilia towards the door, her hand on his arm.

Ilia smiled at her. "You've had a snack?"

Aili nodded. Once Ilia was through the door, she joined them outside and hugged the bony old woman.

"Good. This will take a fair bit of energy, but it's nothing you can't handle." Ilia hugged her, her grip strong despite her age.

Aili linked arms with her and walked down the steps with her. Ilia grinned at the little wagon waiting at the bottom of the stairs. Aili waited as Kyson settled Ilia into the passenger seat.

"Hop in back if you want a ride." He nodded to the flat deck with short sides behind the seats.

She hesitated, her fingers gripping the sides. Certainly, he'd be careful driving Ilia around. Aili let out a slow breath and hopped in the back. She sat with her back to the seats and curled her legs up, her arms wrapped around them.

"Ready?" Kyson set his palms on the control panel.

Aili glanced over her shoulder and saw Ilia grin. The main hall door opened, and Andvari stepped through. His eyes widened, and he opened his mouth. The wagon shot off, speeding down the hill. Aili gripped the tool rack and hunkered down, slamming into the low side as the wind rushed over her. The wagon caught air, and the magic held her down.

"Yeah," Ilia whooped, her hands in the air. "Faster."

Aili pressed a hand over her mouth. The wagon zipped and weaved among the trees, rushing at the dome. Aili slid as he veered left around a boulder, hitting the side again. Ilia cheered as dirt sprayed from the wheels in the skid.

The wagon slid to a stop, missing the dome by inches. Aili lay on her back, her fingers white where she still gripped the tool rack with one hand. Her legs ached where they were tucked up under her, pressed against the back of the wagon.

Ilia eased from the wagon. She reached over the side and held Aili's cheeks in her hands. "You'll be fine. I've seen the way you and that pony gallop." Magic flowed from the old woman and through her.

Her nausea eased. Her body stilled, the trembling just a recent memory now. Circulation flowed back into her fingers, and she let go of the metal rack. Aili took Kyson's offered hand and scrambled from the wagon. "You enjoyed that?"

Ilia beamed at her. "I can't tell you how seldom I get to go out and go carting. They get incredibly upset if you do it in the city. Every time I come to a camp someone takes me for a ride."

Kyson laughed. "As much as you talk about me, her driving privileges were revoked after an incident. We're happy to drive her."

"Incident?" Aili raised an eyebrow.

Ilia winked. "When I was young, we used to compete in wagon races. It was a way to cheer people up and help them adjust as magic was changing. Gave them something to look forward to. We were always testing spells to give us an edge. So many new spells were developed because of us racing."

Aili's jaw dropped. "You used to race?"

"Oh, yes." Ilia beamed at her, grinning widely. "I was champion of the northern circuit, where the tracks were wilder, and you had to watch for bears and cliffs and such." She thumped her chest.

"Did you teach him to drive?" Aili narrowed her eyes at Kyson.

The old woman laughed. "Oh, forests, no. Though he is my favourite driver." She leaned against Kyson, her arm around his waist. "He's not afraid to break me and will go the fun routes."

Another wagon emerged through the trees, Andvari driving Gavi at a walking pace ahead of the rest of the Scouts.

'You could have warned me,' she shot at him, through the link.

Andvari smiled as he pulled the wagon up beside them, parking with more skill and attention. 'It was too late. Anyway, you seem fine, despite the terror moments ago. You were with Ilia. Do you really think she'd let anything happen to you?'

The group gathered beside the wagons. Their attention was on her and Andvari. Aili shifted her weight from foot to foot as she considered the dome.

"Is everyone going to be allowed in?" She watched the magic shimmer and dance across the surface of the dome.

Ilia touched the dome, sending ripples of power through it. "Yes. I've already talked to Mother. She's waiting for us. The magic will let everyone in."

"Alright, everyone. We'll set up just inside this first barrier. Nobody is to go close to the inner dome. Do not go inside it under any circumstance." Andvari waved and began walking toward the entrance to the outer dome.

Aili walked beside him, leading the group. She glanced back to where Kyson and Ilia trailed behind. All these people following, all trusted her to do something, but what?

"Lead us through," Andvari stated calmly, as he stopped at the barrier. "They're ready to follow."

She pressed her fingers to her lips and walked through the barrier. Andvari stayed beside her, a trusted guide and advisor. She reached over and gripped his sleeve as the magic coated her, overwhelming her senses. He took her hand in his and kept walking, not letting go until she could see and feel again.

They went in a short distance, though nobody strayed close to the inner domes. Even with the middle dome to help shield them, the Darkness inside gave her the shivers. Their temporary reinforcements barely held.

"Aili, are you ready?" Andvari quickly glanced over the group, the mages gathering with those of their own kind.

"No," she whispered. "I have no idea what to do." Aili played with the hem of her sleeve, her fingers rubbing the fine fabric so hard she could feel the stitching.

Andvari rested his hand on her shoulder. The familiar soothing energy rushed into her. "That's not a problem.

Why don't you ask the one person who knows?" He tilted his head towards Ilia.

Kyson brought Ilia through the crowd of mages and stopped beside Aili.

"It's okay to not be ready. We can do it anyway." Ilia draped an arm around her shoulders.

Aili took a deep breath and straightened up. "How do we do this?"

"You have an expert on shields and barriers. He will shape the magic. The other mages will give power from each school of magic. You and I will provide the power of nature, channelling what Mother has to offer. We will weave the magic all together in the pattern he provides. Let him guide it as we work. I'll show you how." Ilia took her hand and squeezed lightly.

"Right. I'm ready." Aili frowned as a tendril smashed into the innermost dome, straining against the magic.

The mages formed a circle around the three of them. A quick glance and Aili noticed they stood in a pattern: an Earth Mage, a Water Mage, an Air Mage, and a Fire Mage, with three of each type spread around the circle.

Andvari began chanting, his hands raising. Magic flared around him. The mages around the circle raised their hands, their own power flowing to join his. Closing her eyes, Aili saw it all with her magical senses.

He directed his magic over the inner dome, the middle dome letting the power through with no direct guidance. Aili sensed a warmth in it, a familiar presence. Mother? She smiled as the ground under her warmed.

Ilia chanted, her voice slow and quiet. Her power threaded through the magic gathering from the mages. This extra power flowed over Andvari's shaping magic, weaving among the frame he lay over the dome.

I see what she's doing. I can do that. Aili smiled again. Pulling energy from the ground, wind, and sun, Aili sent it among the magic Ilia shaped and held. Guiding it directly into Andvari's magic, Aili blended it all into a solid thread.

Andvari opened the link fully and grasped this bundle of magic. With her help, they shaped it and blended it right into the outer edge of the innermost dome. He altered the pattern, adding to it and weaving additional magic she gathered from the land.

They coated the dome, covering every crack and fissure, sealing any forming gaps. The tendrils of Darkness smashed at the dome, shaking it, weakening one spot. Her bones rattled with the force as another deep purple tentacle of power hammered the spot.

'Focus. You're stronger than it is, especially with us.'

Aili smiled. Andvari was right. She worked over the weakest spot, thickening the magic they added as Andvari laid another pattern over that crack. Ilia kept weaving magic from the mages around the lower part of the dome, following the pattern Andvari set.

Closing the magic over the top of the dome, pressing firmly over the cracks, Aili flowed more power from the sun, sending it down the sides. That tendril was still down there, reaching into the soil. With Andvari's strength as an Earth Mage and her ability to touch the planet directly, they sped beneath the ground.

Taking more power from what Ilia spun from the mages, Aili blended it with extra sunlight. She and Andvari approached the tendrils from opposite sides, bringing this magic around it. Their quick patch was holding, though it was stretched. Aili coated the tendril, stopping it again.

"Now, Aili. You and I will cleanse the interior." Ilia took her hand.

CHAPTER 18

Ilia's power rushed through her, so like her own. Aili pulled from her inner lights, adding more energy from around her. Sending a blast of sunlight and Nature Magic directly inside the dome, Aili kept the magic coming as Ilia directed it into the crystals.

Light collided with Darkness. Explosions rocked the dome, dark smoke obscuring the inside. Aili pressed the Light in, spreading it like Ilia showed her. The ground shook. Light hit a pile of massive crystals. Lightning flashed, releasing power. Shards of crystal flew, hitting the inside of the dome.

The tendril shivered as the Light coated it. The ground rolled. Aili stretched her arms out and caught herself. Andvari kept Ilia upright, with an arm around the old woman. Sending more Light down, Aili focused on the tendril. Ilia added to the magic. The tendril burst. Smoke rose inside the dome, obscuring everything inside from view.

"Done." Ilia brushed her hands together.

Aili pulled a snack bar from her pocket and devoured it in seconds, not leaving a single crumb. A second followed, and a third. Ilia took the bar Andvari offered her and ate it.

"Is it safe to go and inspect it?" Frida stared at the dome.

Aili patted her pockets, looking for another bar. She glanced up at the dome. The smoke inside was clearing and turning white. "If we did it right, yes."

"Stay here with Ilia and Gavi," Andvari instructed. He handed her another bar. "We'll be careful."

She took the bar and unwrapped it, tearing the paper off. "What happens to the crystals now?"

"They can use them again. They're empty and clean. They can even keep storing them in here, as long as no more contaminated crystals come in." Ilia licked her fingers clean.

Aili swallowed the last of the bar. "Can we find a way to cleanse the crystals instead? Maybe make an artifact or something? If each camp had one, or at least the four big camps, they won't need to store them like this. Look what it did to the forest."

Bracing her hands on her hips, Aili looked around. A few trees and plants still grew under the outer dome, but they were spindly and weak.

"Now we can send a regrowth team in. With no Darkness in here, they can come and go safely. We'll leave the barriers for now, though. Maybe after you create this mystical artifact, we can take the barrier down, too." Andvari set his hand on her shoulder. "Ask Rei. He knows more about the ancient artifacts than anyone else in the Scouts."

"I can tell you, too," Ilia whispered. "It can be our project."

Aili grinned. She threw her arms around Ilia and hugged tightly. "That sounds like so much fun. Will the normal mages be able to use it if we make it?"

"If we do it right." Ilia grinned back at her. "You've never done a magical research problem before, though it's a lot like herbalism research. This will be good for you." She squeezed Aili back, her arms around Aili's ribs. "Now, I'd like another snack, if you don't mind."

Kyson handed her an unwrapped snack bar. Andvari and the others headed down towards the dome. They didn't stop at the building for any protective clothing. There was no need now. Frida led the group beside Andvari, her magic active. Even this far away, Aili sensed the spells with ease.

Aili turned to Gavi. "How have you been? You look good."

"Thanks to you and the others." He tapped his chest. "That lung is working great. My endurance is back and I'm on full duty. I'm not sure how you kept Andvari from going forest mad when he was recovering. Being idle like that is hard."

She laughed. "Most of the time I'd go for walks in the forest, leaving the link open. He could feel the grass and hear the birds and all through me. At least, when I wasn't busy helping you all."

With the air inside the dome nearly clear, Aili watched the others move around inside. They followed Andvari back to the entrance and started back up the path.

"Congratulations." Ilia took her hand. "You just did something that took your sister years to master."

Aili shuffled her feet and stared down at her boots. "I had you helping. If I had to figure it out on my own, it would have taken me years."

Gavi chuckled. "Only because you'd be cleansing those one at a time. Not because you didn't know how. Remember the boy you cleansed?"

She nodded. How helpless had she felt, sensing what was wrong, and not knowing how to fix it? Andvari guided her through it. Did he know for sure it would work?

"Everyone, head back and rest. You have the day off training. We still have stolen artifacts out here somewhere, so that's our next focus." Andvari split from the group and rejoined Aili's small group. "If you want to ride back with us instead, you can."

"Absolutely. They can get themselves killed without me."
Aili bounded over to the small wagons and leapt into the
neatly parked one.

Ilia smiled at Aili as she settled into the passenger seat of
the other wagon. "If you ever get as old as me, you'll take
your excitement where you can get it."

Aili leaned against the seats and closed her eyes. The enormous domes still glowed in her senses, the strongest magic
in the wider area. Still, something pulled at her beyond
that. Without the mass of Darkness, her range was now
many times greater. What was she sensing, though?

The wagon rolled back to camp, a smooth ride at a walking
pace. Aili stretched her awareness out, seeking the energy
she somehow knew was there. One wasn't far away. The
dome was still interfering, but now she had somewhere to
look.

Opening her eyes, Aili watched Andvari drive past the
main door. Kyson stopped his wagon there and was offering Ilia his arm. Turning around the side, Andvari drove
the wagon to a large door partway down the building.
Driving smoothly inside, he parked the wagon among the
others.

Leaping down, Aili looked around. Wagons of a few different sizes waited along one wall. The other wall was
equipment storage. A couple of doors led off somewhere,
one probably into the building itself and the other might
be food storage.

"Go join Ilia. Get another snack. I'll be right there." Andvari pointed at one of the doors.

Slipping through, Aili found herself in the hall near the communication room. Ilia wouldn't be in the main dining room. The chairs weren't padded enough. Aili smiled. She knew just where to find her. Passing through busy halls, Aili snuck into the third recreation room.

"Perfect, child. The tea is ready." Ilia gestured at the small table, where a tray held tea and biscuits.

Aili poured herself a cup of tea. This room almost looked made for Ilia. She looked so snug in that big, padded chair, with a warm wrap around her, her feet up on a padded footstool. The fireplace held fire crystals, giving off a soothing heat. Cradling her mug in her hands, Aili sat near the fire with her.

"You did well, child." Ilia smiled as she lifted her teacup to her lips.

"It's not over, though." Aili took a sip. Cinnamon. Her insides warmed.

"No, it's not. We cleansed the crystals, true, but not the source of the taint." Ilia selected a biscuit with fruit pieces in it. "There's more to this."

Aili blinked at her, her teacup partway to her mouth. "More?"

With a wave of her hand, Ilia set a barrier around them. "Remember what I told you about the dragon eggs? Remember how they were hidden?"

"Yeah, that story was incredible." Aili sipped her tea. "Wait, the eggs are connected to this?"

The old woman smiled. "Yes. Imagine what it would take to get through the barrier, knowing there aren't any griffins around now."

"Huh." Aili watched the flames dance on the surface of the fire crystals. "You'd need a way to disrupt the massive winds—"

"Exactly." Ilia beamed at her. "What might do that for most mages, knowing they don't have spells powerful enough, not even as a mass magical working?"

Aili shook her head. "Only an artifact from the old days. Magic was stronger back then. But I thought mages couldn't use the pins? Rei has been trying to activate one carefully, and he can't."

Ilia smiled. "The ocean changed just from having an unshielded pin nearby. Imagine if someone flew into the barrier with the pin?" She tucked a lock of her wild grey hair back under her scarf.

"You're saying they don't need to use it directly. It'll just interact with the barrier anyway. Is it the same kind of magic?"

Pulling the cord around her neck, Ilia raised the small vial where Aili could see it. "I fear so." The vial glowed deep orange, almost red, instead of the usual swirls of green. "The eggs are in danger. I believe it's related to the taint and the mages gathering the pins."

Aili rubbed her cheek. "Okay, but how? Why?"

"Dragons are creatures of air, like we're creatures of the land. Imagine what might happen if the eggs were submerged in taint? In Dark Magic? Do you know how it might affect them?"

She shook her head. "Nothing good, I imagine."

"Dark dragons would hatch. We can't allow that. Imagine if they begin affecting magic again, spreading the taint throughout the land?"

Aili took another sip of tea. "So, we need to keep the eggs safe and cleanse wherever they were planning on submerging them. I don't know where that would be, though. It could be anywhere, right?" She stared up at the map on the far wall. "It's a big country."

"Yes, but what do they need?" Ilia tapped her teacup. "Water with a magical presence. Without that, the Darkness can't affect the eggs. It's not strong enough. The shell would protect them."

Shifting in her seat, Aili curled her legs up under her. "Like the heart of the forest? I've never felt magical water anywhere else." She cast her mind back. Was that true? Her pond back east was magical, but was it because of the water?

"There are a few other places. One isn't far from here. They're all well hidden. There's one up north. When you were there, you hadn't yet grown into your powers enough to feel them. There's another near your camp in the east but also locked behind magical protection."

"What kind of magical protection?" Andvari strolled into the room. He took a teacup and filled it.

"Most is ancient magic placed by mother. Ethala set some as well, when the camps were established near the springs. I'm not sure she made notes in her writings for the Scouts." Ilia took another biscuit and bit into it.

Andvari pulled a chair over and sat with them. "I don't recall anything about magical springs. How is the water different?"

"It's infused with mother's magic. Theoretically, only a nature mage should be able to access them. The magic should stop anyone else from sensing them. Magic has only become more structured over time, making the protections even more powerful." Ilia held her teacup out. "Aili, dear, would you get me some more?"

Aili set her own teacup on the little table. "Of course." Taking the cup, she refilled it and handed it back.

"Wouldn't that same magic prevent anyone else from finding them, including whoever might want to submerge the dragon eggs?"

"But what if the taint is letting them feel it?" Aili settled back in her chair. "We know their magic looks closer to what I do. Since cleansing the dome I'm feeling all kinds of new magic around us. What if they can as well?"

Andvari focused on her, not frowning, but intently serious with his slightly pinched brow. "What kinds of things?"

"The best I can describe it is I'm sensing spots where the magic is strong and different. It's like the water pin, but not quite the same. I think we need to go look." Aili picked at the fabric covering the chair's arm.

"Can you point them out on a map?" Andvari glanced over at the huge map on the wall.

She shook her head, her tea sloshing in her cup as she picked it up again. "No. I can sense direction but not point to a spot. I know which ones are closer by how strong they feel, but not well enough to guess."

"Have your snack and a rest. We'll do a meditation session and see if we can help you find them. We'll get as close as we can."

"I will help." Ilia smiled at her. "My magic isn't linked to yours like theirs is, but that might make it easier, with me also being a Nature Mage."

Aili glanced at Andvari. 'Did you tell her?'

'No.'

"I can feel it, child." Ilia winked at her. "Your magic is so tangled up with theirs, it had to be your doing. It's wrapped around their hearts and magical cores. I can see it plainly when I feel for magic."

"Has it ever been done before? Has any other Nature Mage done it?" Aili straightened up in her chair.

Ilia was silent for a long moment, a distant look in her eyes. "No, but each sister had unique skills. Go and rest."

CHAPTER 19

A ili stopped. "What's that for? Are we getting even more people?"

Andvari stopped beside her. "Something like that."

Kyson and Hana knelt on the grass near the building with a tent spread out before them.

Aili recognized the mesh sides as a research tent right away. "People don't sleep in those."

"Not usually, no." Andvari smiled that knowing smile. "We have a special case."

"Oh?" She followed him closer.

Furniture and bedding were stacked beside the building. Kyson and Hana had the tent set up in moments, only using magic for the poles out of reach. Once the tent was up, they set spells on it for stability and protection. Kyson levitated the heavier furniture in as Hana carried the writing table inside.

"You'll see soon." Andvari headed for the wooden steps. "We've been too busy to practice your sword work outside of Drill. I'll be busy for a short while, so maybe you want to do that?"

"You bet." Aili bounced up the steps behind him.

She sprinted for her room, dashing past him in the entryway. Taking her sword from the hook near her bed, Aili belted it around her shoulders. In every other camp, there was a door out back near the communication centre. She smiled as she found it, slipping out into the quiet field behind the building.

Glancing back, she nodded. Few windows on this side, since the living areas were to the sides and front. Perfect. Aili stood still, closing her eyes and settling her breathing. With plenty of space, she could move with full energy and speed, hitting nothing.

Drawing her sword in a steady motion, Aili flowed into the first pattern. Taking her time as she stretched her body, Aili stepped and slashed, fending off her invisible opponent. Each movement connected to the next until her sword slid back into the scabbard at the end. Aili opened her eyes and smiled.

Letting a slow breath out, Aili focused. Whipping the sword from the scabbard, she repeated the pattern at full speed. With sharp focus and a warm body, the movements were effortless. Her sword slid back into the scabbard, and she stilled herself again.

"Oh, wow."

Aili spun. Karil stood at the corner, leaning against the building. Her cheeks were red.

"Hey." Aili smiled. "Were you looking for me?"

"I—um—no. I was just out for a walk. How did you get so good? Where did you get such a beautiful sword?" Karil pressed her hands to her cheeks.

"Andvari gave it to me. Would you like to see it closer?" Aili unbuckled the belt and held the scabbard in her hands.

Karil walked closer, each step tentative and halting. Her eyes widened as Aili drew the sword. Aili held the sword still.

"He got you that? It's beautiful." She lifted her gaze from the blade and looked at Aili. "How long have you been practicing to get that good? I though you only joined a short while ago?"

Aili slid the sword back into its scabbard. "I've been with Andvari for about a year now. The man who looked after our horses was a former Scout. He's actually a Scout again. It's complicated. Anyway, he taught me starting when I was a small child."

Karil raised an eyebrow. "You started as a child."

She shrugged. "I didn't have a normal childhood. What about you? Do you like sword practice?"

The young woman shuffled her feet, her gaze down. "I'm not the best at it. Not like you or the others. I'm better with animal care."

Aili had the urge to hug, but Andvari's talk gave her pause. "It just takes practice. If you want to grab your sword, you can practice with me."

"I won't slow you down?" Karil looked up and met her gaze, her body tense.

Smiling, Aili shook her head. "It's always good to go over the basics. That's why I practice all forms regularly, and not just the one I'm working on."

"Dare I ask which one that is?" Karil grinned.

Aili hesitated. Would it sound like bragging? "The fourth," she mumbled. "I'm not as practiced with it yet, but I'm consistent, at least."

Karil's jaw dropped. "The fourth? That explains the sword."

"He said all Scouts get a special sword when they master the third form. He gave this to me for practice and use when in the field."

"That's partly true." Karil moved around her and stared at the hilt. "People do get a duty sword after form three. They rarely get a sword like that until they master form five."

Was it true? Aili's thoughts stalled. Darik had a sword like hers. So did most of her Scout friends, but they were Master Mages and senior Scouts. Theirs had never held elemental magic like hers had but were perfectly capable of it if needed.

"Would you help me with form one?" Karil shifted from foot to foot.

"Sure. Get your sword. I'll wait." Aili closed her eyes. 'Do you have a minute?'

Andvari warmed in the link, answering immediately. 'What's on your mind?'

'My sword. Is it higher quality than normal for my level?'

The warmth pulsed and grew with amusement. 'I'm surprised you haven't noticed that before. Not that it matters, but yes, it is. Your sword was chosen for you to make the most of your abilities. Darik, Ilia, and I chose it. It has served you well, has it not?'

Aili pressed her hand to her heart. 'Yes, and I love it. It feels like a part of me when I use it.'

'Ilia thought it might. How's form four feeling?'

She smiled, letting her emotions through clearly. 'I wouldn't say I'm confident, but I can do it fully without obvious mistakes.'

Karil dashed through the door, sword in hand.

'Karil's ready. Gotta go. I'm helping her.' Aili backed from the link.

Andvari's presence in the link glowed brightly for a moment.

"Is there something specific you wanted to work on?" Aili offered.

"I'm having a little trouble with my hand position, and it's throwing the tip of my blade off," Karil admitted.

Thoughtful for a moment, Aili nodded. "We'll go through it slowly, move by move, and see what we can figure out." She relaxed into the ready position. "Work there so I can see you."

Karil stepped to where she pointed, just far enough away that their blades wouldn't touch stretched out. Once she was also in the ready position, Aili nodded.

"We'll go half speed, a single move at a time. Begin," Aili instructed.

They drew their swords, moving together. Aili matched Karil's pace, keeping her head turned just enough to see how she moved. They advanced through the first few moves with Aili calling the pace.

"I think I see it already." Aili slid her sword into the scabbard and stepped closer. "It's not your sword, it's your elbow."

Karil raised an eyebrow. "You're sure?"

"Not exactly, but the whole body is connected, right? Change any one part, and the rest will adjust. I had a similar issue with a move in form four, when I was newly learning it. One move didn't feel right. Try keeping your elbow in line with your body. Don't let it move forward."

Drawing her sword again, Aili showed Karil what she meant. "Here. At this point. Keep your elbow back so your arm stays in line, at least until here in the movement." She swung her sword slowly, showing Karil. "Now see it the way you were trying, and how it changes?"

Moving at only a quarter speed, Aili repeated both ways again. Karil stood close enough to touch her. With all the practice she had, Aili wasn't concerned about hitting her, but was it getting warm out here? Had she spent too much time in the sun?

"Let me try." Karil moved away and raised her sword.

Keeping her elbow back this time, Karil tried the move again. She grinned at her steady sword tip, pointing right where it was supposed to be. "Why wouldn't anyone see that sooner?"

Aili shrugged. "Sometimes adjusting the hand position will correct the arm position for the same reason. Women are just a little different because we're usually more flexible right? It's a tiny difference in our shoulders, too, so sometimes we need an adjustment in how we do things."

"Is all form one like that? I need to keep the elbows lined up?"

Smiling at Karil, Aili moved back to her starting place. "Let's try it and see. We'll go a quarter speed. Think about moving your body and upper arms together, but don't get stiff. Wherever the elbow allows, the arm will go."

They went through the form again, Aili calling each move one at a time. They moved slowly, but Aili called it so they flowed between moves. With her attention on her body so firmly, Karil's brow pinched. When they stopped, she grinned at Aili.

"That was better. Now I just need to practice that a lot more, but it feels better. Elbows. Who knew?" Karil sheathed her sword and beamed at Aili.

Aili grinned back at her. "In the fourth form, there's a movement that starts as a stabbing attack. After that, you bring your arm back for an elbow strike. I didn't even know that was a thing until Kyson showed me. He even showed me how to add power to it. Since then, I've been paying more attention to my whole body during the forms."

Karil frowned. "I need more practice. I'm not ready for full speed now. Not anymore."

Sliding her sword back into the scabbard, Aili shook her head. "It'll be worth the effort. When you do speed up again, it'll flow better. You won't have to think about it anymore. They're not going to judge you for this. If anything, they'll be proud of you putting the work in. I promise."

"Thanks, Aili." Karil bounced on her toes and grinned again.

"Any time." Aili's stomach flipped. Is this what it is to get the metaphorical butterflies inside? It was definitely hot here. Maybe she should find some shade. "You're welcome to stay and practice. I'm going for a short walk."

Karil waved and smiled. Aili waved back before turning and scooting around the building. Stepping into a stronger breeze, her cheeks cooled again. What was wrong with her?

Coming around the front again, Aili looked up. She'd recognize that tingling anywhere now. Dinna was coming back. A glance showed the tent was up and the furniture inside now. Was the new guest here?

Andvari came through the door and down the steps. He smiled and waved Aili over as he waited for the air box to glide in. Dinna piloted the small box to the grass, touching down beside them.

"How was the flight?" Andvari offered his hand to the passenger.

They wore a thick cloak. A pale hand stretched out and took his. The person stretched their legs out and stood. A light blue cloak instead of Scout green? Her hood fell back. She looked around. Her pale blonde hair shone in the sunlight, almost the same colour as the sun itself. Her eyes were the colour of the sky on a clear day.

She's so slender, a stiff breeze might knock her over. Aili stepped back, giving her room to climb over the edge of the air box. There's no way she's a Scout. Even little people like me are strong physically here.

"It was fabulous." Her voice was light and breathy. "I rarely get to go that high." She grinned. The fine lines around her mouth and eyes gave her age away.

"Aili, this is Renni. She's a specialty consultant for us. An expert on all things related to the atmosphere and wide weather patterns." Andvari bowed his head to her.

Not a regular Scout. She didn't think so. Aili bowed her head as well. "It's a pleasure to meet you."

"Thank you." Renni took Aili's hand. "I've heard about you, and it's amazing. You've really managed some Master level spells? You're so young."

Kyson chuckled. "She's as young as you were when you first started levitating." He strode over from the steps.

Renni shrugged. "Levitation came easily. Staying on the ground, now that was the hard part."

"We have the tent set up, as you requested it. Would you like to rest first? The staff are bringing food and refreshments out any moment now." Andvari gestured at the mesh tent beside the hall.

"I appreciate it so much. I'm fine in normal quarters and looking after myself, but—" She shrugged.

"I understand. We're grateful you've come, even while your experiment is running. I know you'll share the results once you're finished, and we'll all learn more." Andvari bowed his head once more. "We'll support you however we can."

She shook her head, her light blonde hair swinging slightly. "You've already given me everything I need. I just need to stay outside in the air currents." Renni tucked her hair back behind her ears.

"I saw the research proposal." Kyson offered her his arm. "Every Master Air Mage who deals with the atmosphere is eagerly awaiting your results."

Aili stayed out of the way, following behind as they headed for the tent.

Renni patted Kyson's arm. "I already have some results, if you'd like to see them." She glanced over her shoulder at Aili. "I also have a project in mind to research the sun. I understand you might be able to help me."

Aili raised an eyebrow at Andvari.

He laughed lightly. "As a full mage now, you can choose to assist any Master Mage in any research you like. If she requests you specifically, you can set the timeframe for when you're available. We'll make sure you get the chance, if you want to help."

"I'd like to learn more. It sounds interesting." Aili caught up and walked on Kyson's other side.

"Once I'm finished with this experiment, I'll send you the full proposal. Your mentor can help you understand it if you need, especially if you've never seen one before."

Andvari opened the tent flap and let them pass before following as well. "There's a slate here to contact the support staff. They're ready to help with anything you need." He gestured at the desk.

Renni bowed her head this time. "Thank you. I will need some time to settle after the flight. It was most stimulating." She grinned. "A snack will help."

Andvari looked over at Norial, who was bringing a tray down the steps. "Right on time."

CHAPTER 20

There were so many stars above her that the sky was bright with the tiny dots of light. How big and vast was space? Somewhere out there, were there people staring up, wondering if they were alone in the vast universe, too? Did one of them also have a destiny, maybe, or were they free to enjoy life while someone else saves their world?

He glowed in her senses, a familiar presence leaning against a tree behind her. Aili smiled. She'd never be able to sneak out, so she didn't bother trying. With their link, he could find her as easily as she feels him.

"Can't sleep?" Aili turned and faced Andvari.

"I could ask you the same question." He walked over to her side, staring up at the patch of sky she had watched moments ago.

Aili shrugged. "I was thinking about the Darkness." She looked up again, the black peppered with stars above her. "I mean, there's more than one kind of darkness, right?

There's the absence of light kind, like this. Then there's Darkness. The corrupted and polluting kind. How did it get that way? How does it become a thing like the Light, instead of just being a lack of light?"

"Well, everything is either matter or energy, right? Perhaps the difference is in the wavelengths or speed. Maybe something happens to turn darkness into Darkness. Maybe they're not actually related at all. I have no idea how Darkness becomes what it is."

"If we knew, maybe we could stop or prevent it," she whispered. Aili wrapped her arms around herself.

"Don't get cold." With a snap of his fingers, warm air flowed around her.

"I think the chill is in my soul," she muttered.

Setting off, she strolled through the trees. Andvari matched her slow and steady pace, a silent companion in the chilly night. Sending her awareness down into the soil, Aili reached out with her senses.

"I wonder if there's a sentinel tree around here, too."

"A what?" Andvari glanced at her before turning his attention back to the dark forest.

"Trees tied directly to mother. She said they were scattered across the country." Aili pulled her senses back and reached out among the trees this time.

"We call them sacred trees. Writings mention them, but we don't have any locations noted. Can you feel one?"

She stopped and searched. Frowning, Aili rubbed her chin. "I don't feel one here, but I didn't feel the one by our camp until this spring, either. I only sensed that one because it was active when the others were nearly fully dormant."

Aili peered out into the dark forest. It was easy to see the stars above, with how thin the trees were. The domes were behind her, out of sight but still a powerful presence in her senses. Closing her eyes again, Aili reached out into the forest.

The domes still yanked at her attention, but there were a few places that felt different. She recognized one right away. The soil around the tree felt more alive than normal. The sentinel tree. What were the others?

"I'm ready to go in." Her visit to the tree could wait. Tomorrow was soon enough, and something inside whispered to her. That visit should be private.

"Have some tea if you need. We'll be busy, so make sure you're well rested." He stayed by her side as she turned and headed for the dark building, a few lone lamps all the light to guide her back.

"I'll be fine."

Her feet slipped through the long grass without tangling. The dark building blended into the forest around it, with only the roofline visible where it blotted out the stars behind. Only the living wood it was made from kept it warm and welcoming, especially to her.

The door swung silently on the hinges. She walked down the dark hall, his ball of mage-light just bright enough to help her find their room. Kicking her boots off inside their door, Aili grabbed her nightclothes and headed for the bathroom. He settled at his desk and went through papers as she changed.

Tossing her dirty day clothes into the hamper, Aili washed up. Leaving the light on for him, she went straight to her bed. Snuggling under the covers, Aili curled up. She burrowed deep under the soft blankets and closed her eyes.

***

Aili rested her palms against the tree. "Mother?"

"Yes, child?" Familiar energy flowed from the soil, up the tree, and into her palms. It circulated within her, blending with her own energy.

"I think we're getting closer. I'm feeling a bit lost, though. Why would they steal artifacts they can't use? At least, they're not supposed to. Maybe one of them found a way."

Her mother stepped from the tree, taking Aili into her arms. She held the girl close, hugging firmly. "They don't need to use them. Having them unshielded is enough to affect the forests. Only you and your sisters can use them, unless someone is so deeply tainted they're no longer just a mage."

"I did use the water pin once. It was so powerful, it was amazing. What are they planning, then? Why bother taking them at all?" Aili relaxed into the hug. She hugged back, her arms around her mother's waist.

"After you cleansed the crystals, I could feel this part of the forest fully for the first time in centuries. Already I've begun rejuvenating the land. I know where the Darkness is coming from. I found the source."

Aili wriggled and looked up at her mother. "Really? There's one spot where it's concentrated?"

Her mother nodded, the mossy green hair swinging with the motion. "Yes, all taint spread from it. Help me cleanse and seal it and the taint will be gone for a while."

"Where is it?" Aili whispered.

Strong fingers rubbed small circles in her back muscles. "South. You'll feel it when you get close. Be careful. The Darkness is thick and strong there."

Her mother faded, the hug easing as she blended back into the tree.

"Be careful, Aili," the wind whispered. "I am always with you."

Standing still for a long moment, Aili wrapped her arms around herself. The memory of the hug lingered, the feel of arms around her. South. She'd feel it when she got close? How close?

She strolled through the forest back to camp, going wide around the domes. The potent magic still messed with her senses. Aili stayed in the trees as she rounded the camp. Andvari would know where she was; he always did, but she didn't feel like explaining what she was doing to anyone else.

Crossing the smaller protective barrier around camp, Aili headed into the forest to the south. Once the barrier was behind enough her skin no longer tingled, Aili sank to the soil and crossed her legs. She slipped into meditation breathing with ease.

Small points pulled at her focus, magic and power gathering where she didn't expect. If they're shielded, the pins will be hard to sense, no more powerful than any other strong magic in the area. Multiple places glimmered to her, spread around the forest to the south. At least one spot was inside the camp somewhere.

Were any spots caused by the artifacts? Were they hidden camps? Something else? Aili sighed. She needed their help. As good as she got with magic over the last year, there was still so much she didn't know. Getting to her feet, Aili let the dirt drop back to the ground. She returned to camp.

He was hunched over the desk, papers spread in front of him. When she came in, he looked up. "What's up?"

Aili walked over to his desk and took the map, unfolding it on the bed. "I feel things now. I think I started to sense them when we cleansed the dome, but I wasn't sure. I'm still not sure what I'm sensing, or where exactly, but it could be the artifacts."

Setting his quill down, he turned to face her. Andvari leaned over and looked at the map. "Alright, what do you know so far?"

Her finger tapped the spot on the map where the camp was. "There's something out this way. It's past the domes, wherever it is." She traced a line on the map. "There are more out in these directions as well."

He straightened up and rubbed his chin. "We should check these out. I'll send teams out to investigate. If the artifacts are hidden, they may not find them, but they may find signs something is unusual. That's almost as informative. I'll let you know what they discover." He reached for the desk and took a coloured wax stick. "Mark the directions and I'll send people out."

Aili turned the map until it matched north. Taking a moment to double-check what she felt, Aili took the wax stick from him. She drew some lines radiating out from camp.

She drew a large circle around the edge of her senses as near as she could tell, almost a couple of miles now.

"Have them look beyond the circle for these two." Aili marked two lines. "I think the others are closer."

Andvari took the map and examined her markings. "I'll send people out."

***

Aili walked a couple dozen paces, counting as she went. At the end, she stopped and turned. Kyson faced her, hand up and ready, spell at his fingertips. Glancing over, Aili saw everyone lined up along the building in the shade, watching. Renni reclined in a chair, her attention on Aili.

Andvari strode over to her. "You've felt Darkness attacks before. First, send a ball of Light energy at the target. Don't try to mimic the Dark, but see if you can match the amount of energy we face. Kyson will try the new spells, and we'll see what works."

She nodded. Raising her hands, she closed her eyes. Pure Light was easy; she could do that in her sleep. Adding power behind it took more focus. Don't blind everyone. Add power, not more Light. Aili released the energy.

The ball of Light sped to the target. Kyson's shield snapped into place, the familiar shimmer of magic in her senses. Her ball hit the shield. The shield glowed as most of the energy was absorbed, the rest scattering as harmless rays of light.

"Fascinating." Renni leapt to her feet and charged over. Holding her hand close, she cast spells on the shield.

Aili closed her eyes and focused. It was a sensing spell, but not one like she'd ever seen. This one was specific for air and gases, and waves of light?

"Your shield is effective, but if you make a couple slight changes, I bet it will contain all the Light. It'll only be for Master Mages, though. I do have a spell you can try for the other Scouts." Renni pulled a journal out and sat.

Moving closer, Aili watched her draw a pattern, an intricate copy of the one Kyson used in his spell. Two changes? Oh, there they were. Aili glanced up at Kyson.

He stared at the page, his brow furrowed. "Oh, I see." Kyson smiled. "I'll try that. How did you discover it?"

Aili rubbed her cheek. What would the changes do? The pattern was already complex, easily one of the most complex she'd seen them do. It resembled the levitation spell he once helped her with. That spell had the same adjustment, but in a different place.

Kyson nudged her shoulder. "It changes how the energy in the spell behaves. This one makes it solid, like the air platforms you use to levitate. Hers is stronger, so I'll use it instead. This other one holds the energy instead of releasing it. It'll recycle the power in the spell so I use less energy to hold the shield up. Ready to try again?"

She nodded. Aili jogged back to her spot. Raising her hand, she called her Light.

"Ready." Kyson raised his hand.

Releasing her spell, Aili watched it speed over. Her Light hit the shield. Raising her hand to shield her eyes, Aili peeked through her fingers. Light reflected onto her from the shield, just bright enough to be uncomfortable.

Aili used her senses to guide her over. Once behind the shield, she lowered her hand. The target was completely untouched. The shield glowed strongly, trapping the magic inside.

"I'm not holding this up, your Light is." Kyson shrugged. "It works."

"What happens if you hit it with a normal spell?" Aili reached for the target. The air was cool and comfortable, like being in the shade. "If you need shields, you'll probably be facing more than Darkness."

"Excellent point." Andvari headed around the shield, walking a dozen paces away. "Everyone get behind cover."

Aili and the others backed up, away from the target. She threw a dome over the group. Kyson tapped into the link and added to their shield, helping it spread over everyone.

Andvari released his spell. A whirlwind full of dust sped at the shield. It hit the surface and soaked in.

"Jeril, try something." Andvari headed for Aili's dome, passing through easily as she made space for him.

Jeril took Andvari's place across from the target, the shield still glowing. Renni examined Aili's barrier with a spell. Aili's nose itched. Kyson rested a hand on her shoulder and added more focus to their dome.

Hurling ice at the target, Jeril released a powerful spell. Icicles hit the shield and disappeared into the magic.

"Hana, your turn," Andvari ordered.

Rubbing her hands together, Hana grinned. She and Jeril traded places. With the group protected, Hana called a fireball. It sped to the target. The fire faded, sucked into the shield with the rest of the magic.

"It's starting to vibrate," Aili warned. She tugged on Andvari's sleeve. "How do we safely get rid of it?"

"Can we get closer?" Andvari raised an eyebrow.

Aili nodded. Bringing her barrier with her, Aili led the group over to the target. "Maybe I should only let Kyson's power through, since I know it well. The shield is his, after all. If something goes wrong I can keep this barrier strong."

"Good thinking." Andvari nodded to Kyson.

CHAPTER 21

K yson cast a sensing spell, his hand up and near her barrier. Aili let the magic pass through, his energy as familiar as her own.

"It gathers the power and will keep it going until it gathers more than it can hold. If using this in combat, it will need to be released and refreshed every few hits. If not, it will explode at some point." Kyson lowered his hand again, letting the sensing spell fade.

"How do you do that?" Aili reached for the shield with her senses, but the glare was blinding, even more than what she saw with her eyes.

"As an Air Mage, I can release it into the sky. Andvari can send it down into the soil. We all have our ways."

Aili glanced over her shoulder at Hana. "I shudder to think how you do it."

Hana laughed. "Fire Mages have many ways to dissipate magic. I can release it as heat into the air most easily, but it's slow. I don't want to burn anyone. In combat I'm better off letting an Earth or Air Mage cast a shield for me, unless I want to release the heat at an opponent. That's kind of a last resort thing, since they'd probably die."

"It's vibrating more now." Aili took a slow breath to steady herself.

Kyson raised his hand. Chanting softly under his breath, he drew circles in the air with his fingers. The shield dispersed, the energy scattering harmlessly in the breeze. Waves of magic washed over her barrier, ripples in the power around her. The air warmed from the fire magic. Aili followed the ripples as they flowed out, just like ripples in water do.

"Yes, those shields are not without side effects. All great magic leaves energy waves behind." Renni reached out and touched her barrier.

"How did it work, though?" Aili dropped her barrier. She stepped to where the shield had been moments ago.

"It works just like our atmosphere," Renni explained. "The shield has layers, and each filters out a different wavelength of magic. I will make notes for you. The Master Mages can help you make sense of them if you need assistance. You weren't around when we adjusted the shield, so now you can learn more about what we changed."

"Thanks." Aili smiled at her.

Andvari clapped his hands, and the group went silent, all attention on him. "This isn't one we'll practice often in camp. Everyone here who is able can try it now, though. All Master Mages, spread out in pairs. Call the shields, but only throw minor magic at it. We'll test it better away from camp in smaller groups later."

Aili waited with Kyson and Renni as everyone else paired up. She smiled. The CDF and Scouts were working together, not separating like she expected. The regular mages moved back to the shade of the building and watched.

"So, the shield isn't what causes the ripples? It's the magic stored and released? Does each spell make it stronger?"

Renni nodded. "A regular Scout might be able to cast this spell. They probably won't be able to release it safely afterwards, though."

Closing her eyes, she sensed when someone released their spell. The magic rippled out, washing over her with a warm breeze. She opened her eyes again. "What would a regular Scout do, then? Aren't most Master Mages?"

Kyson rested a hand on her shoulder. "Most field Scouts are, yes. Apprentices are not. Most support Scouts, those involved heavily in the sciences and research roles, many of them are not yet. There are always plenty of Master Mages around, though. We do prefer people train to be independent, but all partnerships have at least one Master Mage."

"Stronger together?" Aili raised an eyebrow.

He nodded. "Yes, but part of why that works is we train to our strengths, and for independence. We do cover each other's weaknesses and help those less experienced. Consider this, though. If I'm shielding you, I have less focus and energy available to subdue an attacker. If I know you can shield yourself, I can focus on getting them in custody, right?"

Renni turned to Kyson. "I think I have successfully altered one for the regular Scouts. Are you ready to help me test it?"

"I am." He paced away, counting his steps.

Aili ducked back, out of their way. She stayed near Renni, her senses open and ready. The woman chanted as she cast, moving her hand as well. Aili examined the pattern as it formed. The shield closed, hanging in the air before her.

"This will deflect the Light or Darkness, so it's less ideal in battle, but it'll save a less experienced mage." Renni smiled at her. "I've had student mages in their final years use the base pattern against lightning strikes."

"They can cast it fast enough?" Aili tapped her chin.

Renni nodded. "I cast this slowly for your benefit. When the spell is memorized, it can be up in moments."

Aili's stomach growled.

Kyson shook his head. "Once we're done here, we have a meeting. Go get a snack and wait in the room for us. This won't take long."

She glanced over at Andvari. He was deep in conversation with one of the CDF. Leaving the mages to practice, Aili went back inside. The dining room was empty except for a young Scout sipping tea by the fireplace. She grabbed a plate and tossed a filled bun onto it, followed by some berries and cut fruit.

The meeting room was dark and empty. She snapped her fingers, and the light came on. Settling at a table where she could see the door, Aili waited. Taking the stuffed bun, she devoured the first half. She took her time with the rest, enjoying the sweet sauce now that her hunger eased.

Three tables wrapped around the room, with the chairs primarily facing the wall map. She shifted in the un-padded wooden chair. Did they keep these uncomfortable so meetings didn't run too long? Licking her fingers clean, Aili grabbed her bowl of fruit.

Andvari wandered in as she was halfway done. "Did you get enough?"

She nodded, berries still stuffed in her mouth.

"Great. The others are on their way. We'll begin soon." He flipped through the papers he held, searching for something.

One of the support staff wheeled a cart with tea and snacks in. They set everything on a side table, many plates with biscuits and snacks, along with at least two teapots. Hana and Kyson came in as they were leaving with the cart again.

Andvari glanced over from where he was examining the huge map on the wall. He nodded to the CDF mages as they entered. They nodded back, heading for the snack table. Frida smiled at her as she took a couple of biscuits.

"Great. We're just waiting on our Water Mages." Andvari turned and faced the tables.

"We're here, Boss." Jeril came in, Dax following him.

Kyson and Hana brought their snacks over and sat with Aili. Jeril and Dax grabbed snacks and settled near the door. The CDF sat along the table facing Andvari directly, ready and professional as they waited.

"Since we cleansed the crystals, Aili sensed some points of interest to us. With all the extra help here right now, I sent some teams out to investigate many of them. One team came back with an interesting report. They found signs of a number of people moving about this area." Andvari pulled up a spot on the map, enlarging it for everyone to see. "They couldn't track them far. All traces disappear here." He pointed to one specific spot.

"The track just stops?" Kyson folded his arms across his chest.

Andvari nodded. "They couldn't detect any magic beyond old spell fragments. The kind any of us might leave behind. The best thing to do is get her out there to see what she senses. We'll take this as an opportunity to do a joint training exercise on tracking. Working in small teams, we'll investigate the area as fully as we can."

"Are you not worried about spreading us out there?" Theron set his teacup on the table.

"Not at all. We won't be far from each other, and the Scouts laying practice tracks are all experienced sneaks. You will be spread among the teams, so if any group does encounter the hideout, we're as strong as possible."

Frida nodded. "We're ready."

Vinnia perked up. "We get to try and follow the tracks?"

Andvari chuckled. "Absolutely. We'll keep you from straying too far off course, if it comes to that, but you've worked hard with us. You'll be fine. We'll check out this area." He drew a circle on the map with his finger. "You might also detect things we don't as we check it out."

A young woman stopped in the doorway. "The wagons are provisioned and ready."

"Thank you." Andvari nodded to her. "We'll sort teams there. Any questions?"

The group was silent as everyone finished their snacks and tea.

"Clean up and head over." He gestured at the door, dismissing the meeting.

Kyson and Hana led the way, setting their dishes in the bin and leaving the room together. Aili hung back, waiting for the others to go.

"What's on your mind?" Andvari leaned against the table.

"What if I don't find anything?"

He shrugged. "Then we keep looking."

Getting to her feet, Aili collected her dishes. She set them in the bin as she passed and walked with him behind the group. They all filed down the hall and out the small side door, where the wagons waited.

Two wagons sat parked outside the door. Each had a supply trunk fastened near the back. Andvari nodded to Dax, who climbed into the control seat of one wagon. He gave Aili a boost before settling into the control seat near her.

Aili grinned at Kyson, noting his down-turned lips and pinched brow. "What, not driving?"

Kyson shrugged. "Dax will benefit from the experience. Up north he doesn't get to drive as much. The camp is too busy, with too many people taking turns."

"Cheer up. We may not die in a crash along the way, but we might still get locked in mortal combat or something instead." Aili poked his shoulder.

He narrowed his eyes at her. "I've never hurt anyone with my driving."

"All those near heart attacks you've given me don't count?" Aili rested her hand on her heart, giving him the saddest eyes she could.

"No." He turned his nose up and looked away.

Hana snorted. "What about the poor crafts mage you were bringing back? Didn't he slip a disc when you leapt the ditch and the wagon landed hard?"

Kyson shook his head. "One time, and they healed him right away. That didn't count on my record. Nobody else ever got hurt."

Aili stared out at the forest as the trees rushed by, the wagon rolling smoothly down the packed road. Hana and Kyson debated what counted as a wagon-related injury as they recounted near mishaps from their past. A few made Aili shudder and appreciate Andvari's driving even more.

The wagon slowed as they left the road, climbing a slight rise. The gigantic wheels covered the ground, passing over minor obstacles with ease. Magic and shock absorbers took care of the rest. She glanced back at the second wagon following, Dax smiling as he steered.

Andvari parked the wagon among the trees. Everyone leapt off the back. Dax pulled up near him, parking the second wagon. People stretched and paced lightly as they gathered nearby.

Andvari held his hand up, and everyone gathered closer. "Aili and Dax will lay one trail. Jeril and Hana will lay the other. I will take Theron and Vinnia while Kyson assists Frida, Horgin, and Rylor. Remember, we're not far from a possible camp location, so keep an eye out for any sign of other people as well. That especially goes for you four." He nodded to Aili and the other trail layers.

"One of you will leave a magic trail, advanced level. The other will make sure there's physical sign at intermediate level. Go. Your lead time begins now." Kyson waved them off.

Dax grinned and followed Aili through the trees. "I love tracking games. I'm guessing you need me to leave the magic trail?"

"Yeah." Aili tuned into her senses. "They'll never follow my abilities. It's over here somewhere." Following the sensation, Aili picked a path through the trees.

Aili glanced over her shoulder. Jeril and Hana picked a different direction from them. She snatched a glance at Dax as they walked. He saved her from drowning once, but she didn't really know him. He lived at the northern camp. It was massive, and a great many Scouts lived there.

"Something wrong?" He leapt up the rock beside her, scrambling over the boulders as they climbed.

Her cheeks burned. "No. Sorry."

Dax chuckled. "I'm just as curious about you. Wonder student? Who wouldn't be curious?"

The warmth spread down her neck.

"I imagine you get that a lot?" Dax looked around. He shifted their path to cross the stream.

"Sometimes. Even I don't understand how my abilities work, so I understand, I guess." She reached her senses ahead. "There's a good spot that way." Aili pointed. "We can split around a cluster of shrubs."

"Sounds good." He smiled as he waved her ahead.

She eased past him, leaving enough sign for someone to follow. It took a little concentration to leave a path. After spending so much time sneaking, she almost had to think about it now.

"You're confident in the bush. I've never seen it in someone so young."

Aili glanced up at him as he caught up beside her. "You're not that old, either. Not compared to most of the others."

Dax raised his eyebrow. "You must spend a lot of time in the field if you think that."

She took a winding path around a thick tree trunk. "Why do you say that?"

Dax laughed, keeping it soft and quiet like his voice. "How old were the people on the survey teams?"

Aili thought back to their time in the north. Even the memory quickened her heartbeat. She got to try so many new things and meet new people. Had she even noticed? "Oh. Right. There were older people, but most were younger. Even in the healing centre there were plenty of apprentices."

"In the camps, there are many young people. That's if you don't spend all your time hiding in the healing centres and around the senior staff." Dax smiled. "I'm betting nearly everyone helping you with magic has been a Master Mage, because of how unique you are. There's no point you attending normal lessons, is there?"

Aili shrugged. "I guess not. Yes, I've met many Master Mages here. There's so much about the Scouts I still don't know."

Something tugged at her deep inside, making her stomach churn. She slowed, staring off into the trees. What was that? Magic, but there was something different about it.

"What?" Dax slowed and matched her pace.

CHAPTER 22

Aili shook her head. "I'm not sure. This is it, I think, but I don't know what 'it' is."

Dax raised his hand and muttered, chanting a spell. "I'm not sure I'm sensing anything. We can lay the track anywhere. Want to check it out?"

"It's why we're out here." Aili headed towards the sensation. "Hopefully I can tell more as we get closer."

"Lead on. I've got your back."

Andvari's words flowed through your mind. You can trust any Scout anywhere in the country. He was right. No matter where she went, they were always looking out for her. Leading him through the forest, Aili set a path right for the magic.

'Everything alright?' Andvari brightened in the link.

'So far. I feel something, so we're checking it out.'

'Don't take risks. Listen to Dax if he tells you to do something. We're not far behind and will catch up soon if you need us.' Andvari faded into the link again.

She leapt over the small stream and headed up the rise.

"We're getting close." She was almost whispering now.

"Just ahead?" Dax scrambled up the rise beside her.

Aili nodded. "At least it's not underground this time," she muttered. "I don't sense anyone around."

He crouched with her behind the shrubs and looked through the trees. "Have people ever hidden from your senses before?"

"Yes, in certain kinds of magic fields. I don't feel those, either, though." Aili closed her eyes and felt around. "They're not far behind us. We'll have backup soon if we need."

She scooted around the bushes and towards a short cliff face. The rock was smooth and almost vertical, a few dozen paces wide and high enough even Andvari wouldn't be able to reach the top. Whatever she felt, it was coming from the rock. Aili pointed.

Dax stopped and knelt behind a clump of bushes. Trees didn't grow within a few feet of it, like they were held back by magic or had been cleared away. Traces of magic shone on the rock.

She gave the hand signal. Nobody was around. He nodded. A quick series of signals, and she had her instructions. Approach slowly and stay close to him. Aili signalled back that she understood.

They crept over to the rock wall together. She laid her palm flat on the rock, her senses flowing freely into it. There was a cavern inside. The entrance was close. Aili walked along the rock, keeping her hand on the cool surface.

There. The cavern was just inside. Only a thin layer of rock kept her out. She could move it easily, but who covered it? The cavern was natural, but the rock keeping her out was not.

Aili opened the link. 'We found something.' She shared what she sensed with both of them.

'We're almost there.' Andvari glowed with how close he was. 'Wait for us.'

'I will.'

'I'll alert Jeril and Hana, and we'll head that way.' Kyson brightened in the link, before backing out again.

With her senses open, she felt Andvari approach. He and the others came right over. Andvari stopped beside her, his hand on her shoulder. Aili opened the link to him, inviting him into her senses directly.

'The cave feels natural, but they don't usually form like this. There is no natural opening. What does it remind you of?' Andvari focused on the thin rock layer keeping them out.

It was familiar somehow, but from where? He smiled, brightening the link. Aili looked closer.

'Crystals?' That couldn't be right, could it?

'This is what they feel like in their raw form.'

Aili rubbed her chin. 'So, it's not the people we're looking for?' Did she wreck the training exercise for nothing?

His warmth flowed around her like a magical hug. 'It's not them, but it's something even more important. I'll let the researchers know about this. They've been looking for a long time for new crystal formations. I can now tell them why it's so difficult. They'll be thrilled.'

Andvari straightened up and stepped back. "Stand down, everyone. It's natural, but important."

They all turned their attention to him.

"I'll explain soon. Aili, Dax, lay a trail back to the wagons. They're doing well, so make it a good one. Late intermediate difficulty."

Aili and Dax grinned at each other. Without a word, they faded into the forest.

***

When they returned, Andvari spent some time in the communication centre. Aili had a nap and a snack while she waited. When the summons came camp-wide, she perked up. Everyone who was free was assembling in front of the building.

He was already there, the CDF with him. Aili joined the line leaving the building, as they all flowed out into the grassy area. The younger mages hung back, but the more senior staff gathered right around him.

"Since we have a unique opportunity here, we'll take advantage of it." Andvari paced the new sand ring. "We're going up against mages who are skilled and enhanced. In the spirit of cooperation, we'll share techniques for subduing and controlling."

Aili glanced around as she hung out at the edge of the senior mages. The young mages gathered at the benches near where Gavi sat. Even Ilia was there in the shade with him, a grin on her face. They both smiled at Aili.

"There are more of us than our CDF friends, so we'll work in smaller groups led by experienced Scouts. Everyone will get a chance to try the skills."

Frida lifted her hand and got his attention. "Will we get a chance to try sparring with Aili? If we're facing magic a bit like hers, it would help."

Andvari smiled. "Of course."

He split the mages into groups based on their magic type. Aili joined the Earth Mages, young Jorlo and Mowen among them, along with Vinnia. She smiled to herself as she walked over. Normally, the Scouts had more Earth Mages than any other type. Not with this group. They were pretty evenly split.

Vinnia rubbed her hands together and bounced on her toes. "Aili, Jorlo, have you had any experience in combat and subduing hostile mages?"

Jorlo shook his head. "Almost daily training, but I've only ever used my skills once."

Aili nodded. "I've survived my share of battles."

"Mowen, if someone attacks you and you need them under control immediately, what is your strongest method?" Vinnia asked.

He scratched his cheek. "Like Andvari, I use barriers a lot. My partner could move in after that, since she's an Air Mage."

"We also split duties among partners, so we take advantage of our strengths." Vinnia smiled. "All of our pairings have a Fire or Air mage when we pursue fugitives."

Aili raised an eyebrow. "Why fire or air?"

"Fire and Air Mages, especially Air Mages, they're strongest at stunning people. Just like Earth Mages are strong at holding them. Have you ever seen a group of

Water Mages working together on a crowd, calming them down to prevent a riot?"

"Riots? In the capital?" Aili shook her head.

"It's sometimes a risk at the university, where they do plenty of competitions and magic shows. When young people get excited, emotions sometimes run hot. Magic can quickly get out of control. We always attend and help keep things calm. We control things before they get to that point. I know you were in the city last fall when Darkness was running loose. Water Mages patrolled the streets and helped calm people." Vinnia crossed her arms, though she still smiled.

Jeril had used magic to help her with her emotions before. She depended on him for a while after lightning magic got trapped in her body. Even with his help, she was a mess. Would she have survived that without him?

"I do have a spell we'll go over that blends lightning with Earth Magic to stun someone. As long as you can control it, lightning is the best way to stun. Too much power and you hurt them, though. Sometimes permanently." Vinnia frowned. "Always practice, and start small until you get used to the strength in the spell."

Vinnia chanted, performing the spell slowly for Jorlo. The ground before her sparked with lightning, the magic rising from the soil.

"Like that. The charge is always under you, waiting to be called. We just usually ignore it. Who wants to try?" She gestured at Jorlo. "If you're ready, give it a go. I'll help. Our goal is to make Mowen's feet tingle with the power."

Jorlo straightened up. "You bet."

He practiced the chant a few times as Vinnia helped. Aili shivered. The idea was sound. Could she do it? Yes. Would she? Leaving the others to practice, she joined Andvari and the Water Mages.

Andvari wrapped an arm around her shoulders. "It's fine. Join any group you like."

She nodded, staying beside him.

"So, if you time it right, send a burst of emotion through them. It'll disrupt their spell." Rylor gestured at Jeril.

Jeril tensed as tears flowed from his eyes. Teya watched raptly, her mouth slightly open. Jeril shook his head and shrugged, wiping the tears from his eyes. Aili curled up against Andvari, taking slow breaths.

"Here." Jeril stepped up to Aili and rested a hand on her head. "Calmly."

The magic flowed into her. Her body calmed, the urge to shake flowing down and into the ground. Her heart slowed with her breathing. She knew that spell. It was the one Andvari sometimes used for her, but so much stronger.

"You'll be fine. Most people have some emotional scars. Us old people just hide them better." Jeril patted her shoulder.

"You, too?" she whispered, looking up to meet his gaze.

"Many." Jeril nodded. "I've seen you calm animals. Think you can calm a person?"

Aili glanced up at Andvari. "I've never tried." She shrugged.

"This sounds like a great time. I'll check on the other groups." Andvari gave her a quick hug before leaving her with Jeril.

Aili watched Teya try a spell on Rylor. "You really think I can do this?"

Jeril nudged her. "You won't know until you try."

She straightened up. "Okay. I can't imagine it's too different. Your energy isn't the same, and I have less to work with, but I'll give it a try."

Jeril stepped back. "I can't wait to see what this feels like. Try as if I were an animal first. Once I know what effect you have on me, I can help you adjust the magic as needed." He spread his arms out. "Ready."

Aili stretched her focus around him. Healers calmed people all the time. Even she had put people in a magical slumber or coma to heal them better. Slowing his energy, Aili settled his body and quieted his mental energy.

"I feel that. It's subtle, but effective. Now, send energy through me. Excite me. Make me mad, or sad, or scared. Overload me with sensations." Jeril winked at her.

Aili's eyes widened. "What if I hurt you?"

He pointed at Rylor. "We have another Master Water Mage right there." Jeril turned and gestured at Gavi, sitting with Ilia as he watched everyone. "Gavi's right there. They can undo anything you do. Come on, Aili, mess me up."

Wincing, her eyes closed, Aili let energy loose in his body. Jeril twitched and fell to the sand. She cried out and ran over, dropping to her knees beside him.

Rylor kneeled behind her and took her hands in his, keeping her from touching Jeril. "Teya, come learn. You won't get a chance like this often."

"Is he okay?" Aili's voice shook. She blinked back tears.

Soothing magic flowed through her. "He's fine," Rylor murmured. "You did exactly what he asked."

She took a deep breath, allowing the calming to ease her panic. Gavi was walking over, just as calm and steady as ever. If he wasn't in emergency mode, then Jeril must be fine. She nodded.

"This is an amazing chance for Teya to learn. Would you like to watch?" Rylor relaxed his hold on Aili's wrists.

Aili nodded.

Gavi knelt beside Jeril and did a quick medical scan. "He's alright, Aili. He's not in pain, either."

She waited with Gavi, listening to Rylor talk Teya through how to rebalance Jeril's emotions and energy. Even with Rylor's help, her stomach flopped around. Gavi sat beside her and hugged her to his side as they watched Teya cast the spells.

Jeril sat and smiled. "Excellent. Maybe a little less power in training? In battle, that would be most effective."

Gavi held his hands out and waited as Jeril touched palms with him. "He's fine. Teya, that was thorough and well done." He let go of Jeril and turned to Aili. "You still need some help."

She slid her hands into his. Powerful calming magic settled through her. With Jeril safe and back to normal, she took another slow breath. Her body settled. She let her mind relax, allowing the magic to work on her emotions fully, too.

"See, we're both fine." Jeril smiled at her. "I wouldn't have let you try if I didn't trust your abilities. You did great."

Teya rubbed Aili's shoulder. "That was unforgettable. Thank you."

Gavi stood and offered her his hand. "Come. We'll have a snack."

She accepted his hand and stood. Walking over to the bench with him, Ilia slid over and made room for Aili between them. He handed her some dried fruit. Aili nibbled as they watched the groups work. Keeping an eye on Jeril, Aili nodded to herself. He really seemed fine.

The groups changed around, and people got to try things from the other magic schools. Aili kept her senses open. While it was interesting seeing how normal mages worked, and she got some new ideas, Aili wasn't ready to try some of them herself.

"Excellent work, everyone. Time for some light sparring." Andvari clapped his hands, gathering the groups together.

"May I have the opportunity to spar with Aili?" Theron asked. He bowed his head to Andvari.

Andvari smiled. 'Are you up for this? It'll be good for you.'

Aili nodded. She finished her fruit and stood. Would her legs carry her back over there?

CHAPTER 23

Andvari came over and handed her a canteen. "Just spar with him like you do with us. He'll have new spells to test yourself against. You'll be fine."

She opened the canteen and took a long sip. Juice? Perfect. She took another long sip. By the time she recapped the canteen, everyone settled in the grass around the ring, waiting. Wait, was everyone going to watch this?

Aili walked to one side of the ring and stepped onto the sand. He stood opposite her, calm and imposing. He wasn't any bigger or more powerful than Andvari or Kyson. No, but he dealt with stressed-out people and their problems far more often than Scouts did. It was only part of what Scouts did, but that's what the CDF trained most for.

Wait, was being intimidating a CDF technique as well? Vinnia could do the same thing when she wanted. He was friendly enough any other time she saw him. Aili gathered her courage and stepped forward, her hand up and ready.

"He will use any skill or spell he knows. Any stunning spells will be a fraction of normal power. Use any skill you would during sparring. Your balls of light with no power are also fine, just like you'd send against us." Andvari stood nearby, somewhere behind her and just at the edge of the ring. "Begin," he called.

Theron raised his hand. Power gathered. A shield? Aili smiled. It was the new one Kyson used the other day. If he really wanted to test it, who was she to deny him?

Aili flicked her fingers, sending a light ball at him. Two more followed right after. The first hit the shield. She spun the others past and brought them back around. He whipped his hands around, forming a bubble instead. A sliver of her light made it inside. He dodged, and she let it fade.

Theron raised an eyebrow at her. She allowed the corners of her lips to turn up. That barrier was fast. She'd need to be careful.

Focusing beneath him, Aili touched the sand. She piled it around his ankles, sinking him down into the soil below. Theron dodged, cartwheeling off the soft spot and back onto solid ground. No magic? Interesting. He was every bit as strong and fit as a Scout.

Fireballs hurled towards her. She pulled her bubble up, fading inside as she warped the air around her. He blinked and hesitated as she disappeared from his sight. With a wave of his hand, the sand rose. It hit her barrier, giving away her position.

Aili ducked and rolled, dropping her barrier. She sprang to her feet; her breathing hard and fast. What else should she do?

A stunning spell sped towards her. Gathering her light in an instant, she flung it out, forming a net. Her net wrapped around the spell. The magic exploded in a burst of sparks. She turned her head away and blinked, seeing white. Calling a bubble up, she let her vision clear.

He breathed as hard as she did now. She fought the urge to gasp, her hands on her knees. Aili straightened up. Were the Scouts going easy on her all this time?

Andvari glowed in the link, warm laughter surrounding her like a hug. 'No. You're just used to how we fight. You're doing great.'

"I think it's time for a simple demonstration." Andvari stood and walked to the centre of the sand ring. "In sparring, we deliberately test magic against another. This time, they will subdue their opponent as if it were an actual battle. No testing, no games. Each will have a turn to contain the other. Theron will go first. Aili, you may resist, but sparring rules still apply for safety."

Her hands shook. The last time the CDF subdued her, they had a spell that pressed everyone to the floor. Would he do that? Would he use something else as a Fire Mage? Vinnia mentioned they like to use stunning spells. She straightened up and nodded.

Andvari backed away from the ring. "Begin."

Magic gathered around him, instant like lightning. Compact and fast, it hurled towards her with a wave of his hand. She spun and leapt sideways, a shield forming in front of her. The magic grazed her shoulder. Her legs tensed, and she toppled to the sand. He knelt over her, his hand on her shoulder, restraint cuffs in his hand.

"You'll be fine." Theron's magic flowed into her shoulder, pulling the stunning spell from her. "How did you almost dodge it?"

She stretched her arms and legs. "That was incredible. I felt it coming. I just wasn't fast enough."

He tucked the cuffs back into his pocket. Offering her his hand, Theron helped her up. Her legs wobbled a moment before she steadied.

"Best to walk it off," he suggested. "Using the nerves restores them faster."

Aili smiled. "That wasn't full power, was it?"

Theron chuckled. "No. Full speed, but not full power. At the strongest, it can completely incapacitate someone. I didn't need to do that, just get you down."

She walked in a slow circle. Her legs were solid under her again. "Well, you did that."

Andvari walked over. "You're good?"

Aili nodded. "That was an experience. It was different from the time at the tower." She glanced over at the crowd, all watching intently.

"That time, there were so many of you, and you were all fighting. We worked together to lay a stun field out," Theron explained. "We just got everyone and sorted it out later. With all six of us combining magic, it was the safest way. That, and we don't get to use stun fields often."

"You're welcome," she muttered.

Theron laughed. "Still, I've never had anyone feel my stun spell before. Not even Master Mages could identify it and react in time. How did you do it?"

"I didn't identify it. I just felt the magic and tried to dodge. Tried." Aili shrugged.

"Her ability to detect magic is just like another sense for her, like sight and hearing," Andvari explained. "It's a Nature Mage thing." He nodded to Aili. "Your turn. Subdue him as if you were going to arrest him. You don't need to actually finish the arrest, just make him harmless."

Aili grinned and bounced over to her spot. "I'm ready."

Theron walked over to his place and raised his hand. Aili focused on him, blocking out the crowd of Scouts and CDF watching from around the ring.

"Go."

Her barrier snapped up around him. Aili sidestepped the counterspell as it sped towards her. She lifted her globe off the ground a few inches. Theron tested the barrier, trying a few spells, before standing quietly. Aili grinned. Spells couldn't affect pure magical essence. She had him trapped. Aili lowered him to the ground and let the barrier fall.

Frida came over. "Can we make something like that for our spell users? Can you put it up again?"

"Here, do it on me, so they can inspect it," Kyson offered. He stepped to the middle of the sand.

With a thought, the barrier formed. Aili hovered him just off the ground, only the bottom of the globe touching the soil. The CDF mages circled the barrier, casting every sensing spell they could at it.

"How long can you hold him?" Frida looked over her shoulder at Aili.

"As long as I can focus and stay awake." Aili shrugged. "Hours, maybe, if I'm feeling good to start?"

"We've been trying to make one for a while now, but it's something unique she can do. It's not based on a spell as much as a concept. I have a few that are similar, but I can't hold a Master Mage long in one before they break out." Andvari shook his head and shrugged. "Fortunately, by then Kyson has them in custody."

Frida shared a look with Theron, a whole silent conversation in an instant. She rubbed her chin. "I think we might help. Think we can try later?"

Andvari nodded. "Sure. Great session, everyone. Stay and practice if you like. Get some food and rest up. I'll call some of you soon for a mission."

Most of the Scouts and the CDF headed for the building. Aili picked up the canteen and sipped from it, downing the cool juice.

"You, too. Get a proper snack." Andvari nudged her towards the steps.

She handed him the canteen and followed the others. Gavi was walking with Ilia through the archway. Aili fell into step behind them, the others already inside. Taking a plate with pastries and fruit, Aili walked with Gavi and Ilia to one of the closer tables.

"You've come a long way, child." Ilia beamed at her. She picked up her teacup and took a sip.

Aili grinned. "You think so?"

Gavi laughed. "You just sparred with one of the top public defenders and did better than most mages. I'd say so."

She glanced over to where the CDF all sat with a few senior Scouts. They looked excited as they talked, smiling and moving their hands as they gestured with enthusiasm. Theron met her gaze and smiled. Aili smiled back briefly before looking away.

"You've learned to wield your abilities like they used to in the olden days." Ilia patted Aili's hand. "You weave it into being like mother does."

"Most of the time I feel like I'm making it up as I go," Aili whispered.

"That's okay," Ilia admitted. "I have a few spell books from the old days. Possibly the last ones around. Next time you come to visit, I'll show them to you. They're not written like modern spells at all. They're talked about as concepts, ideas, and things we form from our imagination. I bet you can make use of them." She popped a berry into her mouth.

Aili perked up, straightening in her seat. "Really? I didn't think any were left. The oldest I've seen were from after the—well, you know."

Ilia smiled, but her gaze grew distant as she stared towards the table. "Yes. Anyway." She shook her thoughts free and looked up at Aili. "Nobody else can make use of them, so I thought you might."

"Don't you still use them?" Aili devoured one of her pastries.

"Not in a very long time." Ilia touched her wrist, where Aili knew a dragon-scale bracelet was under her sleeve. "When I bonded, my magic changed. It's a blend of Nature Magic and charms. I prefer to use my magic in making potions. The herbs concentrate my power."

Many of the senior Scouts and all the CDF got up and left the room.

'Aili, come to the meeting room when you're ready.' Andvari briefly flared in the link.

'On my way.' She stuffed the last pastry in her mouth, chewing like a starving dog. "Gotta go. He's ready."

"Don't choke," Gavi warned. "If we have to save you from yourself, you'll never hear the end of it."

Taking her plate of fruit, Aili got up. She left her empty teacup in a bin as she passed. The halls were quiet already as she headed for the meeting room. Their blended conversations seeped into the hallway as she approached. The room sounded full.

Slipping inside, Aili looked for an empty seat. Kyson waved her over to the far side, close to the map again. She settled into the end chair and took an apple slice, biting into it. Glancing around, she saw all the CDF, as well as all the senior-most Scouts.

Andvari turned from where he was drawing on the map with a magic pen. "I got word of a hideout. It was occupied, so they marked it, but didn't approach too closely. We'll all go in force and check it out." He touched the map, and it zoomed in on one area. "It's one of the places Aili identified earlier."

"Is it another cave?" the Scout from the southern camp asked. What was his name? She met him; she was sure of it.

"It is underground. The entrance is hidden and leads down into a hillside. We don't know yet fully how extensive, but they did sense a tunnel network. Powerful magic overwhelmed their sensing spells, so they couldn't see as far as normal."

"How many people?" Hana shifted in her seat.

"They either saw or detected at least six. Be ready for anything. We work in teams. If we need to split, groups of four or five. Frida, you'll be with Kyson, Aili and I. Theron and Vinnia, work with Hana and Edlyn. Rylor, Horgin, you'll be with Jeril, Dax, and Jinan. We'll take two wagons. Standard field gear for fugitive pursuit. Scouts, meet at the wagons. CDF, come and we'll get you geared up."

Everyone stood, the sound of chairs shifting on the wooden floor echoing through the room. Aili waited a moment, still in her seat.

"Come on, Aili." Hana waved her over. "We need to get your sword and gear."

Andvari nodded towards Hana. "She'll help you. I'll meet you at the wagons."

Aili slid from her chair and darted over to Hana. They followed the other Scouts down the hall and to the guest quarters. Aili's was in the closer side hall. She headed for their shared room. Hana followed her inside.

"Get your sword. Make sure you have your small toolkit. Do you usually carry spare meal bars, or does he?" Hana leaned against the doorframe.

"I take some, and he and Kyson always have some." Aili took her sword from the hook by her bed. She retrieved her little toolkit from her trunk and slipped it into a pocket in her pants.

"I'll take a few as well, since he's busy. Now, do you have any cuffs?"

Aili shook her head. "I've never carried them before." She took her healing kit and tucked it under her shirt. Taking her cloak, she followed Hana from the room.

"Once I get my stuff, we'll grab a couple sets from the storeroom. It's time you started having them, even if you just carry them for others to use." Hana led her down the other hall.

It took only moments for Hana to be ready. They stopped in the dining hall for some spare meal bars before swinging past the small storeroom for some cuffs for Aili. She slipped them into a pocket and fastened it closed. Ready to go, they went outside through the main door.

The wagons were already parked out front. Dax and Edlyn leaned against one, talking quietly together. Jeril came around the corner and joined them. The others gathered in small groups nearby, also talking as they waited.

Pacing around the wagons, Aili stared off into the forest. When she reached the back of a wagon, she stopped and closed her eyes. The sensations were still there, off in the direction she identified. That's all she could tell, though. What if it wasn't the right place?

CHAPTER 24

"Is everyone ready?" Andvari led the CDF over to the wagon, Kyson walking with them.

The Scouts nodded.

"Mount up."

Dax gave her a boost up into the wagon. Aili scrambled towards the front, leaving room for everyone else without them crawling over her. The CDF weren't wearing their usual black, but had Scout clothing on. They didn't have any shoulder patches showing rank, so the clothing must have come right from the storeroom.

Hana swung up into the control seat. She glanced down at Aili and smiled. Aili curled up right behind her, leaning back against the side of the wagon. Andvari sat beside her, though Kyson joined the other wagon with half the CDF.

Hana was a fast and smooth driver, leading the way through the forest. Relaxed, Aili closed her eyes and felt for the spot. The closer they got, the easier it was to pull from the mess of magic around her.

They were close when she first started sensing the tunnels and caverns. It wasn't as strong as she thought it should be. Either this place was partly shielded, or there wasn't a pin here.

'What are you feeling?' Andvari's presence strengthened in the link.

Opening her senses, Aili invited him in fully.

'Maybe it'll get clearer when we're close.' He rested his hand on her knee. 'You're right, though. It might not be the pin. That's alright. Who knows what else we might find?'

The wagons rolled to a gentle stop near some thicker bushes. The wagon shook as people piled out. Aili waited until it was nearly empty before hopping down from the back. A couple of Scouts, including Kyson, cast spells for everyone to move silently. Aili smiled. The Scouts didn't need it, but the CDF wouldn't feel singled out now.

Andvari led the way closer, Aili right behind him. Keeping her link open and her senses active, they crept closer. If she were storing something incredibly powerful, she'd have guards. There wasn't anyone above ground at all other than her group.

Giving a hand signal, Andvari stopped and crouched behind bushes and boulders. The group settled in behind him. The entrance was ahead, with no sign of mages around, other than the magic she sensed left behind.

He signalled again. Aili and Kyson followed him partway down the hill while the others stayed hidden. She could feel them in her senses as glowing beacons of life, but looking back, she'd never know it. The three of them crept down the hill about halfway, to another cluster of bushes.

Closing her eyes and sinking her senses down, Aili searched for the tunnels. 'It's not big. A couple branches at most. Three caverns. I don't feel anybody.'

Andvari memorized her mind map. 'We'll keep a watch for hidden tunnels or magic as we get closer.'

'Simple enough floor plan.' Kyson slipped into the link fully.

'What's got you thinking?' Andvari laid a hand on her shoulder.

Aili rubbed her chin. 'If the pin were here, I should feel it. Even shielded in a box, I should feel it. I felt the water pin across the sea. There is something magical here, but not that powerful.'

He shrugged. 'Either way, we need to check it out. We know they're around here somewhere. I don't see anything else noteworthy here. We'll go in.'

Turning, Andvari gave a hand signal to gather. Jeril and Vinnia snuck down the hill first, darting among the cover. Everyone followed in pairs or threes until the group tucked into the bushes with them. Andvari gave a series of Scout hand signals. They were going in. She didn't recognize the rest of the hand signals. It must be what the CDF uses.

Checking again, the tunnels were still empty. She dashed after him to the tunnel entrance. Aili searched ahead, looking for traps around the entrance.

'Anything?'

'Nope.'

He led the way inside. Staying right behind him, she kept careful watch. Within a few feet, the tunnel narrowed down. Andvari had to crouch. Many of the bigger Scouts would find it a tight squeeze. Aili and Vinnia were the only two likely to stand upright here. It narrowed as well, just barely wide enough for massive Theron to fit.

Andvari called a shield up. 'Follow me. Kyson, have the others space out.'

'Will do,' Kyson replied.

Waiting for him to get an arm's length ahead, Aili followed him. Why did he always have to go first? Probing the darkness with her senses, Aili searched for any danger. A hand reached from behind her, and magic tingled through her.

Her sight adjusted, showing her the tunnels as if it were daylight.

'Thanks.'

Kyson warmed in the link. 'Any time.'

The rough walls were packed dirt, mostly clay. If she touched them, the soil crumbled a bit. Magic shone from behind her as other Earth Mages added stability magic to the tunnels. Their spells reached ahead past Andvari.

He stopped before the first chamber and crouched. Aili tucked in right beside him, sensing ahead. Everyone else pressed low against the walls. She peeked over his shoulder. Her eyes and senses told her the same thing.

Crates were piled in a chamber not much bigger than a Scout bedroom. Each had magic infused in the wood, protecting whatever was inside. A storehouse? Two tunnels led off from there, one on either side of the room.

'These aren't the source of the magic. I still don't feel anybody. No traps, either.'

Andvari nodded. He slipped into the room, staying along the wall. Aili stayed with him. Kyson went the other way, passing between crates and the wall. The group behind split, spreading out around the room.

Stopping at one tunnel, Andvari cast some spells. Aili reached down it, also looking. The rough walls were wide, big enough that they could stand well. Turning, Aili checked the tunnels coming in again.

'It makes sense now.'

Andvari turned to her. 'What does?'

Even Kyson stopped to listen, from where he investigated the other tunnels.

'That tunnel in has been narrowed with magic. Possibly to protect their stockpile. That's why the soil feels so—odd.' She reached down the closer tunnel again. 'There is something this way, though.'

'Let's have a better look.' Andvari followed her senses down the closer tunnel.

Something pulled at her from down this tunnel. Pretty sure it wasn't the artifact, Aili couldn't figure out what it was. Some kind of magic, but what?

'Crystals. Full and ready to go. I wonder if they're preparing to power a spell of some kind?' Kyson leaned into the link, exploring as Aili examined the sensation.

'We'll go check it out. It explains the power she felt, and that our own people detected with standard spells. Leave a group to watch our backs. We'll take this path, send a group down that one.' Andvari gave a quick hand signal.

Kyson gave a series of hand signals to Dax. Dax nodded and spread his group around the room. Andvari gathered their group together and started down the tunnel. Aili stayed close, almost right against his back, as they headed down the tunnel.

This tunnel was higher and wider, designed for someone to move down with ease. Nobody needed to crouch. Made of packed dirt, it had a sense of being carved with magic. It wound back and forth a few times, always heading in a rough direction towards another chamber. The chamber was small and unremarkable, just big enough for everyone to stand in.

A tunnel led on. Stopping to investigate, Aili frowned. Something about this chamber felt wrong, and not just its carved nature. Shaking herself free of her thoughts, Aili scooted after Andvari. Frida and Kyson had their backs, and Dax's group was in the main chamber. Still, why leave something so powerful unguarded?

'An excellent question, is it not?' Kyson asked in the link.

'Are you listening to my private thoughts again?' Aili glanced back over her shoulder.

'That one was rather loud,' Andvari agreed. 'It's an excellent question, though. Interesting—'

Aili peered around him. A wooden door blocked the tunnel ahead. A door? Opening her senses, Aili reached for it.

'It's not really there. Why didn't I feel it sooner?'

Kyson's large hand rested on her back. 'Let's look closer.'

Andvari pressed himself against the wall, letting them pass. Aili stopped right in front of the door, with Kyson immediately behind her. Raising her hand, she stopped just short of the illusion.

'It's just like in the vault. It's blended in with the natural magic around it. What spellcaster could do this?'

Andvari cursed under his breath. 'It means whoever was at the vault has access to rapid transport. Our people are all accounted for, even the area field Scouts. It must be one of them.'

Aili glanced back. Frida was the only one not in the link, not part of this conversation. 'Frida was right? It's one of her people?'

'Most likely. What can you tell me about this door?' Andvari gestured at the illusion, the door only visible to her through magic.

Turning back to the illusion, Aili touched it with her senses. 'Don't touch the doorknob or try to turn it. It's alarmed. I bet we can walk right through the rest of the door. There's nothing but illusion there.'

Kyson raised a hand and cast a spell, avoiding the doorknob. 'Amazing. It feels like a solid door to me, even with advanced spells. I can check it out.'

'Be careful, partner.' Andvari pulled Aili back against the wall beside him.

Kyson eased past her. Pressing against the wall away from the doorknob, he passed through the door, disappearing from sight. 'It's safe.'

'No alarms,' Aili confirmed. 'Stay away from the doorknob and we should be good.'

'Follow Kyson. I'll warn Frida and leave a marker rune. We'll be right behind you.'

Aili took a deep breath and let it out. She slipped through the door. Kyson waited just on the other side, a couple of feet down the tunnel. He inched forward, peeking around the tunnel curve. Tucking in beside him, she felt for the room. Simply furnished, she sensed a bed and a trunk. The trunk glowed with magic.

'I see it.'

Aili glanced back. Frida passed through the illusion. She blinked and shook her head. Her eyes told her one thing and her senses another. Her brain ached. Turning back to Kyson, she followed him around the curve.

Stopping in front of the chest, Kyson crouched. He raised his hand and muttered under his breath. Aili crouched beside him. At his gesture, Frida came over and cast a few spells. Andvari approached, giving the hand signal for report.

Kyson gave the all-clear signal, followed by the signal for locked. Frida gave a signal, but Aili didn't know it.

'That's their signal for the same thing,' Kyson explained. 'Scout mentors and Field Scouts learn both sets. We're the most likely people to work with other groups.'

'Fabulous,' she muttered. 'I don't even know the Scout sets.'

Andvari chuckled in the link. 'You're learning fast. Most Scouts take their entire apprenticeships to learn them. A solid four or five years. Give yourself time.'

'Dare we open it?' Aili touched the trunk with her senses. 'I don't feel any traps, but there are locks and wards.'

Frida gave a series of signals. Andvari nodded. She pulled a tiny crystal from her pocket and held it. The crystal glowed. After another hand signal, Andvari nodded again.

'Vinnia is on her way. She knows about the door.' Andvari guided Aili away from the trunk until they stood by the opposite wall. 'She's an expert with locks of all kinds. She'll get it open.'

'Better than the Scouts?' Aili raised an eyebrow.

Andvari nodded. 'They need to enter buildings all the time, and most are locked. Some have magical traps on them, especially if they're chasing a fugitive. We can open any lock, but not with the ease and speed they can.'

Soft footsteps approached. Vinnia came into the chamber. Kyson shifted back as well, giving her room to work. Settling in front of the chest, Vinnia raised both hands. Aili opened her senses fully again. She would not miss this.

Vinnia began her spell, chanting softly as her hands moved. Aili watched the spell weave into existence, covering the chest. It was related to the one the Scouts used, but significantly more complex. Aili could only guess at what some parts did.

'This part is a shield, in case she missed a trap or something,' Kyson pointed at a part of the pattern. 'This part, well, I have no idea.'

Andvari looked closer. 'It's another barrier of some kind. I'm not sure what it does. You probably shouldn't be looking too closely at their spells without permission. If they want to share, they will.'

Aili turned pleading eyes on him. 'It's new magic. I see stuff like this in the university library. Maybe not this specific spell, but others like it. How else will I learn more?'

'Yeah, partner. How else will we learn more?' Kyson folded his arms across his chest.

Andvari's laughter filled the link. He crossed his arms over his chest and gave Kyson frowny face, which quickly broke into a grin. 'You two are incorrigible.'

The lock clicked. Vinnia grasped the lid and lifted, just barely enough to make a crack.

"Wait," Aili urged. "Hold it there."

Tendrils of Darkness slithered through the gap. Aili threw a barrier around them and filled it with Light. The tendrils pulled back, sliding deep into the chest. Snapping her barrier closed around it, Aili chased the Darkness into the corner of the trunk. Sending a burst of Light in, the Darkness faded.

Frida chanted, her hands moving. "It's clear. Darkness?"

Andvari nodded.

Vinnia opened the lid fully. "Crystals?"

CHAPTER 25

T he trunk was full of crystals, from slivers as small as her little finger to larger ones that would fill her palm. They glowed faintly with magic, though not as strong as before she sent her Light through them. Someone had stored Darkness inside most of them.

"These are from a shipment travelling through the area. When it arrived, they were a crate short. Nobody knew where it went, though. We couldn't track it, not where it went missing, or who took it." Andvari reached down and picked up a crystal the size of his palm.

Kyson nodded. "It was on the wagon when it came into this forest, but even a mind scan couldn't reveal what happened. Their memories were blanked. The crystals were there, and then they weren't."

Aili tapped her chin, pacing slowly. "An invisibility potion only works on one person. The crate would still be visible. Someone would have noticed it floating away. I didn't feel magic at the site. It was like they erased all traces of it with those stones you carry."

Frida frowned down at the trunk. "Teleport magic takes time to set up. The spell would be detectable after they leave. Not to mention how dangerous it is for living things to use."

"Their memories didn't have traces of magic in them. They looked like the normal gaps we all have." Kyson crossed his arms. He shook his head. "The only unusual thing was they all had a memory gap at the same time."

"Well, these are cleansed." Aili kneeled beside the trunk of crystals. "What do we do with them? Oh." She reached inside and pulled a crystal out, holding it in both hands. "This one feels different, like it's magnifying the others." She held it up towards Andvari.

"This is why the shipment was so heavily guarded." Kyson cast a mage-light ball beside the crystal.

The light grew, shimmering and pulsing. It filled the room, blindingly bright. Kyson snapped his fingers, and the spell stopped. Aili blinked, but the spots in her vision remained for a few long moments.

"How did it do that?" She brushed her fingers over the smooth, cold surface of the crystal. It was heavier than the others.

"Crystals grow in patterns. We don't fully know how they form one over another. What we know is a few can reflect or magnify magic around them when shaped and polished. It can take a trunk like this and enhance the power by many times. The magic in the trunk probably feels weaker with that in your hand, doesn't it?" Andvari nodded to the crystals still piled in the trunk.

"Will this work for me? If I try to sense the pins while holding it, might I find them better?" Aili smiled as the last of the spots cleared from her vision. If it were that powerful, what might it do for her?

Andvari frowned deeply. "We have no way of knowing how it'll affect you. Are you sure you want to risk it?"

Aili brushed her thumb over her reflection, staring back at her from the crystal. "If it might work, even if it's just a chance, I have to try, right?"

Frida and Andvari shared a look. What was it? Skepticism? Disapproval? Something else? It wasn't quite frowny face, but it was close.

He shook his head. "Try something tiny first. Just use the barest hint of power. At the first sign of anything going wrong, stop. We'll stay ready to help."

Nodding, Aili moved to the middle of the room. She sat with her legs crossed. Cradling the crystal in her hands, Aili closed her eyes. Something small. She could do that. With open senses, Aili felt for the soil beneath her.

Magic shone all around her. Her nerves burned. Searing pain shot through her body. Fear. She felt fear. Hers or theirs? Too much. Way too much. Her senses went black as all sensations faded.

Soothing warmth flowed through her body. Her nerves calmed. Hands touched her face. Arms supported her body. Forcing her eyelids open, Aili looked up.

"Take a moment," Frida soothed. She held Aili in her lap. "Don't try to move yet."

Andvari squeezed her hands lightly. "Slow breaths. We're not done helping you."

Her hands shook, steadied by his. Each breath got easier. Where was the blood from? It was on her hands, and his now, too. It spilled onto her lap. Aili flexed her fingers. New skin showed pink on her palms and fingers. The crystal lay beside her on the floor, blood covering the middle.

"What happened?" Her voice trembled. Feeling in her body came back fully, magic still flowing into her. The extra hand on her shoulder was Hana's.

"Your senses were overwhelmed." Frida brushed Aili's hair from her face, where loose strands came free of her braids. "Kyson and I got you under a sleep spell and calmed your nerves. They're just finishing your hands. You gripped the crystal so hard it cut right into you."

"Don't touch those crystals," Andvari warned. "I'm not sure what you tried, but it came right through the link and almost got us, too."

"I only tried to sense the rock," she whispered. "There shouldn't be magic in it. There is, though. Mother's magic is everywhere." Aili pressed a hand against her head. "Ow."

"Jeril." Andvari stood and moved aside.

"Here, now. It'll pass." Jeril laid a hand on her forehead.

Her emotions calmed with his magic. Her muscles relaxed. The last of the pain faded. Even her fear disappeared. Was the fear hers, or something from the crystal?

"Thanks. I feel more like myself again." Aili sat up.

She wiggled her fingers and toes. Looking around, she noticed Hana's team was here. Jeril was with Dax's team, though. Were they still guarding the rest of the tunnels?

"Take it slow." Jeril took her hands and helped her up. "There's no rush."

"There might be." Dax came into the now-crowded chamber. "A barrier came up over the entrance. We can't leave until we dispel or outwit it."

"I'll check it out." Kyson headed for the tunnel, following Dax back to the entrance.

Theron and Vinnia followed Kyson. The others waited as Aili steadied herself.

"Take it slow if you need." Andvari offered her his arm.

She clung to him as she took a few wobbly steps. Pulling energy from the soil, her body calmed. Her steps grew stronger as she walked with him through the tunnel. He stayed beside her as they walked, moving only to ease past the illusion trap. The others followed.

Had someone touched the trap by mistake? Was there another one down the other path she didn't know about? Where did the barrier come from? Maybe she'd get answers when they investigated the barrier.

She could see the barrier as they approached. Kyson and Theron stood before it, casting spells and debating how it was triggered. Aili opened herself. The barrier hummed.

"Pull back." Andvari pulled her behind him, turning to shield her.

Aili closed her senses. The barrier calmed and went quiet.

Andvari turned again, watching the barrier. "Interesting. Kyson?"

"I'm not sure what's powering it. It feels a bit like her magic, but not quite. It's the magic from the vault. Whatever it is, it stops just past the entrance in the rock, anchored somehow." Kyson scowled at the magic.

"Stay with Jeril." Andvari stared Aili down for a long moment before joining Kyson at the barrier. He rested his hand against the stone. "Hmm. Vinnia?"

The small woman snuck past everyone else and stood beside him. She laid her hand on the rock beside his. "Yeah. I see it."

"What?" Aili went to step forward, but Jeril wrapped an arm around her.

"There are tiny fragments of crystal embedded in the rock. They're so small, I only sense them by the magic in them. We can try and track where the thread of magic goes. Maybe we can reverse the trigger." Vinnia pulled her hand from the rock.

"That, or we just make a new entrance away from them." Andvari smiled at Aili.

"What, really?" Vinnia raised an eyebrow.

"Why not?" Andvari shrugged. "The magic doesn't extend past the crystal grid."

Vinnia pressed her hand to her cheek. "I've never gone through anything thicker than a wall. Do you think we can?"

Andvari chuckled. "We can. We'll need to be careful and not touch the barrier at all, though." He eased past the others, rejoining Aili down the tunnel. "Open your senses. I'll direct it, just in case."

Kyson offered Vinnia his hand. "Anyone not involved should head back towards the first cavern."

The others moved past, spreading down the tunnel. Aili opened herself and waited. Andvari directed her senses to the rock, away from the crystal grid inside it. The barrier stayed quiet. With some care, this might work.

The rock was warm and pliable, bending to her energy with ease. Moving it like clay, they pushed it around, creating a weak spot. The rock shifted under her energy, thin and weak. Andvari pushed, breaking through. Sunlight streamed into the cave through the new gap as well.

Aili pushed on the opening on the side away from the crystals. In moments she had a gap big enough to get even the largest people through. She walked through and into the sunlight. Turning her face to the sun, Aili smiled.

"That was pretty amazing." Vinnia stepped through and grinned. She examined the opening, running her hand over the rock. "You made that look easy."

"You've never done that?" Aili gestured at the tunnel.

"I've gone through walls, but never solid rock like that. Stone walls have mortar and weaker areas. You just went right through solid rock." Vinnia held her hand against the rock. "It's still warm."

Aili nodded. "I use the heat from the planet to warm and shape the rock, just like if it were underground. It is easier with support, though. If I were alone, I would have made a much smaller opening." She grinned as the massive Theron still had to duck.

"Aili, rest." Andvari handed her a snack bar. " The tunnel is solid, so we can come and go. If anything happens, I can still contact you. We'll bring the crystals out."

She took the snack bar and sat with her back to the rock. Demolishing the bar in a few bites, she took another from her own pockets. Aili nibbled this one while she waited. Should she be in there helping? What if they set off another trap?

'We'll be fine. We dealt with everything thrown at us before you came along. You're also right here if we need you.' Andvari's energy pulsed in the link, like he was laughing.

Her cheeks warmed. Was she thinking out loud again? 'If I lose contact with you, I'm coming in after you.'

'Good. We also found the trigger for the barrier. It was down the other path. There aren't any others. How's sentry duty going?'

Aili muffled her laugh with her hand over her mouth. 'Is that what I'm doing?'

'Someone should. It's one thing to come in here and clear the place out, but they can always sneak back in while we're not looking. With your senses, who's better equipped?'

Dax and Theron came out of her new opening, the trunk of crystals carried between them. They're not levitating it? Might it affect the crystals inside if they do? Edlyn followed close behind with a box of papers and scrolls in her hands. The others trailed behind, some carrying more boxes or items from inside the tunnels.

"Come on. You can rest in the wagons while they get everything loaded." Kyson offered her his hand.

Taking his hand, Aili stood. They walked up the slope to the wagon together. She hopped up into the back of one and reclined against the side. A crystal that magnifies magic? She had read about one once, in a book old enough that it was written in ancient. She thought them gone with the rest of magic from the golden age.

She still used magic from the golden age, though. It wasn't gone, just out of reach for normal mages. Magic was everywhere. Touching the crystal and seeing the tiniest traces of magic only confirmed that for her. Maybe Rei had a fragment of a crystal she could experiment with? One small enough it won't overwhelm her?

The wagon shook as the others climbed on. Aili braced herself in the corner as the wagon rolled back towards camp. She yawned. Normally, magic made her insatiably hungry, but holding the crystal just made her tired.

Frida glanced at her again.

"I'm fine." Aili smiled at Frida.

Frida smiled back. "I'm glad to hear that. I've never seen a reaction like that to magic before."

"Never ever?"

Frida shook her head. "Being around you has been most educational. You're certain you're fine?"

"Yeah. They'd know right away if I weren't." Aili glanced up at Kyson beside her.

"She's mostly fine. When we get back, I'll have Gavi go over her. She can relax while we do the paperwork and catalogue everything we found." Kyson rested a hand on her knee.

"You mean Andvari and the others will do the paperwork while you somehow have something else to do?" Aili nudged him in the ribs.

"If you want to stay fine, you'll be quiet now." He narrowed his eyes at her.

"If anything happened to me, he'd make you fill out the paperwork." Aili grinned up at him.

Kyson folded his arms across his chest. "Right now, that's the only thing saving you."

She leaned her head against his shoulder. "I knew you loved me. You pretend you don't, but you do."

"Like an annoying kid sister who won't go away." Kyson rolled his eyes, exaggerating it, but he rested his arm around her shoulders.

The wagon rolled onto the road. The ride smoothed out. Wind rustled her hair as the wagon picked up speed, loosening the fine hairs around her face with the force. She curled up against Kyson's side and closed her eyes.

CHAPTER 26

Aili looked up from her book. "Come in?"

The door creaked softly as it swung open. Karil poked her head inside. She smiled at Aili. Were her cheeks pinker than normal? "Do you have a moment?"

She set her book down and straightened up. "Of course. Do you need help with something?"

Karil closed the door behind her and walked over, a hand held up against her chest. "I was hoping you could help me with an animal."

"Sit." Aili gestured at the end of her bed. "I'd be happy to."

She sank onto the mattress at Aili's feet. Reaching into her shirt pocket, Karil eased a tiny hummingbird from inside. "I nursed her back to health and she's ready to go. She won't fly away. She keeps coming back. Is she okay?"

Aili held her hands out. Karil placed the little bird in her palms.

"What's going on with you, little one?" Aili held the bird close to her heart. Opening her senses, she touched the bird.

The bird chirped softly, settling in her hand. Flashes of memories poured into her. The bird lay on the ground with a broken and bent wing. Pain rippled through her. She lay in a box, her wing wrapped. The pain was almost gone now. Karil holding the bird up, feeding her drops of honey and seed paste. Warmth flowed through her.

"She's fine," Aili assured her. "She's grateful and thinks of you as a friend."

Karil blushed. She stared at her boots for a long moment. "What about her going home, though?" She looked up and met Aili's gaze.

Aili held the little bird up and looked her in the eye. "Well, what about your home?"

An image of a forest filled her mind, seen from above the trees. After spending time flying around, Aili knew roughly where it was.

"I see." She stroked the bird's tiny feathered head with her smallest finger. "Her family migrated on. They were heading south."

Karil wrapped her arms around herself. "What do I do now? Keep caring for her until they come back? They're gone, right?"

"You have a couple of choices." Andvari leaned against the doorframe.

Karil spun, gripping her shirt with her hand. She grabbed at the blankets as she slipped from the edge of the bed. Stumbling to her feet, Karil stood, staring at him with wide eyes.

"My apologies. You can look after her until they come back in the fall, or we can send her to her summer range. We relocate migratory animals all the time." Andvari stepped closer and offered her his hand.

Karil stretched a shaking hand out to him. Aili sensed his calming magic flow as he guided her back to the bed.

"What does she want?" Karil asked Aili.

"Would you like help getting home, or would you like to stay a while?" Aili whispered to the bird.

Images of the forest filled her mind.

"Okay. We'll get you home." Aili looked up at Andvari.

"Could she show you where? How close? The forest is a big place." He held his hand out.

Aili stood and eased the bird into his palm. "I can mark a map for you, close enough for her to find them."

"I'll arrange a transport." Andvari looked the bird over. "You did a great job with her. Did you want to take her home yourself?" He smiled at Karil.

She grinned back. "Can I? Am I allowed to, being here and all?"

He nodded. "You're scheduled to move soon anyway. No apprentice stays here long. It's not good for your social or skill development to be so isolated for too long. Frida and Aili can confirm you're free of Darkness before you go."

"Will you be a Scout short if I go?" Karil gripped the blankets, her body tense.

Andvari held the bird out to her. "You can take her home on the way when you get reassigned. Your replacements will be here before you leave. I can always have Dinna do a special run."

She cradled the little bird close to her chest. "Thank you."

"I'll set it up and let you know. It will take a few days at least. Dinna has some runs to do for us first." Andvari smiled at Aili.

"Thank you." Karil stood, the bird safely in her palm. "That was amazing," she said to Aili. With a quick wave, she left with the bird.

"You're staring," Andvari commented, half under his breath. He smiled again.

"Huh?" Aili pressed her hands to her cheeks. "Am not."

He shook his head, still smiling, as he went to his desk.

"I need some air." Aili stuffed her feet into her boots and headed out the door. Was it hot in here, or just her?

Juice might help. Maybe a tea. Aili headed for the dining hall. It was quiet again. Where was everyone? Passing through the arch, she heard a small group talking, though she couldn't make out the words yet.

Going straight for the drink table, Aili poured herself a glass of juice. She turned. Aili froze in place. Between meals, the place was almost empty. The CDF sat at a table near the window, talking. So, it was them she heard.

Now what? Would it be rude if she just sat over here? Should she just turn and go outside? How long had she been standing here, staring at them? Why did social situations have to be so complicated?

"Hey, Aili. Come and join us." Frida waved her over. "If you're fine with it, we'd like to ask more about your magic."

She took a slow sip of juice. What do I do now? Her traitorous feet carried her over to the table. Was she supposed to talk about her magic? What could she tell them? What shouldn't she tell them? She obviously wouldn't mention their magic suppression cuffs don't work. That much she knew already.

Aili sank onto the bench beside Frida, facing the window. Vinnia sat opposite Aili. Theron and Rylor were beside her, and the old man was on Frida's other side. What was his name again? She really hadn't had anything to do with him yet.

"It's fine, Aili." Vinnia smiled at her. "You look like a startled bird."

She set her glass on the table, begging her hand not to shake.

'Are you alright?' Andvari burst into the link, opening it fully. 'I can feel your fear from here.'

'Help.'

Frida wrapped an arm around her. "Are you alright? Do you need a healer?"

Aili shook her head. "I'm okay."

No, she was most definitely not okay. First, she talks to a cute woman while her body feels like it's on fire. She must have been bright red. Did she embarrass herself? Now the CDF want to talk? Was it friendly? Were they actually trying to interrogate her? What was she supposed to do?

Andvari strode into the room. She spun at the heavy foot-steps, the sound so unlike him. When he saw her sitting there, he raised an eyebrow.

'Aili?' Confusion filled the link.

"Andvari. Come join us if you have time." Frida raised a teacup to him.

"Aili, I'd like to ask you something." Theron's gaze fixed on her, his expression neutral.

"Uh, yeah?" Would they notice if she pulled a bubble up and disappeared? Maybe she could slip out?

"I understand you snuck into our headquarters. I saw the report you wrote for our commander. That day the wind blew chaos through our atrium, that was you. Wasn't it?"

She curled up, hunching her shoulders. "Yeah?"

Andvari settled on the bench beside her, a teacup in his hand. He set it on the table. The delicate porcelain clinked lightly. Aili glanced at the intact cup, magic protecting it from any wear and tear.

"We tried tracking the source. There wasn't any trace of magic at all to follow. How do you do that?" He sipped from his teacup, his gaze not leaving her.

Aili squirmed. "I didn't actually do anything. I kind of lost control. She was saying things about Andvari and I got mad. The air just sort of—did that." She stared down at the table. Her face warmed again.

Frida smiled and rubbed Aili's back. "I understand you've been studying magic for just over a year now."

She glanced up at Frida and nodded. "Yeah."

"Most magic students have outbreaks for a few years at least. Their magic simply isn't powerful enough to do much yet." Frida winked at Aili.

Aili smiled.

"Still, why no trace of magic at all?" Theron rested his chin on his hand, still watching her.

She glanced up at Andvari. What was she supposed to say?

"Aili doesn't use magic as we do. You know she doesn't use spells. That's why her magic went so long without being identified and drawn out. She can manipulate any magic around her without setting a pattern if she chooses, so there's no trace left to detect. I only know when she's using her abilities through my link to her as a mentor." Andvari touched his neckband, his finger resting on the little cube with her name on it. "It makes teaching interesting, but I love a challenge."

"How do you use magic, then?" The older man leaned forward and looked down the table at her. "What do you do to make magic work?"

She glanced at Andvari, who nodded. "I think about what I want to happen. I have to focus on it. I don't call on my own power. I pull magic from whatever is around me."

Vinnia raised an eyebrow. "You potentially have unlimited power?"

"Power, yes. Focus, not so much." Aili grinned sheepishly.

"Still, what she can do is amazing." Andvari rested a hand on her shoulder.

"Like regrowing a damaged lung?" Rylor chuckled. "That's Master Healer level magic, and she did it in a fraction of the time."

Aili squirmed again, shifting on the bench. "I'm sure you all can do amazing things, too."

"Well, sure." The older man laughed. "It's just unusual to see someone so young doing such powerful magic. It took a couple of custodian specialists to clean the atrium. Some of the papers you flung around didn't want to come unstuck from the walls."

"Sorry." Aili buried her head in her arms.

"Don't be. Our spell weavers came out to help. Even they couldn't figure out how you did it. We got to watch them work, though." Rylor raised his teacup towards her.

"Spell weavers?" Aili raised her head and straightened up.

"Master Mages who specialize in creating new spells or modifying existing ones. They trace patterns and identify new magic. Surely the Scouts have them?" Vinnia looked at Andvari.

"She's never heard us use the term. All Field Scouts at master level are spell weavers, and most senior healers are, too. For her, it's normal for any Master Mage to assess or create new magic," Andvari explained.

Aili drained her juice glass as he talked, listening carefully. Why hadn't she read about spell weavers before? That sounds like something a book on advanced magic, or even magic creation, might want to mention.

"Now, Aili and I have a magic lesson, so we'll head out. Enjoy your tea." Andvari stood and nodded to her.

Aili rolled her shoulders as she stood, stretching herself out again. Leaving her glass in the container by the door, she followed him out. He kept going, turning towards the main door. They passed through and stepped out into the sunshine. Andvari led her down the steps and to the edge of camp.

"Why no stables?" Aili looked back at the building.

"We don't bring the horses this close to the taint. Now, what was that all about?" He leaned against a tree and waited, watching her.

She wrapped her arms around herself. "I don't know. Everything was fine, but then I saw them. I didn't know what to do, and—" her words failed. How could she explain something she didn't understand?

A smile slowly spread across his face. "So, you've come a long way with your magic but you still feel uncertain in new social situations."

Aili nodded.

"You know, as Scouts, we tend to attract people who are comfortable being alone or in small groups." Andvari straightened up and began walking around the edge of camp. "You might be surprised at how many of our people don't like going into cities or interacting with a group of strangers."

"Really?" She matched his pace, a relaxed speed she could keep up with easily. "They all seem so confident and all. I just felt so—I don't even know."

"Panicky was the word I'd use, or I wouldn't have rushed over like that." Andvari took her hand and held it in his for a moment.

"So, what do I do? I don't want to be rude. I don't know what to do." Her voice trailed off, fading into a whisper.

"You know what I advised a young Scout with once? They said it helped them."

She shook her head. She couldn't even guess.

"Pretend it's a training exercise. Have a goal no matter how small. In social situations, maybe you want to learn one thing about each person you meet. Maybe you want to find one thing you have in common with someone you don't know well. Maybe you just want to ask what their favourite spell is. Keep it simple and small, and you can change your goal when you achieve it."

Aili rubbed her chin. "An exercise. Hmm."

"It's one way to get started until you feel more comfortable around new people. The more practice you get, the easier it is. We aren't born with social skills. We develop them and practice, and sometimes fail. You didn't get to attend classes and events with your peers when young, so it's only natural you'll feel behind, right?" He lightly nudged her.

She blinked tears away. "They avoided me," she whispered.

Andvari stopped. He wrapped her in a tight hug. "Then it makes sense you're not used to being social. There's nothing wrong with you. You're not broken. You just need time and practice."

She rested her head against his shoulder and cried, letting the tears flow. Her magic was a gift, and she loved it now, but growing up was so hard without it.

"All the pain won't go away just because you have a family and friends and a place now. You need to feel it and let it pass. It takes time." He rubbed her back.

Kyson slipped into the link. 'I'm going out with Frida and a few Scouts.'

'What's up?'

'Something happened to a wagon shipment. There aren't any details yet, but they requested Master Mages with Mind Magic. We'll check it out and I'll keep you informed.'

CHAPTER 27

'Do that. I'll check for requests and reports when we get back. Once we know what we're dealing with, we'll go from there.' Andvari relaxed his hug and looked at the hall, visible through the trees. "While I see what's going on, why don't you work on the sword forms? Keep smoothing form four and I'll teach you the first few moves of form five."

Aili perked up, smiling. "You bet." She ran for the hall, leaving him behind.

Dodging Kyson and the small group of Scouts gathering with him on the steps, Aili charged up the steps and down the hall. Dashing into her room, she grabbed her sword. Aili walked back towards the training ring out front of the building. Kyson and the others were gone, the wagon just disappearing among the trees as it rolled down the road.

She stopped on the step beside Vinnia, who also watched them go. "Not going with them?"

Vinnia shook her head. "They've got a full group, and I'm not gifted with Mind Magic. I'll wait here." She glanced at Aili's sword. "Which forms do you know?"

"The first four. Do you also know them?"

"No, we don't carry swords in the city. We have batons that tuck into our robes, but seldom even use those. Mostly we depend on our magic." Vinnia smiled. "Would you show me?"

Aili smiled back at her. "Will you show me the batons? I don't think I've ever seen one."

"Sure. I'll get it and be right back." Vinnia turned and headed through the door.

Aili wandered over to the practice ring. It was so much smaller than the large camps had, holding a dozen people at most. Did they practice Drill as a group here like she did at the eastern camp? Fastening her sword belt around her shoulders, Aili took a few slow breaths.

Vinnia emerged from the building, with no baton in sight. It must be in her robes. She sat at the edge of the ring. Aili closed her eyes for a moment. After another slow breath, she opened her eyes and drew her sword.

Moving without thought, Aili flowed through the first form at full speed. Aili sheathed her sword and took a moment to be still. Fluidly, she drew her sword and went through the second form. Another pause and form three followed. Finally, Aili went through form four at a leisurely training pace.

"That's impressive," Vinnia admitted. "I sometimes wish we learned sword, too." She got to her feet and walked over to Aili. Pulling a thin, yet sturdy stick from her robes, she held it out.

"This is a baton?" Aili touched the smooth wood.

"Yes. We can use it so many ways to control a person or crowd, with less risk of hurting them. We have forms, too."

Aili dashed to the edge of the ring and sat, her focus on Vinnia. The baton slid back under her robes, completely hidden from view. She whipped her outer robe back and pulled the baton, flying through a form so quick Aili almost couldn't catch it.

"Come on over. I can safely show you some things we do with it." Vinnia twirled the baton between her fingers.

Leaping to her feet, Aili charged over. Vinnia showed her some ways they could use the baton, including joint locks. Using light pressure, Vinnia moved Aili around.

"That's effective." Aili straightened up as Vinnia let go. "I can feel the magic in it, too." She held her hand over the warm wood.

"The magic keeps mages from using spells on the baton. They can't do anything that would prevent us from using this. Imagine how awkward it would be if an Earth

Mage turned it into wood shavings or something." Vinnia smiled, brushing her fingers over the smooth wood.

Aili laughed. "I'd try something like that if I had the chance. It's a helpless feeling, being in someone's control." Her smile fell.

Vinnia rested a hand on her shoulder. "I read that report. It's not often they use a full stun field like that, especially not on another law enforcement group." She squeezed Aili's shoulder lightly. "That whole situation was awkward."

"That's one word for it," Aili muttered.

She looked over at the sound of a wagon coming down the road. Another wagon followed, much bigger and with crates on the back.

Andvari burst out of the building and strode over to them. "Aili, can you help Gavi with health checks? They were attacked. Nobody was reported as seriously injured, but still."

"Absolutely."

She waited beside him as the wagons rolled up to the steps. Gavi came down to join them as the wagons rolled to a stop. Under his direction, she set to work. First, they went over everyone and dealt with minor injuries. Aili set a broken wrist in seconds.

"You're going to help me perform a deep dive with Gavi."
Kyson led her to one of the men. "I bet with your help, we
can go deeper."

Aili took the man's hands in hers. "Alright."

Kyson brought Gavi into the link. Keeping herself open,
Aili let Kyson lead. He went deeper into a brain scan than
Aili had ever seen, poking about in the actual brain tissue
and not just the blood vessels around it like she usually did
with injuries. He wasn't affecting the brain, though, just
looking for traces of magic. He found some.

"Let's go share what we found." Kyson backed them out
of the brain.

Aili pulled her abilities back as Gavi left the link. Scouts
were bustling around, bringing the people in for a meal
and a chance to rest. Aili followed Kyson back to the
meeting room as Gavi went with the freshly healed mages
instead. As the senior-most healer in, well, all the Scouts,
he was ultimately responsible for them until they returned
to their duties.

The senior-most Field Scouts and all the CDF were here.
Andvari nodded toward the food table as she came in. Aili
collected a plate and carried it to her spot. She sank into the
chair as Kyson joined Andvari at the front of the room.

"It's confirmed. Half a shipment of supplies went missing
not far from here. The escorts don't remember anything.
The wagon wasn't tampered with. No Mind Mage could

find any magical trace of spells affecting them. With Aili and Gavi's help, I did a deep dive, though. There are traces of magic on one of them, just not as a spell." Kyson paced the front of the room slowly. "What they remember is a black fog moving around them. They woke to half their cargo gone."

Andvari tapped his chin. "Black fog. I haven't heard of anything like that before."

Theron shook his head. "Nothing in our reports, either."

Aili set her wrap back down on her plate. "Can I see the memory?"

Kyson walked over to her. "The driver has the clearest memory."

Closing her eyes, Aili sat still. Kyson rested a hand on her forehead. She opened the link fully for him.

Perched on the control seat, Aili had a perfect view of the road. Trees bordered them on both sides of the packed dirt, so tall they blocked all direct sunlight. A pair of Scouts sat behind her, talking quietly about—something. Their words were muffled, like she couldn't remember, or maybe it was her focus on the road.

"What—?" She spun to the side, taking in the sight of black fog pouring from the trees.

A thick mist formed first, growing thicker with each breath. The air was choking, almost too thick to breathe.

Swirling up around her, she saw the others fall asleep or unconscious; she couldn't tell which. It flowed up over her, choking her.

She tasted acid on her tongue as she breathed the fog in. There was no way to recoil from the bitterness, the pain. The fog coated her, clinging to her clothing and skin. Darkness. Aili tried to touch her Light, but nothing happened.

'You're in a memory, remember?' Kyson's presence was quiet in her head. 'Feel. Watch.'

The fog covered her eyes. She couldn't see clearly. She tried his other senses, but they were as dulled. Even sound didn't travel well in this fog, muffled thumps all she could make out.

'You'll only sense and feel what he did,' Kyson warned. 'They can't feel as you do. Do your best to pull what you can from his experience.'

Shadows moved through the fog, circling the wagon. Her head turned down. The Scouts lay just below her in the back of the wagon, their eyes open and unmoving. Her own body stiffened. Even the smallest movement was all she could manage.

The wagon shifted and wiggled as something moved in the back. Wooden crates scraped over the back deck. Garbled voices were too distant in the fog. She toppled from the wagon, hitting the ground. She heard the crack, but nothing hurt. There was nothing but cold that seeped through her.

Shadows ran past, crates in their hands. The fog swallowed them. It retreated into the trees. Sunlight shone down, filtered through the leaves. Her wrist ached, sending stabbing pains through her. She woke fully; the pain pulling her into sharp awareness. She rolled and cradled her wrist in her hand.

"Did this happen in the morning or afternoon?" Aili pulled herself from the memory.

"Just over an hour or so ago, near as we can tell, though their sense of time was altered. They found the wagon half empty. You pulled from the memory before the headaches started." Kyson smiled at her. "I'm still going over the memory for clues."

Aili rested her chin on her hand. "I've never seen fog like that before. It was definitely Darkness blended with a spell. I don't need to feel it to know that for certain." She went quiet as she considered the memory again. "There's something wrong with the land, though."

"What?" Andvari crossed his arms over his chest, his gaze on her.

"I'm not sure. His senses aren't like mine, so I've only got what he experienced in the memory." Aili shook her head. "Still, there's something there I need to see."

"If a shipment is missing, can you track it in the forest?" Theron shifted in his chair. "I'm guessing you have ways?"

"We do, but the Field Scouts couldn't find anything. We're going to take Aili there to have a look." Andvari tapped his chin. "You're welcome to come and observe, or even help, if you like."

Frida grinned. "Happy to help."

"It was the fog." Aili straightened in her chair. "It wasn't normal fog, but was too heavy. Much too heavy."

Theron's brow wrinkled. "How can fog be too heavy?"

Aili glanced at his neckband. Right, fog is more of an Air Mage thing. He was a Fire Mage. "Fog is normally moist air, right? This fog also had Darkness in it. It came from somewhere. I might be able to track it. They couldn't track the spells under it?" She looked to Andvari.

He shook his head. "It was like someone walked the area with an erasing crystal. They still might have a few."

"I have an idea." Aili smiled.

"We'll take a wagon. I'll drive." Andvari headed for the door.

"We're right behind you." Theron gestured to the other CDF.

***

Aili strolled along the road, taking her time. The wagon tracks were deep here. Scuff marks in the dirt around the wagon showed where tendrils of fog moved along the ground, a trace of the taint still present. Fog shouldn't do that.

"They followed these marks?" Aili pointed at the scuff marks.

Andvari crouched beside a set of the marks. "A dozen feet into the trees they just stop."

Picking a deeper mark, she followed it into the trees bordering the road. Sure enough, they faded just past the bushes. Fortunately, she could still feel traces of the Darkness in them. "This is where they cast the spell."

Andvari came over, followed by the others. He crouched and cast a spell. "No traces left. Someone erased it all."

"Ages ago, back when I was a new mage, you showed me a spell. It asked plants to help show a memory of what happened. Remember that?"

Kyson shared a look with Andvari.

"The Field Scouts would have tried that one," Andvari pointed out.

"Well, yes, but they can't talk to plants or animals, can they?" Aili closed her eyes and opened herself, searching.

She held her hand out. A tiny weight dropped into her palm. When she opened her eyes, a little brown bird with spotted feathers stared up at her.

"Hello, little friend. Did you see what happened here?" She pulled a few seeds from her pocket and dropped them in her palm.

The bird cheeped. He pecked at the seed, grabbing each one.

"You can talk to birds?" Frida raised an eyebrow.

"Animals have a lot to say. Most people just don't listen." Aili raised her hand to eye level. "What did you see?"

The bird peeped. Aili closed her eyes. She perched high in the branches, watching the road. Insects were easier to see on the road. Movement caught her attention. It was something significantly bigger than an insect.

"There were four of them hiding in the trees, one where each of the marks stop." Aili pointed in the directions, keeping her eyes closed.

"They called the magic together, like a great magical working, channeling it through the one that feels wrong. I bet it's the man with the taint. There's something about his memory, though—"

Aili waited and watched.

"The Darkness was tied to a point. It's over here. I think I can follow it." Aili opened her eyes and headed for the spot.

"Can birds see Darkness? Why wouldn't Master Mages detect it?" Frida knelt beside the shallow grooves at the road edge.

"He didn't see the Darkness directly. Nature Magic leaves ripples the animals can see. The mages funnelled their power to the tainted one. That taint transformed it into Nature Magic, so there's no traces of spells left behind." Aili offered one last seed to the bird.

He chirped and grabbed the seed before taking off again.

"This way." Aili headed for the spot the bird showed her.

CHAPTER 28

Opening herself, Aili searched for the ripples in the natural magic around her. The faintest traces were still there, Darkness holding it still. Nature didn't want to absorb it again, keeping it at a distance, diluted though it was. It lingered in the air and on the ground, barely present still.

The others trailed behind, silent and watching. Andvari and Kyson stayed right behind her. They cast spells as they walked, but Aili focused ahead. Whatever the bird detected, it was just on the other side of the bushes.

Aili stopped at the edge of the clearing. Something about this place just felt wrong. She shivered. There was something familiar about it, too. Looking closer, she saw a spell pattern written in the Darkness left behind. The tainted one performed a spell here.

'Help?'

Andvari set his hand against her back. 'Look as closely as you can.'

Kyson warmed in the link, joining them. Aili examined the pattern, trying to make sense of the lines and spaces.

'I know this pattern.' Kyson guided her attention to the middle. 'This is nearly identical to what the kitchens use to move food between rooms. It's a teleport spell, but only designed for objects, not people.'

'What, really?' Aili followed his attention, examining the threads of the pattern again. Many lines crossed and re-crossed the pattern. 'This must have taken time to set.'

'Hours,' Andvari confirmed. 'How might the Darkness affect this pattern, I wonder? Did they try and use it as well, taking the crates with them? Did they teleport the crates and walk to wherever they sent them?'

Casting around, Aili searched for traces of Darkness beyond the clearing. 'They walked. I bet they only sent the crates through. How far out would the Scouts search?'

'I'll share what we found with our guests.' Kyson backed from the link.

'They would have looked maybe another dozen feet or so. Follow the footprints. Let's see if they're heading in a straight line.'

Aili glanced back at Kyson. He stood with the others, his hand held out. They all had their hands stacked on his. The group glowed with magic, visible with her senses open like this.

'He's sharing the pattern. They might track where it goes. Those spells have a range, and it's not far.'

Keeping away from the magic in the clearing, Aili circled around the edge. She slipped into the bushes, following the trace of Darkness.

"I'm getting tracks now." Andvari pointed at the soil.

Aili pulled back from her senses and looked closer. Sure enough, tiny traces of someone passing through remained.

"You keep tracking the magic, and I'll follow the physical trace. Let's see if they stay together." Andvari smiled.

Opening her senses fully again, Aili followed the magic. She stayed behind him this time. The trail led away, veering only to avoid large trees or rocks in its path. They passed between bushes, emerging onto an animal trail. Two sets of wheel marks remained, the grass slowly bouncing back. Deeper impressions showed where the wagon had parked a while ago.

"There's a road that way." Andvari kneeled and examined the tracks closer. "The wheels are smaller than on any Scout wagon. They couldn't drive this quickly on rough terrain. A good-sized tree root would stop this wagon."

"They know the area, then?" Kyson stared off to where the track disappeared from sight.

"Scouts usually know the locals. Don't they here?" Aili felt along the track, seeking the traces of Darkness.

Kyson shook his head. "This camp isn't like the others. It's hidden, remember? There's a tiny Scout outpost nearby where locals can come and get help. We can ask when we get back."

"Why don't you go get our wagon?" Andvari asked Kyson. "We'll follow this and meet you at the road." He pointed off where the tracks led. "Aili can ask if there's anyone else who saw anything." He smiled at her.

"Can Ilia talk to animals like this?" Vinnia asked. "It would be great to have another way to solve crimes."

"She talks to plants in a way I can't, but her gift isn't with animals like mine is." Aili shook her head. "She can feel their energy and communicate with them, but can't talk to them like I do."

"Shame." Frida shrugged.

"Come on. Let's see if anyone saw anything." Andvari draped an arm around her shoulders and guided her along the track.

Aili walked with him, her senses still active. "Wait, this wagon doesn't have any enchantments like I'd expect. It can steer and stop like normal, but there's no comfort or safety enchantment like we have. They're like wagons I'd find in the city."

"Not taken from Scouts, any CDF, or the Council," Theron commented. "Maybe they bought or stole it from a market or farmer."

"I'll have someone go through the records when we get back. It might take time, but we have people who do this sort of thing." Andvari cast a spell on the track.

"There." Aili pulled away and darted ahead.

She dropped to her knees near some bushes. Andvari stopped a few feet back, letting her look around.

"Come out, little friend. I won't harm you," she whispered.

A sleek and shiny rabbit poked her head from the bush, her nose wiggling. She turned and stared at the Master Mages.

"They're my friends. They won't hurt you, either. Can you tell me where the wagon went?" Aili reached out slowly and scratched the rabbit under the ear.

An image flowed into her mind, a memory from low to the ground. The wagon rumbled past, towering over the little rabbit, and turned left onto the road.

"Thank you." Aili pulled a piece of herb from her pocket and offered it to the rabbit.

The rabbit grabbed the herb and hopped back into the bushes.

Aili stood. "That way." She pointed.

They followed the trail south. Andvari picked the occasional sign from the wagon from the undergrowth. Looking ahead through the slightly sparse trees, Aili saw Kyson and their wagon waiting on a road for them. He leaned against the wagon, watching as they approached.

Aili kneeled at the edge of the road. Opening herself, she sought any sign of magic. The wagon left no traces behind. She shook her head.

Andvari cast a spell. "Anything anyone else can sense?"

The group spread out over the road. All the magic they cast shone in her senses like miniature fireworks. Most were too complex to watch, and gone almost as soon as they were cast.

"It didn't have a tracker," Theron muttered.

Frida shook her head. "I can't find anything, either."

"Mount up. We'll head back. We've been able to gather information from other Scouts in the area, and we might be able to narrow down where to look." Andvari walked to the back of the wagon.

"Drive slow and I'll see what I can find." Aili scrambled up into the back.

She crawled to the front corner and wedged herself in. The wagon shifted as the others climbed in as well. Andvari sat beside her, his back to the side. He took her hand, and she opened the link. The wagon eased down the road, smoothly picking up speed.

Aili scanned the magic around her as they headed back to the main road, such as it was out this far. Wait, was that a faint ripple in the magic over there?

'I see it, too,' Andvari assured her.

Kyson pulled the wagon over, and it rolled to a smooth stop. Aili waited for the others to get out before hopping down as well. Following the sensation, she wandered through the trees. Stopping at a larger gap between some trees, she reached her hand out. The air almost hummed, though so low she barely felt it. What kind of magic was this?

'More teleportation magic?' Aili poked the ripple in magic with her senses. 'No, this is more familiar than that.'

'Invisibility spells,' Kyson corrected. 'I think it's still there. See those marks?" He pointed to where something pressed the undergrowth flat.

Andvari reached for it. The magic crackled and brightened in her senses, visible to him through the link. He pulled his hand back. "There's something hidden here. Everyone, we'll try and unravel it, but it's mixed in with nature magic and a hint of taint. I'll guide Aili. You all know what to do." He took her hand. 'Kyson and Frida will lead the group. You follow my lead.'

Frida and Kyson pressed their palms flat together. Magic flowed as the others cast spells, sending the power into their joined magic. Aili followed Andvari, giving Kyson her powers directly through the link.

Closing her eyes, she experienced the magic unravelling. Nature Magic, including the tainted part, held the spell together. Flooding the magic with her light, she chased the taint down and dissolved it. Andvari tugged at the spell with her powers. The spell collapsed.

Aili opened her eyes. Crates filled the space before her, stacked roughly. They shimmered with magic, but all normal spells this time. They were identical to any other crate she saw holding crystals inside.

She tried to watch and examine every spell the others cast, but there were so many. Aili recognized many of the spells. A few used by the CDF were unfamiliar to her. Some parts she thought she recognized, but she wasn't sure. The spells were over in moments.

"They're safe." Frida held her hand out to the crates.

"We need to get these back." Andvari walked over and lifted a crate. He set it down again. "They're heavy."

"Of course they are," Kyson muttered. "No magic help, either."

Aili grabbed an edge and tried to lift a crate. She barely got it a couple of inches before letting go. "There are so many protective spells. Is that why they couldn't teleport them, you think?"

"Probably." Theron lifted the crate she had abandoned with ease. "It's a wonder they got them this far. It doesn't answer the question about where the wagon is, though."

"Could that be what the teleport magic was for?" Aili stepped back as the others grabbed the remaining crates. "Something happened to the wagon, and they sent it somewhere?"

"If so, they need to be incredibly fit to carry them this far." Rylor picked up the last crate. "Unless they teleported the wagon and the crates happened to come along for the ride."

"Teleport magic has a limited range." Kyson looked around, peering through the trees. "If they brought it all together, the wagon must be nearby."

"Aili and I will look while you load the wagon." Andvari rested his hand against her back. "If it's nearby, we should be able to find something."

"Wagons aren't something you just throw away," Frida offered. "They might even have taken it first to repair it, so they can come back for this." She waved at where the crates had been, the undergrowth still pressed down.

"I have an idea." Aili smiled up at the hawk overhead. 'Might I borrow your sight?' She touched the bird with her abilities, keeping herself open in the offer.

A sensation of hunger filled her. Aili smiled as she imagined a full belly. The bird flew lazy circles overhead, looking down for her. The canopy was thin, especially compared to the northern forest.

"There." Aili grinned. "I found it. Get a predator stick out."

Andvari pulled a wrapped bundle from his pocket and took the waxed paper off. Crumbling it with his fingers, he set it down where the crates had been. He stepped back with her. The hawk swooped down and landed beside it. They stayed back as he snatched at the pile, tilting his head back to eat.

'Thank you.' Aili backed away, leaving him to eat.

Giving the hawk space, she led them through the trees. Rylor and Horgin stayed with the wagon and crates as she took the others to the spot the hawk noticed. They dropped into a ditch.

The remains of the wagon lay at the bottom, partially on its side. The middle was cracked, and some side boards were missing completely, while others lay shattered under the wagon.

"That answers one question." Kyson held his hand out, magic at his fingertips.

"Everyone, learn anything you can. Who owned it? When was the magic stripped from it? Everything." Andvari walked over to it and touched a wheel. "This wood is ancient."

Theron walked to the control panel. "The wagon is older than modern registration numbers." He tapped the panel. "There's a registration mark here, though. Old."

"Any support spells faded long ago." Kyson walked to the back of the wagon, his hand stretched out over it. "You can only refresh them so many times over the centuries."

Frida nodded. "It's been a while. This wagon was waiting to fall apart. It might not be reported missing if they knew it was barely serviceable at best."

"What can you learn from this?" Aili touched the registration numbers, carefully carved ages ago.

"All manner of information. Who owns it? Is it reported stolen? Where is it supposed to be? We also have specialist spells that can tell more about it, once it's back in the lab. If we have a suspect, we can use that knowledge during the spell sweep and confirm if they were involved or not." Theron wrote the number down.

CHAPTER 29

A ili stepped closer and watched the paper. The numbers faded. Text appeared instead. "You don't use mirrors?"

Vinnia grinned. "We don't need to in the city. We have these, tied right into our information specialists. It's all connected, so we can learn things about people fast. It's helpful when trying to sort out a large crowd."

Andvari moved beside her, also watching the text scroll onto the page. The text shifted as Theron scanned it, moving it with his finger.

"We can take people back to camps and sort things out with our archivists instead. You didn't think they were only librarians, did you?" Andvari laid his hand on her shoulder.

"Maybe?" Aili smiled and shrugged.

"They are all information specialists. They keep the records and maintain the database. It's tied in to others, like the city databases, so we pool our information together. We just access it differently because our situations are unique."

Aili glanced up at Andvari and nodded. "That makes sense. "What about the wagon?"

Theron scrolled back through the information and showed it to her. "It was stolen a week ago from a farm near Dinlark. I'll make a note and have the Dinlark CDF ask the owner about it."

"Are they with you, or separate?"

"They're separate. They run the same way we do, though. Same command structure. If anyone moves between cities, they can transfer smoothly."

"There's dirt under here that's different." Vinnia pointed under the wagon.

Aili wandered over and knelt beside the mud and drying dirt. "This doesn't feel like the local dirt."

Andvari joined her, crouching down. He took a pinch of soil between his fingers. Pulling out his mirror, he held it in his palm.

"Yes, boss?" Mowen's face appeared on the mirrored surface.

"What can you tell me about this soil?" He set the soil on the mirror surface.

"That's not local. I can tell you at a glance. It's found southwest of your location, in the lower and wetter areas. It's formed when a plant breaks down that only grows out there, so I'm certain about this." Mowen's voice sounded clear, despite the soil over his image.

"Can you show me where?" Andvari flicked his fingers, and the dirt fell to the ground.

A map appeared on the surface, with an area marked in red shading. Their current position also showed. Following the map back to where they came from, the marks all lined up.

"Thanks, Mowen." Andvari closed the call, though the map stayed visible longer as he frowned over it. "I'll have a recovery team come for this. We'll head back. I don't want to leave our wagon long, either. We'll lock this down until they arrive."

Andvari chanted, forming a barrier. Kyson joined him, using a different spell Aili hadn't seen before. They added a few layers of magic, each different from the last. She watched with her senses, curious. They ended each layer differently, not like a normal spell.

'That's so any Scout can take the barrier down.' Kyson warmed in the link. 'See this part of the pattern? If someone wearing a Scout mirror reverses it, the whole spell network will collapse, giving them access.'

'Neat.' Aili examined the spell closely, especially where he had just showed her.

"Alright, let's get back." Andvari strode back through the trees. "We'll go at speed."

"Alright," Kyson cheered, raising his fist.

Aili groaned.

"Cheer up. We'll be back before supper officially ends." Kyson wrapped an arm around her shoulders and propelled her towards the wagon.

"Who's going to find our mangled bodies in a ditch later?" Aili fingered her mirror through her shirt.

"So little faith in me." Kyson shook his head. "Frida can always put you under a sleep spell if you're that scared."

"Is he really that bad?" Rylor raised an eyebrow as they approached.

Aili rubbed her chin. "To be fair, I hear he hasn't actually killed anyone. The only injury made a full recovery."

She squeaked as Kyson picked her up and tossed her in the wagon. She scrambled into the corner and tucked herself in snugly, her feet braced wide.

"You will want to use spells to secure yourselves, though." Andvari climbed in beside her. "Just in case."

***

Aili shifted from foot to foot. The mirror seemed so much bigger this time. She played with the hem of her sleeve, the fine threads barely detectable under her sensitive fingers. Was she ready for this? Could she really do this?

Not much more than a year ago, she didn't even know she could use magic. She even tried to leave, tired of being the only person in all of Athia without magic. Now they want her to run the Scouts?

Andvari rested a hand on her shoulder. "You'll be fine. We're not throwing you into leadership right away, are we? You'll ease in and learn your role. Besides, we're here to support you in looking after the forests. You might want to make a few changes one day to make the Scouts yours."

Aili rubbed her temples. "I don't know. I don't know enough. I'm an apprentice. How's this even supposed to work?"

Andvari smiled. "You keep your rank until you are ready to take over officially. Until you step forward, ready to lead, you stay with me and learn and study. Breathe. Relax. Don't stress over something that hasn't even happened yet." He took her hand and held it.

"Easy for you to say. You didn't go from being an outsider to being a full mage in a year," she muttered.

"No, but I know someone who did. I saw her change and grow and blossom. I watched her deal with uncertainty. She bravely stepped forward and met each challenge, no matter how scared she was. I also had to remind her repeatedly she's not alone." He sent soothing magic, easing her nausea.

Aili smiled back at him. "Thanks."

The mirror flickered. She turned back to it and watched the smoke swirl before fading.

The commander appeared before her in the glass. "Andvari. Aili. How can I help? Has something happened?"

Andvari smiled and shook his head. "Nothing mission related. Aili has learned about her position now, and is looking to her future. In recognition of your knowledge and service, she wishes you to stay on as Commander for the foreseeable future, and is considering you for her council."

The commander bowed her head. "I am honoured."

"With everything we've faced, Aili has a request to make." Andvari nodded to Aili. "Go ahead."

Her eyes widened. Her chest tightened. No, if she's going to be my advisor, I need to do this. Aili took a deep breath and let it out. "I would like Niru or a mage of equal standing to do a check for Mind Magic. I wish to know you're advising me without any interference from anyone else. After the whole University thing—" Aili shrugged.

The commander bowed her head again. "Understandable. I agree."

Aili let out a breath she didn't realize she was holding. "Thank you."

"The transition will not be immediate," Andvari acknowledged. "I'll send the request to Niru and he can make the arrangements for everyone she is considering."

"I will make time for his visit." The commander smiled at her.

The mirror went dark, smoke filling the glass again. Within moments, the reflection of the room returned. Aili stared at herself in the reflection for a long moment.

"What's on your mind?" Andvari rubbed her back.

She shook her thoughts free. "You don't know?"

Kyson flowed into the link. 'He wants you to say it. It'll help you organize your tangled mess of thoughts.'

"What if I choose wrong? What if someone betrays me?" Aili hugged herself.

"We're here to help you. When have we ever left you alone to deal with things?" Andvari rested his hands on her shoulders, turning her to face him. "When you were separated from us those few short times, you did well on your own. Trust yourself, and trust us. Whatever happens, we'll deal with it."

Aili nodded slowly. "You're right. It's just, the Scouts are so big. They're everywhere. It's a lot."

He wrapped his arm around her shoulder and guided her from the communication room. "Yes, and you have people already running things, who know how it all works, right? Planning on firing me?"

She grinned. "Well—" Aili drew out the word.

Andvari laughed as he led her around the corner. "Sure. Good luck running the Scouts."

Aili poked his side. "If you keep doing your job, I won't have paperwork, right?"

"Taking lessons from Kyson, now?"

'Hey,' Kyson protested, bursting into the link.

"If you want a scribe, you can have one."

She raised an eyebrow. "Really?"

Andvari nodded. "But not until you officially take your place. Until then, the paperwork will help you understand how the Scouts work." He guided her through the arch-way and directly to the table with snacks. "Now, we'll be going out again after lunch, so eat well. There are some places we need to check out."

She grabbed lunch, her mind whirling. Andvari gave her space to work through her thoughts, keeping her company, but letting her sit in silence. They were early, so the room was empty except for them. She finished her meal and left her dishes in the bin.

A little day wagon sat out front, waiting for them. Aili climbed up into the back, her belly comfortably full. Kyson was already here doing the wagon check for them. She settled with her back to the control seat. With both hands out, she could reach both sides. It was just long enough for someone to lie down back here. Only one person fit on the control bench. She pressed her lips together.

Kyson leapt up and sat with her in the back. "Wagon's all good. We can leave when you're ready."

Andvari swung up into the control seat. "As we get closer, you two will scan for anything unusual. Look for any signs of mages or magic that is concentrated where it shouldn't be. We're going for stealth, not speed."

"Ready." Aili spread her feet, bracing herself without effort.

"Same." Kyson leaned against the side of the wagon near her foot.

The wagon rolled smoothly along the road under Andvari's direction. Aili almost didn't feel the first turn. She
closed her eyes and opened her senses. There should be
more animals around than there are. How could she prevent the taint from building up, even behind the dome?
Was it whatever the mages were doing that harmed the
land so much? She wished she knew.

The wagon left the road and headed cross-country. The
ride was still smoother than she expected. Or was Andvari
better at reading the forest than Kyson, who seemed more
concerned with having fun than his passengers' safety?

'Go that way.' Aili pointed, shifting until she kneeled behind Andvari.

'What do you feel?' Kyson crawled closer, looking where
she pointed.

She shook her head. 'I'm not sure, but it's getting stronger
as we get closer.'

What was it, though? She felt it in her heart, not her senses.
Power rippled out at her like waves after a stone lands in a
pond. She barely felt it, but it touched her deeply in some
way, like the warmth of the sun on a cool day.

'Stop here.' Aili leapt from the wagon and ran to a small
cliff. Whatever it was, it was through here.

As she approached, power surged under her feet. Heat
rushed up through her. The rock face shimmered and dis-

solved. A dark cave opening just big enough for her stood before her. Magic pulsed beneath her feet, pure Nature Magic. She pressed a hand to the rock as she peered inside. Runes glowed on the rock beside her hand.

"What's in here?" Andvari caught up, standing right behind her. He looked in over her shoulder, crouched down a bit. "I don't recognize these runes."

"I do," Aili whispered. "I've seen them before."

"Where?" Kyson traced a rune with his finger, the magic in it unchanged by his touch.

"On something Ilia has. These are incredibly old. No wonder the pin was hidden all this time." Aili frowned at the rune, her full attention on it.

Andvari reached out, but his hand stopped at the cave opening. "There's a barrier here I can't feel."

Kyson came closer and pressed against the barrier. He chanted softly, calling to the magic. "I can't sense a pattern, either. It can only be one thing." He and Andvari shared a look.

"It's not a spell," Aili whispered. "Mother."

Andvari raised an eyebrow. "How do we get inside? Do we try?"

Aili straightened up and took a deep breath. She let it out and took a step forward. This wouldn't harm her. Probably. Her skin warmed. She kept walking. Two steps later, and the heat passed. Aili turned and looked back at them.

Kyson stood at the barrier, his mouth slightly open as if to protest. Andvari pressed against the barrier, his brow furrowed. Aili walked back through. The heat surged and faded as she slipped past them, under Kyson's arm.

"How do we get in with you?" Kyson braced his hands on his hips.

Aili touched the runes. "I'm not sure you do. This one means wild magic. It usually refers to Nature Magic. I don't see a symbol for any other magic kind. Maybe I'm supposed to do this alone."

Emotions surged through the link. For the first time in a long time, they weren't her emotions. Fading almost as soon as she felt them, the link calmed. When was the last time one of them worried that much?

"Are you certain you'll be alright?" Andvari took her hand. He held her gaze, his normally relaxed expression tight this time. "We don't know what's in there. You might walk right in, or there could be trials and tests. We don't know."

"You don't have to let her go." Kyson rounded on Andvari. "We can always go ask Ilia before sending her in there alone."

CHAPTER 30

"I can do this," Aili protested.

Andvari crossed his arms over his chest as he turned to the cave. "She's a full mage now."

"She's an apprentice. She's still under your command. What you say goes." Kyson balled his hands into fists.

"For how much longer? She's growing up."

A flash of sadness rushed through her. Was it Andvari's emotions or Kyson's? It just felt so weird not to be the one losing control. It shocked her into stillness for an instant, her protest lost on her tongue.

With a last glance at them, Aili stepped through the barrier. They stood facing each other, Andvari frowning and Kyson with a clenched jaw. Pushing her confusion aside, Aili followed the tunnel into the darkness. It spiralled around and down.

'Are you both still with me?' Aili opened the link to them.

'Get back up here. He didn't say you could go.'

'If the link is affected, come back immediately. Remember, we can't come save you, so don't take chances.' Sadness and worry rushed through her for an instant with Andvari's words, his emotions almost covering his voice.

'I will. I'll be fine. Mother would never harm me.'

Aili set a steady pace downward, following the path laid before her.

'What do you see?' Kyson wasn't panicking, but there was a tone of worry in his voice she didn't hear often.

'So far, it's just a tunnel. It's getting warmer, but nothing I can't handle.'

She rounded the corner and stopped short. A door of black stone blocked her path. Red flames were carved into it. Paint or another rock type? Who makes a door of rock? Closing her eyes, she reached for the door with her inner lights. The moment she touched the door, it swung open.

She froze. The room was full of flames, dancing and flickering on every surface. Her palms sweated and her body shook. So much fire? It took a moment to realize the flames were silent. The room was silent. Only her breathing echoed in the stone chamber. The pin sat on a rock pedestal at the far end.

'Breathe slow and deep.' Andvari's voice cut through her panic. 'What do you see? Are you safe?'

'Yeah, I'm okay. I'm not sure what I'm seeing, honestly. It just startled me.'

It wasn't just the lack of noise that bothered her. There was no roaring heat. Her skin was warm, sure, but not like it should be. This much fire should be unbearable. She still had flashbacks where she could feel the heat and hear the deafening roar. These flames shimmered with magic, almost as if they were an illusion instead of actual fire.

Was it a test of bravery? No, there was no way. The pin has been here so long the runes outside are as old as it gets. There's no way whoever put the pin here would know how it would affect her. It must be related to the fire pin and not her, then. It wasn't personal.

'Okay, I'm fine. There's powerful Nature Magic here, but it's not hostile. The pin is right here. I'll take it and come out.'

'Be careful,' Kyson urged.

'Worried about me?' Aili tried to fill the link with her tease, but fear still flowed through her.

'You little—of course I'm worried about you. I wouldn't have saved you all those times if I didn't care. If you were annoying, I'd have chosen the paperwork instead.'

Aili smiled as she took a step into the room. The flames under her feet faded, letting her pass untouched. The flames around her leaned in, like they wanted to touch her. She closed her eyes and felt for the magic instead.

The pin glowed like a beacon. The flames were little more than a trace of magic in comparison. Aili examined the pedestal. There could be some kind of trap or mechanism protecting the pin. She didn't want to trigger one if there was.

Nature magic ran through the pedestal, filling it and making the runes shine a bright red. Nothing seemed out of place. If anything, it felt just like the barrier keeping her friends out. Reaching out, she touched the pedestal. Warmth flowed through her, like a hug through the link she shared with them. She moved her hand away, and it stopped.

She reached out and touched the glittering crystals in the fire pin. Images rushed into her mind, overwhelming her other senses. A mountain exploded, fire and rock spewing from a hole in the top. Heat and ash coated everything, making the sky dark. Hot red ooze melted down the side and spattered the surrounding land.

Aili gasped and yanked her hand away. Was that a volcano? Like, an actual working volcano? Athia once had volcanoes in the northwest, but they've been quiet since before the golden age. The soil there was special, allowing plants to grow that didn't grow anywhere else in Athia. Kyson's family grew coconuts there.

Her hand trembled, hovering over the pin. The pressure on her was immense when she touched it, as if she were a rock about to be flung into the air by the mountain. Taking a deep breath, she touched her fingers to the pin again.

Heat and pressure pressed against her. Aili rushed down this time, into the mountain in a fiery stream of molten rock. Her lungs ached and burned. She coughed. The air was thick and hot.

'Aili!'

The sensations fled. A cooler warmth, more like a summer day, filled her instead. Aili fled up to the light, a brightness like the sun that came from her link. That voice meant safety. She sped up towards it, emerging back into her own body.

'Breathe, Aili. Ground yourself in my voice. Can you wrap the pin in something? Do you have a handkerchief with you?'

Aili patted her pockets. 'Yeah. I hope it helps. The water one was pinned to my shirt and it still affected me.'

'Try with the handkerchief. The magic inside should help protect you. Once it's out here, one of us will take it. We don't feel it like you did.'

Pulling the handkerchief from her pocket, she draped it over her hand. Aili dropped it onto the pin before touching it again. Wrapping her fingers around the edges of the pin, Aili picked it up. Holding the handkerchief by the corners, she held it up.

'I've got it. I'm okay.'

'Great. Get back here.' Kyson's voice was hard, rough, and a little shaky.

She turned, heading for the door. The stone doors swung closed, moving silently as the flames grew higher and brighter. Heat washed over her. The fire crackled, making noise for the first time. Smoke flowed up the walls and spread over the ceiling.

'No. No, no, no, no, no!'

'Aili, what's going—' Andvari's voice faded as the doors slammed shut.

She reached out through the link. He was there, but just a distant glimmer, like when they were across the country from each other. Spinning, she looked for any way out. The smoke grew thicker. Only the runes on the doors let her know where the way out was.

Think, Aili, she urged herself. You didn't survive that fire only to die in another one. She wiped her forehead with her sleeve. Was she a Nature Mage or not? There was always a way out. If she couldn't find it, she'd make one.

Stone. Reshaping rock and stone was easy. Aili reached for the wall with her abilities. The flames blocked her energy, threatening to pull her into the magic. Aili yanked herself back and sank to the floor. The heat made each breath an effort.

The pin swung against her in the handkerchief, bumping her leg. Was that the answer? Feeling the pin through the cloth, she traced its shape. Power called to her, the raging strength of the volcano. She could be the power, bringing fresh growth to the land around her. She just needed to use it.

Could she, though? Aili coughed. If she wanted to live, she had to. Opening her handkerchief, she gripped the pin with trembling fingers. Heat rushed through her. She commanded it now. Strong. She had to be strong.

Focusing on the door and the flames around it, Aili pressed the fire down. Heat belonged deep down, far under the soil, where lave lived. She moved the heat down her body as well, through her feet and the stone floor. The surrounding flames dropped, the fire less intense. Soon, only a glimmer of flames remained.

Now, how to get out? Aili felt for the door. Her senses slid right off the stone, unable to look closely at the doors. Her fingers brushed over the tiny crystals in the pin. Something inside urged her to melt the doors and be done with it.

She could melt the entire cave if she wanted to. With her abilities, she could bring lava up and reshape the world.

No. She stuffed the little voice down. It might be right about the doors, though. Maybe she didn't have to melt them, just soften them a bit wherever they were locked together?

Holding the pin out, Aili called on the flames and heat in the room. She pressed it all into the doors. The instant the heat touched the doors, they swung open. Aili squeezed through the widening gap and sprinted up the tunnel.

Stumbling, her knees hit the stone floor. Blood flowed. Staggering to her feet, she pressed forward. Her muscles burned. Heat surrounded her. How much could she withstand before her body gave out?

Sunlight called to her, a massive fireball burning so far away. Still, it called to her. Following the urge, she scrambled along, racing the heat threatening to engulf her. She burst into the light, through the cave entrance, and landed in the soft undergrowth. Aili panted, her lungs full of ash.

Andvari peeled her fingers open and pulled the pin from her grip. "She's burning up."

"She can't breathe. Cool her and I'lll clear her lungs." Kyson's hand lay on her forehead.

Why was his skin cool? His skin was never cool. Aili blinked in the daylight as she coughed. Air flowed into her lungs, scooping the ash up and pulling it out. She coughed harder, rolling to her side. Where did it all come from? There was no ash in the cave.

Water flowed over her, soaking her skin and clothing. Would she burn or drown first? She coughed another gob of sticky ash, spitting it onto the soil. Neither. She would suffocate. Her fingers gripped the grass, the skin sore from the heat and edges of the crystals.

Closing her eyes, she waited for the darkness to take her. She wasn't enough. She tried, though. Maybe someone else could finish what she started. Sound faded. She couldn't feel the plants beneath her. Everything went cold.

***

A page turned. She knew that sound. A book? Her fingers twitched, itching to hold it. She grasped soft blankets instead. She shivered, despite the steady warmth the blankets gave off. Warm and moist air flowed into and out of her lungs, soothing her nose and throat along the way. Magic. Someone is helping me breathe.

"Aili, are you with me?" The book closed. Andvari's warm fingers wrapped around hers.

She forced her eyes open. He sat on the edge of her bed, the mattress dipping slightly under his weight. His book lay on the chair. She shivered hard.

"Warming rocks." A healer approached with another blanket, draping it over her. He tapped it and the enchantment activated, warming her through.

"What? How?" Her voice was raspy and rough. She blinked up at him.

"Rest. The magical heat overwhelmed you. You need time to reset. Ilia said you might feel cold while your body figures things out again." The healer leaned down and peered into her eyes. He laid his hand on her forehead, and magic flowed into her. "She's fine. She's recovering well. I'll let Ilia know she's awake."

"Aili." Kyson stood in the doorway, a plate of pastries in his hand. "How are you?"

He was using his caring voice. Was she that ill? "My lungs ache."

Kyson walked over and sat on the chair, barely missing the book as Andvari snatched it and tossed it aside. He set the plate on the small table nearby. "I'm not surprised. The ash I pulled from your lungs dried them out something fierce. Ilia said you might still feel a bit raw inside while you get rehydrated fully."

"If this is what Gavi felt when I regrew his lung, tell him I'm sorry." She pressed a hand to her chest over the layers of blankets. Her heart beat steadily.

Andvari smiled. "He doesn't regret that moment for a second. He's grateful every day that you saved him."

"Don't speak too much. Breathe through your nose as much as you can." The healer held his finger under her nose, adjusting the spell.

"I couldn't do it," she whispered. Aili closed her eyes as tears streamed down her cheeks.

"You did amazing. You came back to us." Andvari held her hand between his.

"I almost died. It was too much."

Andvari cradled her cheek in his hand, brushing her tears away with his thumb. "Listen. Kyson recovered your memory. You were incredibly brave and resourceful, and you made it out. Nobody could ask more from you."

Kyson bit into a pastry. He held one out for Andvari. "Eat. You need to stay healthy, too." He held Aili's gaze. "Nobody should be asked to wield that much magic, not even you. Don't beat yourself up for not being perfect."

Okay, his caring voice was gone. She would probably be fine, after all. "If I hadn't, I wouldn't have gotten out. If mother put it there, what if she expects me to control those pins?"

"Nonsense. I asked Ilia about the cave. She said it was made with Nature Magic, but mages were involved. That magic has been dormant for centuries. How could anyone know you'd come along? Even if your mother set it, how would she know who or what you'd be? Your father is a normal man, remember. At least half of you is unpredictable, depending on what genes you inherit." Kyson stared her down.

"What else did she say about the cave?" Aili pressed herself up on her elbows.

Andvari slid a hand under her back and helped her sit. He steadied her as she clung to his shoulder.

Kyson smiled and shook his head. "She said the fact you found it at all is remarkable and proves you're special. She believes you can drive the Darkness back and make another few hundred years of peace for us all." He raised his half-eaten pastry to his mouth. "Now hush so I can eat."

"Where's mine?" Aili challenged, the corners of her lips turned up.

He held the plate out. She snatched one and took a bite. Exploring the familiar flavours, Aili named the herbs in her head as she tasted each one. Taking small bites, she nibbled as they ate.

"Ilia says you can come back to our room tonight, but the healer insists you stay here until then." Andvari licked his fingers clean. "I think he only relented because otherwise I'd be sleeping on the floor in the way, and Kyson would need his bedroll in the hall."

Aili smiled as she chewed her pastry. These rooms were smaller than at most camps. Whenever she needed healing, they always stayed right nearby. Given the choice, she'd much rather be in her own bed. They could face everything tomorrow. For now, she was with her friends and safe.

CHAPTER 31

There was still so much to do. Sure, they cleansed the crystals, but the Darkness was still out there. So was whoever was spreading it. If Darkness was like Light, it wouldn't have a mind of its own. Someone was contaminated and was spreading it.

She walked around the corner of the building and into the shade. Moving helped her think. She still needed to find the air pin. It could be anywhere. If she didn't feel the fire pin, might the air pin also be right under her nose, undetectable?

"What's got you so deep in thought?"

Aili spun, dropping into a defensive stance. Letting out a breath, she straightened up again. Ilia sat on a bench in the shade, leaning back against the wall.

"You startled me." Aili pressed a hand to her chest. Had she been so deep in thought that she didn't feel the other living embodiment of Nature Magic? She sat beside Ilia. "I was just thinking about the Darkness. What brings it back? How does it spread? Can it ever be defeated or banished completely?"

Ilia wrapped a bony arm around Aili's shoulders. "Once cleansed, it will eventually come back, most likely. It always has before. Often close to four hundred years later. I think it needs time to gather and get strong enough again. It doesn't spread on its own, not that I've seen. Someone came across it and got infected, spreading it as they go."

"Like a bacteria." Aili tapped her chin. "A little won't make us sick, but a lot can kill us." So, it was as she thought. Someone is spreading it like a disease.

"That's a good analogy actually." Ilia laughed. "Just like bacteria are part of the world around us, maybe Darkness is, too. After all, we're unaware of it most of the time. Maybe it's a natural part of life?"

"If so, it's not an enemy to be fought but a force to keep in balance, like flood waters or a forest fire." Did that feel right, though? Did it fit the evidence? If so, Ilia would know better. She's seen more cycles of this.

"I have something for you." Ilia pulled a notebook from her pocket. "I've been looking into those charms you wanted." She handed the notebook to Aili.

Taking the notebook, Aili flipped through the pages carefully. "Thanks. Do you think I can do it? Make charms? You never had me try when younger."

Ilia laughed. "Your magic hadn't grown active when you were younger. You were spreading passive powers everywhere, but you need active control to make a charm. Get those mentors of yours to help you. Don't try it alone. Oh, and not in camp the first few times, just in case. You'll be dealing with the wildest form of magic."

"Thank you." Aili tucked the notebook into her pocket. "I'll be careful."

Ilia grabbed her wrist as Aili stood. "The most important thing to remember if you want your charms to be strong, separate yourself from the magic once you set the charm. Otherwise it'll be tied to you. You want them protected whether they're near you or not, right?"

Aili nodded. "Separate. Right."

"I put instructions in the notebook. Go on. I know you want to get started, and I'm enjoying being out in the wilds again. I don't get out of the city much anymore." Ilia grinned and winked.

Grinning back, Aili spun. She darted around the hall. Dashing past some Scouts coming from inside, she charged up the steps and through the doors. Heading straight for her room, she closed the door and collapsed on her bed.

She pulled the notebook out and began reading. Devouring every page, hungry for the information inside, Aili took in every note Ilia ever made in here. Separating magic would be easier than she feared. She's already done it before.

Finding something worthy of holding the magic might be trickier. The most powerful artifacts were fancy jewellery, metals that would last with a little care, and stones made deep in the planet. Where would she get something like that?

Aili looked over at the wooden box on his desk. So close like this, even the shielding didn't stop her from feeling the power inside. Setting the notebook inside, she went to the desk and sat. Her feet swung back and forth as she touched the smooth wooden box.

Did others feel this? Ilia might. Andvari already confirmed they can't use the pins, but could they feel the power inside? She brushed her fingers lightly over the lacquered lid. Even with the wards, this box shone in her senses.

The lid creaked as she opened the box. The pins sat on the velvet lining, resting on the cushioned bottom. Each little gemstone shone as if the sun were inside it somehow. The sunbeam streaming through the window wasn't even near them. The metal gleamed, calling to her. Pick me up. Hold me. Use me.

She touched the emerald gemstones, her fingers feeling each edge and facet. Her body lurched. She was at the highest mountain, and down to the deepest ocean trench. Pressure was all around, but not pressing in. Yanking her hand back, the sensation faded. She slipped off her chair.

"Aili." Andvari rushed through the door, reaching for her.

Gripping his sleeve, she opened her eyes. Halfway to the floor, he caught her before she landed. The magic glowed around her when she looked. It slowed her enough he could catch her.

He sat her in the chair and knelt in front of her. Cradling her cheek in his hand, he peered into her eyes. "Are you alright? What happened?"

She still held his sleeve in her shaking hand. "I was thinking about what she said. I need to find a way to use these. I don't know how, though. It's too much." Tears flowed, rolling down her cheeks. "I know how important this is. What if I lose myself and fail? I can't even touch the earth pin without problems, and that's my best element." She let out a sob and collapsed against his chest.

Andvari rubbed her back, letting her cry. "Have you asked Ilia about it? She knows more about some older artifacts than even the Scout researchers."

"We were just talking, but not about the pins. I want to make some charms. Hopefully they'll protect you and Kyson when we go after the Darkness. If I can make enough, I can protect everyone here. These are the strongest charms I know, and I can't even examine them without being overwhelmed." She pushed the box back on the desk. "I need help." She pointed to the notebook abandoned on her bed.

He retrieved the notebook and flipped through it. "Those are charms?"

Aili nodded. "The magic inside isn't spells, it's wild like mine. Nobody makes them except Ilia, because of that. First, I need something of good quality to hold the magic."

Andvari smiled as he stopped at a page. "Like something from this list of suitable objects?"

"I saw that, but those aren't just laying around. How would I get any like that?" Aili wiped her eyes with her sleeve.

He brought the list over and tapped a name. "We're in a camp full of these, right?"

Aili leaned over and looked closer. "We are?"

"They were in the dome when we cleansed it. There's a whole crate full of them, ready to hold enchantments. Why don't we grab a few and try this? If you succeed, we can take as many as you like." He handed her the notebook back. 'Hey, partner?'

'What's up?' Kyson slid into the link.

'Get a handful of the empty crystal necklaces from the storeroom. Meet us at the edge of camp in the forest, away from the dome. We're going to try some new magic.' Andvari pulled a snack bar from his pocket and unwrapped it. "Eat as we go. We'll walk slowly for you."

She took the offered snack bar. This was it. She was going to do something helpful, something she thought up completely on her own. Taking a bite, she got to her feet. They walked through the halls and to the door, Aili eating as she went.

They rounded the building, heading away from the rest of the camp. Kyson came from the storage area, a bunch of the necklaces dangling from his fingers. Gavi, Frida, and Theron walked with him, each with more necklaces in their hands. They joined Aili and Andvari on the walk past the protective dome.

"They couldn't pass up the chance to see this," Kyson explained. "We were talking when you called."

Aili smiled sheepishly. "I'm not sure there'll be anything to see. I've never done this before."

"I have faith in you." Gavi fell into step beside her. "Even if you don't succeed the first few times, you'll learn something from each attempt. Your next try will be better. I know you, though. You won't give up until you get it."

"Charms can be used to heal, right? I'm sure I've seen Ilia use them for that." Aili took a necklace from him and examined it.

"Yes, she's even sent a bunch up north for us. When done right, they last longer than spells." Gavi lifted his hand, letting the necklaces hang. They swung with each step.

"When you figure this out, I'd love to see if we can make some more."

Aili grinned. "Of course."

"This should be far enough." Andvari looked around. Camp was behind them, barely visible through the trees. "Now, we've never done this before. Aili will be using magic directly from nature, so it should be safe enough. Have a barrier ready, just in case."

Aili took a slow breath and settled her nerves. "I don't expect this is too different from putting magic in things. I did make that ever-hot rock for the snake that one time. That sounds like a charm to me."

Andvari laughed. "I almost forgot about that. Yes, from what the notebook said, that's how you make a charm."

"Is there a difference between a charm and an enchanted object?" Frida set all the necklaces down but one. Holding it up, she cast a spell on it. "There. Now it'll allow you to see in any conditions. Dark or fog, even blinding light, it won't matter."

"From what we've learned, enchanted objects are done with modern spells. The enchantment is on them. They can last a few hours to almost a lifetime. Charms are where Aili will put the magic into the object, making it a part of the object. It'll last until the magic is used up. For a powerful object, if she loops it in with magic around her, that might never happen," Andvari explained. "As Aili realized earlier, the pins are charms that are tied directly to the planet. They will be active until the planet itself dies, as long as the user can wield Nature Magic."

Aili opened her notebook and flipped to the page she wanted. "Hold this?" Handing Andvari the notebook, she cradled a necklace between her palms. "Now for the only part I've never really done before," she muttered under her breath. She read the instructions one more time, all the way through.

"Is there anything you want to ask about before you begin?" Kyson offered. "You do have access to an impressive amount of experience and knowledge standing around you."

Pressing her palms against the necklace, she felt the crystal and the sharp ridges at the corners. "I've only ever used magic to influence a thing. I've never used it to have the thing do a thing, I don't think. Is it different?"

"It's a bit like making a potion," Gavi offered. "Your focus and intent change from the potion itself to the intent or effect you want."

Aili looked over at Frida. "You just enchanted that necklace."

"She used the same spell I put on you to shield your eyes when lightning got stuck in you," Kyson commented. "The same spell, but a different focus."

"When I use a spell on someone, I focus on them. When I enchant a thing, I focus on both the thing and the space around it. For jewellery, focus on the part that touches the user. For sunshades, I focus on the back of the lenses they look through." Frida turned the necklace in Aili's hands and pointed at the back. "This surface and the chain."

"Try an enchantment we can test first," Andvari suggested. "How about a shield? You're good with those."

CHAPTER 32

A ili dropped to the ground and crossed her legs. "That's a good idea. After all, I want to make a shield against the Darkness. Okay, a general purpose barrier—" Aili felt the back of the necklace with her thumbs. "Here goes nothing."

Cradling the necklace in her hands, Aili concentrated on the barrier magic. Okay, pour it into the object. Now extend the effect. Tie it to nature and let the magic around it power the spell. Aili smiled as the necklace glowed faintly, a green just like her barriers. When the glow died down, she held it up.

"That should have worked if I did it right? I guess? How do we test it? What happens if I did it wrong?" She held the necklace out to Andvari.

"If you did it wrong, this is going to sting. Kyson, stun me." Andvari draped the chain around his neck, letting the necklace fall against his chest.

Gavi wrapped an arm around Aili's shoulders and pulled her back. Everyone else moved away as well. Aili watched, hands pressed over her mouth, as Kyson strode across from Andvari.

Kyson raised his hand. The magic shot towards Andvari, visible to her magical senses. Her nerves buzzed. Andvari stood still, his hands held out a little, smiling. The spell hit him and fizzled out, gone. He took the necklace off.

"I didn't feel a thing. One thing we need to adjust, though. Nothing passed through the shield at all. Not even the air I needed to breathe. You're used to making shields around people, where there's still plenty of air available. I was holding my breath because I had to." He pocketed the charmed necklace.

"I'll show you how to fix that." Kyson flowed into the link, setting a pattern in her mind. 'See how I alter it here? I know you don't use spells, but if you focus on the effect the alteration has, it should work anyway. Try again.'

Aili took the necklace Gavi offered her. "What do we do with the ones I mess up?"

"We'll focus on undoing the magic later. Try again." Andvari gestured at the necklace she held. "Whenever you're ready."

'Do you want help?' Kyson flowed into the link again.

'Watch that I don't forget anything?'

369

'You got it.'

Aili sat. Kyson came over and stood closer. She focused again, starting at the first step. Everything felt good, so she focused on the effect.

'Make the adjustment here,' he suggested. 'Let them breathe. There. That's it.'

Let air pass for breath, she willed. Protect, but let them live. Now, set the spell to a new source of magic. Aili tied the magic to the flow around it, powering the spell. She stood and offered him the necklace.

Andvari put it on. "I can breathe, so it's better already."

Leaving Aili with Gavi, Kyson moved to where he had a clean shot again. He raised his hand. Aili took a step back, bumping into Gavi. She scooted behind him, peering out from under his arm. The spell hit. Andvari smiled.

"Excellent. Now a gas attack." Andvari nodded.

"Gas attack?" Aili stared with wide eyes.

"Air Mage thing." Frida smiled. "We can displace oxygen in your lungs until you pass out or disperse a chemical agent in the air you breathe. It can distract you, letting us take you into custody."

"You've seen us do it in the healing centre to help people." Gavi wrapped an arm around her. "We've even given potions as a mist directly into the lungs."

"Right," she whispered. Niru did that to help Gavi a few times after she regrew part of his lung for him. "Doesn't it hurt?"

"Not for healing. Not if it's done right." Gavi rubbed her shoulder.

Kyson shot a spell at Andvari. Aili examined it as it sped towards him. What was he doing? She'd never seen that one before. Andvari stood calmly as the spell covered him, his hands on his hips. He didn't react, aside from the smile stretching across his face.

"You did it." He beamed at her. Taking the necklace off, he held it up. "I wouldn't be able to eat or drink with it on, but it's combat worthy. I would give it to someone I was trying to protect for an escort mission. We'll keep this one for the Scouts to use."

A thought flitted through her head. "It'll block the user's magic, too, won't it? If they were wearing it, they couldn't cast spells?"

"Right," he confirmed. "You'll need to tailer each one to the person you intend to wear it, so their magic can go through. For a general shield, anyway. Now you want to create a shield just against Darkness, not magic, so that will be easier."

Aili paced slowly. How would she set that magic? Normally she'd use pure Light Magic. Nothing stops her from trying. It only affects Darkness. There's no way to test it, though. They would wear these into battle, hoping she got it right.

She sat and crossed her legs. Kyson handed her a fresh medallion. Closing her eyes, she called to her Light. Her heart warmed. Mother? Aili smiled at the presence. Together, they shaped the magic, setting it within the necklace.

Opening her eyes, she watched the glow fade. The metal was still warm in her hands. Aili sat still for a few more moments, soaking in the warmth of Light Magic.

"I think I did it." She got to her feet and held it out to him. "I can't test it, though."

He slipped the necklace on. Raising his hand, he called a normal barrier up. The magic shimmered around him. "Everything feels good. I can feel the warmth in it, like being with you in the link."

"You're not worried that we can't test it?" Aili crossed her arms.

Andvari shook his head. "I can feel this necklace is different. I trust you. Besides, I'm still going to avoid touching Darkness if I can. I'm not just going to walk into it just to test this. This is just one more defence for me in case I can't avoid Darkness. How many would you like to make?"

"Kyson will need one for sure. Being around me, he's more likely than other Scouts to see Darkness." Aili tapped her chin. "I want at least one for the healers, and anyone else who cleanses Darkness. Umm—"

"How many can you make and not get tired?" Andvari took the medallion off and handed it to Kyson, who examined it.

"If I get to snack while I do it, as many as we want. Mother helped." Aili kept her gaze down. Gavi didn't know, did he? About her mother? She wasn't about to look at the CDF.

"Can you put an invisibility charm on one of these?" Kyson asked.

Aili grinned. "Easy."

"Hang on. We can't even detect her if she's invisible. Are you sure you want something like that out there?" Theron asked. "If it does fall into the wrong hands, that could be a problem."

"That's a good point." Gavi took another empty necklace from the pile and handed it to her. "Consider what kind of magic you want loose in the world. Don't make things just to see if you can. You never know who will get a hold of it."

Aili took the offered necklace. She stood on tiptoe and whispered in his ear.

Gavi smiled widely. "I think that's exactly the kind of magic you want out there. Yes, I can help you with that spell. We'll save a few for that. Do the shields first."

Settling on the grass, Aili took a few deep breaths. She accepted the first offered necklace and held it in her lap. Infusing it with magic, she handed it off and took another. After a handful of necklaces, Aili's stomach rumbled.

Andvari gave her a meal bar. "Eat before you do anything else."

She took the bar and devoured it. Kyson handed her another. It was gone just as quickly. Andvari handed Theron and Frida each a necklace before tucking the rest in a pocket.

Gavi sat in front of her. He placed three necklaces on the grass between them. Reaching out, Gavi took Aili's hand. She let him in, inviting his magic to blend with her abilities.

'Pain relief or inflammation reduction?' She worried her lower lip between her teeth.

'Why not both?'

Aili grinned. 'Both is good.'

Now, how to set the magic? She picked up one of the necklaces. Focusing inside, Aili let her inner light shine. Let this soothe and heal and mend. Let it make the body strong. Whoever wears it will find peace and strength.

Tapping into the patterns Gavi shared, Aili set her intention in the necklace. She pressed the magic into the metal and crystal, tying it deep into the natural magic around her. She opened her eyes. The necklace still glowed strong in her senses.

"That was incredible. May I see it?" Gavi held his hand out.

"Of course." She passed the necklace to him.

Andvari handed her another snack bar. Aili wolfed it down as Gavi examined the necklace, casting sensing spells on it.

Gavi smiled and nodded. "This will do nicely. May I try it on?"

Aili grinned. "Absolutely. If they all work, you can take the other two up north."

He eased the chain over his head and let the medallion rest on his chest. Aili felt the stir of magic around her as the charm activated.

Gavi raised an eyebrow. "Can you do the others just like this?" He pulled the necklace off and set it beside his foot.

"Sure." She picked up the next necklace. Something didn't feel right, though. "Can you join me again? Something about your presence helps me organize such complex magic."

He took her offered hand without hesitation. "Of course."

The moment he held her hand, her focus settled on the patterns. Having done one, the last two went swiftly and smoothly. So, when using Light, she was strong alone, but when dealing with other kinds of magic, having someone linked helped her? Interesting.

Gavi tucked the two new charms into his pocket. "I appreciate this."

"I wonder if it matters who I link with? Linking helps." Aili rubbed her cheek.

Andvari took his cloak pin off and set it in her hand. "Let's find out."

His presence in the link was strong, as always. Aili focused like she did with Gavi, using Andvari's stability and steady nature to ground herself. The magic settled in the pin, staying with ease. Aili released the magic, tying it to nature instead of herself. This should outlast him, even if he lived a long life. Hopefully, he would.

Gavi took the pin and examined it, casting a few spells. "That's impressive, young lady. Do you think it's stronger because it's his pin, he was the one in the link with you, or you're both connected like family?"

"Ilia is family, too," Aili reminded him. "The pin feels like him. It's like a trace of him is in it, like it absorbed a bit of his magic just being around him for so long. The necklaces don't have that, so maybe that's it?"

"If you don't mind later, once we've dealt with everything, we can make more healing charms for the other camps. We can experiment a bit and see if having different people affects the charm." Gavi handed the cloak pin back to Andvari. "Cherish that. It will heal nearly anything."

Andvari took the pin, holding it tenderly between his fingers. He traced the edge with his thumb. "It's your magic. What would you like to do with it?"

Aili smiled widely. "It's yours. I want you safe. Wear it." She picked up the first healing charm she had made. "I need to go give this to someone."

"Get a snack when you're done if you need," Andvari called after her as she dashed back to camp.

She waved back at him as she ran for the building. Where would Ilia be? Wherever there was tea and warmth. Heading inside, Aili went straight to the smaller lounge.

Ilia was inside, resting in the big armchair by the fireplace. A fire crystal glowed beside her, warming the room. Her steaming cup of tea sat on the table beside her, within easy reach. A soft wool blanket was draped over her legs.

"You look happy." Ilia waved her over.

Aili bounced across the room and sat in the closest chair. "I have something for you." She held the charm out.

Ilia smiled and took the offered charm. "You're a quick study."

"I had good reason." Aili grinned. "I hope it helps."

Holding the charm to her chest, Ilia closed her eyes. "Your magic is so like mother's. Yes, this will help." A tear rolled down her cheek. "This will help when nothing else does." She placed the chain around her neck, tucking the medallion right against her skin under her shirt.

"I'm so glad. Gavi has the others, but I made that one specifically for you."

"Thank you, child."

"The magic isn't interfering, is it?" Aili tapped her wrist.

Ilia shook her head, her hand going to the dragon scale bracelet under her sleeve. "No. Your magic and hers are of the same nature. It feels like a blending of powers. Different, but alike. It's not a surprise, since mother made you both."

"My magic is like the dragons?"

Ilia nodded. "Mine was more so than most mages, but yours is even closer to hers than I've ever seen. None of our sisters' magic was quite like yours, either."

"Aili, meeting rooms." Kyson poked his head through the doorway. "How're you feeling?" he asked Ilia.

"I'm well, thank you. I appreciate the extra blanket, but I might not need it much longer." Ilia winked at Aili.

"I'll see you soon." Aili got up and followed Kyson.

CHAPTER 33

"I don't feel it nearby." Aili stared down at the map again. The mark was just up ahead. She looked out over the valley. "Are you sure it's here?" She could see the line of sick trees, see where they led, but something didn't feel right.

"Certain." Kyson pulled his compass out. Holding it to the map, he tapped his finger against the shiny surface. The mark on the map glowed. "Right there, according to their coordinates found in the journals. That's if they were decoded right, and we don't doubt they were."

"Could they have been left to throw us off their trail? Take us in the wrong direction?" Aili squinted as she peered through the trees. "I don't detect any magic hiding things. Especially nothing strong like at the vaults or ruins."

"Maybe we're still too far away. I'll get us closer." Andvari steered the wagon down the hill, rolling between the trees on the smoothest path.

"I can get us there faster," Kyson offered.

"No." Aili narrowed her eyes at him. "I'd rather get there alive than fast."

"That's the attitude, little sis." Hana bumped her fist lightly against Aili's shoulder. "Besides, even with Dax driving, they'd never keep up." She waved at the wagon behind them.

Jeril waved back from the control seat. He gave the signal that all was well, tipping his hand up.

"He can't be that bad." Frida raised her eyebrow.

"Depends on who you ask," Aili admitted. "And how big a thrill seeker you are. Do you use wagons much in the city?"

Theron shared a look with Frida, the corners of his lips turning up. "Not often. We tend to walk everywhere unless we're doing a prisoner transport. With the packed streets, we don't ever go fast. Imagine how it would look if we ran over someone? How can we enforce the law if we break it?"

"Yes, Kyson, how can we enforce the law if we break it?" Aili stared at him. "Surely there are laws on the roads out here, too?"

Andvari laughed. He glanced over his shoulder at them before turning his attention back to steering. "There are on the roads, but in emergencies, we can break the laws in certain ways. Also, once we leave the roads and are on uncultivated land, there are no laws for how we drive."

"He never told you?" Hana leaned back against the wagon side and stretched. "Most wagons made for the public have speed limiters and load limits for safety. They're not capable of doing half the things our wagons can do."

Theron chuckled. "Even our city wagons can't match yours. We have no need for speedy offroad travel. When tracking fugitives outside the city, we call the Scouts."

Aili gripped the wagon side as it tilted more, heading down a steep slope.

"Well, almost always." Frida smiled at her. "We managed on our own when we were chasing you."

Aili looked up at Kyson across from her.

"According to the rules, if they were looking for a Scout, they'd go through official channels to get our help. Since you were running alone in the forest, and only a student, they chose to find you first." He reached over and bumped his fist against hers. "A win for Scout skills."

"There." Aili spun and got to her knees, pointing ahead. "I feel it now. It's like the power collected in the valley, and it couldn't spill out for me to sense."

"Guide me closer." Andvari patted the control seat beside him. He slowed the wagon and levelled it out at the bottom of the steep bit.

Aili scrambled over the seat and perched beside him. Closing her eyes, she opened herself to the forest. "Over there, among the rocks. Of course, more rocks." She shared what she sensed in the link.

Andvari guided the wagon closer, staying behind thick bushes and out of sight. He stopped the wagon behind another rocky outcrop. "We'll park here and check it out. Any sentries?"

"Right at the cave," she confirmed. "Two at the entrance. I don't feel much of anything deeper yet. There is some kind of shield I don't recognize."

Dax pulled the second wagon over, and the group gathered. The Scouts cast silencing and camouflage spells on everyone.

"Slow and steady. We'll move forward in small groups," Andvari instructed, his voice low.

He gave a series of hand signals. She recognized the first set. The CDF nodded after the second set. Everyone split into their groups. Kyson looked them all over and nodded. He gave the ready signal.

Andvari headed down the hill, leading the first group. Aili stayed behind him, only a pace back, as he slipped between bushes. The spells would allow the CDF to follow, even in denser brush like this. Did they have silencing spells, too? What might they look like?

'I'll have them show you later. Focus.' He was calm in the link, not angry or upset, but there was a slight edge to his voice all the same.

Sticking close, they crept down to a thicker cluster of bushes near the rocks. She glanced at him. They rarely came this close to sentries to make plans. He gave the hand signals for traps. Closing her eyes to focus better, she reached out. Aili shook her head as she opened her eyes. He nodded.

He held two fingers up and pointed. Theron nodded. He gave a swift set of hand signals to Frida and Rylor. She didn't understand them at all. Were they going after the sentries? They snuck off, around the bushes and closer to the sentries. How often did they sneak in cities?

'Still only the two sentries I feel. I don't feel anyone inside yet.'

Andvari nodded. 'Watch closely. You won't often get to see this.'

She peeked through the bushes. Magic burst in front of the sentries. Stunning spells went off. The sentries dropped. The CDF were out and converging on them so fast she almost missed it all. Was that the same spell he once tried on her in training? If that was it at full strength, she was grateful he went easy on her that time.

They had restraints on the sentries and dragged them back into the bushes. Theron waved for Andvari to come down.

She stayed close, still scanning for threats. As they approached, she finally saw the cave entrance.

Andvari gave the signal to scan. Aili tucked right against the rock and opened herself, reaching into the cave. Ignoring the others also scanning with spells, she focused deep.

'There are traps, locks, and things I want to look closer at.' She let him look through the link.

Andvari nodded. He signalled the rest of the groups down. All Aili saw was the occasional flicker of movement between bushes as the Scouts and the rest of the CDF came down the valley side. They emerged from the brush and gathered. Everyone huddled close.

"We're going in. There are some traps and locked tunnels. The next pair of people are behind one of the locks. They might know we're coming. Follow my group. We know the way." He also gave hand signals as he talked, so the Scouts behind the CDF didn't have to strain to hear.

He gave another series of signals. Aili nodded and moved closer to Kyson. They would take Theron and Dax down the tunnel she most wanted to investigate. Andvari would take Vinnia, Frida, and Hana down another branch, and the remaining groups would check the last branch and stand as sentries.

Aili stayed near Kyson, watching ahead with open senses. She pointed each trap out as he went, giving him a chance to disable them. He stopped at one point and pulled her closer. Kyson pointed at the wall. She examined it carefully, feeling ripples she couldn't identify. He gave the signal for trap. Aili nodded. She knew she wasn't perfect. That's why an experienced Scout was leading.

They took the first branch, heading towards the closest magical lock. She didn't feel anymore traps, but she missed that other one.

'There.' Aili shared the lock in the link, showing its exact location.

'Look closer?' He stopped, waiting, watching through the link.

Aili investigated the magic, looking for any pattern. Kyson directed her attention a few times, checking certain parts of the magic.

'Hey, partner.' Kyson nudged Andvari in the link. 'I think I've figured this one out. Have a look here, though.'

Andvari slipped fully into the link. 'Yes, it's a locked barrier. Unlock it to disable it. Our standard spell might not work because of this.' He directed their attention into a specific part of the pattern.

'Stop,' Aili insisted. 'You have a barrier in front of you, too. Don't touch it.'

Andvari glowed, like a smile or hug. 'Thanks. Any others we can't see?'

She spread her senses around, covering as much of the tunnels as she could. 'Not that I feel. Just whatever is down this way, and a few scattered traps.'

'Aili, are the locked barriers the same?' Kyson asked. He cast a sensing spell over the barrier.

She really had to focus to feel the barrier near Andvari. 'I think so? They feel it, but I'm not near that one. I'd say yes, probably.'

'Hana informs me a grandmaster revealing spell will show the entire pattern,' Andvari shared. 'Aili, is there any taint or Nature Magic in these barriers?'

'No. I'm certain. It's a normal spell, though an incredibly complex one.'

'Kyson, Frida says Theron can cast the reveal spell, if you're not confident.'

'Thanks, partner.' Kyson turned to Theron and gave a couple of quick hand signals.

Kyson pulled Aili back against the tunnel wall. Theron squeezed past them. Aili pointed at its exact location, and the massive man nodded.

'When it comes down, have Aili shield you all. I barely got this one up in time. There's a built-in tracker if it touches you,' Andvari warned.

Kyson let Dax know what was going on with hand signals before warning Theron about the tracker. Aili prepared a barrier. Once she nodded, Kyson gave the signal. Her barrier snapped into place, a full sphere to shelter them fully. She focused, letting Theron's magic through.

He snipped at the pattern of magical threads with a spell she'd only read about. He snipped a thread, and a tidal wave of magic rushed towards them. Aili held her shield in place, bracing against the force. She waited until the wave of magic faded completely before relaxing and releasing her magic.

'I think it's done.' Aili let out a breath.

Kyson nodded. 'How about you, partner? Everything alright?'

'Yes. There's nothing else magical in here. Be careful and don't let anything happen to her. We're on our way to help.'

'I'll guard her with my life,' Kyson assured him, his inner voice like steel.

'Who just saved whom from magic?' Aili raised her eyebrow at Kyson.

Andvari laughed in the link. 'Guard him, too. He needs you as much as you need him.'

Aili smiled, warming the link. 'I will. After all, one day I want to see him doing paperwork, and I can't if he's dead or captured, can I?'

Andvari laughed again. 'Focus. Keep me informed.'

Kyson took the lead, Aili right behind him. Theron followed, with Dax watching their backs. She kept her senses ahead. Somewhere, there were still people ahead. There.

'Two guards.' Aili shared their location with him.

Kyson turned and gave signals to Theron, who nodded. It wasn't until he informed Dax as well that Aili understood. No, most Scouts take years to learn them all. I have time.

'Especially with the link to help while you do,' Kyson reminded. 'We'll keep working on it. On my count, we burst in silently and subdue them. You and Dax wait in the tunnel until we're done. Listen to him and follow his lead.' Kyson signalled, asking if she understood.

Aili signalled back with a yes. She wiggled back behind Theron, next to Dax. Kyson counted down on fingers. When his last finger fell, he and Theron charged around the corner. Their boots were silent, the spell working fully.

Keeping her awareness locked on them, Aili watched from where she crouched beside Dax. Theron had one guard down almost before she could blink. Kyson's spell bounced off a hastily made barrier. That was the mage who set the lock spells. They were in for a fight.

His magic bounced around the chamber, ricocheting off every solid surface. Aili snapped up barriers around her friends. Knowing Kyson's magic, she let his through right away. It took a moment to tune into Theron's magic and let it through, but she managed swiftly.

'Well done. You've never protected anyone like that who you haven't linked with before.' Andvari kept his presence quiet in the link, letting her focus. 'We'll be there in moments.'

She turned her focus back to the mage. His defences must have a weakness somewhere. There. Now, could she exploit it? Aili reached for him, but he crumpled to the ground. Kyson saw the weakness through the link and got him while Theron had the man's attention.

'Thanks for that.' Kyson let out a breath. 'Come on in. It's safe.'

Aili gave the hand signal to Dax, who nodded. They came around the corner. Stepping closer, Aili examined the guards. They weren't dressed alike. Their equipment didn't match. This wasn't an organized group. Who were they?

A box in the corner caught her attention. Two torches flanked it, each in a metal bracket on the wall. Both burned with a magical flame. No heat or smoke came from them, just light. Light, and a touch of taint. The box radiated tainted magic.

"Don't touch that," she whispered, pointing at the box.

CHAPTER 34

Kyson snapped magical cuffs onto the guard he subdued. Theron restrained the other guard. Both men nodded.

Andvari led his group into the room, quick and silent. "Vinnia, you and Dax watch over them." He pointed at the restrained men. "The others are outside, watching over our other guests," he explained to Aili.

Dax signalled and moved over to one of the mages. He dragged the man against the wall, near the second one. The guard stirred, though the other slept deep under the stunning spell.

"It's in there?" Andvari stood over the box, his hands on his hips.

Aili stared down at the black cloth draped over most of the box. "The cloth shields it a bit, but it's like they've never seen a shielding cloth before. Maybe they don't know how to make one?"

Kyson knelt beside the box and cast a spell on the cloth. "They probably don't. The Scouts developed the original spell. We shared it with the CDF groups. This one is a variant on how the university does them, and despite the mage's power, there's little skill in it."

She rubbed her cheek. "Then they really don't know what they're doing," she almost whispered.

"It's possible they were taught how by someone who was in the research department at the university." Andvari cast his own sensing spell. "They missed a few vital points in the spell and focused on some spots we don't usually."

Alii followed Frida in her senses as the woman walked over and cast a sensing spell. Her spell was different, though related. She'd have to ask about it later.

Andvari opened the lid with one finger. The power of the pin reached for her, tugging at her essence, like a wind spout trying to gather leaves. Aili gripped his sleeve and tethered herself directly to the rock beneath her. She watched a torch flame, keeping her focus away from the pin.

"Are you alright?" Andvari added a touch of magic to her tether.

"Yeah, thanks. It's real." Aili took a deep breath. His magic added to hers gave her the stability she needed.

Kyson wrapped the pin in a cloth and tucked it into a small box. The box glowed with magic to her senses.

"I said, stay still." Vinnia raised a hand as she glared at one of the captives.

He glared back and opened his mouth to speak.

"Solensum," she whispered, pointing at him.

The captive went silent, his eyes closed, and he went still. The other mage stirred and looked over before staring up at her with wide eyes.

"That'll make the trip more pleasant. You, too?" She pinned the second man with a glare.

He closed his eyes for a long moment and stayed still. When he opened his eyes again, he stared up at the ceiling.

Aili turned to Andvari, eyebrow raised.

'A quiet prisoner is a safe prisoner. They're quicker to use stasis than us, but it's within the rules. It does work,' Andvari explained.

'Why the difference?' She watched as Dax got the one prisoner up and on his feet.

'It's safer for us to walk prisoners to wagons, because we have farther to go over uneven ground. We escort them carefully and only levitate when we have to. They take people shorter distances over smooth roads. If we trip and lose control, the person in our custody could be hurt badly.' Andvari tucked the box Kyson offered him in his pocket. "Anything else interesting?"

Frida gathered some papers from a dark corner. "These might be. We can analyze them when we're back." She tucked the papers in her cloak. "These have the best pockets. It's incredible."

Hana laughed. "Yeah, we might carry evidence over long distances, so the weightless charm is a real boon. Expanding pockets are one of our most useful tools."

"What's the limit?" Frida stuffed her hand in the pocket, her arm disappearing to her shoulder.

"The whole cloak can only hold a few dozen pounds between all the pockets, and the items need to fit into the pocket opening." Hana took Dax's prisoner by the other arm. "Nice and slow now. Quietly."

Aili watched Hana escort the man out, Dax right behind them. She turned her gaze slowly around the room.

"What's on your mind?" Andvari laid his hand over her shoulder.

"That's all four pins. We did it. Now what?" Are the eggs safe? What about the taint? Someone was still behind this all.

"We go back and talk to Ilia. She still has a part to play in all this. Her powers are easily equal to yours, right?" He wrapped his arm around her and walked her back down the tunnel.

Aili smiled when she saw the sun again. Someone had brought the wagons down to the entrance and parked them just outside. They were loading the prisoners in the back and securing them in place. Vinnia stayed beside one, and Rylor sat with the silenced prisoner.

"Come ride up with me," Andvari offered. "It's your choice."

She smiled, following him to the control seat. The other Scouts were loading a few boxes into the wagons, no doubt found down the other tunnels. She climbed up beside him and stared back up the valley side.

The ride back was smooth and uneventful. She was grateful to be here with him, where she had room to stretch her legs and wiggle. Nobody complained about the crowding, though. Even the prisoner sat quietly, his gaze down at his lap. Mind you, if she had one of the CDF watching her like that, she'd be keeping to herself, too.

She spotted the camp through the trees and smiled. Andvari guided the wagon right to the storage doors. Why?

'In these small camps, we keep those in custody in part of the storage area,' Kyson explained. 'Same with injured animals we're treating, if they're too large to keep in our rooms.'

Frida leapt from the wagon and strode over. "Andvari, we need to talk now."

He nodded. "Kyson?"

"I'll see to it." Kyson leapt from the back and gestured to the Scouts guarding the prisoners.

Frida and Andvari headed away from the wagons. Aili hesitated. Should she help Kyson or go with Andvari?

"You can come," Frida waved her over.

She darted over, catching up as they neared the edge of camp.

He stopped just inside the barrier and set a privacy spell. "What do you need?"

Frida pulled the papers out and flipped to a page. She held it out to him. "We found our leak. Our traitor."

Andvari took the page and scanned it. He frowned deeply. "How do you want to deal with this? We'll support you fully."

"Who is it?" Aili whispered.

"Horgin." Frida crossed her arms over her chest.

Aili glanced back at the main building. Nobody was in sight, and her senses couldn't pick someone out like that. There were too many people moving around after the mission.

"I need to inform the others. We can surround him and subdue him. He's smart, so he might notice us getting ready." Frida kicked a rock, sending it through the barrier.

"He just did." Aili pointed to where someone was peeking out around the building. "I can't think of anyone else who would spy like that. Yeah, he's running." Aili looked up to Andvari.

"He won't get far. We can track him, no matter where he goes. I'll gather a team. Get your people ready and meet on the training grounds." Andvari dropped the barrier and jogged back to the building.

Aili had to run to keep up, Frida keeping pace beside her. Something seemed off about the spot she spied him at, so she stopped. Andvari turned and stopped, waiting.

Scanning the spot, Aili opened herself. "It's not Darkness, but more like a memory of it? Like he crossed its shadow or something? He's not tainted, but was close to someone who was."

Andvari cast a spell. "He can't get anywhere without leaving a trace. If he hides his tracks with magic, we can follow him. He shouldn't be able to hide his physical track. Let's get everyone and get out there. Keep an eye on him. He went that way." Andvari pointed through the trees.

Aili opened herself, touching the forest directly. His trail led through the trees, standing out to her because of the odd magic in it. She followed it to another spot along the edge of camp.

"I'll get the others." Frida ran to the hall and up the stairs.

'Kyson, it's Horgin. He ran off. We have his trail. Gather everyone not on guard duty and get them organized. Meet outside.' Andvari followed Aili to the barrier.

'Done.' Kyson faded from the link, his focus elsewhere.

"There's something else we can do." Andvari snapped his fingers.

A trail of footprints headed off into the trees, shining bright silver. It headed off into the bushes, easy to follow for anyone.

"You've never shown me that before." Aili nudged his shoulder.

"It's not a spell," he explained. "Not like other magic we do. When we loan clothing to people, certain enchantments are added. If someone gets lost, it's easier to find them that way. Most consultants don't have our bushcraft, and they get lost easily."

"Have you ever tracked me this way? Could they have, when I was running from the CDF?" Aili kneeled beside the boot print and touched the edge of the magic. She couldn't feel anything, no spell to assess. It was only a puddle on the ground to her senses, though it had a slight magical glow.

He shook his head. "We don't use it on standard Scout clothing. We're expected to know how to survive in the bush, and we carry mirrors. I always sensed you through our link as student and teacher, and in your link ever since you made it. The only people who could track you were people I gave guardianship of you temporarily."

There had to be something here she could use. Aili crouched and checked again, her hand on the soil beside the boot print. "Wait," she whispered. Aili pressed a hand to her mouth.

"What?" Andvari crouched beside her. He patted a pocket. The magical suppression cuffs clinked.

"There's Nature Magic. It's in the direction he ran. He's not a Nature Mage, so what is it? How did it get there?" She wrinkled her nose. "Why can I feel it now? How did it get so strong so fast? Why not before?"

Andvari slid into the link and looked closer. "I can't even detect it without you. It's in the same direction he went. I bet we'll have our answers soon." Andvari stood and stared down at the boot print. "He stayed to look into something CDF related while we were on the mission. I need to check something. Go get some more snack bars and wait with Kyson."

Aili jogged beside him back to the building. His mind was so focused he didn't even notice. What did Andvari suspect? He would tell her when he had time or knew something. Aili turned her attention to her own task instead.

Had she ever sensed Nature Magic on any of the CDF? Not that she could recall. Aili ran her hand along the wall as she headed for the dining hall. She hadn't felt the pin right away, either. Whoever they were following had some kind of shielding that was messing with her. Could it be the dome where the crystals had been? It was still there, standing empty.

Stuffing pockets full of snack bars, Aili raced back outside. The Scouts and CDF gathered out front, buckling weapons belts in place. Aili charged down the stairs and joined them, her sword still on her back from the mission.

"Took you long enough." Kyson waved her over. He nodded to Theron and spoke in a low voice as she approached. "He'll be here in a moment. Everyone is organized. You're with us." He rested his hand on his sword hilt.

Andvari burst through the doors and down the steps, joining them. "We see the track. You can follow the magic?"

Aili nodded. "So far the tracks lead there."

"Let me know if that changes. Move out, everyone." Andvari headed across the grass and over to the edge of the dome.

She stayed up front with him, her senses open. Andvari and Kyson were partially in the link with her, but mostly

occupied casting sensing spells. Everyone else came behind, spreading out a bit as they also cast magic or tracked
the physical signs.

"It reminds me of the heart of the forest, in a way," Kyson
commented, keeping his voice low.

"Yes, and no," Aili replied. "It's ancient, but this magic
isn't alive. It's the best I can describe it. The heart of the
forest is alive, and almost part of mother in a way the other
forests aren't."

"He's leaving track all over the place, moving fast." Andvari pointed to a bent twig. "He's heading right for it."

Frida sighed. "We don't need to hide like you all practice.
We can blend into crowds and shadows, but we don't train
being hidden. I guess that's to our benefit now, though."

They crossed a sidehill. Aili kept close to the rock face as
they passed under the cliff edge. Vertical rock stretched up
over her, topped with ferns peeking over the edge. They
were getting close. Whatever it was, it was just up ahead.
Aili laid her palm on the rock and felt inside it.

"His tracks disappear." Kyson scanned the area, joining
the others as they spread out.

"There's a cave here." Aili pressed both palms to the rock.
The illusion dissolved, revealing a narrow cave entrance. "I
had to get close to feel it. It's mother's magic. It felt like it

was sleeping." Aili pressed her lips together. 'It felt like the fire vault.'

Kyson moved to her side, wrapping an arm around her. "What's in there?"

Aili reached into the darkness. The tunnel curved around and headed down. "It goes deep. There's a cavern at the far end." She invited them in the link to look. "I don't feel any traps or anything."

Kyson wrapped his fingers around his sword hilt. "We check it out?"

Andvari nodded. "He might be inside. There's no sign he went anywhere else. The track just ends. Our own magic might not work right, if this is a wild place."

"I have to go inside," Aili mumbled. "I know it."

CHAPTER 35

"Go slow and be careful. We're counting on you to sense things we can't. We might not have useable magic inside." Andvari frowned at the cave entrance. He cast a communication spell over the entire group. "Just in case."

Aili stepped into the cave, stopping where the footprints did. "This isn't like the other place. That was a vault. This is more like a meditation room." She took a few more steps. "I think we'll be fine."

Andvari stepped forward, his hands up in front of him. He passed into the tunnel. There was no sign of a barrier. He lowered his hands and smiled. "Take us in."

Kyson snapped his fingers, and a ball of mage-light hovered over him. A dim beam of light shone ahead, just enough to show where the walls were as they curved. Aili headed down the tunnel, her senses a better guide than the light. If he was waiting, they didn't want him to see them coming.

The ball of light passed her, stopping a few feet in front of her. It moved when she did and stopped with her. Aili grinned and turned to Kyson. 'New spell?'

He chuckled. 'You bet. Since we spend more time underground with you than I have in all the rest of my life, I thought it was a good idea. Besides, this one was fun to work on.'

She shook her head as she followed the winding path down. Occasionally it turned and headed back the other way, but always down. She stopped at a sharp bend.

'He's just up ahead. I don't feel any traps. I'm not sure he can set any right now. Something feels odd about him.'

'Odd how? Show me.' Andvari rested a hand on her back, strengthening their connection. "He's tainted. Know where we felt that before?"'

"The vaults," Kyson muttered. "It's him."

"Tainted how?" Frida moved closer, keeping her voice as quiet as she could. "That explains why he didn't want a protective charm. Drew back from it when I tried to give it to him." She touched the charm hanging around her neck.

"It's not normal taint, though." Aili rubbed her chin. "It's like he's been so tainted he's changed inside. How could I not sense it?"

"Maybe it got worse when we were on our last mission?" Kyson suggested. "We don't know what he was up to while we were gone. He chose to stay back."

"Changed or not, we need to get him. Everyone be careful We don't need anyone else getting contaminated." Frida pulled her baton out and held it ready.

Theron rested a hand on her shoulder. "Do we give him a chance to talk, and give himself up?"

Vinnia shook her head. "He's powerful. Is he likely to? If he has warning, can we even get him in custody peacefully, or will he fight?"

Frida shook her head. "This isn't like him."

Theron rested a hand on her shoulder. "He hasn't been himself since the incident at the university a year ago. I'm not sure what else is going on in his life, but he's not the same man I worked with even five years ago."

"Our best shot at keeping everyone safe is to go in fast and be coordinated. No long or drawn out battles. Aili has a barrier he can't get through. We can help her with it. Once we've got him subdued, you all can make the arrest." Andvari looked at Aili, who nodded.

Kyson pulled his mirror out. Sending a message silently, he activated the magic inside. Kyson winked at Aili. "Let's go get him."

The ball of light magic floated ahead, into the cavern. It floated close to the ceiling. Magic blasted it, a stunning spell, shaking the cavern rock at that spot.

Andvari gave rapid hand signals, sharing the plan. Aili and Kyson shared a look, and they nodded. Placing a hand on her back, Kyson joined with her magic. She shaped a barrier ahead of them as he set more magic behind hers. Andvari slipped his magic into the blend, pulling the shield along their sides a bit.

At Andvari's signal, Aili and Kyson led the group into the cavern. Horgin stood across the cavern, near another tunnel. His hand was raised, magic gathering on his fingertips. His eyes were black. Something dripped from him, a black oily mess pooling on the floor beneath him.

Magic burst from his hand towards them. Aili adjusted the shield, strengthening where it would hit. His magic hit her shield. The Darkness was pulled into her Light layer, and the rest of the magic ricocheted away.

"Don't touch any Darkness," she warned.

Another streak of magic sped towards them as they advanced. It spun wide, arcing back at their side. Aili and Andvari pulled their shield around. Kyson grabbed Frida and pulled her deeper behind the shield. Darkness splattered against the newly placed shield.

"Thanks for that," Frida whispered, as she clung to his sleeve for a moment.

Another burst of magic hit the rock beside them. Aili adjusted the shield, but the Darkness was faster. Kyson threw himself between the liquid and Hana. Darkness hit his hand, and he hissed in pain.

His necklace charm glowed. The Darkness dropped from his skin, landing as water on the floor by his feet. His hand had angry red patches where the liquid struck him. Tucking in behind her shield, he examined his hand.

"Let me see," Frida demanded. She grabbed his hand and hauled him closer.

Her heart pounded as she focused on Horgin. Emotions flooded the link, hers and theirs. Nobody else could get hit. Her charm worked, but would it work a second time? Aili stood still, holding the shield. With her not moving, she could extend it over them more.

"You're clean," Frida declared. She let his hand go and turned back to the threat.

Kyson let out a breath. "It stings, but I'll be fine."

"Anything in your healing kit for that?" Andvari asked.

"The cure-all, maybe." She kept her hands up, holding the barrier while their attention was elsewhere. "Top row, third vial from the left."

Kyson eased the kit up from around her neck by the little cord it hung on. Andvari helped her with the barrier as Kyson opened the kit. Dabbing some cure-all on his wound, he returned the vial and closed the kit.

Horgin eyed the tunnel. He charged away from them, towards the opening. Andvari snapped a barrier up over the tunnel end. Horgin hit the barrier and bounced off, landing on the floor. His body went limp, as if something had happened to his bones. What? Still, this was her chance.

She raised a dome around him, dropping their shield instead. Layering the Light thickly around him, Aili poured her entire attention into holding him in the globe. He shrieked and writhed, his magic blasting from his body wildly. Her shield cracked. Aili poured more light in, but her shield shook and vibrated with the force of his magic.

'Here.' Andvari added his magic, holding hers together.

His focus steadied hers. She strengthened her shield against the sparks, flames, and Darkness flying around inside.

Frida, Theron, Rilor, and Vinnia gathered around the bubble. They raised their hands, ready. The Scouts formed a second circle around them, giving the CDF space.

Black smoke filled her shield. Sparks glowed purple inside, barely visible through the smoke. A bolt of lightning struck. Sweat beaded on her forehead as she held her barrier in place.

"He's going to hurt himself," Aili whispered.

"What would happen if you dropped the shield?" Andvari reminded her. "What would that do to us?"

She nodded, a tear rolling down her cheek. "Better him than us."

Kyson gave a couple of quick hand signals to Frida, who nodded. Frida's magic joined theirs, with Kyson's help.

'Let our spell through,' Kyson requested.

Kyson's magic could already pass, so Aili tuned into Frida's energy. Andvari kept their shield up for her as she made space for Frida's magic to pass. The instant their spell was ready, she let it through, adding Light Magic to the mix.

Their spell blanketed inside of the barrier. The lightning and sparks stopped. Nobody moved or spoke. Everyone stared at the barrier as the smoke settled. Was he alive? Was he human? She was done with spirits, thanks. The last one was bad enough.

Something charred and blackened lay under the bubble. It twitched. A thin black arm stretched out, ooze dripping from it. A misshapen hand braced against the stone; long fingers spread over the ground. A head rose, two red eyes staring at Aili.

"What is that?" Vinnia's hand shook as she pointed at the thing. "What happened to him?"

Dax wrapped his arms around Vinnia and pulled her back. He hugged her, turning her away from it. Tears flowed freely down her cheeks.

"Aili, can you let a sensing spell through?" Frida asked. Her voice trembled.

"No need," Andvari assured her. "We'll let you see through her senses." He squeezed Aili's shoulder lightly. "Deep assessment. We need to know what we're dealing with."

He's scared too. Even Kyson gave off fear vibes. Had she ever felt him this anxious? Yes, but only when she was in mortal danger. I guess I'm not the only one who's never seen—whatever that is; she thought to herself. Aili nodded.

The thing flopped back, the sleep spell finally taking hold of it. Aili left the barrier to Andvari as she sank into her own Light for a moment. Covering herself fully, every bit of her essence, she reached for the creature.

The instant her Light-wrapped senses touched it, the creature dissolved. A withered old man lay there, barely more than a skeleton with skin. His hair was completely white, and he was pale, as if there was no blood left.

His chest rose and fell with each shallow breath. She scanned him like any other patient, starting with his vital systems. His brain was shutting down, the electrical activity more erratic with each moment. His heart slowed. Even his breathing grew shallower. He didn't have any magic left in his body anywhere.

"I don't see Darkness. Is he safe to touch?" Frida gripped Kyson's hand.

"He should be? Don't kneel in that." Aili pointed at the sludge around his body.

Andvari let the barrier go. Without magic, there was no threat left. He probably couldn't even raise his finger anymore. Aili stood frozen in place. She couldn't do anything for him. With all her abilities, there was no way she could help.

Frida and Theron knelt beside him, keeping clear of the sludge. Dax guided Vinnia towards the cave entrance, blocking her view. Did Vinnia just whisper something about a mentor? Was he hers from many years ago? How would she feel if that were Andvari lying there?

Pulling herself from her heart-breaking thoughts, Aili kneeled beside the pool of Darkness. Doing something was better than standing around. She examined the sludge. His magic was inside it, trapped and quiet.

Forming a Light bubble, Aili rolled it into the Darkness. It pulled the Darkness in, trapping and dissolving it. She kept her focus until every bit of Darkness was gone. Only a clear liquid remained.

"Water?" Aili narrowed her eyes at it.

"Let me see." Jeril crouched beside her. He held his hand over it and cast a few spells. "Yes, it's just water. It has all the usual minerals I'd expect to find in an underground spring."

Canvas rattled and buckles tightened. Aili looked up at the noise. They were wrapping Horgin in a bag and fastening it closed. The cloth shimmered with magic. She pressed her hand to her mouth. Did the CDF carry those like the Scouts carried tools?

Kyson knelt beside her and wrapped her in a firm hug. "You didn't do that. It's not your fault."

"I'm not sure what freaks me out more," Aili admitted. "Whatever just happened, or you not being all tough love on me."

He laughed. "Don't get used to it. This is a one-time thing."

She rested her head against his chest and listened to his steady heartbeat.

Andvari walked over to the other tunnel and dropped his barrier. He glanced back at her. 'It'll be okay. Just breathe. This is scary, so it's normal to feel everything all at once.'

She took a slow breath and let it out. Her friends were all safe. Kyson's hand was already healing, too. Even Vinnia would be okay in time. Vinnia. Aili glanced around. Dax took her out. Did she need help?

"I'll go check on her," Jeril offered.

"Do you have any tablets with you?" Andvari asked. He reached into his pocket, where he kept the herbal calming aids.

Jeril nodded. "I'm stocked up." With a nod to Andvari, he headed back to the entrance.

Aili straightened up and stood, her legs shaking. She could trust any Scout. That's the one thing Andvari was always adamant about. Other than a single incident when Rei was contaminated with Darkness, not even his own fault, Andvari was right. But if both university mages and the CDF could be contaminated, was anyone safe?

When Rei was contaminated, he wasn't like the others, though. Was he aware of it, or fighting it? Even sick as he was, he was trying to do what was right and uphold the law. He didn't hurt her. He could have.

Andvari took her hands. "I've checked as far down the tunnel as I can. Would you help me look deeper?"

Aili nodded. Focusing her thoughts, she let out a slow breath. She sank into her inner lights and sent her awareness out. "I don't see anybody. It's just the cavern and—whatever that is."

Andvari's presence grew strong beside her as they examined the sensation. "Why don't we find out?"

She pulled herself back fully into her body. With her hand still in his, they headed into the tunnel. Aili glanced back. Norial levitated the canvas-wrapped body and headed towards the entrance. No, don't think about it. Focus on the mission. Feel later.

Turning her senses farther into the tunnel, Aili followed the winding path down. Each step in took her deeper into the hillside. Her senses let her feel every inch of rock between her and the sky. Why couldn't missions take her somewhere in the open? She sighed and kept going.

The tunnel straightened out. Kyson's ball of light cast her shadow long on the tunnel floor. The cavern was ahead, and she could see the back wall. The space was small, no bigger than her old bedroom where she grew up.

A well ringed in stone waited in the middle of the space. Aili approached slowly, her senses fixed on it. Peering over the edge, she stared into the depths. Kyson's light didn't reflect off the water surface. It felt like water, anyway. Water, and—

"Darkness," Aili whispered.

Kyson glanced around. "Wait. This isn't—" his words cut short as he brought a hand to his mouth.

Andvari nodded. "I think it is. I think we found a magical wellspring."

"A what?" Aili searched her memory. Didn't Ilia talk about these recently, or was it something she read?

"It's a legend recorded in the Scout archives. Wellsprings hold Nature Magic and bring it up in water, but only in a few special locations. It's old magic, so we can't touch it, but it can still affect us." Andvari stood beside her, his hands on the stone ring. "We can drink it and it's supposed to cure any magical malady."

"This camp was here to guard it, originally." Kyson walked around to the far side of the well. "So the notes say, anyway. Its location was lost with Ethala Minis."

The murky liquid rippled near her. "Did she seal it away? That's pure Nature Magic. Who else might have?"

Andvari shrugged. "Any Nature Mage before her, maybe?"

The water called to her, tugged at her. She leaned closer, watching the ripples form right in front of her. What made it move?

The water rushed up and grabbed her, pulling her down into the well. Her wet hands slipped on the rocks as she grabbed for the edge. Darkness surrounded her. She sank below the surface and plunged into the gloom.

CHAPTER 36

R emember who you are.

Aili clawed at the rocky sides, searching for any hand-hold. Darkness tugged her deeper. Thicker than water, the sludge sucked her down. Each movement took more energy.

No. I'm strong. I can still get out.

Cold filled her. Moving was hard now, each inch taking more effort than before. Heat burst through her, burning her nerves. Raising her face to the light growing distant above her, Aili reached up. Cold shot through her again, freezing her body.

I must get up.

You're alone, a tiny voice whispered.

No, I'm not. I'm never alone.

Where are they then? What happened to that precious link of yours? You're too weak to stand alone. They abandoned you.

Aili grabbed for the rock wall beside her, but the side was smooth now. No, they didn't. They're fighting for me. They always fight for me.

Then where are they?

She clenched her jaw. Why must the voice taunt her? Was it blocking her link with them? If the sludge could do that, was she doomed?

You don't have to fight. Give in. Join us.

Her lungs ached. Which way was up now? How could she tell anymore? Where were they? Her tears flowed, mixing with the sludge.

With us, you'll never be alone. Never forgotten. We won't abandon you.

Her lungs ached. Where was the air she so desperately needed? Which way? Had she finally failed? 'I'm sorry, mother.'

'Aili.' A beam of light shone down on her, thin but strong. The sludge parted, opening a tunnel of pure water. A hand reached down towards her, barely visible in the distance and Darkness. 'Leya's waiting.'

Leya. Her heart hammered in her chest. Energy burst through her. Kicking with all her might, she propelled herself up towards the hand. Still too far!

Wrapping her hand around her sword hilt, she drew the sword. Aili thrust the sword ahead of her. The Light in the blade brightened the well, driving the Darkness down. She could move with ease again, though her muscles ached and her lungs burned. She kicked again, heading up.

'Keep coming. We got you.' Kyson's magic reached down for her, wrapped in another magic. Ilia!

'Grab on, child. We don't have all day.'

Aili's sword broke the surface first. She grabbed the hand and clung to it. Andvari gripped her snugly, pulling up. Magic wrapped around her; a familiar levitation spell infused with Nature Magic. Warmth and Light rushed through her body.

Her skin scraped against the rocky edge of the well. She wiggled over, ignoring the discomfort. Andvari lowered her to the ground, still gripping her hand. She coughed, sending water from her lungs. Her sword clattered against the rock as she let go of it.

"Lay her down. Stay still." Ilia charged over to her side and pressed a hand over her heart.

The aching in her lungs stopped. Each breath came easier. Aili shivered.

"The Darkness is clinging to her, trying to take over. I'll need help." Ilia rested her other hand on Aili's forehead.

"Anything." Andvari kept a hold of her trembling hands.

Aili gripped his hands as hard as she could. His skin burned against hers, but she couldn't feel anything but the heat.

"I can use your link, blasting it open. Once I do, pour every bit of love, care, and healing in her you can. I'll guide the magic. We'll chase it right out of her. Place a crystal on her throat, against her skin," Ilia ordered. "She can't do this alone, but she doesn't have to."

Kyson squeezed in beside her. He held a crystal to her skin, his other hand on her shoulder. "Ready."

Andvari squeezed her hand. "Ready."

Wait, I can feel it. The warmth in his hands seeped into her, down her wrist and into her arm. Warmth blossomed in her heart. There it was, the love of a friend, mentor, teacher, guide, and father figure.

"Kyson," Andvari urged.

Warmth spread from his hand on her shoulder, down to her heart. "You're going to be fine," he whispered.

The Darkness shivered, fleeing the spreading warmth. Ilia rested a hand on her ankle, her other hand still on Aili's heart. Curling into a ball, the Darkness sped up the channel Ilia held open for it. Her shivering eased as it passed up towards her neck.

Her throat tightened, each breath more effort. Light rushed up through her, pushing the Darkness on. She couldn't get air. Aili opened her mouth and gasped.

"Almost there," Ilia soothed.

A burst of Light flooded her, coming from Ilia. The woman glowed so brightly Aili closed her eyes. The Darkness left her, fleeing into the crystal. She took in a lungful of air and panted.

"Easy, now." Kyson's magic moved air into her lungs and out again. "You'll be fine."

Aili coughed a glob of black sludge from her lungs. It hit the ground beside her. Kyson dropped a cloth over it as Andvari pulled her up to sit. She leaned against his arm as she got her breath back.

"Don't you ever scare us again like that, you hear me?" Kyson snapped.

"Anger is fear on the way out." Ilia patted his shoulder.

Kyson closed his eyes and pinched the bridge of his nose with his fingers.

Aili reached up and touched his arm. "You can't save everyone, but you did save me." Her voice was rough, and it hurt to talk, but at least she was alive.

Kyson took her hand and held it. He smiled at her. "Yeah, we did."

"Why couldn't I feel you, though? I was alone down there." Her voice broke as tears filled her eyes.

"You weren't alone, but the Darkness was so thick, it blocked us for a bit. You held it off long enough for us to push through." Ilia rubbed Aili's shoulder.

"I was about to give up," she whispered. Aili clung to Andvari's arm.

"We all have our limits," Andvari soothed. "You fell right in a source of taint and came out alive. I thought we lost you for good." He hugged her tightly.

"Says the guy about to dive in after her." Kyson raised an eyebrow at Andvari.

"And you would have followed had they not been here." Ilia pointed at Frida and the others.

"What happens now?" Aili took a slow breath, enjoying the clear air.

"Now we cleanse that and protect it." Ilia pointed at the well. "We'll need some help, from both the Scouts and mother."

"Mother?" Aili felt inside, where her inner light still burned strong.

Ilia pulled a box from her shoulder bag. She opened it. All four pins sat on the velvet cushion, the gemstones glimmering in the mage-light.

"I can't control those," Aili admitted.

Ilia shrugged. "You didn't know how. I can help."

"First, I need to make sure you're alright." Frida stopped by Aili's feet and held her hands out. "If I may?"

Kyson stood and stepped back, making room for her. Aili stretched her hands up, staying quiet as Frida kneeled beside her. The woman took her hands and held them. Aili closed her eyes and took a slow breath, allowing the magic to flow through her.

"That was the worst case of contamination I've ever seen anyone come back from." Frida shook her head. "You don't have a spell for that, do you?"

Ilia shrugged. "That is a gift from the source. Only Aili and I carry it."

Frida cupped Aili's cheek in her hand. "I've never seen anything like that. How did you survive?"

Aili smiled and opened her eyes. "I wrapped myself in Light and held onto those I love. I only panicked when I ran out of air."

"With these you should be able to resist the wellspring's call." Ilia touched the little emerald crystals on a pin. "The earth pin should tether you fully and ground you."

"Take as long as you need first," Andvari insisted. He helped her stand, supporting her until her legs steadied.

"We should wait in the sunlight." Ilia closed the box and tucked it back in her shoulder bag. "It'll help you recover."

Kyson offered Ilia his arm. Aili stayed between Andvari and Frida as they all headed for the entrance.

"How did you get there in time to save me?" Aili glanced over her shoulder at Ilia.

The old woman smiled. "Mother called me. I sped over in a wagon right away."

Aili tripped as she turned, her jaw dropping. "You can drive?"

Ilia laughed. "Are you kidding? I was quite the menace on the roads in my twenties. Back then, the laws were changing, so we had wagon races in the forest. I often won, as I went places the others wouldn't dare." She grinned.

Aili smiled widely. Which twenties, though? When someone was as old as Ilia, time was harder to pin down. "Hey, you're moving better."

She wasn't imagining it. Ilia was walking with Kyson, but she wasn't using him for support. She kept up with the group. Her steps had more energy, her feet lifted higher, and her legs swung normally.

Ilia touched the chain around her neck, partially hidden under her robes. "The charm works well."

She couldn't help grinning. Aili hoped it would help, but this was beyond what she had hoped for. Ilia's hands still had some swelling in the joints, but she walked almost normally for a woman in middle age. No wonder she got here so fast.

The sunlight greeted her like an old friend, wrapping her in a hug. The warmth seeped into her, chasing the last of the chill away. Andvari guided her away from the entrance so the others could come out as well.

Dax sat with his back against a tree. Vinnia lay on a blanket beside him, curled up and fast asleep. Norial and the canvas bag were gone.

Dax nodded to Andvari. "She took it back to camp. It seemed cruel to keep her here with—his remains." He nodded to Vinnia.

Frida walked over and knelt beside her. "When she's awake and after we deal with that," she glanced back at the cavern, "we'll help her. If a Water Mage could assist?" She looked up at Andvari.

Jeril bowed his head. "Anything you need."

Frida's smile was shaky. "I appreciate it."

"Why did he do it, though? What made him give in to the Darkness?" Aili kept her voice quiet.

Theron shook his head. "He hasn't been the same since we began investigating the university mages. Orlo Mindar was his classmate during their advanced studies. While we knew that, we didn't know they were friends. He wouldn't have been allowed on the case if we knew."

"When the Darkness gets inside, it whispers all your fears." Aili shivered and leaned closer to Andvari.

He hugged her to his side.

"Here. Stay warm and dry." Jeril snapped his fingers, and the water fell from her clothing.

"Thanks." Aili curled up, her head against Andvari's shoulder. Her eyes snapped open. "Kyson, your hand."

Kyson raised his hand and showed her the pink spots, already fading. "You need rest, and the oil is helping."

"I don't need rest." Ilia grabbed his wrist and examined the spots. "Just a touch now." Brushing her fingers over the spots, his skin healed fully. "Done."

Wagons rolled through the trees towards them. The people riding them wore familiar green cloaks. Her friends were coming to help. She grinned as she spotted Gavi in the front wagon. Norial drove it right down to the cave entrance. Even Dinna was with the group. A quick count confirmed there were at least three Master Mages from each magic school.

She glanced at Vinnia. The woman was in no shape to help. There were enough mages from the Scouts here. Were the CDF not helping this time?

'They don't know our rituals. Only Master Mage Scouts will be involved. Well, us and you and Ilia.' Andvari rubbed her back. 'This is Scout business, caring for the well-springs.'

"Boss?" Dax nodded to Vinnia, still sleeping despite the commotion. How much herbal calming did Jeril give her?

"I'll stay with her." Theron walked over and settled on the grass beside Vinnia. "Frida is better at detecting Darkness than I am. She'll verify the cleansing and your safety."

Dax and Frida joined the group forming around Andvari and Aili. As he was explaining the situation to everyone, Ilia pulled the box out again. They waited for him to finish before she handed him the box.

Andvari accepted the box, tucking it under his arm. "Everyone helping with the ritual, follow us. Frida, you as well. Anyone not involved should stay out here."

He guided Aili back to the cave. She stayed beside him as they walked down the tunnel. All those people following, all ready to help, and she considered them all friends. She really wasn't alone, even when she was by herself. Aili pressed a hand over her heart.

Andvari stopped in the larger middle cavern. He opened the box. "You're ready for this. We're here to help. We'll spin our power in, infused with our love of nature. Use the power in the pins for everything else."

The group parted, letting Kyson and Ilia through.

Ilia touched the box. "Those are as strong as ever. Do you know the order to use them?"

"Order?"

Ilia shook her head. "It's a wonder you survived. Mother must be helping. Yes, these were designed to be used by four different mages, and in a specific order. Now, you're young and strong, and mother is always with you. We'll help through the link. Which would you start with if you were to choose?" She opened the box.

Aili touched the pins, barely brushing her fingers over each. "The water pin calls to me."

Smiling, Ilia nodded. "Yes, that should be first. Next?"

Touching the earth pin, Aili didn't hesitate. "This one."

Ilia chuckled. "Those two work together well. And then?"

She glanced between the air and fire pins. Her body trembled at the memory of fire. Her fingers hovered over them, hesitating. "Air?"

Ilia nodded. "With the earth pin on, it'll ground you. You shouldn't get the strong feel of floating or being spread apart. Tether yourself to the soil if the pin feels too strong at any point."

Aili pulled her fingers back. She wasn't about to touch the fire pin.

Reaching a hand to Aili's shoulder, Ilia squeezed lightly. "The planet can handle the heat from that one. You just need to channel it. Stay deep in your earth magic and let the water protect you from the heat. Let him help, too. He's strong enough." Ilia nodded to Andvari.

CHAPTER 37

Taking a deep breath, Aili let it out. She couldn't put it off forever. Aili picked up the water pin. Her body pulsed with the tides. She fastened it to her shirt with shaky fingers. Ilia added the earth pin. The tugging sensation dimmed as the rumbling from deep underground joined it. The grating of the planet's plates vibrated her bones. Aili touched the water pin, and her body stilled again.

Sinking down into the soil first, Aili picked up the air pin. The crystals were such a pale blue they were almost clear. The world around her spun. Was this what being in an air funnel felt like? Andvari's hand rested on her shoulder, and everything went still again. Her body calmed. She pinned it beside the others.

The crystals in the fire pin seemed to glow, shifting between yellows, through oranges, and to a deep red. Heat shot through her as she picked it up. Andvari helped her pin it beside the water pin. The heat faded, a background sensation like the tides, breeze, and ground pressure.

"You will lead." Ilia took the box and tucked it back in her shoulder bag. "I no longer have the endurance. I will help, though. Trust the Scouts to know what to do. They keep these rituals in their memory for times just like this."

Aili smiled and crossed her arms over her chest. "I never saw anything about stuff like this in the manuals you gave me." She fixed her gaze on Andvari.

He shrugged. "Some things are kept among the highest ranks. Rituals have been passed down since Ethala's time. We do have a special book we study once we reach a high enough rank and proficiency. There's a copy in your office when you're ready."

Aili stared down the tunnel. "Let's get this over with."

Andvari took her hand and held it firmly between his. "We're here for you. I'm not letting you fall in again. Seriously, before you became my student, I didn't have a single grey hair. Now look at me."

Aili laughed and nudged him in the ribs. "That's genetics."

"Stress can cause it, too." He walked with her down the tunnel. "I'll show you the research if you don't believe me."

Her stomach clenched. With each step closer, the empty pit inside her surged. No, she wasn't alone and forgotten. She tightened her fingers on his hand. He was right here. They all were. It would not take her again.

She reached up and touched her sword belt. That fear was so deep, it seemed a part of her, though. Of never being good enough, not being the right person, not being wanted. Deep in her soul, she knew she wasn't alone. They'll never give up on her. Even as a child, she had people who loved her.

Aili felt the intricate designs carved into her sword belt. Andvari gave this to her. The sword could have been plain and durable, but he got her a work of art capable of channeling even the strongest magic. With the power from her mother stored in the blade, she could cut through the Darkness. Even alone, she carried the power of others with her.

They rounded the corner. The well waited, illuminated by the mage-light ball hovering over it. Cold seeped up from her feet, making her shiver. Power from inside the well called, tugging her towards it.

Aili pressed a hand to her heart and called to her Light. The link surged. Leya. She'd do anything for Leya. Anything at all. The gloom lifted as she felt the pony in the link. Grazing in the sun, heat on her coat and grass in her mouth, Leya sent warmth back at her. Nothing would stop her from protecting Leya.

She stopped in front of the well. Andvari stayed with her, her hand in his. His earth magic flowed between them, rooting her deep in the soil and rock. She sank her own abilities down beside his, strengthening the anchor.

"We're ready when you are. We know our task, so focus on what you need to do." His fingers tightened around her smaller hand.

"Ready." Kyson laid a hand on her back, his magic joining theirs in the link.

The Scouts stood in a circle around her and the well. They began chanting, calling on their magic and weaving it together. Aili waited, listening to the chant. Her skin tingled as the magic grew. It was time.

She rested a hand on her heart. Sinking inside herself, Aili touched her inner lights. Following her blended magic down, Aili nodded. Andvari had her well grounded. Gathering magic from all around her, her body hummed with power now.

Aili turned her focus to the well. She flooded the cavern with Light, centred on the well. She closed her eyes and still saw white through her eyelids. Touching the pins one by one, and in order, she blanketed the well with their power.

Darkness pushed back, thrashing against her bubble of power over the well. She held her barrier in place as Kyson weaved the magic from the group in. She spun the threads together as a reinforcing net while Andvari kept her grounded.

Her grip on the Fire Magic slipped. Heat flowed into her. Kyson pulled the Fire Magic back into the weave. No, not Kyson, Hana and the Fire Mages through his magical conduit. The heat surged down into the well; the Darkness infused water bubbling beneath her magical weave.

The Darkness lashed out, a tendril snapping against her power. She pressed her magic layer down and in, surrounding it with the blanket of magic. Tapping into the pins again, Aili pulled more power. Her bones vibrated. The Darkness wailed.

Drawing the Darkness up, Aili used heat to guide it. As she pulled it near the surface, the Air Mages formed a bubble around the Darkness, supported by the Water Mages. They brought the bubble up and over the well, hovering in the air.

Ilia's powers joined hers. Aili filled the bubble with their joined Light. Darkness fought back, smacking the bubble with stinging slaps. Her shield rattled where it was struck, thinning and cracking. Andvari helped ease the magic back in place, holding her shield firm.

With a last burst of focus, Aili snapped the bubble closed, suffocating the Darkness. It fought with one last gasp of effort, pressing hard against her magic. She snarled. Her magic suffocated the Darkness. It was gone.

Her clothing was soaked with sweat, clinging to her. Heat surged through her body. Aili swayed.

Andvari wrapped an arm around her, holding her up. "Almost done. We need to be sure."

His presence steadied her, giving her the strength to stand. She searched the entire cavern, including down the well. The magical waters soothed her essence as she slipped into it with her abilities.

"It's done," she whispered. "It's gone."

Frida burst through between a couple of Scouts and kneeled in front of her. "Hands." She held her hands out, waiting.

Aili rested her hands on Frida. Too much, the magic was still too much. The pins. She scrunched her nose up and focused on her next breath. Andvari held her to his side as her legs shook.

"She's clean. I'll check the well next." Frida let go and moved to the stone circle.

Kyson took the fire pin from her, setting it in the box. Energy drained from her, into the rock below. His strong fingers deftly unfastened the air pin. Her legs buckled as more energy was released. A breeze rippled through the cavern before flowing down the tunnel. Andvari removed the earth pin. Her blood surged with the tides. The water pin joined the others in the box. Coldness seeped through her.

Gavi kneeled next to her as Andvari sat her on the rock. "How do you feel?" He rested a hand on her forehead and took her hand in his.

She burst into tears. "Empty."

Ilia laid a hand on her shoulders. Magic flowed through her. "Breathe. Let it flow naturally. Ground yourself."

Aili took as deep a breath as her shaking body allowed. Ilia drew magic up through her, guiding it around Aili's body.

"Artifacts are like a stimulant. They'll give a boost of power, but they can overwhelm you and knock your own energy out of order." Ilia squeezed her shoulder. "You'll be fine in a few days. Think of it like an herbal overdose, followed by withdrawal. With some quiet and a little care, you'll be back to normal soon. Oh, and a cool drink of freshly cleansed well water will help." She winked at Aili.

Kyson muttered under his breath. A cup formed from air, translucent and shining with magic. He dipped it in the water and filled it. Jeril held a hand over the cup, a quick spell to check for impurities, before nodding. Kyson handed the cup to Andvari, who held it up to Aili's lips. She drank deeply, the liquid soothing her dry mouth.

"While you recover, we'll help." Gavi sent calming energy through her. He coated her raw nerves with it. "It's a wonder you didn't burn up."

"You all helped with that. Is everyone else okay?" Aili glanced around at the group.

"They're fine," Kyson assured her. "We're more used to working with others and can channel a lot of power. That, and you were the focus this time. We just had to give magic and help direct it."

"It doesn't help that you don't know how much magic you can actually use yet," Andvari reminded her. "The answer seems to be—a lot." He hugged her with the arm still supporting her.

"Ilia, can you use the pins?" Aili looked at the box sitting beside Kyson. The pins weren't glowing, were they?

Ilia shook her head. She closed the box and tucked it into her shoulder bag. "Not anymore. My body is too old." She touched the bracelet around her wrist, hidden by her robe sleeve. "Among other reasons."

"Are the eggs safe now?" Aili kept her voice down. Was she supposed to mention anything, or was this a secret?

Bony old fingers tugged on the leather cord, drawing up the little vial. The surface swirled with the ever-changing green mist inside. "I think they are." Ilia smiled at her. "With the taint gone and the pins back in our custody, nobody can contaminate them."

"But someone stole the pins once. Can it happen again?" Aili shivered at the thought of going through everything again.

Andvari and Frida shared a look, a conversation Aili didn't understand.

"Perhaps they're better stored in the Scout vaults," Frida offered. "Fewer people have access to it and it's harder to get to."

"If we may?" Kyson held his hand out.

Ilia pulled the box out and handed it to him. Gavi, Hana, and Jeril stepped over and all rested their hands on the box. With a short chant, their magic coated the box, sealing it with multiple layers of protection. The box glowed with a magical halo now.

"That will do until we can get it in the vaults." Kyson handed the box back to Ilia.

"You need a meal and rest, and we all could do with a drink." Andvari helped Aili stand.

"Come with me." Gavi wrapped his arm around her, hugging her as she walked to the tunnel with him. "You supported me in my time of need. Let me do the same for you." His magic flowed through her, giving her strength.

"Thanks," she whispered. "I've never felt so odd, not even when struck by lightning."

"When we get back, she needs the advanced nerve tonic for physical restoration," Ilia instructed, walking behind them with Kyson. "She just channeled enough magic to kill a half dozen regular mages, and her body is a bit raw."

"See? You're in excellent hands. I prescribe a good firm hug from a friend of your choice, and some quiet time with that pony when you return to your camp." Gavi caught her as her foot slipped on a stone.

Aili took a moment to steady herself. "That's a remedy I can really look forward to."

She grinned when she finally stepped back into the sunlight. The heat soaked through her far faster than usual. Gavi cast a spell over her. The sunlight still warmed her now, but only a bit. Aili sighed, content.

Theron levitated Vinnia into the smallest wagon and settled beside her. Jeril and Frida joined him, kneeling around her sleeping body. Aili and Gavi went to a larger wagon with Ilia. Kyson helped them up into the back before joining them. Aili curled up in a corner, leaning against Gavi, her head on his shoulder. The Scouts split between the two large wagons, huddled together.

Aili closed her eyes and listened to the forest as the wagon took them back. Her stomach growled. She opened her eyes as she patted her pockets. Kyson held an unwrapped bar out for her. She grinned and took it, taking a massive bite without waiting. With the first gone in seconds, he handed her another.

She was finishing her fourth bar when they finally rolled back into camp. Vinnia stirred and shifted. Jeril and Frida tended her as the wagons stopped at the front steps. Aili waited as Andvari and Kyson helped Ilia down, though Ilia needed far less help than before.

"Come with me. We'll go to the healing room and get you looked after." Gavi leapt from the wagon before reaching back up to her.

"Do you want me to come, or I can see you when I'm done?" Andvari turned to Kyson. "Take that to the main office. I'll be there soon."

Aili waved him off. "You're busy. I'll be fine."

"You're sure?" He looked her over again, his face pinched with worry.

She smiled. "Ilia and Gavi are looking after me. I'm fine, and I bet you have a lot of paperwork to do."

He grimaced. "You have no idea." Andvari headed up the steps, stopping at the door. 'Let me know if you need me,' he added in the link. 'I'll come right away.'

'I know.' She sent a warm hug through the link to him.

CHAPTER 38

Gavi kept an arm around her as they walked to the treatment room. Aili settled on the thick mattress. Gavi rifled through the potions in the cupboard, his fingers closing around a bottle.

Ilia sat beside her on the bed. "You've grown so much. I'm really proud of you." She took Aili's hand between her own wrinkled, old hands. "They've been good for you."

Aili looked down at her knees. She smiled to herself.

"I hear you're ready to begin easing into your proper role here."

She opened her mouth, but words failed her. How could she say everything she wanted to? The words collided in her brain and didn't reach her mouth. "I'm not sure I'm ready," she finally managed.

Ilia laughed softly. "No one is ever truly ready for something big like that. We do it anyway and count on the people around us to help and support us. I can't think of a better team to support you, either." She squeezed Aili's hand gently.

"Here." Gavi uncapped the bottle and held it out to her. "You know the routine. Drink it all."

Aili wrinkled her nose as she inhaled. "It's going to taste like dirty socks, isn't it?"

Gavi raised his eyebrow. "How do you know what dirty socks taste like?"

Without answering, Aili raised the bottle to her lips. She took the potion in a few swallows, not stopping until it was gone. Aili grimaced. "It needs sweetener."

"You know, as leader of the Scouts, you could command the healers to develop a better tasting nerve tonic." He grinned as he took the empty bottle from her. "Though we both know why that's unlikely."

"No, but leading the Scouts might have a few perks after all." Aili tapped her chin.

Gavi chuckled. "You'll do fine. Count on them to guide you while you learn and listen to your heart. You can go whenever you're ready."

"How about some tea?" Ilia offered. "We can share a pot and I'll tell you all about running the Scouts if you like."

"I'd like that." Aili stood and stretched. "I have so much to learn."

"You go ahead. I feel like taking my time." Ilia also stood, with more ease than Aili had seen before. "This thing works great."

Aili wrapped her arms around Ilia's waist. "I'm so glad."

Ilia hugged back for a moment. "Go on. I smelled fresh pastries."

Aili grinned at her. She dashed from the room. It was a short walk through the halls to the dining room, though she jogged it. Ilia was right; someone had made fresh pastries, and the smell wafted down the dining room hall towards her. She followed the smell.

Frida saw her come into the dining room first. She raised a cup of tea to Aili. "Come join us."

"Sure."

Aili took a cup and filled it with tea. She wandered over to the table. The Scouts and CDF were sitting together; the group mixed like she hadn't seen yet.

"Those are quite the abilities you have. Are you sure you don't want to join us in the city instead? When you're not at work, you can enjoy the city life," Vinnia offered.

She smiled and shook her head. "I have everything I want and need here." Aili glanced around. "Well, maybe not in this camp," she gestured around the room, "but back home I do."

"With your skills and training, you could work with the elite response team." Theron raised his teacup to her.

She grinned as Andvari walked in, Ilia beside him but not holding his arm like she used to. He collected two teacups as Ilia joined her on the bench.

Andvari set a teacup in front of Ilia before sitting across from her. "Not trying to steal our Nature Mage, are you?" He smiled.

"I don't know, it might be fun to let them have her for a week. See what they do with someone who doesn't take orders well." Kyson grinned wickedly at Aili.

"I take orders just fine," Aili retorted. "Just not from you." She smirked back at him.

"Now that our little Nature Mage has grown, she's ready to take her place." Ilia patted Aili's hand.

"Maybe I'll enjoy bossing you around for a change," she challenged Kyson.

"I have a feeling being a Scout is about to get more interesting." Hana winked at Kyson.

Aili laughed. The thought of being in charge made her want to shake so hard her boots would fall off. She wasn't alone, though. She already had experts who knew how things worked. Did the CDF even know she was destined to take leadership here? Did anyone outside the most senior Scouts?

Dinna finished her tea and set her cup down. "I'll get the transport ready. There's no rush, so finish your tea."

Theron drained his cup and stood. "I'll come help. I'll make sure our cargo—I'll help load."

Vinnia's hand shook. Tea sloshed onto the table.

Frida took Vinnia's cup and set it down. She rubbed the younger woman's back. "Do you want to get some air? I can help you pack, too."

Vinnia nodded, tears forming in the corners of her eyes. She reached for the chain holding the charm against Darkness.

"Keep it," Andvari offered. "You all helped, and you deserve protection, too."

Vinnia nodded, her gaze distant. Frida helped her up and walked her from the room.

"It was quite an experience getting to work with you all." Rylor looked around at the group.

"It was good for all of us," Dax agreed. "Some of your techniques will be useful, too."

"Do the CDF in Dinlark work the same way?" Aili asked. She took another sip of tea.

Rylor nodded. "We train together, too. Our new recruits go to a shared school for basic skills, and our experts develop new techniques together. While we have differences because the cities are different, it's easy to transfer if we ever move." He finished his tea. "I may as well help. Safe travels, friends."

Andvari stood with him and clasped hands. "Safe travels."

The room seemed emptier after he left, like a blanket was smothering the sound. She looked around. Everyone had dark shadows under their eyes.

"Using magic in grand workings drains us temporarily," Andvari admitted. "Everyone here is on light duty for two weeks while we all recover. At least, with the Darkness cleansed fully, it'll be quiet out there. The others will cover for us while we rest."

"When do we go home, boss?" Hana took a pastry and bit into it.

"Dinna takes the CDF home today. She'll be back for the rest of us tomorrow, so we can fly in daylight. Everyone from Dinlark and the north get the first flight back. The rest of us go in the afternoon." Andvari settled on the bench again and took a pastry.

***

The sun peeked over the top of the trees, casting long shadows with the early light. Aili drew her cloak tighter around herself. Despite the thick cloak and Andvari's warming spell, she still shivered. Gavi and Ilia assured her that would pass in a few days. If she didn't freeze to death first.

Clutching the box to her chest, she stared up at the cave entrance. Her legs trembled. If she couldn't face her fear again, was she even ready to lead?

Ilia rested a hand on her shoulder. "We'll do this together. What's the Scout motto?"

Aili laughed. "Stronger together."

Andvari rubbed her back. His magic flowed into her, easing her nausea. "We'll be with you in the link the whole time. If anyone can help you with the magic in there, it's Ilia, right?"

She took a deep breath. "Right. Let's get this over with."

Walking slowly, with Ilia beside her, Aili stepped into the cave. No heat this time? It looked like a perfectly ordinary cave, other than the hidden entrance. Just a glimmer of magic covered the surrounding rock.

Ilia linked her arm through Aili's. They walked side by side around the curves, following the tunnel down. The cave was silent, not even an echo of their footsteps or the sound of their breath. Ilia waved her hand. A ball of mage-light floated ahead, lighting the way. It finally stopped at the doors of stone.

The doors were pure black, with no sign of flames. They were closed tightly, not a single air gap anywhere between them. Without the light, it would seem like a shadow that might swallow her whole.

Reaching out with her senses, Aili touched the doors. They swung wide open, exposing the dark cavern beyond. The mage-light ball floated inside, casting a long shadow behind the pedestal.

Aili walked over and stopped at the pedestal. She opened the box. The pins reflected the mage-light back at her, sending slivers of light around the room. Aili reached inside and grasped the fire pin. Lifting it from the velvety cushion, she braced herself.

Nothing happened. No heat and pressure, flames, or burning sensation. Aili blinked. She looked around. Flames grew along the walls, stretching to the ceiling as they danced and flickered. The room glowed a gentle orange colour, like embers in a fire.

Reaching out, she set the pin on the pedestal. It settled into the indent, fitting perfectly. The flames brightened, spreading along the pillars as well. Aili's heart raced. Ilia rested a hand on her back, calming magic flowing into her. Her heart slowed again.

"Let's go. We seal it from out there."

Aili forced her legs to carry her slowly, fighting the urge to bolt for the door. Ilia walked beside her through the room full of magical flames, their arms linked. Holding the box under her other arm, Aili clutched it to her side. She sucked in a deep breath once she stepped out of the room.

"Close the doors with a touch of your magic," Ilia advised.

Reaching out with her senses, Aili touched the doors. They swung closed without making a sound.

"Now touch the doors again and think of protection."

She took another slow breath, filling her lungs with cool air. Aili reached out, touching the magic in the doors. Magic slumbered in the rock, waiting to be awakened.

Protect.

Power surged through the doors, knocking her back a few steps. She clung to the box, holding it to her chest like a shield. Flames rushed up the doors, covering the surface. The carved flames glowed red.

"It is done. Once we leave, we call on the last protection." Ilia took Aili's arm and guided her down the tunnel.

The link warmed her, reminding her how close they were. She fought the urge to run, focusing on slow and steady steps at Ilia's pace. She smiled when the sliver of sunlight appeared ahead, growing larger with each step.

The instant she emerged from the tunnel, Andvari wrapped her in a hug. She leaned against him and let out a sigh. She did it.

"You did great," he said to her. "Take a moment if you need it." Relaxing his hug, Andvari handed her a canteen.

Aili passed the box with the remaining three pins to Kyson. She took the canteen and drank. Cool water soothed her dry throat. She gulped down a few mouthfuls before handing it back to Andvari.

Ilia touched the rock beside the entrance. "You must do this one as well. Only Nature Magic can activate this. Again, think of protection, but also concealment."

Straightening up, Aili squared her shoulders. She turned to the entrance again. Power already flowed under her feet, active since she sealed the inner doors. Aili reached out with her abilities and touched the entrance.

Protect. Hide.

Flames shot up over the entrance. Aili stumbled back, bumping into Andvari. He wrapped an arm around her and held her up. The flames shimmered and danced as they dissolved, forming again as rock covering the entrance. She sensed the power, felt the tunnel beyond, but her eyes told her there was a solid rock wall. The power faded, going dormant like before when she found it the first time.

"What about those three?" Aili nodded at the box Kyson held.

"We can prepare a hiding place for those like this one." Ilia brushed her hand over the rock. "We'll find a place where the elements are strong."

"Why don't they already have one?" Aili rubbed her chin. "Why just the fire pin?"

"It was most dangerous," Andvari explained. "Ethala thought so. She wrote about them in a journal. There wasn't time to make hiding places for the others before she disappeared, so we've been hiding them in vaults and other secure places ever since. Until recently, we were successful."

Aili stepped back from the slumbering magic. If she got too close, she might wake it. "Now what?"

A wind blew around her, swirling up and rustling her hair. 'You did it. Go home.'

Mother? Aili glanced at Ilia, who smiled and nodded.

"Yes, we go home." Ilia gestured to the wagon parked near them.

Aili walked over to the wagon and scrambled up into the back. Kyson helped Ilia with a levitation spell, though the old woman managed better than before. He hopped up beside them and settled with the box in his lap. Andvari settled in the control seat.

"The water pin belongs up north, doesn't it?" Aili leaned back against the side as the wagon set off up the hill.

Ilia nodded. "Where would you put the others?"

She stared at the box for a long moment. The shiny surface showed off the lightly stained wood grain. "The earth pin goes east. That just feels right. I think I know exactly where, too. It'll take some serious magic, though." Her mind wandered to the waterfall. Something about that place called to her.

"And the air pin?" Kyson rested a hand on the box, his fingers stretching over the sides.

"Where else?" Aili smiled. "It belongs down south. We'll do that in spring or summer, though. I'm not going there in winter again unless I can't help it."

"You know, we were only there in winter because our trip got delayed. With everything that happened in the fall, we couldn't leave earlier." Kyson nudged her boot with his own.

"That wasn't my fault."

He laughed. "Nobody said it was. You did help Rei when nobody else could. Sometimes things happen and we have to change our plans."

"It'll be good to get back to my workshop again." Ilia stretched her arms over her head.

"Is someone looking after it for you?" Aili wrapped an arm around Ilia's shoulders.

"Darik and some city Scouts." Ilia leaned her head on Aili's shoulder. "Still, there's something about being home that just feels right."

Aili smiled. Even just thinking about the eastern camp filled her with warmth. So many good things happened there. Many of her friends were there, too. She couldn't wait to get back.

CHAPTER 39

A ili sank onto her mattress. Her trunk was empty, and everything was packed in her bags. A new team would come in and help support the forest. She was still on light duty with the others. Her forest would be fine. It was time to go home.

"What's got you so deep in thought?" Andvari dropped his own bag by the door, stuffed full of his clothing and gear. He sat beside her on the edge of the mattress.

"I guess—I guess I'd like to say goodbye to Karil before we go." Aili pressed her fingers together, twisting her hands in her lap.

"Are you sure?" He grinned.

Aili rolled her eyes. "Why wouldn't I be sure?"

A light knock pulled her attention to the open door. Aili looked over. Karil stood there, her pack over her shoulder. She beamed at Aili.

"Come in. I was just about to tell her." Andvari waved Karil in.

He stood and went to his desk, busying himself with packing the magic mailbag.

"Tell me what?"

Karil dropped her pack at the door and darted in. "I'm coming with you. Norial is going to the eastern camp, and I'm coming with her." She radiated excitement as she perched on the edge of the bed.

Aili glanced at Andvari before smiling back at Karil. "That's wonderful. It's a great camp. There's so much to do there." She reached for Karil's hand, her hand open and waiting on the mattress in silent invitation.

Karil stretched her hand out and rested it in Aili's. "I knew coming here wouldn't be for long, though it sure felt like it. I miss the busier camps." Her fingers wrapped around Aili's.

"Where all have you been? Just up north?" Aili felt her cheeks warm.

"Mostly. I spent a month each in a small western outpost and down south, too. Fortunately, it was warm when I went there. There're more people in the south in summer." She leaned closer to Aili. "I'm glad I got out before it got cold. I'm not used to the cold."

Aili laughed. She pressed her hand to her mouth. "If you're used to the north, I'm not surprised. I was there last winter, and it was definitely cold. If you love the northern camp, I bet you'll love it out east, too."

"I can hardly believe it. I was hoping for a larger camp. I feel so lucky." Karil glanced at Andvari, who still had his back to them as he packed some quills away in the bag.

His amusement was clear in the link. Andvari turned, picking up the full bag. "It was time you left here, anyway. Norial wants to work with Kyson on a project, so she requested it. I approved it."

"You'll be flying home with us, then?" Aili glanced between Karil and Andvari.

"Yes, they'll come with us. No sense sending two transports, when one is going anyway. It'll be here any moment, so make sure you both packed everything. Other than a brief stop to take a little bird home, we fly direct." He strode to the door and set the mailbag with his gear.

"I should check one last time." Karil darted past him, grabbing her bag on the way.

Andvari glanced around the room one last time. With a nod, he sat beside her on the bed again. "Now that you're aware of your future place with the Scouts, there are a few things you should know."

"Okay?" She took a slow breath and let it out, just like in the calming meditation Darik taught her all those years ago.

He chuckled. "You don't have to look so worried. You know the room right across the hall from mine?"

"The one no one ever goes into?" Aili drew her knees up and wrapped her arms around her legs.

"That's the one. It was once Ethala's room. It's close because my position has been aiding her as long as the Scouts have existed. It's yours if and when you want it. If you don't want to live alone, you can take a roommate of your choice. You can stay in my room until you're ready. It's up to you."

Aili opened her mouth. Words wouldn't come out. She pressed her hand over her heart. He'd be just across the hall. It's not like she'd be alone. Wait, she spent her whole life before being a student alone, effectively. It had never bothered her before. Why did it bother her now? No, he wasn't kicking her out. Did she want to move yet?

Andvari rested a hand on her knee. "Consider it, but you don't have to decide now."

"Okay, what else? You said a few things?"

"You have your own office. It's beside mine. As long as you're still a mage and not a Master Mage, your focus will be on lessons and learning. Still, it's a place you can keep maps and notes, write your own journals, and so on. Later you might use it more for Scout business."

"That doesn't sound terrible," Aili admitted. "Anything else?"

Andvari laughed.

Maybe growing up wouldn't be so scary after all.

***

"That clearing over there." Aili pointed. She wrapped her other arm around her stomach.

"Got it." Dinna banked the air box and steered it for the opening in the trees.

Aili glanced at Karil across the aisle from her, the little bird cradled in her hands. The bird cheeped and fluttered her wings.

"You're welcome." Aili smiled at the bird before pressing her hand to her mouth.

Andvari rested a hand on her shoulder. His magic flowed through her, calming her stomach. She almost missed the box landing on the grass; it was so smooth. Aili tumbled over the edge, pressing her palms to the soil.

Kyson leapt out of the air box and leaned against the side. He hid his smile behind his hand.

"I suppose you love that as an Air Mage." Aili narrowed her eyes at him.

"What's not to love?" Kyson grinned and shrugged. "The breeze on my face, the coolness, the views? What other way do you get to see so much of the land at once?"

Ilia laughed. "I can think of a few." She winked at Aili.

Aili grinned back at Ilia. As terrifying as the air box was, what would riding a griffin feel like? Would Kyson love it as much? Knowing him, he probably would.

"Are you ready?" Andvari steadied Karil as she climbed over the side, the bird cradled in her hands.

"Yes. And no? Mostly yes." Karil stroked the tiny head.

"That's alright. We all get attached to the animals we heal. I think she's ready, though." Andvari touched her little feathered back with a fingertip.

The bird called. Birdsong filled the air, distant and getting closer. The little bird perked up and wiggled. She ran across Karil's hand and leapt from her finger, wings spread. Flying with ease, she took off into the trees, heading for the sound of her flock.

Aili turned to Karil. The young woman had an expression Aili knew all too well. She stood still, with both hope and longing at war inside her.

"I guess she's home," Karil whispered.

Aili walked over and wrapped an arm around Karil's shoulders. "It's hard, but hear how happy she is?"

Karil nodded. She curled in against Aili and rested her head on Aili's shoulder. Her arms snuck around Aili's ribs as she hugged back. "Yeah."

Ilia rested a hand on Karil's back. "She'll think about you, too."

Karil didn't move, so Aili hugged her with both arms. She waited until Karil took a breath and straightened up before relaxing her hug.

"I guess she's back where she belongs," Karil said softly.

"Yes, and you helped make that happen," Dinna reminded her.

"Is everyone ready to go back? Apple tea in the private meeting room for everyone," Andvari offered. He gestured at the transport.

"Come on. You'll love the eastern camp. It's not as damp as the north, so it feels warmer. We're close enough to the city you can go shopping sometimes, and there are so many people to make friends with." Aili guided Karil back to the box.

Kyson snorted a laugh. "Since when did you care about shopping? You even make him order books for you, so you don't have to go yourself."

Aili smacked his shoulder. "Says the guy who goes every month for a stash of those candies. Don't think I haven't seen you sneak off. I know about the backup supply you keep in case a mission prevents your usual trip."

Andvari glowed in the link, his laughter clear. 'Get in.'

With a sigh, Aili leapt back into the box. She curled up on the seat. Ilia took her seat right behind Dinna again, where she could see the best. Kyson sat across from Ilia. Probably for the same reason, Aili figured.

Aili glanced behind her. Norial was reading a book, calm as anything. She looked up and squeezed Karil's hand as the girl settled beside her. Andvari sat across from Aili again.

"Next stop, the capital city," Dinna called.

***

Aili pushed the door with her palm. It swung open with little pressure; the hinges moving with ease. There was no dust, despite the room being sealed away. The air smelled fresh and clean, like someone had left a window open.

She took a step forward. Everything she might need was in here. One corner by the window had a bed and nightstand. The trunk waited at the end of the bed, standard Scout issue, but painted with leaves and nature scenes. A desk sat along one wall, small and sturdy. There was even a plush reading chair by the window.

Crossing the room, she looked out at the camp. She didn't look out over the stables like in Andvari's room but had a magnificent view of the meadows and the herbalists' gardens from here. Most of the camp was visible, including the training grounds right below.

"You can decorate as you like. Don't feel you need to move right away. We'll keep your space in my room until you're absolutely certain you're ready." Andvari leaned against the doorframe.

Aili examined the wall of bookshelves. Most titles were old enough that they were written in Ancient. "I might want some more current books."

Andvari scanned the titles, stepping beside her. "Easily done. Any you don't want to keep in here we can put in the library and archives. She had quite the collection, but you can adjust it as you want. It hasn't been added to in about four hundred years."

"I can work with this. It's comfortable. It doesn't look out over the stables, though." Aili sighed dramatically.

He pulled something out of his pocket. Unwrapping the cloth from around it, he handed her a mirror. Aili looked at the glass. She saw Leya grazing in the paddock with the bigger horses. The pony nipped at Charger, driving him from the pile of hay. Charger ambled away, flicking an ear at the pony.

Aili laughed. "How?"

Andvari smiled. "That's an easy enchantment for the communication mages. When I asked, they were happy to make it for you." He took a little metal frame and set it on her nightstand. "Put it wherever you want it."

Aili hugged him, her arms tight around his ribs. "Thank you. I'm not really ready to move yet, but I do want to start spending time in here."

He rubbed her back. "There's no rush. I bet she left more journals in her desk drawer, too. It's locked against spells, but I bet you'll have more luck."

She set the mirror on the stand and went to the desk. The locks hummed with magic. With a touch of her abilities, they clicked open. Opening the drawer, Aili found several journals inside.

"How did you know?" Aili set the journals on her desk.

Andvari shrugged. "I also have a journal passed down from all the people who held my position, including the woman who worked with Ethala. It has some notes like that. I bet she left notes for you, too." He nodded at the journals.

Aili pointed to where her reading chair waited. "I could use a little table for books and tea."

"I'll arrange it."

She rested a hand on the journals. Her whole life was ahead of her. The Darkness was gone for now. She had a future where her unique skills would really help, and an entire team of people who loved the forests as much as she did. What would her sister have to say to her? What notes did she leave?

"I'll get a pot of tea, and we can go through those journals together if you like," Andvari offered. "We're both supposed to be resting, after all."

Aili grinned. "Sounds good." She picked up the journals and wandered over to the chair. "Maybe a second chair would be a good idea, too."

"Done."

DEAR READER,

If you enjoyed my book, please consider leaving a review. It helps other people find my books, so they can enjoy them, too.

You can find more information on all my books at www.aliings.com. Sign up for the newsletter for bonus content and scenes, tips and facts, book information, and more.

ABOUT AUTHOR

Ali spends her days with her horses and ponies, dreaming of adventures and magic. She enjoys martial arts, especially swords and edged weapons, though she practices for self-improvement. She also practices meditation, both sitting and moving varieties.

ALSO BY

Forest Guardians

The Last Dragon

Runaway Magic

Facing the Fire

Healer's Strength

Scout's Honour

Shadow Hunter

Apprentice Scout

Chasing Shadows

Nature's Legacy

Tales From Athia

A Healer's Promise

Legends of the Mountain

Phoenix Rising

Other Books

Rogue Magic

A Flash Of Light